The Dark Side of Ecstasy

THE DARK SIDE
OF
ECSTASY

Roy Harvey

White Knight Publications

British Library Cataloguing in Publication Data
A catalogue record for this book is available from the British Library.

ISBN 978-1-9164885-0-2

Typeset by Amolibros, Milverton, Somerset
www.amolibros.co.uk
This book production has been managed by Amolibros
Printed and bound by Lightning Source

Acknowledgements

It is said that we all have a book in our heads and this was certainly true in my case. I have to thank the Crime Writers Association, who sought my assistance on another matter, for planting the germ that has resulted in *The Dark Side of Ecstasy*.

I also have to thank Terry Rowe (who sadly died when the novel was being developed) Ken Parsons and Barry Kimber for specialist advice in areas where I lacked the necessary expertise. I have to thank John and Lesley Lindsay for re-igniting the spark when the manuscript had lain dormant for some years. Finally, I have to thank Jane Tatam of Amolibros for expert guidance in the publication process.

All profits from the publication of this book will be for the benefit of charities or organisations working with those afflicted by drug addiction.

About the Author

Following military service, the author spent some years as a police officer with experience in the CID, Scene of Crime, Crime Prevention. This was followed by a move to the commercial security world, where he set up a security consultancy whose services were used by a number of UK/international companies and high profile entrepreneurs. These included Porsche Cars, NM Rothschild, Fisons, Pirelli General, Peter de Savary etc. One of the successful specialisations provided was countering industrial espionage by de-bugging premises and telephone systems.

After some years as an independent, he joined previous clients Mecca Leisure and Rank Leisure, to act as their Security Advisor, dealing with problems posed in nightclubs and multi-leisure centres across the country. By necessity this period concentrated on drug and drink misuse and related violence.

Published work includes a chapter on industrial espionage for the *Crime Writers Handbook*, commissioned by the Crime Writers Association, an in-house Operational Security Manual for Rank Leisure and sundry minor articles for magazines.

Contents

Prologue

Friday 1st January 1988
1.33 a.m. Cavendish Square, Southampton, England

The heap of cardboard seemed carelessly positioned. Discarded by the janitor? Awaiting collection by the refuse truck? In fact the placement of it had been carried out with great care. At that point on the inside of the building was the boiler room, providing a small degree of warmth over an area of a few square feet on the outside of the building. Not that the increase in temperature went very far in combating the cold of a winter night. The shivering body beneath the flattened cartons bore testimony to that, but any lessening of the cold was welcome, no matter how small.

He wasn't anywhere near sleep yet, too cold and too much noise for that, so when the high pitched cry came, followed by a low rustling 'whoosh' – as of branches swept aside – and a dull thud, he raised on an elbow and peered through his cardboard window towards a brightly lit first floor flat, whose laughter and music had haunted him since his arrival. Beneath the flat and below the still quivering branches of a tree, was what had been an empty flower bed; it was now occupied!

The first instinct was to stay where he was. He'd learnt the penalties of unnecessary movement. To move from his layers of newspaper and cardboard now would lose what little warmth he had gained. Then with a reminder from his empty belly there came the thought that the body might have pockets, a purse, a bag – and that might have money! The day had gone badly. His old fur hat and unspoken pavement plea had generated only a few pounds in coins – hardly enough for the necessary fix, let alone food. He hadn't had a half decent meal in a week. Wriggling out of the cardboard and newspaper sandwich, glancing left and right, he approached cautiously.

No one else had seen the fall; no alarmed voices from the party in the flat above. Crouching over her he saw that there was no blood. Just a head at a grotesque angle; earth in the curly coppery hair. Eyes wide open staring sightlessly. No breath visible.

Neither were there pockets in the pretty party dress, nor a purse. He shuffled back to his makeshift bed, then thought of a warm police station, perhaps a cup of canteen tea, and changed direction.

1.34 a.m. Archers Road, Southampton

He awoke with a start, jerking upright in bed. In the preceding minutes his sleep had been disturbed by what might have passed for a nightmare. Echoing still in his ears was a cry, the despairing cry of his own name and now he sat amongst crumpled bedclothes, breathing quickly and forcing his mind to accept that the cry had been in his dream. Swinging his legs out of bed he sat for a few more moments then felt his way to a small basin in a corner of the room. Running the cold tap he held cupped hands beneath it, splashed his face and ran wet fingers through curly copper coloured hair before using the towel and returning to bed. Lying there he wondered about the dream that had so violently disturbed his usually sound sleep. Forcing his mind to empty itself he waited with closed eyes, expecting to drop off. It did not happen; his mind refused to release the confused dream, the despairing cry and he wondered whether, despite the hour, he should try Susie's phone. Deciding against it he spent the rest of the night in a restless dozing, waking turmoil.

9.20 a.m. West Quay Road, Southampton

The small single storied building off Western Esplanade bore no external signs to signify its macabre contents and activities. The City's Public Mortuary, enclosed by walls on all sides and with only one point of access, did not invite curiosity. Anonymous to passing pedestrians, whose attention would likely be on the imposing ancient town walls opposite, it crouched like a red brick nonentity, small and insignificant.

To the tall dark suited man, hurrying along with overcoat collar turned up against the chill easterly wind, the scene was a familiar one, as was the inevitable smell of human decay and strong disinfectant, as he punched in a code to open the inner doors. Slipping the coat from his shoulders, he opened a brief case, producing a brown manila file. Across the centre in bold print was the legend 'Hampshire Constabulary'. In the top right hand corner were the words 'Coroners Officer' whilst, in the bottom right hand corner, was a hand written number.

At that moment an inner door opened and a heavily built man wearing a full length green apron and short white rubber boots appeared. They greeted each other and, in that matter of fact way of men who spend much of their working lives in the company of the dead, ignored the body on the stainless steel slab in the middle of the room. It was not until the cold weather, the performance of 'The Saints' in losing three nil and the probable late arrival of an investigating officer not noted for early rising had all been discussed, that the first man turned to open his file and look at the subject of the morning's enquiry.

His first thought was that the body on the slab was Caucasian, a woman and then that she was one of that somewhat rare breed, a natural blonde. He wondered whether 'blonde' was accurate; the hair spread on the slab had a tinge of soft reddish. Despite the glaze of death on her eyes he was struck by their unusual green colour. The waxen features were beautiful. She was of more than average height and slim with small breasts; perhaps in her twenties? Opening the file to check and for the first time seeing the name he glanced quickly at the face again and then said quietly, "Oh shit, no!"

"What is it?"

"This is Martin Wild's sister, Susie."

"Who's Martin Wild?"

Scanning the other papers in the thin file, he said, "Detective Sergeant in the Civic." Then, reading aloud, "Admitted to Casualty just after three this morning. DOA with a broken neck. Only other external injuries are abrasions to the back of the head and left shoulder."

He turned to statements taken by the night duty officers who had attended. "Found beneath a balcony at the flats off Cavendish Square. Had been to a party in the flat above; quite a large one, up to thirty people at one time. Uniform are still making enquiries."

"Has the family been informed?"

"Martin is the family. Both parents are dead. This'll hit him hard. They were twins and very close!"

*

The autopsy would later confirm the findings of the Duty Doctor in Casualty. Death due to a fracture of the spine in the cervical area. It then added a potent comment; the blood toxicology produced traces of Lysergic Acid Diethylamide – the mind bending drug LSD.

The attached witness statements were of little use to the detective who later arrived to take over the Sudden Death enquiry.

Susie Wild had been taken to the party by a female friend. She was seen to drink only orange juice and later coffee. The girl friend who had brought her disappeared quite quickly with a man that she knew into another part of the house. No one noticed the attentions of another man who supplied a bowl with sugar cubes to sweeten the coffee and who, on turning away, surreptitiously pocketed the remaining cubes. He continued to be attentive until she made it clear that his presence was not welcome, but she was conscious of his eyes, always on her, watching.

At just before 1.30 a.m. she was said to be anxious and seeking the girlfriend who had brought her. Another of those present said that a few minutes later Susie left the main room, supporting herself on the wall and door and was thought by that person to be drunk. What the witnesses could not know was the contamination of the sugar cube, or the effect that the powerful hallucinogen had on the unprepared mind of a woman with no experience of drugs. Alone amongst strangers, Susie was suddenly restless, searching her bag, plucking at her dress, getting to her feet, looking for the missing companion. Then, with no warning, dizzy and grasping a chair back for support, having to sit down. Her anxiety turned to fear as suddenly she saw distortion of the people around her. Their shapes changed before her eyes, their voices changed, some coming from afar, others as though whispering in her ears.

Frightened, she got to her feet, looking frantically now for the friend who had brought her. Not seeing her in the room she made for the door which, as she approached, seemed to move as though with a life of its own. She staggered and almost fell. In the corridor outside she did fall and, on her hands and knees, felt time altering, her years slipping away. She was a young girl again, in her school dress. The half light of the hallway was the darkness of a shuttered room remembered from an earlier life. The muffled party voices were from a lounge, they became the voices of an army officer and a policeman, whom she had seen enter the house to speak with the aunt that she was with. They were subdued, talking quietly of an aircraft crash. She wished her brother, Martin, could be there and cried out in a young girls voice for her mummy, daddy, knowing – without knowing how – that they could not come.

As the drugs effect grew she staggered along the dimly lit corridor to glazed doors at the end, pushed against them and, on the balcony, crying, calling out, clambered onto the balustrade and, raising her arms like wings, reached upwards to the dark sky from where her parents had fallen all those years before.

10.25 a.m. Vitrolles, near Marseilles, France

In the principal bedroom of a large white house on the wooded hills above Vitrolles a maid, carrying in one hand a silver tray bearing freshly squeezed orange juice and black coffee, shook the shoulder of her mistress, a young woman lying, despite the drapes just pulled back allowing winter sunshine to stream in, motionless in her bed.

The deep late sleep on the feather filled pillows followed a New Year party fuelled not only by champagne but also – for the first time – by an introduction to cocaine. The drug, presented prettily gift wrapped by a female friend, was accepted as something fresh and sophisticated, to be tried in the company of friends; an aid to the party spirit, an exciting new dimension in an already privileged life.

The maid placed the tray on a bedside table and shook the shoulder again, noting the lightest of shadows under closed eyes. She thought that her mistress, so fortunate with a wealthy husband to supply the grand house and the servants to service it, should not lack sleep. The maid knew nothing of the after dinner antics on the previous night other than the debris downstairs, now being cleared by the cleaner. The champagne bottles, glasses and ashtrays were innocent enough; the faint dusting of white powder on a mantle shelf and side table was not noticed. If it had been it would have elicited no more than a moment's curiosity followed by a shrug of the shoulders and a dismissive Provençal comment from the older employee about the modern woman and her use of face powder. Had the husband been present there would not have been 'face powder', for the female friend who introduced it knew his opinions well enough. The party might have lacked the exhilaration and exuberance that his absence and the consumption of the white powder engendered; the sleep might have been less deep and the waking mood less grey.

At the third shake eyes of the deepest brown quivered open and the very female form beneath silk sheets stretched in waking. The maid, despite her years of service for Marie Thérèse Tabard, marvelled again at her mistress's appearance; with a flawless olive complexion, the blackest of hair spread across the pillow, high cheek bones and the slightest of 'Roman' noses, she was typically Mediterranean and startlingly beautiful.

*

Thus in the space of a few hours, as the world celebrated the turn of the year, in two countries far apart, the lives of two beautiful women altered permanently. For one it ended, dramatically. All that was left was the dreadful disfigurement of the autopsy, the cold and decay of the grave. For the other, no drama, but new experiences, new sensations, new acquaintances; the white powder bringing subtle changes in attitude, growing with the passing months and years.

Life also altered for Martin Wild. The loss of a loved sister; a twin who had occupied much of his world for all of his years, was accompanied by a change in direction. What he did not know, could not know, was the strand of fate which, four years later, would form a trail of death and destruction from Scotland to Provence, completing the unknown connection that had started that night, between a much loved sister and a black haired Mediterranean beauty.

Part One

'The Scales of Justice'

Four years later

The black Citroen SM was being driven just a little too fast. St James Road in Shirley is a convenient 'rat run' for drivers avoiding the rush hour traffic. At just after six in the evening these were still plentiful; they made little difference to the big saloon's progress. The car ate up the short straights and deceptive bends, the driver keeping it in third and fourth with the V6 Maserati engine held between 3,000 and 4,000 revs, drinking four star in sufficient quantities to make an environmentalist choke on his carrot juice.

Martin Wild was enjoying himself. He was pleased with life, entertaining his senses with the surge of immediate power, the lift of supple long travel suspension, the twitch of precise steering. The seat of his pants and the wheel beneath his hands transmitted a dozen different sensations which did not require thinking about, just reacting to. He was relaxed in the contoured seat, in control and more at home in this high speed cocoon than many people are in an armchair.

The Citroen was a modern classic. Only fifteen hundred of the ultra long streamlined coupes had been built in the early seventies at a specialist plant in France. Never common, they were now a rare sight, turning heads in an age of uniform Euro boxes. Martin had found the car in an upmarket showroom at a price which did not reflect its condition and had bought it on the spot. In the twelve months since he had been generous with time and money, as the gleaming paintwork and healthy engine note told.

The smile on his lips was not due only to the sensual pleasure of driving. The London meeting that he was returning from had gone very well and, not for the first time, he blessed the ex-Detective Chief Inspector from Hampshire's Special Branch who had provided the contact. The call from the ex-DCI had come some six months after his own move from the police to the commercial world.

"Afternoon Martin. Norman Gee. How are things?"

He had not known Gee very well. Special Branch people did not mix with the CID General Duties men – or any others – a great deal. Regarded themselves as an elite. He recalled Gee as one of the Northern Ireland Liaison Group who had retired perhaps a year or so earlier and was now Head of Security for United Shipbuilders, the Portsmouth, Southampton and Plymouth based specialists in small fast naval vessels.

"Very well, Norman. Much better than I had anticipated."

Not strictly true. Only the previous day he had been discussing cash flow with a not so friendly bank manager, resisting the suggestion that money spent on his small sailing cruiser would be of greater benefit if ploughed into the business. He had done well during his short time in the commercial world, though hardly well enough to warrant the `very'. But you did not talk in half measures to potential clients. His intuition had told him, correctly, that people like to be associated with success.

"I was talking with Jimmy Durrant this morning," (another ex-CID man known to Martin and now Security Manager for a hotel chain) "and he tells me that you do some 'sweeping'. Says that you did a job for a company that had hired one of his Conference Suites and picked up a bug?"

"Yes, though I think he first thought that we were having the organisation on. Had to go back the next day and take ceiling tiles down to find the thing." Martin grinned at the memory; the look of disbelief on the faces of both Jimmy Durrant and the Chairman of the company concerned had been worth seeing when the device was found. "Pretty sure that it was not aimed at them though; battery life was too low. We lost the signal within an hour of first picking it up. Found the bug by physical search eventually. Probably a problem for the company who had hired the Suite in the previous week."

"Haven't called only to ask your health, Martin. Fact is an old Box 500 contact has a friend in London with a problem. They're looking for a small 'out of town' specialist to sort it for them. Have their reasons for not wanting to use a London company. If you make a phone call to this number you might do yourself some good."

Martin took the number and made the call. On finding whose organisation he was talking to, he knew that if he handled things well, concern about keeping his boat would be a thing of the past. He had handled them well. The first job led to a second, then a regular contract, then to other work for the organisation and now, in turn, for two of their clients. Thank you, Norman!

Right foot moving quickly from accelerator to brake as the bend before St James Church appeared, he pressed gently, almost caressing the pedal, avoiding the nose dive that is a hallmark of those less experienced with older Citroens. With the ball of his right foot still on the brake, he swivelled the heel to the right, giving the accelerator a brief blip to raise the revs, snicking the gear lever from third into second, avoiding a protest from the slightly worn synchromesh.

Left into Church Street, fifty yards with the engine singing in second gear, right into Parksyde Avenue, to brake gently and stop outside the block of maisonettes that overlooked the park. For half a minute he sat still, the motor idling, allowing the oil cooler time to reduce the engine temperature and, with senses slowing, enjoying the contrast of stillness and quiet in this little back water, after the swooping rush of the journey. Metal railings surrounded the park. Tall horse chestnuts, still with spring's fresh green in their leaves, cast a shadow in the late afternoon sun. The only noise, apart from the tennis courts twang of racket on ball, was the distant hum of traffic from nearby Winchester Road.

How should he break the news to Eileen? He was pleased, but she would not be so happy. The job just secured would take him away for some days. Their life styles meant that this was not unusual, but he knew that she had been looking forward to this weekend. Wondering how he should tell her, picturing blue eyes framed by short wavy brown hair, the slightly retroussé nose and, for him, the warm secret smile. He decided that they would eat out; treat the news as a celebration. They had been living together now for almost six months, but he anticipated his return to her after a day away. The feeling was heightening that he had been single too long!

It was just after six o'clock and he guessed that Eileen would have finished work at Shirley Police Station an hour before. By now she had probably changed from her uniform. Her 'metamorphosis' they laughingly called it: work gear off, into a shower and then something more feminine. He pictured the athletic body and slim, firmly muscled dancer's legs, comparing the cool professional woman known to the Shirley police and public, with the bubbly life loving girl who, increasingly, was the centre of his life. Chrysalis into butterfly he thought.

Switching off the motor he swung long legs out of the car and straightened with relief. The journey had taken longer than usual due to an IRA bomb scare backing up the London traffic. Once clear of that he had not stopped, enjoying the fast smooth drive in the late afternoon sun.

*

From an upstairs window Eileen watched Martin emerge from the car. As usual she felt the quickened heartbeat and slight breathlessness that sight of him caused after even a short separation. "Girl, you're in danger of making a fool of yourself over this man" she thought, but not with concern, aware that at last, after several years of caution, with this man she could be trusting and carefree.

At 6'2" with short, almost coppery, curly hair, a very tanned complexion and unusual green eyes, Martin Wild could be described as handsome. The good looks were not total. Years before, the straight nose had been broken and still bore signs of damage. When he smiled his teeth were good in the wide mouth, but the smile was not straight. A three inch scar, visible as a raised white line between the left cheek and the corner of his mouth, gave the smile a slight twist.

Eileen, although struck by his unusual looks when they first met, had been more intrigued by the interviewing technique that she witnessed in a far from luxurious basement flat off of London Road in Southampton. She had arrived in connection with a shoplifting charge involving the girl who occupied the flat. Wild had been present before her, interviewing the boyfriend of her girl thief on an unconnected matter. In the ensuing exchanges between Eileen and the girl, Wild had slipped effortlessly into a role that he knew well, that of a supporting investigator, resulting in a much quicker and fuller confession from the girl.

Some weeks later they met again at the Magistrates Court where the girl, now with a solicitor and subtle changes to the story, was seeking to negate the evidence against her.

The solicitor used a standard form of defence; when facing sound evidence attack the credibility of the witnesses. In this case they were Eileen Padgett, a store detective, and Wild to finally corroborate the confession. Despite innuendos appertaining to Martin's presence in the flat, his evidence and attitude to the court had been professional, polished and unshakable. Eileen was not at all surprised to learn subsequently that he too had once been a police officer.

Over coffee in the court cafeteria they talked. "And what does a Security Consultant do in real life?"

Martin smiled at the question, knowing the doubt and suspicion about his chosen profession in the minds of many police officers. "Oh, I design security systems, mainly for larger companies, ensuring that physical and electronic elements are integrated with manned security. Supervise security guard operations for clients, preparing assignment instructions, that sort of thing. Use covert operatives for occasional investigation work – not marital stuff – commercial losses, large scale theft. I also look after what is euphemistically known as 'corporate confidentiality', that's de-bugging, security audits. I also occasionally organise close escort or protection for VIPs."

Eileen's eyes had widened, then narrowed thoughtfully as Martin, surprised to find himself wishing to extend the conversation, had self-consciously sought to impress.

"If you don't mind me saying, you don't look old enough to have that sort of experience – but it must pay well to have a tan like yours!"

Martin laughed. "I'm older than you may think – and I've been lucky! But really I can thank the army and the police for both the training and the contacts that have made it possible. The only real personal effort was opting to work for a security electronics company for eighteen months after I left the police. The tan comes from spending most of my spare time 'messing about in boats' in this country, not abroad, though I've a long time love affair with La Belle France!"

When she came to enquire about his family there was a long pause whilst Martin stared into the distance. She thought that he had not heard her question, but then he said quietly, "My parents were killed in an air crash when I was at boarding school. Some years later my sister, Susie, was found dead outside one of the flats off Cavendish Square in the centre of town. She had a broken neck. She'd fallen from the first floor. There's no one close now."

"Oh, I'm so sorry!" Eileen was shocked. "Do you know what happened to your sister?"

She saw the hurt in his eyes. "The post mortem found traces of LSD in her blood. The investigation was not conclusive, there was no way of proving whether she had taken it herself or it had been – as I think – slipped into her drink. The Coroner recorded an open verdict at the inquest. I tried to get the investigating officer to dig deeper, but you know how it is, every day brings another case or three and only those that look hopeful get full attention."

"But surely the death was looked at properly?"

"It was looked at, but in my opinion, not properly. The timing was bad, unlucky. It was the post Christmas and New Year period. There'd been a major blagging in the city plus a heavy burglary. The usual winter ills added a shortage of manpower to the equation. When I put it to the DI a second time that not enough had been done, things got rather heated and I ended up putting my ticket in."

For once Martin's reserve about his twin sister's death, a subject that he still found painful despite the passage of years, was missing. He found himself able to talk much more easily and openly to Eileen than was usual. She sat quietly listening, hearing the anger and bitterness that had caused his resignation from the police, the hurt that remained and, especially, the blame that he felt. After their parents' deaths Martin and Susie had been even closer but, to him, when she needed him most he was not there. Eileen pointed out the impossibility of continuous support. It was inevitable that he could not always be on hand. Martin had shrugged and she left the subject, knowing that logic could not deal with the depth of hurt that she saw in his eyes, heard in his voice.

He went on to tell her of his early life in and around Aldershot where his father, an army officer, was stationed and of subsequent peripatetic years travelling with his parents on his father's postings. Of becoming a boarder at Sherborne in Dorset and then having to leave following the death of his parents. Of enlisting in the army as a 'boy soldier' and gaining entry into Sandhurst, only to be RTU'd (returned to unit) after a year following outspoken criticism of a regime that he found elitist. Of then volunteering for the Royal Military Police and, after specialist weapons and explosives training at Longmoor Camp, of buying himself out to join the civil police. They talked together of the police 'family' and she learnt of his selection for CID and training as a Scene of Crime Officer before promotion to Detective Sergeant.

"And what about you?" he asked sitting down with their refills.

"Oh, I've led a very ordinary life. My parents are Scots. I was born north of the border, but dad was in the merchant navy, an engineer and, like yourself we moved around a lot cos of his job. He ended up in Southampton, then they moved back to Scotland when he retired."

"But you stayed down here?"

"I had met a man, fallen in love and married. Unfortunately it was a bad choice. There was a messy divorce after a couple of years and I joined the police on the rebound." She laughed a little self consciously. "Mum and Dad wanted me to go back with them, but I'd flown the nest, had my own place and didn't want to start over where they were concerned. They're darlings but you know how parents are, especially with an only child."

Some days later she took a telephone call at Shirley Police Station; it was Wild. "Hi, you seemed a fairly free agent when we were talking the other day. I wondered whether you might like dinner one evening?" Surprised and pleased she had accepted his offer.

The following Saturday she met another side of a man whose unconventional life and unusual personality intrigued and attracted her. Over the weeks which followed, Eileen found herself falling for his quiet charm, looking forward to their telephone conversations, increasingly eager to see the flash of white teeth in the brown scarred face. Though normally friendly she did not allow herself to be quickly influenced. A broken marriage and several years as a police woman had taught more than a degree of restraint. But, as she came to know Martin, the professional in her admired his commitment and attention to detail in his business life, whilst the woman in her responded to his masculinity and appreciated his thoughtful attentiveness. Her Scottish blood was concerned by occasional excessive drinking – though only of wine, not the 'hard stuff'. As their lives became increasingly intertwined, another concern were the occasional mood swings; black days when Martin seemed to withdraw, preferring his own company. These intrigued and challenged her, they seemed so out of character and she guessed that they went back to the family losses that he had experienced. She made allowances, giving ready support on the one hand and space, without comment, when he seemed to need it.

Now, as she watched pale grey trousers tighten as he reached into the rear of the car, the past twelve months of interest growing through affection into what she now recognized was a great deal more, had its usual effect.

Martin collected his jacket and briefcase from the rear seat. A sticky back to his shirt brought the pleasurable anticipation of a shower as he walked across the road. The door key was in his briefcase so he rang the bell with an elbow. The door opened immediately and, not for the first time, he felt momentarily unbalanced by the face peering round the door. Smiling blue eyes seemed to twinkle, kissable lips parted to show even white teeth, small pixie like ears were half hidden by fair wavy hair. As he stood for a moment, smiling back, all that he could see was Eileen's face. Stepping in he saw why. She was certainly out of uniform! Before him was the delicious sight of a slim curvaceous figure wearing only the laciest of brief panties and bra in a soft, very feminine pink. Her complexion glowed, the curls at the nape of her neck were still damp from the shower. Smiling eyes held more than a hint of a naughty twinkle.

"Do you usually answer the door like that?" feeling a frisson of a different anticipation.

"I saw you arrive and it took you so long to come in." She turned and stepped onto the first stair and then, laughing over her shoulder, wiggled her bottom at him and dashed towards the landing. He caught her before she was halfway up the stairs, the sound of the front door shutting on it's closer echoed by the thump of his briefcase on the hall floor. She cried out in mock dismay as he seized the waistband of her panties, in one move bringing her to a standstill and the flimsy garment down to her thighs. She fell on to the stairs, on her knees, wriggling and full of pretend protest, softly curved cheeks proving irresistible to white teeth. She was hobbled by the froth of lace around her knees, further flight impossible. Kissing his way up her spine he reached beneath extended arms, found the lacy cups and, pushing them upwards, freed small breasts. Her breathing quickened as his tongue and teeth reached her neck and ears. With fingers extended he made small circles, the palms of his hands against pink points. Feeling them harden he gently rolled and pulled. Arching her back, pushing her bottom against him, squirming, then, "Oooh Marty!" and, giggling, breathlessly, "A gentleman would at least take his trousers off!"

8.30 p.m.

Bathed, changed and dressed with care, green eyes toasted blue across raised champagne glasses at a table in the Chewton Glen's Marriott Restaurant. Elegant chandeliers and discreet table lighting vied with warm red luminous from a sun just set, filling the tall west facing windows. Polished panelling, crisp white table linen and glistening cutlery provided a stylish backdrop as Martin gazed over the rim of his glass. Bubbles spiralling upwards in the clear golden wine seemed to express the exhilaration and delight that he felt. She was so lovely! Smooth bare shoulders above a blue strapless dress, the perfect setting for a heart shaped face, golden hair and those warm blue eyes. Eyes that smiled with love. A love that echoed in his heart so much that he felt a physical ache.

"So when do I see this other woman in your life?" she teased, "La Belle France?"

Smiling, Martin tapped the champagne flute against a bottle of Taittinger resting in the ice bucket and then raised it. "September and October are always a good time. The vendage, the grape picking, will take place then and in the Champagne area the celebrations, especially if the year is a good one, are fabulous. They're not as serious as Bordeaux or as much fun as Burgundy or Beaujolais, but the larger houses certainly know how to entertain. I've a standing invitation to spend a weekend with a Director of this House." He tapped the Taittinger again.

"Is this a further sign of a misspent youth?" She teased again, eyes sparkling and the tips of her fingers caressing the back of his free hand where it lay on the table.

"Not really," smiling. "Did a job for their London agents a couple of years ago and was asked to report direct to one of their French Directors. Spent a very enjoyable day at a Chateau that they use for entertaining. Also I love their wine, so different from some of the other Houses, light, elegant and seductive. Just like a very accomplished woman." It was his turn to tease.

Eileen's even white teeth caught the curve of her full lower lip. Quite deliberately the long fair lashes swept down over blue eyes. "I wonder what a girl must do to keep her man on the straight and narrow whilst he's away?" she murmured.

They laughed quietly and happily together, content and confident in one another. His hand now upturned on the table to face hers. Fingertips gently caressing palms and wrists.

Later, in the darkness of their room, she collapsed upon him, full of shudders and little moans. Holding her close, he wondered whether life could improve. Certainly love could not!

Friday 8th May 1992
5.45 a.m. Southampton

Waking early, Martin left Eileen sleeping whilst he shaved and packed a case. Taking tea to the bedside he kissed her neck gently. She smiled without opening her eyes.

"See you in a few days," he whispered. "Put the Citroen away for me. I'm taking the Porsche." A clear sky and cool early morning air promised another fine day as he walked the short distance to a lockup garage. Sliding into the driving seat he turned the ignition key and, as the flat six of the 911 burst into life, felt his blood quicken. The car was a few years old but it was another major plus in his life, as was the thought of driving it off the ferry and across France to the rendezvous in Switzerland.

The journey to Poole took only forty minutes. At a little after 7 a.m. he joined the short queue of cars and was soon driving up the ramp and into the bowels of the car deck. As he did so, suddenly, unaccountably, he felt an emptiness, a loneliness, a wish to turn and go back. The feeling was totally alien to him and, had he been superstitious, he might have paused. But he was not and did not. With a shake of the head he threw the momentary blackness aside.

7.05 a.m.

Outside the maisonette Eileen, smart in crisp white uniform shirt, black skirt and black and white chequered tie, was opening the driver's door of the Citroen. Her hat and shoulder bag were still in the hall of the maisonette, where she could pick them up after garaging the car. She turned the ignition key. The motor fired instantly and settled into a fast tick-over. About to engage gear she saw Martin's sunglasses on the floor of the car, in front of the passenger seat. With a smile at this untidiness, thinking that they must have slid off the seat during the journey home she leant across to pick them up and then, with a little glow of warmth, thought that, once home, Martin had been too busy to tidy the car.

Slipping the glasses into their case and that into the dash pocket, Eileen engaged first gear and, as the big car started to move, checked over her shoulder to see a Post Office van turning the corner from Church Street into Parksyde Avenue. She dabbed the brake pedal and the Citroen dipped its bonnet abruptly. Beneath the car, in a wooden box held in place by a marine recovery magnet, a little globule of mercury ran two centimetres to the end of its glass tube; the electrical circuits completed and the detonator inserted into the rectangle of Semtex activated.

The force of the explosion destroyed the big saloon, lifting the front of the car completely off the ground. The passenger shell reared upwards and backwards, disintegrating into a mass of metal fragments, body parts and internal trim. Petrol from ruptured fuel lines and then the tank bursting into flames, causing a fireball which burnt the leaves from the trees on both sides of the road. The blast caused glass from the windows and doors of the maisonettes to fly in splintered shards, some to pierce the smart uniform hat and leather shoulder bag which lay on the hall table.

*

The ferry's car deck was crowded as Martin collected his cabin bag from the rear seat and then spent some minutes fitting the Porsche's Targa top in place. He smiled quietly to himself, anticipating breakfast and lunch on board with the French roads to come. Making his way to the Purser's office to collect a day cabin key, he was already looking forward to the next trip, when Eileen and he might take some days leave. The thought of sharing his love of France with the woman that he loved was good indeed.

*

In a Cork hotel, Liam Mahoney eased his long rawboned frame into his second hot bath of the morning, methodically soaping and scrubbing, paying particular attention to the hands and wrists. He listened to the news bulletin, anticipating a news flash which would report the death by explosion of an unnamed man in Southampton. "Police are withholding the identity until relatives have been informed." Scrubbing completed, he draped a hot flannel over the top half of his face, leaving the mouth clear for the glass of Irish whisky on a chair by the bath.

The job had gone smoothly. The target had appeared a few minutes earlier than expected in the Pall Mall entrance. Although he was some distance away, it was obvious that the height and build were right. Could not see the hair, wearing a hat, but the complexion was dark as described. The clincher was the car brought round to the front by a doorman. A black Citroen is distinctive.

It was easy to follow through the traffic of St James and Piccadilly, though he was surprised by the direction that the target took. He had anticipated crossing the Thames and taking the A2 to Dover. Instead the Citroen headed west to join the nose to tail, stop start lines of cars in Knightsbridge. Must be taking the Portsmouth, Southampton or Poole ferry?

The heavy traffic made it appear quite natural to spend moments astride his motorcycle at the rear of the Citroen. During one convenient pause it had taken just a few seconds to slip a miniature transmitter on its elasticated loop over the tail pipes of the car's exhaust. Then he had allowed the Citroen to gain distance on him as the traffic thinned out. Once on the M4 he had dropped right back, virtually out of sight and had followed the target by listening to the bleeps coming from the transmitter, through the receiver in his 'Courier' pannier on the rear of the bike and thence through the headphones worn beneath his crash helmet. Only at the approach to road junctions did he open the bike up and close to viewing distance. Occasionally he checked his mirrors and smiled sardonically on seeing the dark BMW saloon keeping steady station a couple of hundred yards behind.

The only difficult part had been staying in touch with the target through the back streets of Southampton. The BMW had its work cut out to stay with him there, and he didn't make it easy for them. The remainder was simple. The transmitter was retrieved and the magnet with its wooden box had clunked into place as he bent to lace a shoe whilst walking past the car ten minutes later. The shortened bright blue pencil that he had used as a final 'safety' was tight and required a slight pull and twist to get it from the hole in the box. In so doing it slipped from his fingers and rolled into the gutter. He left it there.

Back on the 'bike he had made a fast run to Swansea, wondering initially about the target's destination. Not what he had been told to expect; should he make a call to query? Probably an English girlfriend. Not to bother. The people in the BMW could worry about that. He stopped to switch plates on the bike in a quiet lane and, by midday, was on the Swansea to Cork ferry. In the middle of the St George's Channel, the plates went into a weighted bag with his 'Courier' vest wrapped around them and disappeared over the side of the boat. Should there be any enquiries, he had friends in Cork who would talk readily about an all night cards and drinking session. But he did not expect his alibi to be tested. Everything had gone so smoothly.

12.20 p.m. Cross Channel Ferry

The girl standing behind the waiter was slim, dark skinned and with jet black hair. She had a Mediterranean appearance thought Martin and, remembering her accent, probably Italian. She was wearing a dark linen business suit with just sufficient décolletage to raise interest but not temperatures around a boardroom table. He had seen her before; she had joined him as he stood at the ship's Information Desk, had put her shoulder bag on the desk and, in extracting a purse, had knocked it to the floor. Martin had knelt to help her collect the scattered belongings and been treated to the sort of view usually reserved for the Chairman of the Board! Now, with what he thought to be quite seemly pleasure, he listened as the waiter explained that the crowded restaurant had no empty tables and 'Madame' wondered whether she could trespass upon their brief previous acquaintance to share his. Martin rose to his feet, smiled and, as the waiter held the chair for his new companion, assured them both that he would be delighted.

Sitting again he extracted a bottle of Chablis from its ice bucket. "May I offer you a drink?" She paused a moment, smiled again and said, "Thank you."

For a moment she felt herself slightly off balance; a moment of unease. The close cropped coppery hair, the pale green eyes and the easy smile on the open scarred face were attractive. So different from her usual companions. Then she remembered the instructions from the driver of the black BMW, her Number One in the previous day's game of cat and mouse.

"Get close to him. Find out as much as you can. His route, his destination. Phone me as soon as you've got something useful – and before you leave the boat!"

She wondered how difficult this was going to be. The English were renowned for their reserve. She need not have worried. Martins' curiosity led the conversation and, as the meal progressed, it was easy to turn from generalities of the boat, the weather and motoring on the continent to the specifics of recommended hotels and restaurants. Over the main course she enquired directly about his destination and his work.

"Oh, I'm heading for Switzerland this time. I'm a building surveyor." The half-truths came smoothly. He'd had plenty of practice over the years in hiding his true activities. Casual conversations were apt to become difficult when the word 'security' was mentioned.

"That's a long drive. Surely you will break your journey somewhere?"

Martin's preferred hotel was not critical as there was no connection to the client or the job in hand, so he answered freely. "Yes, I like to enjoy these working trips, allow time to deviate a little. I've a favourite hotel in the Ballons des Vosges, a pretty mountainous area in the Alsace region of France. I shall stay there tonight and travel on to Switzerland tomorrow."

"It must be a special hotel to take you into the mountains when you are on business?"

"The hotel is good but it is the region that I find so attractive. The Vosgue mountains are not large, and motoring through them when the weather is as good as is forecast for tomorrow, is something special."

"That's an area that I do not know at all. Would you be kind enough to share your hotel's address with me?"

"Of course." Martin scribbled the name and address on a yellow sticky, adding the telephone number from his diary. "If you do stay there please do not expect a modern hotel. The building is old but comfortable. But make sure that you are in time for dinner! The chef is also the owner and he is very good."

The lunch had passed pleasantly with his unexpected companion and Martin was a little taken aback when, a few minutes after their coffees had been served the 'décolletage' suddenly rose, thanked him for sharing his table and announced that she "had things to do before the ferry docked."

As she left, perhaps for the first time, he looked beyond the dark brown eyes and the ready smile, noting a pallor beneath the olive skin. The ship's motion had been comfortable and she'd eaten a reasonable amount of food. Perhaps she was just tired? Martin's guess was correct. The previous night's attempt to sleep on the back seat of the BMW had not been a success. Her male companion had been uneasy and the route that they had followed was not what he had expected. The sudden appearance of the target in the morning when he was half asleep himself, with Martin leaving the Citroen where he had parked it to drive off in another, totally unknown car, had caused confusion, a rapid exit from the side road and a flurry of telephone calls. It was a difficult 'tail' in the early morning traffic. On arrival at the ferry terminal and without documents for their car, they had been prevented from following Martin onto the boat and she had to hurriedly board as a foot passenger, feeling very much on her own and distant from the companion left in Poole.

*

Even further away, at the rail of a luxury yacht lying motionless on a calm Mediterranean sea, a heavily built man with dark complexion, black hair flecked with grey and a prominent hooked nose, awaited the arrival of a passenger. With coffee cup in one hand and a custom made Havana in his mouth, he watched as the ship's motor launch carrying the arrival curved out from the quay, leaving a trail of white froth on the dark blue water. The boat slowed to arrive with scarcely a bump on the side of the mother ship.

As the new arrival mounted the inclined steps slung from the yacht's deck, the cigar went over side and the men greeted one another with embraces, kisses on the cheeks and back slapping. They made an odd pair, the new arrival was smaller, slim and in a dark business suit, contrasting with the bulk and lightweight white shirt and trousers of his host. They spoke in Italian "Coffee or something else?"

"Coffee will do."

"Did you have a good trip?"

"Very good. The arrangements were excellent and we got the deal – better than hoped! These people are easy. They were so anxious to get the supply we could have asked more."

"How soon do they collect?"

"Within the next two weeks."

"And what about Tabarde?"

"That's built into the deal; they will take care of him."

"Good." Then with a note of concern. "Can we trust them to do it right? We cannot afford a connection back to us on this one. That bastard has too many highly placed friends now."

"Don't worry Patron, it is all taken care of. They have an Irish man in their team with good Republican connections. The death will be blamed on the IRA. Remember the boatload of arms that the IRA lost last year, the trawler that was seized by their Customs and Navy? Our tame policeman is feeding that into their system – that the information came from Tabarde's people!"

"And do we have a fall back? We have not used them for this before."

"We have insurance. Their man will be followed by Toni's people who will stay at a distance, but if anything goes wrong they can cover it."

Saturday 9th May 1992
2.50 a.m. The Vosgue

He awoke with a start, prompted into consciousness by a particularly chilling dream. For seconds he lay in the blackness, heart pounding, mouth dry and foul. Where the devil was he? Memory returned. The strange bed was in a small hotel near the Franco-Swiss border. He had arrived early the previous evening, relaxed by an enjoyable drive, had dined well and drunk too much of the Macon Blanc. Always a danger when eating alone.

Martin raised himself on an elbow, peered at the illuminated figures on the bedside clock and swore silently when he saw that it was not yet three in the morning, and he was now wide awake. What, apart from the frightening dream, had woken him? Lying beneath the warm duvet his mind went back to the first time that he had stayed at this particular hotel, sharing the bed with a pretty girl companion. He smiled in the darkness, thinking now of Eileen.

Counting girls instead of sheep had its dangers. He was on the point of switching on the bedside light to find a glass of water when he heard voices. The sound was faint; he did not immediately recognise the murmurings as such, but knew that this was what had disturbed his sleep. Throwing back the duvet he swung his legs out of bed. The floor of the old building creaked as he moved to the window. From the darkened room, looking into the car park, he was again reminded of the earlier visit. The scene outside was illuminated, as it had been then, by cold alpine moonlight, the stars were huge and clear.

At first he could see nothing, then his eyes focussed on the squat shape of the Porsche, sleeping in the hotel's rear car park, and he saw movement. Two figures were on the far side of the car. After talking quietly for a few seconds they moved out of the moonlight, into the dark shade of a tree, where they disappeared.

For perhaps five minutes he stood and watched, awaiting further movement, debating leaving the warmth and security of his room to investigate; then decided that daylight would serve. Altering the alarm to 6 a.m., Martin drank from a glass of water, checked that the chock of hardwood was under the door and was asleep again quite quickly.

5.55 a.m.

Waking before the alarm, he lay for some moments as morning light illuminated the floral curtains. Quietly he moved about the room, making a first pot of tea and then sitting in the window seat to drink it. The light changed on the surrounding mountains as the sun appeared. The valleys beneath were misty, with pine forests on their flanks, pale grey lower down shading to dark blue higher up. As the sun rose detail became evident. In the distance, on a crest, stood the silhouette of a castle, too far away to see whether it was ruined or inhabited. Closer at hand the scattering of parked cars had a light misting on the windscreens and rear windows.

Tea finished, he threw clothes on, not pausing to shave, and slipped quietly into the car park. Walking to the car, his thoughts now on the mysterious figures of the previous night, he circled round it, checking tyres and bodywork. On the far side of the Porsche, near the rear wheel, he knelt and peered underneath, checking the floorpan and the visible parts of the rear mounted engine. The exhaust pipes swept down from each bank of cylinders on the flat six engine, joining together to run as twin pipes to the rear of the car. At a point close to their junction was a flat black plastic package held in place by two circles of adhesive tape. From one side of the package there ran a piece of thin plastic covered wire which again was taped to the rearmost part of the exhaust pipes; it was about half a metre long.

Martin sat back on his heels, shocked, a curious feeling of tightness in his chest contrasting with emptiness in his belly. Staring straight ahead for a second or so, his brain refusing to believe his eyes. Thoughtfully he gazed at the dusty wheel and surrounding panel, contrasting starkly with the shiny cleanliness of the black plastic package. From past experience he had no doubt about the package. But why? And then what to do? Apart from the disruption to his day, he did not need the interest of the local police or the curiosity of the French anti-terrorist officers. He knew too well the likely extent of their enquiries. The contents of the two customised tool bags filled with 'sweeping' gear, electronic test equipment and search tools packed for his Swiss contract, would require explanation, which undoubtedly would be difficult in the circumstances. In any case he had a deadline in Zurich with a valuable client!

Experience took over. One thing had to be done straight away and mentally he thanked the tough, unassuming Warrant Officer who had been the Explosives Team Trainer in his Longmoor days. He fished a small penknife from his pocket and opening it, without hesitation, cut the wire where it entered the plastic package. Removal of the aerial ensured that if the bomber wished to activate his device now he would have to be within a suicidal two metres if transmitting on VHF or an equally unrealistic ten metres if on UHF – instead of up to 200 or so metres which the antenna's original length would have permitted.

Carefully now he examined the rest of the car's bodywork, checking the dust from the previous days driving. He paid particular attention to the edges of the doors, the front opening luggage compartment and the rear engine cover. The expertise in forensic search, learnt so carefully in his Scene of Crime years, now came into its own. In only two areas was the dust disturbed, in front of and behind the rear wheel arch where the men of the previous night had gripped the panels in reaching under the car. In one of these areas there was the slightest of damage to the bottom of a panel, a very faint indentation with a different sort of debris attached – more like minute fragments of wood than road dust, brownish in colour instead of grey.

Looking around, Martin saw that in the grass at the edge of the car park was a long straight length of pine. It was devoid of branches, apparently part of a logged load. At the thick end of the branch he found traces of gravel embedded on one side, similar to that covering the car park. About half a metre up from that end was a sharp bruising of the wood and bark. The bruising was on the opposite side to the embedded gravel. The branch had been used as a lever to lift the side of the Porsche to the limit of its suspension. They had encountered difficulty in getting under the low slung car. Satisfied that only one area of the car was of concern, he opened the luggage compartment, removing one of the customised cases to extract a mirror on a telescopic handle. Lying by the side of the car he switched on an illuminating ring positioned around the circumference of the mirror's glass and spent some time examining the plastic package. There was no dowel hole therefore the device was not fitted with a tilt switch. Feeling slightly more at ease he unstrapped the car's jack, quickly positioning it and lifting the car on the same side as the two men of the previous night must have done. It took only a few minutes to saw through the plastic tape and release the package.

The plastic covering the package was conventionally wrapped as a gift would be with more tape holding together the overlapping joins at the top. He lifted it to his nose and immediately recognised the marzipan smell of nitroglycerine. Feeling the surface of the package with delicate touches he found that there was an irregularity on top of the package, under the joining flaps.

His penknife was not sharp enough and, rummaging through the small collection of tools carried on the car, he grunted with satisfaction on finding an old modelling knife. Breaking off a segment of blade to obtain a sharp edge he gently cut the top layer of plastic. Beneath was what he had expected. The wire that he had initially cut short was connected to a slim cigarette shaped detonator which in turn was pressed into the plasticine like surface of two sticks of shaped nitro, which were moulded together into a more or less flat package. Removing the detonator, he wrapped the nitro again in its plastic covering, sealing it with the remnants of the adhesive tape Almost carelessly he tossed the package into the tool bag and, with much greater care, wrapped the detonator in a piece of cloth, placing it in the car's dash pocket.

Lowering the car and putting the tools away took only a few minutes. He walked back to the hotel looking for an early breakfast. It felt good to be alive and suddenly he was hungry!

In the small dining room the proprietor and his wife were busy with early morning chores. As the man disappeared into the kitchen, Martin asked his wife if he was too early for the 'petit dejeuner'. He received a cheery assurance that he was not and she bustled over to prepare a window table for him.

"Are you very busy Madame?"

"Oh non, Monsieur. It is too early for the tourists and in any case we are off the main route. Usually there are a few businessmen like yourself, but that is all."

"Your husband's lotte was very good last night. With cooking of that standard I expected your restaurant to be busier than it was."

The wife looked pleased. "The businessmen are all on their way home by Friday. We get many local people, but that will be tonight. Already the restaurant is nearly full."

"I saw two men in the car park late last night, but I did not see them in the restaurant earlier. Are they staying with you?" Madame looked puzzled. "We do not have two men together. Apart from yourself there is only the family, who arrived before you and they retired early because of the children, and a young couple who were at the table by the bar."

*

As Martin Wild rose from his breakfast table, Gordon Wilson sat down to bacon and eggs and all the trimmings in the kitchen of his pretend farmhouse near Cadnam in Hampshire.

Wilson was a big man, over six foot and with a large frame. When on his feet an early beer gut was apparent. His light brown hair was brushed forward and contained a lock of premature grey above the pale blue eyes. The grey in his hair and the protruding stomach made him look older than his forty years.

Almost immediately the telephone rang. Wilson's wife answered it to say, "It's DM for you."

Wilson put down the coffee that he was about to pour and went to the phone in the corner of the kitchen. "Where are you calling from?" Then, "I'll ring you back."

Replacing the handset, he walked the short distance to his office where he picked up a telephone. This was on a different line without extensions. He dialled a long distance number. Dermott Mabbett answered immediately with the words, "I'm told the job wasn't done; someone else in the car!"

"Yes, I know. It must have been a girlfriend."

"We were not told of any other connection this side. We've lost him then?"

"No. They had backup, someone following. They saw him leave earlier – before the event. Took a different car – we didn't know about that either – caught the Poole to Cherbourg ferry. Their people phoned us. We're still looking after it. I've spoken with our French friends."

"Gordon, we cannot afford anymore cock-ups on this one. If we do, we lose respect. And, if that happens, we lose the connection – and a lot more besides." Mabbett was angry and it showed.

Wilson's voiced was also raised; he snapped back defensively "It was your man who cocked up DM, but you don't need to worry. I've told you that it's taken care of."

"Do our French friends know who it is?"

"No. They're doing us a favour. They owe us for the job that Liam did for them last year. They don't know that there is a new French connection."

9.30 a.m. Southampton

In Parksyde Avenue the police barriers were being taken down. The remains of the Citroen, covered in plastic sheeting, were on a transporter. Scene of Crime and Bomb Squad officers had searched and photographed every inch of the road.

Detective Chief Inspector Potter walked from the windowless maisonette, around the one remaining area protected by chequered tape, tarmacadam scorched and melted, to a waiting police car. Using the radio he spoke with the Incident Room, set up in Shirley Police Station, some half a mile away. "Any further news on Wild?"

The detective constable manning one of the six desks crammed into what had been the Parade Room answered in the negative. It was known that Martin was the owner of the Citroen. A curtain twitching neighbour had watched him arrive and saw the couple leave some two hours later. Eileen Padgett's distraught parents confirmed that their daughter had phoned to say that she and Wild were going out for a meal. She normally spoke with them on a Friday evening, but the heartbroken couple knew nothing more.

Potter had known Eileen reasonably well. Her sunny personality made her popular. She was also a competent officer and Potter had frowned upon the romance between Wild, an ex-policeman with a known penchant for pretty girls and the younger policewoman.

9.40 a.m. Essex

It was not only the police who were active that Saturday morning. Crouched over his workbench the stocky figure of Doctor Anthony Drew gave no indication of the excitement that he felt. To a casual observer the disembowelled 35mm camera on the bench of this garage turned workshop would hardly have been exciting. At first sight a layman could have been forgiven for assuming that an enthusiastic amateur of electronics was at work. The more discerning eye would have noted the substantial range of test equipment, the rows of multi-drawered components cabinets, the neat professional layout of tools. A visitor from the shadowy world of commercial security, or a 'junior' from one of the government agencies, would have been more interested in the part finished miniature transmitters and receivers, the larger customised cases of electronic search equipment and the printed circuit boards undergoing soak test. For here, in the heart of an Essex estuary town, worked an individual of surprising talent. Anthony Drew's Doctorate was in Physics and, from the wider spheres of radio, electronics and telecommunications, he had narrowed his vision to become one of the leading designers and small manufacturers of those very specialised items required by any security professional who needs to monitor – or ensure that someone else is not.

Why was the excitement behind the pale blue eyes not shared by a design team in a large modern complex? The answer to that lay within the man himself. An individualist with towering expertise but a temper and tongue which eschewed commonsense, could cauterise conversation and inevitably made teamwork an impossibility. To the select few who were privileged to be termed friends there was quick wit and rough hewn humour, but above all, comradeship. Martin Wild counted himself lucky to be in that small circle. Presented with a technical problem of sufficient interest, Drew was capable of tremendous concentration which would turn day into night and had brought his marriage to the edge of domestic strife on more than one occasion. When the problem was difficult any first signs of success were contained. It was not until it was as good as solved that discipline would be relaxed.

Hence the cause of the present excitement. For weeks he had been working intermittently on the miniaturization of a covert directional microphone. The standard 'rifle mike' was a cumbersome device, difficult to operate and virtually impossible to hide. Martin had suggested that the shell of a 35mm camera with telephoto lens might lend itself as a cover for a close range device, but the problems had been immense. Now at last results were appearing.

The timing was opportune in another respect. Two days before he had received a call from Martin.

"Tony, I'm at Quantum. They're asking for a sweep of their Swiss meeting this Monday. I know that it's short notice, but can you join me?"

"Tell that bloody man Drummond to get his act together. They must have had this on the cards for weeks."

Martin had smiled at the typical Drew reaction. "You're right about the meeting but the sweep is a last minute decision."

"Well, as luck has it I can be free and I've got something to show you anyway, so I can kill two wealthy birds with one stone."

Martin had grinned again. Tony frequently made reference to what he termed as 'Martin's wealth'. In fact the boot is on the other foot thought Martin.

"Can you meet me at Poole tomorrow morning? I'll take the Porsche and we can stop en route at that hotel that we used last time – the one with the good restaurant."

"Not bloody likely! You can collect me from Zurich. I'll fly myself there." Drew's one obsession – apart from his work – was flying.

"Tony, the expenses will be heavy enough without us travelling separately."

"That's their fault for short notice, but don't worry, I haven't had the engine covers off the Cessna for two weeks so it will be something to look forward to. I'll keep the cost down to a normal return air fare. Why don't you join me in the passenger seat on Sunday? I could pick you up at Eastleigh. It will save you two days."

"Thanks Tony, but I've decided to motor. I want to make a break of it too."

"You'd be safer with me at 2,000 feet than on four wheels." Tony goaded Martin gently, knowing that whilst he himself disliked car travel, Martin only flew when he had to.

"I'll take my chances. Let me know your ETA at Zurich and I'll collect you. Don't make it too late on Sunday. I'll book rooms at the usual hotel and we can talk over dinner."

Martin and Tony frequently worked together on 'sweeping' jobs. Drew's expertise in electronics and telecommunications, coupled with Martin's contacts and grounding in forensic search, had made the specialisation a lucrative field. For larger jobs they put a team together, all of whom were very competent. The Swiss job was a small one so they needed no one else.

As he put down the phone, Tony grinned to himself at the thought of he and Martin testing the new 35mm 'toy' on the unsuspecting buxom barmaid who presided over the hotel's bar.

10.05 a.m. The Vosgue

Breakfast over and bill paid, Martin carried his overnight bag to the car. Throwing it into the back, he settled into the driver's seat and inserted the key into the ignition. For several seconds he sat still, mind racing over the incidents of the morning, checking yet again what he had done – and for anything he might have forgotten! With stomach tensed he turned the key. Only the engine burst into life.

"No Big Bang yet," he muttered and waited for the motors beat to settle into an even idle, then slid the gear lever into first and moved off. The short driveway from the hotel led to a typically alpine road. There was comfortable room for two cars abreast but little more. The road surface was good but it undulated and there were bends aplenty.

The Porsche had covered no more than fifty metres, the engine was just beginning to warm up, when Martin saw a grey Mercedes saloon in his right-hand door mirror. It was parked in a small clearing to the right of the road and had been hidden behind a growth of young pines as he approached. The two occupants had a view of the hotel's drive through the pines. Within another half kilometre and on a slightly longer straight he could see that the other car had pulled out and was following at a steady distance.

Martin was not surprised. The planters of the package would need to be in a position to activate their device at a convenient point. Somewhere on the road that would suit their purpose. They would follow until the road and its surroundings were right, then press the button and 'boom'. If their target was not killed outright they would be in a position to finish the job.

For the best part of a kilometre the two cars maintained station, Martin driving at a steady pace, not quickly but not hanging about either. Then he saw that the Mercedes was gaining ground. They must have pressed their button and were now wondering why he had not disappeared in a puff of smoke. Time for their Plan B – whatever it was.

As the big Mercedes closed in, he was not too concerned, confident that he could lose them. The saloon would be no match for the Porsche on these roads. The situation echoed some of his past life and he felt the adrenaline pumping. The excitement and the slight edge of fear that had once been almost a drug. The memories were good and confidence boosting. Checking the internal mirror he realised that his scarred face was smiling its twisted smile. He remembered a jest from comrades in the specialist army unit that had once been his home. "When Wildman smiles you know things are dodgy!" He waited until he could read the French number plate on the car behind, dictated this onto a pocket recorder that lived in the Porsche's glove box, then dropped the gears into third and 'leant' on the accelerator. The rear of the car squatted and the flat six's note rose to a mechanical howl. Swiftly the Porsche distanced itself from the big saloon and as he entered a right hand curve through a growth of mature pines Martin raised his left hand in a wave of goodbye.

The Porsche exited the second half of the right, left double curves and by the end of a short straight was doing almost 90 mph. As he braked for the next sharper bend he checked his mirror, expecting the Mercedes to be just appearing from the last curve but, to his surprise, it was halfway along the straight and gaining ground as he braked.

Martin swore, the smile leaving his face, and settled down to some serious motoring. For several kilometres a game of cat and mouse ensued. Through the frequent bends of the pine clad mountainside he would gain some distance only to see the gain being held on faster curves and the occasional straight. This was no normal Mercedes, of that he was sure. He guessed it to be the wolf in sheep's clothing of the range, the short wheelbase saloon with a massive 6.9 litre engine shoehorned under the bonnet. The suspension and brakes of that model had been substantially modified and it was as fast as or faster than most sports cars.

The road was now descending into a valley, the downhill bends and curves favouring the Porsche. It was a road that he knew – but not well. He guessed that the driver of the big saloon, which was substantially heavier than the Porsche, probably did not know the road at all and was working hard to maintain contact. This was perhaps the only opportunity to put sufficient distance between the cars, enabling him to change roads or duck into a side turning without being seen.

Despite all efforts, he had gained only some two hundred metres on the Mercedes as he sensed that they were nearing the bottom of the valley. Here he knew the road would straighten, which would favour the other car. Then, rounding a series of sharp bends with the hillside on the right and a sheer drop into pines on the left, he saw a glint of water through the trees, confirming that the valley floor was near.

The road plunged downhill steeply. There was a straight of about two hundred metres followed by another right hand bend. Just prior to the bend was an indentation in the mountainside and as he approached it he remembered seeing, on a previous trip, heaps of gravel dumped by road workers. In the few seconds allowed he saw that there were now two large mounds of road surfacing material, the first higher than the second and large enough to hide the Porsche, with what looked like sufficient room between to allow a car through.

Martin hit the brakes whilst the Mercedes was still out of sight. The Porsche snaked viciously, his opposite lock corrections just holding the tail heavy car, unbalanced by the sudden deceleration on a curve. As they approached the first mound Martin allowed the incipient swing of the car's tail to the left to go uncorrected for a split second. The rear wheels lost adhesion and as the car went sideways, slowing rapidly, he caught the start of the spin with a large handful of opposite lock and firm acceleration. The car shot forward, off of the road and between the two mounds.

The gap was narrower than he had thought, the mound on his left shallower and with loose granules lying between the two heaps. As the wheels bit into these the car slid to its left under the remaining momentum. Martin swore as it came to rest. It was behind the first larger heap but the rear wheels were on the slope of the second.

He sensed rather than heard the approach of the Mercedes and slipped the gear lever into first, easing the clutch out to gain more shelter. The wheels embedded in the granules, spun and the car only inched forward. Suddenly the possibilities of a road surface covered with loose granules on a sharp downhill bend, coupled with a heavy car travelling too fast, struck him. He dipped the clutch, depressed the accelerator and as the Porsche's rev counter swung around the clock, dropped the clutch out. A steady shower of granules shot across the road behind the Porsche and in front of the approaching Mercedes. Its driver was braking hard for the corner and on the limit in his efforts to stay in touch with the Porsche. There was the scream of rubber as the Mercedes lost adhesion, the driver battling to hold the big car. Ten metres of loose granules at that critical moment was just too much. Then the sound of splintering wood as the Mercedes went sideways through the red and white marker posts on the side of the road, followed by a rising howl from the engine as the rear wheels left the ground. The car went sideways off the road, hit steeply sloping ground clear of the last pine trees, rolled once and then fell again as the slope became a sheer drop for thirty metres. It landed nose first on rocks bordering the river. The smash of metal was followed by a huge splash as the car somersaulted into the heavily flowing river.

By the time that Martin reached the spot where the car had gone through the posts, there was nothing to be seen apart from the shattered windscreen and broken glass glinting from the rocks bordering the river. The weight of the mountain water had swept the car downstream as it sank. It was out of sight and so were its occupants.

"Not quite the big bang that you planned," murmured Martin and turned to set about rescuing the Porsche. The sheet of plastic from the boot again proved its worth, providing traction under the Porsche's rear tyres. With the car back on the road, he saw that there was slight body damage to the rear nearside and, more importantly, an exhaust 'blow' where the pipes had hit the mound. He drove sedately and thoughtfully to the next town where he found two garages. At the larger and better equipped he left the Porsche for temporary repairs; at the second he hired a small Renault.

The attempt on his life had been a professional one. The only people who knew of his journey – apart from Eileen and Tony – were the clients. The instructions for the job had been a last minute affair. Should he have been told more than he had? But then no one knew of his actual route – or did they? His mind went back to the girl on the ferry and her interest in his job, journey – and hotel! Suddenly the hairs on the back of his neck prickled – and he had not had that sensation in a long time. There was only one explanation and he must speak to the client as soon as possible. If the opposition were prepared to kill him to ensure that privacy could be invaded then others might be at risk. On a personal note it was time to start being evasive.

Martin's assumptions were logical in the circumstances, but totally wrong.

Sunday 10th May 1992
9.10 a.m. Southampton

Detective Chief Inspector Potter looked at his watch. "You've got forty minutes to get me to headquarters," he said. The drive to Winchester was traffic free and within three quarters of an hour he was knocking on the Detective Chief Superintendent's door.

Ray Lawson was deceptive. His manner and presence made him appear bigger than he actually was. Now approaching fifty, a little under six foot and leanly fit, he gave the appearance of a younger man. The piercing blue eyes beneath greying hair coupled with a strongly boned face and authoritative voice commanded respect.

His record as a detective was equally respected. He was one of that unusual breed, achieving senior rank because of success in active policing rather than good administrative abilities – or knowing the right person, in the right place at the right time. Lawson was feared by some; he had a reputation for not tolerating either fools or sluggards and did not mince words when dissatisfied. He had enormous energy and even much younger officers found it difficult to satisfy his desire for progress in a case.

DCI Potter was not one of his favourites. Potter had transferred from the Met and had achieved promotion largely on the merits of one successful major case. Apart from an ability to delegate, little of note had registered in Ray Lawson's mind since. Nevertheless, Potter had avoided 'own goals' and achieved further promotion. He was now DCI in charge of the Divisional CID.

The two men eyed one another. Lawson without enthusiasm, Potter with a degree of wariness. The two were contrasts in many ways. The Met accepted men at 5'8" and Potter only just qualified on that score. Against Lawson's lean fitness, Potter being overweight and out of condition. His complexion was more than fresh and the brown hair tinged with grey, was thin on top. His movements were slow, in keeping with his physique.

Ray Lawson gestured to a seat. "Fill me in. We're due in the Chief's office in five minutes."

Potter was taken aback and it showed. Chief Constables are not normally found in their offices on a Sunday. Seeing Potter's expression, Lawson said, "When it's one of our own, you must expect the Chief Constable to take more than a passing interest." Potter thought that he detected an edge of sarcasm. "Especially when they're blown up by a bloody bomb!"

Potter went through the details of Incident Room set-up, Scene of Crime search, house to house enquiries and Special Branch reports. Lawson leant back in his chair, elbows on the arms and hands together, finger tip to finger tip. His blue eyes did not waver and he interjected only occasionally to ask a question or clear an ambiguity. As Potter finished he said, "And what are your first feelings for the job?"

Potter did not answer directly but said, "We must find Wild quickly. I think he's the key to this business. He was not your usual type of copper when he was in the job. He left suddenly and the word is that he has had some dodgy connections since leaving. God knows what he really does in this security business that he's started."

"I agree that he must be found quickly, also that he was not the usual type of copper, but don't jump to too many conclusions about his resignation. There were reasons that were not generally known, as you will see when you read this file." He slid a thin manila folder across the desk. On the top right-hand corner were the words 'DS Wild – Resignation'. It had a 1988 reference number beneath and on the bottom right hand corner was an adhesive slip which read 'Ref. Susan Wild – Sudden Death.' With another 1988 reference number. "If he had stayed in the job it's odds on that he would have been well promoted."

Potter, surprised, said nothing and Lawson continued, "It's essential that we identify his more recent associations as quickly as possible. It's much more likely that the bomb was meant for Wild than for Eileen Padgett. We don't want the body of an ex-copper alongside that of a serving one. Have you spoken yet with his old colleagues and girlfriends before Eileen Padgett?" He waited, eyebrows lifted.

Potter was saved by the telephone, summoning them into the Chief Constable's office.

10.50 a.m. Putney, London

Rafe Drummond slid the cold box containing chilled Moet et Chandon between two picnic hampers that were already in the rear of the Range Rover. Turning to face the two men following his wife across the courtyard he felt a twinge of annoyance. It was Sunday and the weekend had been set aside for polo at Windsor Lawn. The last thing that he required at that moment was an interruption to a programme that was already in danger of running late.

His wife's face said the same, but with the annoyance was a hint of curiosity.

"These gentlemen are from the police. Some problem with one of the people from your office." As she turned away, "Don't be too long, the children are nearly ready."

The taller of the two said, "I'm Detective Sergeant Williams, this is DC Hill. We hope that you can help us. We're trying to trace the movements of a Martin Wild. We understand that he is retained as a consultant to Quantum Bank."

Drummond certainly knew Wild, had been responsible for engaging him. There had been concern about confidentiality within the Bank's operation. Drummond had approached a friend in the City and, via the friend's Special Branch contact, Wild had been recommended.

Quantum Bank was part of a privately owned commercial conglomerate with offices just off St James. Drummond, a senior Director in the Bank, had passed control of Wild's activities to James Wentworth, who was specifically responsible for administration. Drummond knew that there had been a meeting between Wentworth and Wild during the previous week in connection with a conference scheduled in Zurich for the coming Monday and Tuesday. The Chairman and some Executives were already in Switzerland, entertaining wealthy Middle Eastern 'investors', whose private jet had deposited them and their entourage – including several wives with positive intentions for the local retail economy – some days before. Wild was due there first thing Monday morning to ensure that the boardroom and Chairman's suite were 'clean'.

Cautious and astute, Drummond was not anxious to tell Williams too much. It took some persistence by the detectives and a phone call to the Chairman in Switzerland before he would admit to knowing more than that Wild had been at St James the previous week. Having been given a limited OK and spurred on by his wife's hovering at the kitchen window, Drummond turned to the two detectives.

"Wild has worked for us on an 'as required' basis for some time. He seems to be good at what he does – wouldn't be employed by the Bank if he wasn't. He's an ex-policeman." This last almost as a challenge. Then "May I know your interest in him?"

"Wild's car was destroyed by an explosion – a bomb – the day after his meeting at your offices. He was not in the car and we have been unable to locate him since. What did Wild do for the Bank?"

"He has looked at our operation from a business confidentiality point of view, identifying areas where we could improve and generally tightening up on office practices – mainly middle management and the junior staff, of course." This defensively thought Williams, with an inward grin. "He also surveyed our new offices when we moved and has drawn up specifications for security, the intruder alarms, access control, that sort of thing. He does a regular sweep of our premises to ensure that there are no bugs on the telephone lines."

"Has he ever found any?"

"What has that to do with your present enquiry?"

Touched a raw nerve there thought Williams. Aloud he said, "We understand that Wild was due in Switzerland. You have just spoken with your Chairman, also in Switzerland. If Wild was on his way to carry out a similar operation there then it is conceivable that there is a connection, especially if he has thwarted such an attempt before."

"Bit extreme." Drummond obviously did not believe that the Bank's business would generate such an act and he made his point succinctly. "We have business operations across Europe, in the Middle East and in South America. Bombs are surely the weapons of terrorists. They're not used to negate business deals, at least not in this country or Europe."

"Nevertheless, we have to consider all the options."

Drummond was silent for a moment then said carefully, "We employed Wild originally because we thought that we might have a problem. His continued work for us has been because his background and specialist knowledge were found to be useful. That is all." Mentally he visualised the chairman's disbelieving face when told that Wild had found a bug at the bank's previous premises. He had demanded to see the device. Shown the grey cylinder with its connecting wires and listening to Wild's quiet explanation of placement backed up by the authoritative detail of construction from Tony Drew, he had suddenly gone from an angry red to an almost speechless white. The immediate effect was a sudden increase in the frequency of the sweeps, and a major improvement to Wild's cash flow.

"He's not going to admit it, but they did have a bug" thought Williams. Aloud he said, "Turning to last Thursday, what time did Wild leave your offices in St James?"

Over Williams' shoulder Drummond could see his wife's impatient face at the window. "Wild met with James Wentworth, the director who deals with the bank's administration, on Thursday. You will have to speak with him if you require precise timings, but I would think that it was late afternoon. Now gentlemen, I'm running late already. If there are further questions then James and I will be happy to answer them at some future date, but I really should leave now."

They parted after obtaining details of the Swiss venue.

Back in the car Williams used the police radio to brief DCI Potter on the meeting with Drummond. Before they reached Southampton, on the instructions of Ray Lawson, two seats were booked on a Sunday flight to Zurich. Potter and Williams were to intercept Wild before the curious and not too happy people of Quantum Bank could put him on guard.

*

As Martin Wild followed minor roads across Switzerland, with a careful eye on the rear view mirror of the hired Renault, reception parties were being organised by both his client and the police. Without doubt the more comprehensive efforts were by the latter. Local police, acting on information and requests from their English counterparts, made discreet enquiries into Quantum Banks activities in Zurich. Covert observations were set up on both the bank's offices and the Chairman's home. Swiss plainclothes officers surprised staff in hotels by the attention being paid to visitor lists. Customs officials and border police were instructed to look out for Wild and the black Porsche. They were asked to detain but not interrogate. DCI Potter wanted that pleasure for himself.

5.35 p.m. Provence, France

Some four hundred odd miles away, to the southwest of Zurich, another black Citroen, one of the new XM models, was just approaching the junction of Autoroutes 7 and 8 north of Marseilles.

The driver, apart from straight brown hair, brown eyes and a naturally dark complexion rather than tanned, could easily have been mistaken for Wild at a distance. Slightly shorter, perhaps a trifle heavier but with a similarly erect bearing, he had left the St James offices of Quantum Bank some twenty minutes after Wild, crossing the Channel that evening via Dover/Calais to stop overnight at his Paris flat. The journey south to Lyon, where he spent a second night, had been broken by a stop at Beaune where he lunched with friends, whose dining room overlooked the unique golden roof of the Hotel Dieu. Now he was almost home.

Home to Monsieur Henri Tabarde was a large detached house standing in its own extensive grounds just to the east of Velaux, a small town near Vitrolles. His family had occupied the property for over a hundred years. Built by his grandfather, a successful shipping agent with offices in Marseilles, the house had been the centre of domestic life for his parents and, since the death of his father five years previously, also for Henri. It was more than large enough for his wife and young family and an ideal setting for the businessman turned politician who needed to host small gatherings from time to time.

The family business in Marseilles, now diversified from the existing maritime agency into road transportation, was substantial. It was managed by experienced staff, many of whom had worked for the family most of their lives. His visit to Quantum Bank had been one of several such, concerned with funding further expansion of both the shipping agency and the road haulage company in the wake of increasing European trade.

Henri was not the sort of man to sit back on the laurels of his families efforts. At thirty five years of age he had followed in his father's footsteps as the Mayor of Velaux. Henri was the youngest such in the small town's history. His enthusiasm and energy had quickly propelled him from his local position into National Government and he was now a junior minister.

As Commissaire of the République for the Region, Henri Tabarde was said by those in the General Councils Paris Chamber to be a man going places. As a Junior Minister, he had chosen law and order as his personal crusade and had specifically targeted the drug cartels operating in and out of Marseilles. His local reputation was high whilst his political level gave him the ear of the Prime Minister.

Henri's public profile had not been damaged when, some ten years earlier, he had married Marie-Thérèse Ducheneaux, a tall strikingly beautiful girl some ten years his junior. From a French father and Italian mother she had inherited not only her outstanding looks but also a social position in the Marseilles and Milan hierarchy. The confirmed bachelor was captivated.

A whirlwind romance and early marriage had been followed avidly by the media in both countries. Soon there was a baby and, two years later, a second. The arrivals barely slowed Marie Thérèse's social round.

The location of Tabarde's home was ideal in many respects. Both the A7 and A8 were less than five kilometres from his front door and Marseilles Provence airport was only thirty-five kilometres by autoroute. The house was built on the southwest slopes of the Chaine de Vitrolles, a range of hills, wooded to the north, which looked across a large landlocked expanse of water, the Etang de Berre. On the narrow strip of land separating the lake from the Mediterranean was the town of Martiques.

As Henri took the slip road from the autoroute onto the D10, it was of this town that he was thinking. There was talk of a potential marina and residential complex but, as in so many new business ventures around Marseilles, there was also talk that laundering of drugs money was involved. Henri's impact on the local drug scene had been substantial and, if the suggested origin of the money behind this development was correct, then here was another challenge from the invisible barons. It was a red rag to a bull and he had already planted his flag of opposition.

*

The watcher on the hillside above the D10 raised binoculars as the black Citroen appeared. The car was only a half kilometre away but would have to descend a slow winding road, follow the stream in the valley into the village, cross a narrow bridge and climb a similarly slow route before it reached his position. That would take a minimum of four minutes. He knew, they had checked it by night and day. It would then take a further 30 seconds for the car to reach the gravelled entrance to the gite that was the watcher's base, the other side of a belt of scrub and small trees from his vantage point

With the identity of the Citroen confirmed, the watcher raised a two way radio to his mouth. His French had the guttural patois of the southern Provençal region. "François, set the scene, set the scene. You have less than four minutes."

*

She had been a pretty girl once, tall and slim, with long fair hair and an open smiling face. How long ago was it? Two years? Perhaps only eighteen months. But her habit had bitten deep. Not yet twenty one, she looked ten years older. Had not had a 'fix' for two days now, not since before they had brought her to this awful lonely house, with only that bastard François and his cold silent companion Luis for company. Her need was desperate, limbs trembling uncontrollably, constantly restless with jerky uncoordinated movements. She was itching, her skin crawling in the first stages of withdrawal. She had scratched herself leaving blood on the skin of the wrists and lower arms. Painfully thin arms with the blue veins standing out from the pale skin.

Huddled in a corner of the gite's second bedroom, she hugged her knees to her chest. The room stank. Sweat with the acrid addition of vomit and urine from the bucket in the corner. The soiled sheets on the bed were a knotted heap from her last attempt at sleep. She knew that there would be no rest until François gave her the promised package. That wouldn't happen until the car that they were waiting for came.

"God, come quickly, come quickly!" she whispered, using the name as an expletive without thought. The voice betrayed a Glasgow childhood. She was a long way from home, both in distance and experience.

Her belly turned over emptily, she felt sick again. She had eaten little in the time that they had been in this shabby house. Could not eat, her other needs were too strong. She would have done anything for the package of white powder in François' pocket. Anything! Anything! She had done "anything, anything" many times in the past year for the brief high of heroin.

François had laughed his twisted laugh and kicked her aside when she went on her knees to plead with him. He knew exactly what he wanted of her, had schooled her carefully in the first hours of their stay. He knew that in her present state she would accept whatever he did or said…for that pinch of white powder. Her gear was on the bedside table, the night light, the matches, the discoloured spoon, the heavy rubber band – and the so called disposable syringe that had been used time and time again.

*

The voice from the radio brought François to his feet. He reached the portable propped on the windowsill in two strides. Thumbing the switch he acknowledged the message and, moving with urgency, kicked open the door to the second bedroom snarling, "Up bitch, you're on!"

Stunned, she stared at him open mouthed until he shouted, "Do you want the stuff or no?"

Galvanised into action, she scrambled to her feet and started for the door.

"Jacket and knapsack." He spat the words out and was gone.

Gasping, almost sobbing now that the moment was upon her, she turned and snatched up the dirty denim jacket and canvas rucksack, following him out of the backdoor to where he was already astride a motorcycle. He pressed the starter and the bike's motor burbled into life. She climbed awkwardly onto the pillion and clung to him as he gunned the machine down the dirt drive to where gravel lay scattered on the tarmac of the D10.

"Off, get off," almost before they had stopped.

As she half climbed, half fell from the bike, he killed the motor and deliberately lowered the machine to the road, on its side in the middle of the carriageway. He snatched the panniers, held by bungee grips only, from the bike and, taking a crash helmet from each, threw the panniers into the road a few feet away.

Thrusting a helmet at her he said, "Get that on – quickly! Now remember, French and English, mixed up. Cry Bitch, shout and cry to him for help. Don't give him time to think. Now kneel beside me."

With that, François pulled the second helmet on to his head and threw himself to the road beyond the motorcycle, facing the direction from which the car would come.

A minute passed, then above the sound of her own gasping, rasping breath, Jeannie McKay heard the car approaching. As it appeared she started towards it, a pathetic figure in soiled denims, long straggly fair hair falling from under the helmet as she pulled it off. Running, stumbling in the centre of the approaching Citroen's carriageway, waving her arms, gasping and crying. The car slowed and, with the inert figure of François and the motor cycle on the road beyond, could not have passed even had the driver wished to.

As it stopped, she half fell onto the bonnet, clawing her way to the driver's door as the window slid silently down.

"Help, please help! Oh, envoyez cherchez l'ambulance." From English into French as she clung to the door.

Henri Tabarde took in the scene, the motionless figure by the motorcycle, gravel and debris across the road. The hysterical girl, obviously English from the voice, but with an accent that he did not immediately recognise. He understood her words, both in English and the poor French. Help for her injured companion and an ambulance were needed.

He reached for the carphone and in that second, from the corner of his eye, saw movement from the rear of the car. The girl was pushed aside and there was the cold barrel of a handgun against the side of his head.

"Get out of the car!"

Henri hesitated for just one second, then felt the pain as a hand grasped his hair, jerked his head back and, as he opened his mouth to protest, stuffed the barrel of the gun into his mouth.

"Get out of the fuckin' car!"

The car door opened, for a second the hair was released but his head was still forced back by the gun poked into the roof of his mouth. Then the hand came through the opening door, grabbed his hair again and he was pulled sideways out of the car onto his knees in the road, the gun again at his head.

Reaching into the car, Luis took the ignition key and, with François helping, dragged Henri to the rear boot. He opened it with the key.

"Get in!"

Opening his mouth to protest was the last thing that Henri remembered. The barrel of the gun smashed into the side of his head with vicious force and blackness enveloped him.

Watching the inert body being tipped into the boot of the car, Jeannie was suddenly aware that her involvement had finished – she hadn't been paid! Running to François, she pulled at the arm of his jacket.

"I want my score. You promised me!"

He pushed her away roughly then, to her relief, took a folded envelope from an inside pocket and threw it at her.

"Stick that into you, Bitch." His mouth twisted into a grin. "Have a good long sleep!"

As she stumbled back to the gite, there was the roar of the motorcycle as it followed the Citroen back to the autoroute.

Inside the dirty bedroom, far worse than the Gorbals tenement of her childhood, she sat for seconds trying to control the trembling of her hands, frightened that clumsiness would spill the precious white powder. Lighting the night light she tipped a little water from a bedside glass into the stained bowl of the spoon. Adding a third of the powder from the package, she heated this over the night light until the powder had dissolved then, very carefully, using both hands to steady herself, dipped the needle of the hypodermic into the liquid and sucked it into the syringe.

Hurriedly now she wrapped the elastic tightly around her upper left arm, massaging the veins into greater prominence. Raising the needle she expelled air from the mixture then carefully inserted the needle into a vein, which already bore the marks of numerous injections, some healing, some starting to ulcerate. With half injected, she felt the first, psychological, flush of heat to her abdomen. Pausing, she allowed a small amount of the liquid, now coloured by blood, to re-enter the syringe, paused a moment, then completed the injection. She removed the elastic and falling back onto the bed, stuffed a piece of linen into the crook of her arm to absorb the spot of blood.

*

On the bike, following the Citroen, François' lips twisted into a mirthless grin.

"You'll sleep well, Bitch!"

The heroin in the packet had been almost pure. Jeannie had graduated to her usual dosage on a drug which had been cut and cut again.

After they had finished with the man, they would return to the gite and "clear up". In a few days' time, the body of a British girl, a girl dancer in the Marseilles clubs and a known drug addict, would be found in a public toilet, her gear close to hand. Another OD for the authorities to deal with.

Friday 15th May 1992
12 noon Ballentour, Scotland

He was still shocked. Shocked and confused. Confused about everything. He'd been struggling with disbelief and confusion for days now, ever since returning to the horror that was Parksyde Avenue.

Today was particularly so. It should have been raining. In his mind, it always rained at funerals. The very sky was supposed to weep, as his heart did. Instead, the sun had shone continuously, as it had since the day that she died.

Her parents, whom he had just left, should have looked at him with angry eyes, blaming him that their lovely daughter had been blown to pieces in his car, in an act that was almost certainly aimed at him. But they did not. Though full of anguish and despair, this gentle couple greeted him as they had always, with warmth – and now sympathy.

The service had been in Scotland. With only two exceptions, the mourners were all strangers to him, with foreign accents. Nice people though they were, he could not accept this village as part of Eileen's life. Nearly all of his time with her had been against the background of a busy Hampshire city. So different from this quietly pretty country community, whose tongue he had to listen to carefully if he were to understand at all.

Before that, there was the confusion of finding that this woman – his woman – whom he had known for a year, lived with for six months and loved more than any before, was not his, even to bury. The arrangements that occupy the mind of a bereaved partner were taken from him by those who were closely related. Suddenly Eileen's remains were on their way to Scotland and, to be with her to the end, he had to follow.

Follow that is, only after the police had let him. Confusion again. For years he had been a member of the 'police family'. After his resignation there had still been close links with many previous colleagues. Suddenly he was on the wrong side of the interview table. The eyes staring at him, the voices asking questions, were no longer friendly. They were probing, hard, hurtful.

Most confusing of all were the attacks on Eileen and himself. His work, though specialised and very different from the average, should not hold dangers of that type. His clients were as respectable as any high flown businessmen or wealthy entrepreneurs can be expected to be. Although there might be occasional risks from the denizens of that darker world, they were not the sort that resulted in car bombs or murderous chases.

The final confusion was what to do next. His world was not only upside down, it was literally in pieces. Should he return to Hampshire? Face the friends whose stumbling condolences he had received in an unreal dream with dry eyes? They would not know what to say now any more than they had then. Or ex-colleagues, who would avoid speaking to him, unless they were part of the Murder Team charged with the investigation which patently included himself. The flat had been Eileen's, was in her name. There were personal possessions to recover; a new home to be found. But there was no incentive. He had no wish to retrace his steps. People and the business could go hang for a few days. He needed to sort himself out.

As these thoughts went through Martin's mind, he remembered mention of a particular Scottish place name by one of the interviewing officers and, without really thinking why, the decision was made. His return air ticket could wait.

Two hours later, he stepped out of a hire car office, put his suitcase and bag into the boot of a Mondeo and pointed the car's nose north, away from people, towards the Highlands of Scotland. He had no plans, no itinerary. In his mind was a once mentioned Scottish name and Scotland, or at least the far north, meant emptiness. Emptiness to match that in his heart; that in the foreseeable future.

Southampton

Detective Inspector Potter was more surprised than confused. The enquiry into the Parksyde bomb had been as routine as any enquiry of that nature can be – though not very revealing to date.

Close examination of recent cases and contacts dealt with by Eileen Padgett had failed to identify any which might have led to the incident, which was to be expected. She'd had her share of shoplifters and juvenile offenders, which were the usual lot of an operational policewoman. The city area of Shirley had minimal prostitution and drug problems, which were the slightly heavier possibilities.

It was the rapidly expanding file on Martin Wild that lifted Potter's eyebrows. He had known Wild as a fairly ordinary uniform policeman and subsequently as a more proficient CID officer, whose expertise in certain areas had resulted in early promotion. Then there had been the sudden resignation and Wild had dropped from Potter's view.

The surprise was the obvious success that Wild had achieved in the last three of the five years since he had left the job and 'gone commercial'. Copies of bank statements and the Annual Accounts of Wild's company confirmed the impression given by the list of clients supplied during his interviews. He was earning at least twice Potter's salary and substantial payments were going into pension funds. He ran two cars on the Company and owned a small sailing boat privately. The client list contained respected international and city names. One or two might be considered more successful than respected, but were still impressive to a cynical senior officer. The bank manager's guarded responses had produced only one negative comment, that he would have preferred greater capitalisation in the company. The impression was that Wild knew how to spend at least as well as how to earn. How on earth had he done it? In the last two years he had spent time in many of the nearer European countries and, in Potter's opinion, seemed to be busier than a 'straight' ex-detective sergeant had any right to be.

It was going to be difficult delving into this client bank. The investigating officers assigned to this aspect of the enquiry were already reporting resistance and an unwillingness to communicate by many of the companies and names listed. It seemed that much of Wild's work was of a sensitive nature. There was no way that Chairmen and Chief Executives of certain multinationals wanted enquiring police officers wading through the more confidential aspects of their businesses – explosion or no explosion, death or no death.

*

Gordon Wilson was not only confused, he was angry, and not a little worried. Things had gone badly wrong on two occasions. Mahoney had killed the wrong person – and a police woman into the bargain! The 'politician target' was missing. The French operatives had disappeared, together with their car, and had not been seen or heard from since the day that they received their instructions.

Mabbett was not going to be pleased, not at all amused by these failures. Wilson had witnessed Mabbett's displeasure on previous occasions and the thought that he might be in the firing line this time caused a prolonged visit to the toilet and a mental search for excuses. For the umpteenth time he went through the instructions that had been given. The target had been well described. It was known that he would leave the Quantum offices at around 4.30 on the Thursday afternoon and that his car was a black Citroen. It would be brought to the main door from Quantum's private car park by an attendant.

How on earth had Liam Mahoney ended up killing some policewoman? Mahoney did not make mistakes, normally. He had not where the equipment was concerned, his IRA connections had seen to that. He'd been back to Belfast to set up his alibi and only the previous day had phoned from their Birmingham club. He let slip that he had been to Gateshead after Belfast and Wilson wondered about that. The previous Monday's papers had reported a number of fire bomb attacks at the Metro Centre there, said to be the IRA's response to MI5 taking over intelligence gathering from Special Branch.

Wilson wondered whether Mahoney's supply of 'equipment' and visit to Ireland might have involved a 'quid pro quo'.

Mabbett, however, was a day late. He'd been scheduled back in the country on Thursday, but was now due in from The States today. Wilson would have to give him the news that not only was the target back in France, but that their own Paris connections had also failed. There would be hell to pay – especially if they lost their new Marseilles supplier.

*

Martin's journey north was slow. What was there to hurry for? No longer were there incentives, aims. The immediate shock and numbing pain of Eileen's death was moving to a deeper level. He felt anguish that, since the death of his twin sister he, who until a year ago had never really wished to share, should now after such a short time no longer be able to.

He distanced himself from the pretty village with its funeral memories. Gradually the Highland countryside, with rich patterns of light and dark green where the spruce and pine intermingled, sank into his subconscious. The hills gave way to mountains with snow still trapped in the deeper gullies of the peaks. Gorse yellowed the roadside and blazed in patches on the lower slopes. He came to calm lochs, their waters gently ruffled by the lightest of catspaws. Water was essential to him and a part of his mind came alive at the sight of it. But the stirrings now were slight and served only to double his sense of loss. How he missed her!

Leaving the car, he made his way through a stand of birch and beech to the shores of a loch. As he walked amongst their favourite trees, still with the clearly defined green of early summer leaf, he found, for the first time, tears in his eyes and then on his cheeks. Almost blindly he walked on. They had never been to the Highlands together but had talked of sailing his small boat west to the Scillies and then north to the Western Isles. How he wished that they could have shared the mountains and the lochs. Now he knew that they never would.

Desolate for the loss and what might have been, he grieved for her. Quietly, out of the public eye, away from her family and friends, at last his loss spilt over. Sitting on a moss covered boulder, he gave way to desperate weeping. Buzzards wheeled high in the air. There were the family calls of smaller birds in the tree canopy, trout rose to dimple the surface of the loch. These were the sights and sounds of nature with which he – they – were very much in tune. They now went unnoticed.

He lost track of time and, very much later, was conscious of a chill as the sun disappeared behind the mountains. A pair of mallard wheeled overhead, flattened their wings and skimmed the surface of the loch to land with a splash in the margins. The laughing cackle of the drake seemed to mock and the sound seeped through the black cloud in his mind, rousing him.

Returning to the hire car he pushed it hard, following the A9 north along the Spey Valley. He turned right on to the A95 sign posted Grantown on Spey and, in the gathering dusk, found a B & B sign outside a lonely farm which looked south to the Cairngorms.

For the first time in days he was suddenly hungry and found both a meal and a comfortable room for the night. After dinner, over a quiet whisky with the husband of the house, he felt a degree of normality returning, the black cloud lifting an edge. Then, again for the first time in many nights, he slept until the early hours.

Saturday 16th May 1992 8.15 a.m.

The following morning Martin woke early, refreshed. Sadness still clouded his vision but the shocked apathy of the last week was receding. As he ate a portion of the generous breakfast, he marshalled thoughts, desperate that logic and action should replace the confusion and numbing uncertainty.

The police had all the information that had seemed appropriate and it was sensible to leave that which they did best, and for which they were better equipped, to them. That left the matter of the Mercedes owner. Martin had supplied the investigating team with the number on the French licence plate. One of the older detectives, a man who had served with Wild and whom he knew well, imparted information that the registered owners of the car ran a number of gaming casinos. The Sûreté were following up that line and had been told by the firm's directors that the car had been stolen and its whereabouts were unknown. The Sûreté officers were doing a thorough job though and one other piece of information was of interest, although Potter seemed dismissive. The French company had contacts with a British business which had a registered office in Glasgow and operated a number of nightclubs in England and Scotland. It was this name and the location of this business, which he had remembered after the service for Eileen, that in part had kept him in Scotland.

Healing takes time and Martin knew from bitter experience that he had to immerse himself in a project if he were again to beat his black clouds. He would try to avoid muddying the waters of the police enquiry but Potter's attitude and the need within himself to 'move on' were enough stimulus. He would just have a quiet nose around.

An hour later he pointed the Mondeo's bonnet south and followed the A9 through the Glens. That afternoon he booked into a plastic Glasgow hotel, forced a reluctant window open to gain fresh air and then spent some minutes studying a slim A4 sized directory that always travelled with him on business. It was provided by an organisation of ex-police officers and contained the contact details of members. Its purpose was to assist those like himself who provided services in the commercial security world. There were two Glasgow based members with the sort of CV that he needed. A call to the first resulted only in an answerphone but the second found an ex-Glasgow policeman running a private detective agency. He was not only in his office but prepared to meet and share local contacts, for a 'consideration' of course.

"What is it that brings you all the way to Scotland on an enquiry?" His new companion was curious. It was normal to deal with information gathering by the telephone rather than to travel distances 'on spec'.

Martin was casual. "It's the usual situation. A client is owed money by the owner of a nightclub. It's a fair amount but the indications are that they are difficult people to deal with. He thought it best for me to have a quiet look at their operation. Could be he'd be throwing good money after bad, or that there's a better way of tackling it rather than head on."

"What nightclub is it?"

"The name is Shadows. It's at Govan. Do you know it?"

"Oh, I've heard it, but not had any dealings with it but I know a man who has. Just wait here a moment." He disappeared into the hotel foyer.

Several minutes passed before he returned to take his chair and say "Jimmy's an old friend of mine, still in the job. He's on today and won't be free until six this evening. He uses a pub round the corner from the office. Most of the CID do. Would that suit?"

"Good," said Martin. "That'll give me time to do some of the routines."

6.00 p.m.

The rest of the day was spent between a reference library, the Local Authority's Licensing Office and a fax bureau before Martin reached a pub close to the Glasgow Central CID. The meeting held in this establishment with the 'ex-job' private investigator and Jimmy, his detective friend, was enlightening and put flesh of a not very pleasant kind on the bones of Lowland Enterprises, who owned Shadows and a number of other nightclubs. The company search details had been faxed to Martin earlier. With these to provide the official hierarchy, his meeting with this new contact gave him the necessary background.

"It's a good job that you spoke with us first." Was Jimmy's opening comment when told of Martin's supposed quest. "There's a guy by the name of McAinsh who runs the place, but though he holds the licence, he answers to another who's very much in the background. It's known as a rough place, used mainly by youngsters, as most of these rave clubs are. The Drugs Squad keep an eye on it but they're few on the ground and busy so we're not too sure how hot it is."

"You say a rough place. What sort of youngsters are you talking about?"

"Oh, it's not the youngsters that give the trouble, it's the bouncers. They're over the top when it comes to handling problems. We've dealt with a number of injuries caused by over enthusiastic doormen and we had a 'pusher' badly beaten and found in the street outside. That should have been a GBH but he wouldn't give a statement, they never do. He'd had his warning to stay off their turf and ignored it. A beating was the result."

Two rounds of drinks later Martin, feeling that he had as much background as these two were able to give, made his excuses and left.

9.05 p.m.

Set up by a couple of hours sleep and a quick meal, Martin parked his car outside of what he judged to be a converted cinema. The building looked 1930s and parts of it did not seem to have been cleaned since! The front doors which, in cinema days would have been glazed to provide a view of the interior, were now clad in metal with only small rectangular panels to give a view out rather than in. Over the doors was a canopy with neon lighting shouting to the passing world that this was `Shadows' nightclub, offering the best that Glasgow had in dance and drink between 9 p.m. and 3 a.m. According to Martin's earlier information gathering exercise, it was also the registered offices of Lowland Leisure, a subsidiary of Lowland Enterprises. Posters on the sides of the building majored with visions of scantily clad, over endowed women, promoting Happy Hours, Party Nights and an evening for the Over 30s. Martin had a shrewd idea that he was going to feel very much out of place later.

On either side of the front doors, suspended from the canopy, were two battered television cameras. They were directed at the doors. A third camera was mounted higher up and appeared to be motorised, giving a view up and down the street. As he watched, the two pairs of double doors were opened and a burly black clad figure could be seen removing lengths of chain from inside, where the pushbars had been secured. He disappeared, swinging the chains and calling out to an unseen person. Seconds later another equally large man appeared, to lounge against the frame of the open door with his hands in the pockets of a black bomber jacket.

Not wishing to be the first face in the place, Martin made for a café some fifty yards away. Ordering a coffee, he found a table where, with a lean to the left he could see the roadway outside Shadows. A middle aged woman in a grubby apron was pushing an equally grubby broom around the floor, threatening to clear the debris of more than one day's customer browsing. Martin lifted his feet for her in the mistaken anticipation that she would wish to deal with the scattering of crumbs hiding beneath his table.

As she was poised to send the broomhead on a halfhearted investigation beneath the next table he asked, "Is there anywhere good for a night out around here?"

She removed the cigarette dangling from a corner of her mouth, regarded the end as though the voice had come from there and, without looking at him said, "Yu'll ave to ga inta Glasgee fur that." She spoke as though the city centre was another town.

"What about the club up the road – Shadows?"

"Thas no fur the likes uv yu."

"Why's that?"

"Thas all bairns."

Within the next hour he had confirmation of her description. The customers arriving in a steady trickle were indeed 'bairns'. During the first hour it didn't look as though one of them was over the age of twenty, most were much younger. Then, with the pubs turning out, the age range increased slightly, but still they were all very much younger than Martin. He debated the wisdom of going in. He would stand out like a sore thumb. Quite obviously this was a job for a much younger person. He was just on the point of leaving when two men, who he judged to be in their thirties, arrived to join the little group awaiting admission.

"Hell, what have I got to lose?" He waited a couple of minutes for the group to reduce in numbers before walking across the road to join them from the doorway that had been his hiding place.

Three girls in front of him were giggling as bomber jacketed doormen patted down the pockets of the older men. He stood behind the girls, conscious of the thin shift-like dresses and cheap perfume.

"Yu goin' to search me?" called out one with hair bleached almost white. Martin judged the tone to be hopeful.

The better looking of the two doormen smirked and chewed gum with an open mouth. "We'll 'ave a look in yur bag fust, Blondie."

The girls squealed, giggled and chattered as their purses were given a cursory examination. Then it was Martin's turn and he was aware of hard eyes from the man in front sizing him up. As the other half of the duo patted his jacket and trouser pockets from behind.

"Whas this?" enquired the 'patter' as he found the mobile phone on Martin's belt.

Martin removed it. "Just a phone."

"Yu'll 'aye to switch it off inside – couldna hear it onyway."

Martin did as he was told, making his way to the pay booth. His ticket was punched out by a blowsy woman, also chewing gum, only to be taken from him immediately by another bouncer standing between the booth and double doors to the club. The ticket was threaded onto a string with a spike at the end, to join a thick wedge of similar tickets.

Through the doors he was hit by a blast of sound from the amplified beat. He wondered how many of the staff would still have their hearing in middle age. Bright coloured strobe lights dazzled and flashed, the alternate illumination and darkness making it difficult to adjust. The club was nowhere near full; just groups of young people, mainly men around the bars with a scattering of girls sitting on upholstered couches or standing jigging on the small dance floor.

Martin joined a group at one of the bars where the two thirty something men were ordering drinks. At the rear of the bar was a display of designer bottled beer, which seemed to be the popular drink. He asked for one, paid what seemed to be a high price for it and hid his distaste at the first swig, knowing he would have no difficulty in making it last.

The club filled rapidly, within another hour it was difficult to move about near the bars or dance floor. Many of the youngsters were drinking cokes. Martin felt sure that a lot of the frenetic activity on the dance floor was chemically rather than alcohol induced. Bouncers were moving through the crowds every so often. Others were standing at certain points all the time.

Suddenly there was shouting and turning he saw two bouncers dragging a young man towards a fire exit. A girl was trailing behind screaming at the men. It was her high pitched voice that attracted attention. The double fire doors were opened and the man thrown out with a joint heave by both bouncers. By the force of the ejection it was obvious that he would no longer be on his feet. The girl stood her ground shouting and before the doors closed she was bundled unceremoniously out, though with less force. There were angry comments from some standing around but no one made a move to object more strongly.

By the time that Martin had spent the best part of three hours in the club he knew what he thought were the more important 'faces'. He ignored the girls and boys serving behind the bars and those that were collecting glasses from tables dotted around the edge of the dance floor. He discounted the bouncers on static points, concentrating his attention on three men. Two were both older than most customers and spent their time visiting bars, talking to the servers and apparently supervising activities. One of the men was thin, gaunt and with an apology for a beard. He thought this to be the manager, McAinsh, who had been accurately described by his CID contact. The second of the two was subservient and probably an assistant manager. The third man was dressed as a bouncer. He had a good looking, heavily boned face with a strong jawline and close cropped brown hair. His body more than filled the lightweight bomber jacket that was the uniform of those charged with supervising the conduct of customers. He made regular rounds of the bar and dance floor area, talking to the other bouncers but not to the bar staff. Martin put him down as the head doorman and wondered about the extent of his duties.

Finally, at just after three in the morning, with the premises now empty of customers, the last of the staff left. Some took waiting taxis whilst others had cars parked at the rear of the premises. To Martin's interest the bearded man, whom he thought to be the manager, and the man who he had identified as the head doorman, left together.

"Robert, I need someone who can do a job for me in Scotland. Someone from north of the border would be preferable. He must be able to look after himself as well as do some digging. I need information from inside a rather 'heavy' organisation."

Martin's call was to Robert Hardy, a cultured giant of a man, who ran a London agency specialising in Close Protection. They also did investigations, although these were a recent addition to their portfolio. Robert had been a Guards Officer of the modern school until an injury interrupted his career. In the last two years Martin had used his men on a number of occasions and had developed respect for the organisation. Most of Robert's people were ex-military and considerable care was taken in selecting and training them for work in the commercial world. The slimming down of the armed forces meant that Robert had been able to build a useful workforce around his original group of two or three specialists.

"What's the scenario, Martin? Doesn't sound like your usual contract." Robert owed much of his early success to a cautious approach.

"You're right. It would be very useful if you had a Scots nightclub doorman of above average intelligence, but that's asking too much, I'm sure."

"You're absolutely right. My lads wouldn't be seen dead on the door of a nightclub."

"Not only do I need a pseudo 'bouncer' for some weeks, I'll also need two of your larger guys for a night or two, just to help set a scene."

"Firstly the only true Scot that I have on my books is already committed. The best that I can do is Ewen Handsford. His mother's Scottish and he goes north on family visits. He doesn't have much of an accent though. Secondly I'll need to know more of your requirement before we get into the personnel."

Although their business relations were friendly, they were not close friends. Opportunities to meet socially were limited and they had not spent time together for some months. Robert knew that Martin had a regular girlfriend. He'd met her once, but the introduction had been brief. As Martin sketched out what he required, he avoided all reference to Eileen and the bombing. As far as Robert was concerned it was an investigation into a bent nightclub.

"Ewen hasn't been involved with nightclubs to my knowledge, but he's an intelligent lad and I'm sure that he could cope. Whether he's able to do the digging that you require is something that you'd have to assess yourself."

Robert was being his usual careful self. Martin recognised this and asked that a meeting be set up for the following day at the Heathrow Post House.

Robert was intrigued by the request for two of his larger men but Martin refused to tell more until they were face to face.

"I'll have to charge you for the lads in that case Martin. The meeting will take up their time and you may then decide that they are not suitable."

9.30 a.m. Cadnam near Southampton

"DM wants you to go back up north as soon as, Liam." Gordon Wilson's tone was neutral, deliberately so. There was a lot of flack in the air and, having spent a difficult half hour on the phone with Dermott Mabbett, he had no wish to be further involved in what was turning out to be a very bad deal. Wilson was big and brash but he had no stomach for refereeing between Mabbett and his hardman.

"What about the London visit?" Mahoney wanted to know. "There was a collection to be made there on this trip."

"You could pull that in without losing too much time if you use the M25 and MI."

"Right. How was DM? Did his meeting go well?"

"The States visit went well enough, but he's not happy about the other business."

"The time, the place, the car were all right and the description was as near as dammit." Mahoney's tone was defensive, as well it might be, thought Wilson.

"When that car headed for Southampton instead of Dover you should have double checked. Anyway, you'll have to sort it out with Dermott now he's back."

Winchester. 9.55 a.m.

"Damn these Monday Briefings," muttered DCI John Potter as he heaved his bulk, with briefcase in one hand and files under both aims, through the doors at Police Headquarters.

He signed in at Reception, taking the Visitor badge from the civilian employee behind the screen, fumbling to clip it in place on his breast pocket, only to realise that he'd got it back to front again.

"And damn these stupid badges. Everything for economy rather than efficiency!"

He turned to the lift only to find that it had just gone and he would now be those two vital minutes late in getting into the Detective Superintendant's office. He looked at the stairs, thought of all those flights and the weight of his files, and thought again.

"One of those days, John?"

He turned to see the ACC Personnel, standing behind him. Nice guy but divorced from the realities of operational work, thought Potter.

"Good morning, Sir." Then, as two lifts arrived together "Yes, just like buses!"

Ray Lawson was at his very tidy desk, drumming his fingers, as Potter had expected. He gestured towards the chair opposite and said, with what Potter thought was a deceptively gentle voice "Well John, how goes it?"

Potter launched into a more or less chronological run down of the murder investigation during the last week, leading up to the reason why he had been pressed for time that morning.

"And perhaps the most important aspect is the initial reports from the Lab, which arrived this morning. The indications are that the explosive, the method and what we have recovered in the way of materials, all point to this being an IRA job!"

To Potter's surprise, Ray Lawson merely nodded and then said, "But there has been nothing in Wild's activities to connect him with the IRA or any of its known Units. Am I right?"

He knew about the Lab Reports before I told him, thought Potter. Aloud he said, "Quite right, Ray, nothing at all. Despite all the travelling that he seems to have done, Ireland's not listed. None of his contacts have an Irish connection. None of his clients are Irish based or with any known affiliations."

"Nevertheless, you'd better pop into the Liaison Group office on your way back and share what you have with them. They may come up with something that's not so obvious. Where's Wild now?"

"He went up to the funeral in Scotland last Friday. Apparently he's stayed up that way. He said that we could contact him through his office. He has a secretary who talks to him each day."

"Keep me in touch with developments, John. The Chief's asking every day."

10.05 a.m. Marseilles

The dark blue Sikorski helicopter spiralled out of a pale blue sky to hover just a foot off the ground for some seconds before gently touching down. The man waiting on the edge of the apron raised a black briefcase to shield his face from the dry dust swirling up beneath the blades. Summer had come early to the south of France. Spring rains were a distant memory.

The door slid open and a very large man stepped down, looked around and turned to nod into the open doorway. The man who followed him out was dark, with thick greying hair and a prominent hooked nose. He walked quickly towards the man with the briefcase and they embraced before making towards a terminal building where an empty VIP lounge awaited them. As they walked they talked. By the time that they had reached the terminal door there was a waving of arms on both sides and a heated discussion. They stopped at the door; the man with the hooked nose made a final point, now in a softer voice but with a finger striking the palm of his hand with each word, then turned and walked back to the helicopter.

There was no parting embrace.

Tuesday 19th May 1992
9.25 a.m. Glasgow

Glasgow Airport was a drear sight first thing in the morning. A grey overcast which promised nothing, was echoed by the mood of the taxi driver who took the English £5 note, looking up with mouth opening in protest.

"It's all I've got," said Martin, "why not keep the change?"

"Ai thus time, but yu'll not a make a habit I hope."

Martin collected his ticket for the morning shuttle to Heathrow and made his way to the Departure Lounge. Ten minutes later the BA flight was called, the atmosphere lightening with a cheery smile from a uniformed lass offering complimentary papers at the entrance to the boarding tunnel.

There was no hold up. In ten minutes the aircraft was being towed from the apron and, once clear of its tug, trundled to a take off position. With the brakes applied, the pilot swung the tail around, paused, ran the engines up and, with the whole machine quivering like an impatient beast, released the brakes to send them hurtling down the runway.

Opposite the terminal buildings, Martin felt the aircraft rotate. The bumping lurching ride transformed immediately into a smooth, exhilarating, lifting flight, aimed for the grey murk overhead. Seconds later they were enveloped in wispy mist and then, suddenly, gloriously, broke free into the cloudless blue above. The flat platform of the overcast, now like white cotton wool, stretching away to the horizon.

As always he marvelled at the transition; the total change of spirit which he felt at this moment in an aircraft. One minute earthbound and uncomfortably thrown around in a grey world. The next, smoothly propelled by what seemed limitless power, soaring towards a blue heaven, gazing down onto the beauty of Earth's enveloping cloud mass. This was the only part of the flight that he enjoyed. The rest was boredom tempered with unease at the thought of the myriad of electronics and thousands of mechanical moving parts essential to continued safety. Then there were the millions of germs now being pumped around the re-circulating air system in the pressurised hull. He wondered what he would catch this time.

An hour later, again surrounded by grey murk, the aircraft descended into and was swallowed by a low cloud base, which seemed to cover the entire country. The London cabbie outside arrivals was, if anything, less promising than his Scots counterpart. Upon hearing that the total journey was to be all of half a mile to the Heathrow Post House, he commenced a detailed whinge on the delays experienced in getting a cab into the airport, something which he would now have to do for the second time that morning.

Martin's first port of call was the hotel's Gents where, standing at the porcelain, trying not to listen to the piped music, he was startled by a heavy hand on his shoulder.

"We can shake hands after you've washed, old fellow!"

Then there was the smiling face of Robert Hardy at the next stall.

"Robert, you're early, as usual."

"Never been late on parade in m'life."

"Where are your lads?"

"Ewen's getting the coffee in and you can tell me what this is all about before we join them."

Having given Robert half a story, sufficient to satisfy for the moment though, by the look in his eye not for long, they moved to join the three lads in the hotel bar.

Following Robert's limping 6'3" to a table, Martin suddenly felt shortened as the two men sitting there stood for their arrival. Both were bigger than Robert, all three of them inches taller than himself. Robert made the introductions and, at that moment, a third man, much smaller than the others and a couple of inches shorter than Martin, arrived with a tray of coffee cups.

"And this is Ewen," said Robert Hardy.

Martin found himself looking into a pair of steady hazel eyes and being gripped by a firm hand. Ewen Handsford was not a big man, perhaps 5'10" or 11", but there was an immediate impression of strength above and beyond the firm handshake. As they talked about the job in hand, Martin assessed the three lads and, not for the first time, was impressed by Robert's ability to provide people who were just what he wanted.

The two larger men were both ex-Guards from Robert's old regiment but Ewen, although with a military background, was a different kettle of fish. He sat quietly listening to the conversation but not saying much. When he did join the conversation his comments or questions, with a slight Scot's brogue, were intelligent and to the point. Martin was impressed by the man and even more so when the question of his ability to look after himself came up.

Ewen looked to Robert who nodded and said, "You've no worries there, Martin. Ewen spent time at Hereford and later in Northern Ireland – and he's qualified to instructor status in martial arts."

"Oh," said Martin, interested. "What branch do you follow, Kung-fu?"

Ewen smiled and Martin felt that it was a touch dismissive. "No, I'm into Karate. I've specialised in Shotokan and Wado-ryu."

"Woah, you've lost me already," said Martin, laughing as he caught Robert grinning indulgently at him. Suddenly conscious that it had been a long time since he had even felt like laughing, Martin felt a moment's unease, as if caught in an act that was improper.

"It might pay you to come on one of my Close Escort Courses if you're going to get involved in this sort of business," said Robert.

"You'd probably RTU me after the first day." Martin grinned, falling into and enjoying the easy camaraderie that the little group carried with them and, with the darkness of recent memories clouding the edges of his consciousness, remembering the simpler regular life that he had enjoyed during his own time in the army.

With arrangements made for the lads to join him in Glasgow as soon as possible, Martin left them. He needed to phone Tony Drew, whom he had not seen since their ill-fated rendezvous in Switzerland. Tony was available so Martin hired a car and took the M25 and A12 to Colchester.

Rayleigh, Essex. 3.50 p.m.

There was much for Tony and Martin to update each other on as, although they had spoken on the telephone after their respective police interviews following Eileen's death, they had not been face to face. Like Robert Hardy, Tony had met Eileen only briefly and did not know the depth of the affair between the couple. In Tony's comfortable lounge, with his wife Betty busying herself with a tray of tea, Martin made every effort to keep the conversation away from the personal aspects of the situation. There was no doubt, however, that the very perceptive couple who looked after him that day were aware that this must have been much more than a casual relationship. The unexpected gentleness from a normally brusque man, coupled with the unfailing warmth of his wife, did much to undo Martin's resolve to move on emotionally. It was with more than a small degree of relief that he accepted Tony's suggestion that they spend an hour in his workshop before dinner.

The hour was well spent. When they left Martin was in possession of not only the miniature rifle mike, which Tony had now field tested, but also a selection of his room bugs and telephone taps – just in case! Their conversation had been fruitful as well. It had confirmed the immediate course of action in his mind. He now knew how, if not precisely when, the information gathering exercise on Lowland Leisure was to be progressed.

Of more importance, he felt an increasing degree of recovery from the swamp of despair which had started to enmesh him again during their previous talk. He recognised and pushed to one side the self pity that was part of the problem. Natural distress remained, but was relegated to what he saw as its proper place, in the dark hours of the night, the small hours of the morning. There was a renewed determination to do his own thing where the investigation was concerned. He remembered wryly the criticisms that had been levelled at him on more than one occasion by both the instructors at Sandhurst and senior police officers.

"You're not officer material, Wild! There's a streak of insubordination running through you that's a mile wide," from one and "When will you learn that we are a team, Sergeant? Keeping things to yourself can be a recipe for professional disaster!" from another.

Inevitably the after dinner conversation turned once more to Eileen. It took a long time for Martin to go to sleep and he wondered uncomfortably whether Betty Drew would notice the damp pillow in the morning.

Friday 22nd May 1992
11.30 a.m. Glasgow

Neil Fisher had been 'bouncing' for eight years and Head Doorman at Shadows for the last two. At 5'10" he was not particularly tall, but what he lacked in height was made up for in build and aggression. In common with many of his fellow Door Supervisors, he spent time each day either in a gym 'pumping iron' or working out in some other way. For Fisher this was easy. Courtesy of Shadows bonuses, he had added a conservatory to his home and equipped it with weights, secondhand exercise machines and other training aids. His mini-gym fulfilled all requirements for keeping fit but he still visited the local gym favoured by the bouncing fraternity. This was to keep his finger on the pulse, who was working for whom, what rumours were circulating, all the gossip on other clubs and their management. These were all the essentials of staying ahead of the game.

Home was a small end of terrace house in a Glasgow suburb some three miles from his place of work. It was brightly painted and, to an observant eye, stood out from its neighbours with a neat frontage and quality Austrian drapes instead of curtains. The fence to the small garden had been removed, well laid paving replacing the front path and unkempt lawn. On the paving stood a white three-year-old BMW 318, which looked to Martin, slumped in the seat of his own car some fifty yards away, to be in very good condition.

This was not the car that Martin had seen Fisher drive away from the club the previous morning. That was a very battered and scarred Ford Escort, which now stood in the street outside the house.

"Second 'quality' car. Uses the Ford for work. Doesn't matter if that gets done over by aggrieved punters." Martin's musing were accurate thus far. To a practised eye, the greater affluence set the house apart from its neighbours. "His wife, if he has one, probably works. For whatever reason, he's not short of a pound or two."

It was here that Martin's guesswork went astray. His investigations had revealed that most doormen had a regular daytime job and worked only part time at clubs in the evenings. What he did not know was that Fisher was employed full time by Lowland Leisure. As both cars were still outside the house at midday on a Friday, he had assumed that Fisher had no daytime job.

In fact, the big man's role at the Club included afternoons working to prepare the premises which catered for up to a thousand customers each night for four nights in the week. He spent time taking deliveries, sorting the cellar, cleaning and maintaining the 'pythons', large diameter tubes twisting and turning from the cellars to spaces above the false ceilings, transporting beers from barrels to the bars. He stocked the bars with bottled beers and carried out numerous maintenance tasks.

In the early evening, after a break for a meal taken at a nearby pub, and paid for out of the Club's petty cash, he did the final checks in readiness for the night's business. He took off the door chains, short lengths of heavy chain padlocked to the panic bars, which secured the fire exits out of business hours. They were then placed on numbered pegs at the front of house. Ostensibly this was to ensure that management and any visiting fire officer could see that the fire exits were free and ready for use by the public in an emergency. Unofficially, in that position, the chains were very handy should a fight get out of hand.

Recently Lowland Leisure had been forced to consider new Health and Safety legislation designed to protect staff and customers. Neil Fisher's latest hat was as the Health and Safety Officer for the Club!

When open for business, his primary role as Head Doorman was controlling the team of Door Supervisors or Bouncers. The management of a group of aggressive, muscular and macho men could be fraught with difficulty. Many nightclubs run into problems with unruly customers being dealt with violently rather than diplomatically. It was not unknown for a door team to virtually take a club over, with the management themselves in fear. Lowland Leisure's answer to this problem was to employ a man whom the team themselves feared, and to make him much more than a head doorman. Thus there were other unspecified, and to most people unknown, activities that engaged Fisher. The big man was a small but important cog in the Lowland Leisure wheel.

Now, as Martin watched from the reclined seat of his car, Fisher was readying himself for work. Twenty minutes after Martin drove away, concerned that further time spent would make him stand out and bored with two hours of inactivity, Fisher came out, got into the Ford and set off. Friday was one of his busier days. He had a beer delivery scheduled for three o'clock and another little 'management' job which required his attention.

It was setting up this job that occupied him on arrival. The cleaners had finished and, apart from one member of management and the evening's DJ preparing for a session, he had the place to himself. The staff rest room was empty. Its doorless ex-broom cupboard had been converted into a telephone booth with a payphone on a shelf. It was a line with no extensions. Ignoring the mass of scribbled numbers and graffiti on the walls, he thumbed coins into the slot. He could have made the call from the management offices but, although McAinsh knew of the big man's extra 'responsibilities', he preferred to keep the detail to himself.

He dialled a number. "Duggie, did you have any luck?"

And then, "Do you think he's up for it?"

The answer was in the affirmative. "Bring him to the Roundhouse for eight tonight."

7.55 p.m.

The two men entering the bar at a few minutes to eight that evening could not have been more unalike. He who pushed the door open was, apart from his height, a typical doorman. Bullet headed, thick necked and with long arms that swung outwards at an angle from the big torso. The thickness of the body and the shortness of his legs turned his walk into waddle and he rolled with each step much as a seaman is said to do. The sight could have been comical, but no one laughed. His scowling face, aggressive eyes, disproportionate body combined to provide a threatening appearance. The instinctive thought of those in his path was that here was a man capable of being as ugly as he looked. The man following him, fending off the door as it was carelessly swung back into his face, was slim, well dressed in the casual manner of the nightclub world with designer jeans and a soft shirt, which had probably cost a lot for not much at all. He was of average height, had straight dark hair, was tanned from regular sunlamp use and wore gold about his neck and wrist. If you looked past the bruised cheek and yellowing black eye, he was handsome in an effeminate way. He was also patently nervous, eyes darting hither and thither, shoulders hunched in a way that said rapid departure was a distinct possibility.

Pausing inside the door, number one looked about until he saw Fisher sitting at a table in the corner with the remnants of a meal before him. Without a word, he swung towards the table, gestured to the chair opposite Fisher, said, "This is the man," to no one in particular and rolled off towards the bar.

He with the black eye stood uncertainly until Fisher said, "Sit down then." And, as he did so, Fisher continued, "So you're Denis." He proceeded to quietly detail his address, the name of the girl that he lived with, his place of work and his parent's address. The shifty eyes were now fixed on Fisher as a frightened rabbit might have viewed the approach of a dancing stoat. There was surprise and fear in equal quantities. Fisher had made no threats; had no need to. The fact that this man knew so much was threat enough.

"Now, Denis, you were caught in the club with this little lot last Friday." He threw a polythene packet onto the table. It contained twelve small blue tablets.

"They was just for me and me mates, Mr Fisher." The excuse was made without hope. He knew that he would not be here, like this, if Fisher thought that.

"Denis." There was an edge now in Fisher's voice. "Don't piss me about. We both know that you were chased off, working the queue on Thursday. We've got you on the cameras selling in the club the Saturday before. You're starting to take liberties and you know what happens to people who do that."

The hunched shoulders had now become a frightened crouch. The voice quivered. "I won't do it again, Mr Fisher. I'll stay away. Promise."

"Oh, but that's not the sort of promise that we want, Denis."

"Whatever you say, Mr Fisher." The voice was lower, uncertain, but prepared to listen to anything to avoid a repeat of his visit to the 'Gents' the previous Friday.

You've heard that we've lost our 'Spotter' I'm sure. Duggie over there seems to think that you might like to make us an offer in consideration of these." Fisher poked the polythene package with a stubby finger.

Denis shivered. There had been graphic descriptions of the broken body taken to hospital from a side street near Shadows. The man had been a well known face in the club, always talking to the doormen, seemingly on an inside track. There were those in the local drug fraternity who pointed to the fact that it was after conversations with the doormen that there would suddenly be a concerted move and some unfortunate would be rubbed down, his supply confiscated and he would be bounced out of the fire doors. The suggestion was that the 'spotter' had started to do some dealing on the side for himself. The bruised hands and fractured fingers would not be able to handle tablets for a long while and it was not the broken jaw and missing teeth that stopped him talking to the police. He was a local man with wife and kids to be fearful for.

"What do you want, Mr Fisher?" There was a whine in the voice now which seemed incongruous coming from a personality normally confident, even bold, on the surface.

"What we want is for you to come into the club on a regular basis. We want you to do what you're so good at, sussin' out the punters who're carrying, especially those who are supplying. All you've got to do is tip us the wink. Duggie over there," he nodded towards the bullet head holding a glass at the bar "will be one of your contacts and we'll give you another. Every time you get a result you'll be paid in these." Again his finger poked the packet of pills. "Only thing is that you won't sell in the club. You can deal with whoever you want outside, but inside you work for us."

The frightened eyes were still there, but the voice was stronger. "How many do I get when I spot someone, Mr Fisher?"

That will depend on what we get, but that's not your problem, Denis.

Your problem is convincing us that we can trust you after pushing these on our turf." Fisher picked the packet up, tossed it once in the air and slipped it into his pocket. "Anyway, the better you do the more you get. You can drink for free, but not too much! If you keep your nose clean, we might be able to put something else your way and, of course, we'll keep an eye out for you."

The double meaning was not lost and, when he rose to leave after further one sided interchanges, he had a feeling of inevitability that was not very satisfying. His dealing had bought him the gold around his neck, that on his wrist, the deposit on the pokey flat that he shared with his teenage girlfriend, the body kit and flash wheels on his XRI. He wondered how this arrangement would affect his cash flow and how dodgy this new association would be. But there was nothing that he could do about it. He had stepped into their world, taken a chance, made some money, got caught and was now committed to them first and himself second.

Saturday 23rd May 1992
2.50 a.m. Glasgow

To Ewen Handsford the job up north had sounded like a bit of a gas. Now, entering his second night of waiting for Fisher to appear, he was not so sure. If this was an operation in the commercial security world it was all a bit boring. Three hours sitting in a parked car looking at an unchanging landscape was two and a half hours too much. Oh for some action.

To Martin in a second car a few yards away, and within view of the nightclub's doors, it was far from the light hearted exercise that the three men from Robert Hardy's agency anticipated. If this plan did not succeed, he would have wasted time and money and be back to square one.

On the previous evening they had waited until 3.15 a.m. before Fisher appeared. When he finally walked through the front doors he had the thin bearded man with him, whom Martin had recognised as one of the management. The couple had driven to the rear of some nearby shops in Fisher's Ford, where the bearded man transferred to a black Audi saloon parked there and drove off. Fisher had then taken his normal route home.

At three in the morning, the streets had been fairly empty of traffic. Only the occasional taxi or private car appeared. In these conditions it had been difficult to follow Fisher closely without arousing suspicions. Then, on arrival at his house, the plan had failed completely. Two doors from Fisher's home a domestic row was raging between a drunken husband and his angry wife. The police were present, completely scuttling Martin's plan.

Tonight they had an extra hire car. Martin had the club in view, Robert Hardy's 'heavies' were in the second car some fifty yards away and Ewen was in another round the corner. Each car had a handheld radio, all tuned to the same frequency so that they could talk together 'back to back'. The plan was to follow Fisher to his home without showing out. The first two cars were to change position as required whilst Ewen stayed behind out of sight.

As Martin watched, the staff trickled out to their cars and waiting taxis. Almost immediately, and much earlier than expected, Fisher appeared. He was with two doormen and Martin cursed, hoping that they were not staying together. If they had to run the exercise a third time it would become difficult not to show out.

"He's on the street lads. Be ready to move." There was immediate acknowledgement and he was thankful for trained and disciplined men who did not doze on the job.

"He's moving towards his car." Fisher had separated from the two men and was making towards his car in a side street.

"Ewen, move off towards Fisher's address. Take it slowly and let him overtake you. Mike, John, follow me at a distance."

When Fisher turned off of the main road, Martin intended doing a U-turn, allowing Mike and John to close in whilst he took up the 'tail end Charlie' position.

Fisher's lights came on and Martin eased the Mondeo into first. He waited for the Escort to accelerate before moving away. Keeping well back, he followed and then, only some half a mile from the club, Fisher's Ford swung into the only open, brightly lit premises within sight; a petrol filling station.

"Your location, Ewen!" Martin's tone was urgent.

"Still on the main road, approaching the turn off."

"Turn and get back to the 24-hour service station that you've just passed. Make it as quick as you can. Mike, John, follow Fisher into the petrol station and wait for a call from me."

They did as instructed whilst Martin braked and stopped just beyond the station's exit. He waited impatiently. If Ewen did not get back quickly and Fisher left, he might recognise the Mondeo which had been on his tail the previous night.

Fisher was now out of his car and filling with fuel. No sign of Ewen. Mike and John had stopped by the airline and were handling it as though about to top up a tyre. Again Martin was thankful for Robert Hardy's selection of staff

Fisher replaced the hose, fiddled with the petrol cap and started towards the kiosk.

"Ewen, location!" The words contained an unspoken plea.

"I'm within sight, Martin. On the forecourt in seconds if that's what you want."

"Right, that's a 'yes', Ewen. Action stations Mike and John. Take him as he returns to the car. Remember that you're up for Oscars on this one. I want him still able to walk after you disappear."

Having paid at the kiosk, Fisher started back towards his car. As he did so he saw a man get out of a white Ford Mondeo and stand staring at him. The action made him stare back. He reached for the Escort's door handle and was suddenly aware, with that sixth sense of men who walk in the shadows, that he was not alone.

Startled, he swung round. Two large men, carrying baseball bats were almost upon him. Their soft soled shoes made no noise. There was no time to enter the car. Desperately he reached for the coat on the back seat hiding a length of door chain but the car was a two door. No chance. A splintering crash as a baseball bat hit the windscreen and in that moment he was plucked from the car and thrown against one of the petrol pumps.

Aggression and adrenaline fused as he sprang forward, fists raised at the nearer of his two assailants. He saw bared teeth and heard, "This is fur me wee friend t'other night," as he swung a punch. The man swayed backwards. Fisher's punch found empty air and then, off balance, he felt the sickening pain of the bat thudding into his kidneys.

The force of the blow and loss of balance put him down and he rolled, fighting the nausea and pain, knees and hands going up in protection against the expected boot. There was the sound of breaking glass again and a car door slamming.

"Yu'll think again before setting your men on a wee bairn," he heard.

Lashing out with the feet drawn up to his chest he was rewarded with a crack across the shins. More sickening pain. Fisher, a man who could be considered an expert at beatings, knew that he was in for one himself. Both blows could have been harder. The large man towering over him was only playing with the bat!

Then, through a grey mist of pain, he saw a smaller man step into view. The newcomer seemed to spin and one leg shot out to hit the assailant on the back of one thigh, knocking him off balance and to his knees. He spun again and this time caught the side of the big man's head. The baseball bat fell and the newcomer, without pausing, swooped onto it, scooping it up with his right hand. As Fisher started to lever himself up to rejoin the fray, there was a blow to the back of his head and the greyness turned black as he slumped forward.

For the benefit of the petrol pump attendant Ewen, John and Mike followed their script, engaging in a few seconds of shouting and baseball bat action before John and Mike both went sprawling. Martin was now shouting too. "Get out of it." John and Mike scrambled away to their car, as Ewen bent over the recumbent figure of Neil Fisher, now on his side retching. The Mondeo and its sister car sped away with tyres squealing, leaving Ewen to solicitously bathe Fisher's bruised head and dignity with a length of paper towel dipped into the forecourt's watering can.

Some five minutes later, sitting with his back against a petrol pump and surveying the broken glass of his car, Fisher listened to a graphic account by the forecourt attendant of Ewen's arrival and intervention. The little man was hopping from foot to foot, hyped up by the evening's unexpected entertainment.

"Mon, yu shud 'aye seen this laddie. He saved yu bacon. He knocked the two of them down, one after the other. He did the fust with his feet – spun like a bluddy ballet dancer and the other with the bluddy bat that the fust one dropped. It was brawl! They ran like a pair of rabbits!" Then followed much excited description of Ewen's expertise with feet, fists and baseball bats.

"Ay an' there wuz another wun too – over by a white car in the road. He drove off before them, but he wus wi' them, shoutin, an' all."

With the arrival of the police, Fisher climbed to his feet, holding a towel to his head and gazed at the damage to his car. The Ford's windscreen and both headlamps were smashed. With the police taking details, he listened as Ewen told them that he did not yet have an address. "Just arrived in town and looking for a cheap hotel if you know one?"

Despite his battering, Fisher was still a careful man. There was no immediate offer, just a suggestion that if Ewen cared to visit the club he would be pleased to have a drink with him the following day. Ewen, equally offhand, said not to worry, if he was still in town he might do just that.

As Ewen left, Fisher was refusing the offer of a trip to the local Casualty. It was pleasing to hear the attendant telling the second policeman that the forecourt CCTV covered the pumps but not the airline area. There was no accurate description of either the Mondeo or the assailants.

Sunday 24th May 1992
8.05 a.m. Southampton

Bill Creighton walked into the Incident Room at Shirley Police Station anticipating another boring eight hour shift. He was not an 'office man'. Heavily built, not particularly tall and getting thin on top, Bill was one of the most experienced – and more successful – of the foot soldiers in the Southampton Criminal Investigation Department. Normally stationed at the Civic Centre Police Station covering the Central Sub Division he, along with a number of other CID men from Central and other Divisions, had been seconded to form the Murder Squad operating from Shirley, investigating Eileen Padgett's death.

The Incident Room was staffed around the clock by two officers. They worked in pairs on eight hour shifts, changing at 8 a.m., 4 p.m. and midnight. The investigating officers who carried out the external enquiries worked – nominally – on two shifts of eight hours commencing at 9 a.m. and changing at 5 p.m. to finish at one in the morning. The pressure of a murder enquiry, especially in the early stages, meant that a great deal of overtime was worked by these officers. It was not unusual for those on the early shift to be still 'at it' in the late evening. For this reason there was a weekly change of shifts to ensure that the workload was fairly spread.

"Sorry I'm late." Bill's cheery greeting was normal, in contrast to the officer he was relieving. Bill was an extrovert character and joining the 'Squad' had lifted him from the humdrum of shoplifting, burglaries and thefts that were the routine of Central Sub Division. Additionally there was a personal interest in this particular case which, to his surprise, had been overlooked by the Chief Inspector when choosing those officers who would form the Murder Squad. Although Bill knew Eileen Padgett only distantly, he was on more than friendly terms with Martin Wild. When Martin had been in 'the Job' and first joined the CID, Bill had been his partner, teaching the younger man the practises of plain clothes work. When Martin's twin sister died, Bill supported him through the bereavement and when he decided to leave the Force Bill, although counselling against it, had been there with wise words to smooth the change. The companionship continued, albeit less frequently after Martin's resignation, with meetings for a drink and, before Eileen's arrival on the scene, the occasional meal at home with Bill and his wife. Although the contact had lessened there was still the easy partnership when they met.

"Anything new overnight?" Bill tried again. He had passed the other night duty officer, waiting outside with his coat on for Bill to arrive. The remaining detective was an older man, not noted for cheerfulness at 8 a.m. on a Sunday morning after a night's work.

"We might have found the missing man from the St James list." He handed Bill a Fax sheet with an Interpol heading and turned back to finish the overnight report which would be required by the Duty Detective Sergeant in an hour's time.

The fax detailed the death in Marseilles by shooting of one Monsieur Henri Tabarde, a junior minister and rising star in the French government. Tabarde had been at the forefront of a drive against the Mafia led drugs rackets that used the seaport as an entry route for the distribution of narcotics.

Due to the connection with Martin, part of the murder enquiry had centred upon Quantum Bank, the London client that Martin had been with on the day prior to the explosion. Whilst the identities and location of most staff and visitors had been easy to establish, two were missing. The first, the bank's Marketing Director, was holidaying on a yacht in the West Indies and was confirmed within a day. The second, Henri Tabarde, a regular visitor in connection with funding for an Anglo French business venture, should have returned to France after the meeting at St James. It was established quite quickly that, driving his black Citroen XM, he had taken the Dover/Calais ferry, visited friends in Paris and had then disappeared.

Detailed enquiries by the French police had failed to locate the prominent businessman. Then a barge docking at the port of Marseilles grounded on a submerged obstruction. A search by a diving team resulted in the recovery of a black Citroen complete with M Tabarde, who had died from a single bullet wound to the head.

A suspicion that the criminal activity directed against Eileen and Martin was due to a simple but tragic case of mistaken identity had been growing in the minds of the investigating team since the first week of the enquiry. Now, with this latest information, Bill thought it time that Martin should be made aware that he was no longer the centre of the enquiry. He knew that Detective Chief Inspector Potter would do nothing to ease Martin's concern until it suited him. As Martin had said during their last conversation, "He won't even give me the time of day!"

The two pairs of detectives manning the office had an unofficial arrangement. As soon as the first of the morning shift appeared, one of the night duty would leave for home. The second would brief his incoming colleague before disappearing. The second 'morning man' would arrive at about 8.30 just prior to the appearance of the Detective Sergeant responsible for the day shift.

Now, as the last night duty man filed his report in the 'Eight to Four' tray and picked up his coat, knowing that he would have the office to himself for a few minutes, Bill Creighton lifted a telephone and dialled Martin's office number. When the answerphone cut in he said, "Angie, if you are in touch with Martin, ask him to ring the following number at 6 p.m. tonight or the same time tomorrow night." He gave the number of a pub close to his home which they had both used as a 'local'. "Don't ring me back at the office."

Bill guessed that Martin would be in daily touch with his office and that Angie would recognise his voice.

8.15 a.m. Glasgow

It was not only the police that were active that Sunday morning. As Martin caught up with his late night in a hotel bedroom and the shift changed at Shirley Police Station, a somewhat jaded Gordon Wilson awoke – also in a Glasgow hotel. He had slept badly after arriving in the early hours, having spent the preceding two days visiting Lowland Leisure clubs on his way north. He had driven a series of 'dogs legs' from Hampshire to Glasgow, crisscrossing the country to spend an hour or two at each nightspot. The reason for the extended journey was a call from Mabbett to attend a Sunday meeting at his Scottish home. For his own protection, Wilson needed to know that all was well where the various clubs trading activities were concerned. The only way to get a feel for that was to spend time with the operators, preferably when they were open for business.

Now, as the time approached to join Mabbett at his west coast hideaway on the Isle of Bute, Wilson's thoughts started again where they had left off during his broken night's sleep. What did Mabbett want? Despite careful questions, there had been no indication in the telephone conversation that had preceded the journey. A summons to Scotland was unusual and boded more than routine discussion. It could not be the debacle of the Southampton bomb. That had been settled. Liam Mahoney had spent an uncomfortable time spelling out his actions to Mabbett. Wilson did not know what had been said but guessed that Mahoney was too valuable for Mabbett to deal with as he would most others in the organisation. He did not know that Mahoney had suffered the financial penalty of foregoing the second half of his payment for the job. There was also the unspoken knowledge that he was now considered as less than reliable. A not inconsiderable problem for a man whose stock depended upon that somewhat rare commodity. It should not be the clubs. They were trading well without the hidden factor of their 'unseen' cash streams. If those were included, then the balance sheets were such that an average business man would have thought that he had struck gold!

As Wilson left the hotel and headed for the Isle of Bute, he turned his mind to the opposition. It could be to do with a new challenge to the Lowland Leisure position. Every so often another personality would appear on the nightclub scene, with the bottle to consider changing envy to something more concrete. These had been met and dealt with in the past. Due to the manner in which they were dealt with new challenges were few and Wilson had heard nothing on the grapevine as he questioned the various club managers on his way north.

The dramatic coastal views during the ferry ride from Skelmorlie, on the mainland west of Glasgow, to Rothesay on Bute, and the beauty of the coastal road to Kilchatten, were lost on Wilson. The drive was eventually over and, at a few minutes before midday, he pulled up on the gravel driveway which led to Mabbett's expensively restored Victorian country house.

Before him was a pair of ornate wrought iron gates which gave access to the large house positioned halfway up the hill above the road. From the road itself little could be seen of the building whose tall garden walls and shrubbery acted as an effective screen. Neighbouring properties consisted of a scattering of cottages and a small hotel, all bordering the road. Mabbett's house was the largest and most secluded. From its higher elevation there were extensive views across Kilchatten Bay to the mainland.

Wilson left the car to press the intercom at the gate. He knew as he did so that the positioning of the communication panel was deliberate and allowed a good view of callers via a closed circuit television camera positioned halfway up a massive pine inside the grounds. Mabbett was a careful man and valued his privacy.

12.20 p.m. Southampton

The small 'L' shaped suite of rooms that housed the local Photographic and Fingerprint Office within the Civic Centre Police Station at Southampton was quiet. It was, after all, a Sunday lunchtime.

The corridor outside the offices, with its row of similar cell doors, was deserted. Prisoners arrested for drunkenness and similar minor misdemeanours in the town centre on Saturday night had been bailed to reappear at the Monday morning's Magistrates Court.

Only one person was working in that area and his was a private rather than a police job. Detective Constable Kent, a photographer and fingerprint officer, had spent the previous weekend in London with the very petite Janet, a telephonist on the Civic Centre police switchboard. The weekend had been a swift reaction to their first date which, to Kent's surprise, had been much more 'fulfilling' than expected. During the weekend away he had shot a reel of film which spanned the spectrum from innocent to mildly pornographic. He was now processing – and re-living – the events.

One of the reasons that Kent had chosen this weekend to develop the film was that he knew Janet was scheduled to be Duty Telephonist from 8 a.m. to 4 p.m. With the last of the prints going through the drum of the glazer he picked up the internal phone and dialled the switchboard. "Jan, our photos are done. Can you get down here to see them?"

"My lunch break is in half an hour. I'll see if I can get the office man to cover for me early."

Ten minutes later there was the sound of the cell passage door buzzer. Kent took his keys, let himself out of the Photo Department and opened the heavy cell passage door a few feet away. Janet slipped through the door, looking over her shoulder as she did so.

"No problem down here, I'm the only one in," said Kent.

Shutting the door he turned and followed and, as her high heels clip-clopped ahead of him, Kent was given the benefit of that which had first attracted him.

Janet's 5'2" figure was, with the exception of her breasts, beautifully rounded. Slim ankles led into muscular calves and curvaceous thighs. Her derrière was very full and feminine. Kent gazed with masculine appreciation, he was very much a 'bottom man'. Good job too because above the waist Janet could almost have been mistaken for a boy with wavy brown hair. This odd juxtaposition fascinated him.

Opening the Photo Department door, he ushered Janet in. She turned immediately, encircling his neck with her arms, offering lips in a greeting kiss.

As they kissed Kent felt himself hardening. Janet did too.

"Ooh, that's quick!" she breathed against his mouth and, to show approval, slipped the tip of her tongue between his lips and gently rotated her belly against a now obvious bulge. Breathing quickly, conscious of the door with only a latch, Kent broke free and, taking her hand said, "Come and see the photos." He led through another door, which was a small working area with sinks to one side and the glazing machine on an open work surface opposite.

Off this area was a curtained darkroom to the right and directly ahead another door leading to an even smaller room known as the Developing Room. This room's windows were equipped with lightproof shutters and the door with an automatic latch. It had a small work surface and sink whilst against the inner wall was a small table. The wall against which the table stood was a thin partition which divided the Developing Room from the curtained Darkroom.

Kent picked up the pile of finished prints and led Janet into the Developing Room where he switched on the light and closed the door. He spread the prints out on the table where Janet picked them up murmuring after a few seconds, "They're very good."

As she reached the last print and started to go through them again Kent, standing by her side, could resist no longer. Caressing her full bottom, kissing her neck and nibbling her ear had the inevitable result. The photos fell as she turned, breathing quickly, eyes closing as she again encircled his neck. For several seconds they remained in a kissing embrace with Kent's busy hands caressing curves, tracing outlines beneath Janet's thin summer dress.

She was a very feminine girl and, whilst not the 'station bike', had a small number of 'very good friends' amongst the policemen who operated out of Civic Centre. She was very aware of the effect that certain items of clothing or styles of dressing had on particular males and quite often wore stockings and a suspender belt instead of tights. Now, as Kent traced the outline of suspenders drawn tight over full thighs, he found himself quivering with excitement and anticipation. He could find no sign of the very brief panties that Janet normally wore.

"Is there something missing?" he breathed against her ear.

"That's for me to know and you to find out!"

He dropped to one knee and slid the hem of the dress upwards.

"Oh, you gorgeous girl!"

Freed of the skirt's constriction, Janet leant back against the table with bared thighs parted. Above the stocking tops, Kent's appreciative investigating fingers found a nirvana of silken skin covered in a warm slippery sheen. Anticipation and desire hardened into urgency. In one heave Janet was sitting on the worktop, plump thighs widely spread scattering glossy prints in all directions. There were no further preliminaries, in seconds she was gasping in time to his uncontrolled thrusts. Her back was against the wall, her bottom on the table and her legs clasped around Kent's waist. As his fever mounted, the freestanding table thumped against the partition wall at an increasing rate.

On the other side of the wall, in the darkroom, was the baseplate of a photographic enlarger. On it were a number of items laid out to be arranged, labelled and photographed. They were the debris from Parksyde Avenue, one plastic bag from each square metre of road and pavement. Each bag was labelled to identify which particular square metre it was on a large scale drawing of the scene and in the Scene of Crime photographs.

The contents of this bag were typical of rubbish found in a gutter, ranging from a crumpled cigarette packet, a rusty washer, pieces of broken glass and a short section of pencil, bright blue in colour and with some silver lettering. It was about 2" long and did not have a point, being cut short at too acute an angle to be used as a writing instrument.

The officer responsible for the routines of photographing, re-labelling and indexing had been called away on an urgent 'shout' the previous day.

He had anticipated being only an hour or so, but the job took several hours and, on his return, he followed the inhouse routine, posting a notice on the darkroom curtains advising others not to touch.

No one had, but now the rhythmic thumping from the other side of the wall caused the pencil remnant to quiver. As the tempo increased so did the movement and the stub started to move. Slowly, millimetre by millimetre it rolled towards the rear of the backplate. Seconds before Kent's finale it dropped out of sight between the back of the enlarger and the wall.

Thus was 'lost' the only identifiable object which could have connected Shadows Nightclub with the bomb scene.

12.30 p.m. Scotland

Sunday was proving interesting for Gordon Wilson. On arrival at the lochside house he and Mabbett had lunched on the patio. The view was magnificent. The hillside below dropped down to the blue waters of Kilchatten Bay, beyond which the Firth of Clyde was a deeper blue with an offshore breeze. In the distance, over occasional white sails, the green and brown bulk of Great Cumbrae Isle loomed on the horizon. Whilst Mabbett, lean and relaxed, glass in hand, sat and admired the view with an almost proprietorial air Wilson, hunched over his belly, concentrated on the smoked salmon.

Initially the conversation was routine. How well the various clubs were doing, changes to management, new promotions affecting the 'spend per head' and eventually their hidden margins.

At this point, having finished his dish, Wilson was taken by the arm and walked off of the patio by Mabbett onto the large, carefully manicured lawn. When well out of earshot of the maid clearing the table, Mabbett said, "Gordon, this business that Mahoney and the others fouled up has cost us. You know that we were down to sort that particular problem. We didn't and we've raised a stink into the bargain. It has been sorted now, but by others in Marseilles."

Wilson started to repeat excuses that had been voiced previously in the days after Eileen's death, but was cut short. "Wait 'till I've finished." They walked a few paces in silence.

"The latest news is that the two in France that the Paris people put onto the job after Liam's mistake also made a complete balls up. This guy Wild, who Mahoney mistook for the target, took a different car from the one that he used the previous day. They knew this and picked him up. Until today that was all that was known. Why they didn't do the business is anybody's guess. They just disappeared. Yesterday they turned up – dead!"

Wilson stopped in his tracks. Mabbett glanced at him and noted without amusement that his jaw was actually hanging open. The mouth moved but no words came out.

"They were still in their car, but at the bottom of some river on the Swiss border. Our Paris connection is trying to tell the Sûreté why they employed two known criminals, who were found to be armed and had bomb making equipment in the car. The French police are looking at them sideways!"

Wilson was out of his depth and it showed. "What can we do about it?"

"The Marseilles connection has shown less profit over recent months. This latest business could spell trouble; could well be the finish of it where our dealings are concerned. They don't have time for amateurs and that's about how we look at the moment."

Mabbett paused and they walked on in silence for some distance. "Have you ever been to Russia?" he asked suddenly.

Startled, the answer was "No. Never wanted to."

"Well, perhaps that won't be necessary, but I'm talking to some people at the moment who are in our business in East Germany and they're getting supplies from Russia. The talk is of low prices and no shortage. With the border controls disappearing in Europe and the Channel Tunnel here shortly, it should be easier to move the stuff. I'd like to make the connections and try a first run if it's OK."

"There's talk of delays where the Tunnel's concerned" observed Wilson.

"I know that, but I might be tempted to kick it off by using the boat for the leg across the Channel."

Wilson was surprised. Mabbett was the planner, the financier. It was very unusual for him to accept a direct connection with a job.

"You've never done before DM."

"No, but one of the Germans that I'm in touch with is an electronics hotshot and he's got some gear that's interested me. It could be very useful as insurance if there's any Customs interest and also for transferring stuff. We're talking around modifying it to fit 'Spirit'."

"What about language?" Wilson sounded doubtful.

"Cash in hand talks volumes, Gordon." Mabbett chuckled. "Besides, the man I know could well take a hand in this and he's pretty fluent in Russian."

Wilson was concerned. Another body in the organisation might pose a threat to his position and, the more people, the more potential leaks. He voiced his fears. "How safe are these people?"

"If by safe you mean secure, then that's what we have to find out, but I'll look after that angle. If you're talking about the quality of the merchandise then we have our own safeguards there. I'll take the Chemist with me; he can do some initial checks. We won't buy anything unless it's been past him."

They had reached the bottom of the lawn. Turning, Mabbett said, "You've got some contacts in the transport business Gordon. Start having a nose around, a quiet word here and there. See if you can find a small firm – not too many vehicles – someone who's not doing too well. That shouldn't be difficult at the moment. Someone who wouldn't be unhappy if a lorry took a diversion for a suitable 'interest'. Don't pitch it too high, you know the form. Look for a company that's been using the French Channel ports for some time. I want to steer clear of Holland, the Dutch Customs have been active recently."

For the next half hour they discussed the detail of Wilson's target companies and the potential of using the anticipated Channel Tunnel. It was obvious to Wilson that Mabbett had made up his mind and intended being closer to the action. He wondered uneasily how that would affect him and did not like some of the options that presented themselves.

3.00 p.m.

As Wilson drove south from the Kilchatten meeting, Martin Wild was already ahead of him courtesy of the British Airways Shuttle to Heathrow. It had been several days since he had spent time in the office. His telephone conversations with his secretary, Angie, had reinforced the thought that a business neglected would very soon falter or fail. The investigation into Eileen's death was uppermost in his mind but, without the income from the company, there would be no possibility of him investigating anything. Having made the decision, Martin did not delay and intended spending Monday in the office, catch up with current clients, find out how the police investigation was going and, if necessary, farm out some of the work to a trusted associate. All being well, he could rejoin Ewen in Glasgow the following day.

On reaching Heathrow, Martin phoned Bill Creighton who he knew to be on the day shift at Shirley Police Station. "Bill, I'm on my way south. Wondered if you were free to meet?"

"Good to hear from you. I left a message on your answerphone this morning. Did you get it?"

"No, I've not spoken with the office today. What was it?"

"If we're meeting, I'll save it till then. I finish at four today, all being well. Why not come over to us and stay the night?"

Martin refused his offer of a bed, conscious that Bill's position could easily be compromised. They agreed to meet for a drink in the evening, leaving Martin free to spend the day in the office. Normally he would have looked forward to such a day, but not now. He had a feeling of foreboding, knowing that fallout from the recent past was overdue.

Monday 25th May 1992
9.20 a.m. Southampton

"Monday, bloody Monday." Angie had deposited the post and a cup of black coffee on Martin's desk. The first letter opened was from Rafe Drummond at Quantum Bank. The Bank could not possibly employ a Security Consultant whose activities had cost senior executives much time, aggravation and embarrassment. His services were no longer required. The letter was not a surprise. He had expected a bad reaction to the Swiss trip, but it was still a shock to see it in black and white. Quantum had been one of the first of his major clients, the start of his London success and a steady source of income.

Just under an hour later Angie took a call from another London firm, this time a prospective client. The meeting arranged was cancelled without comment. The caller would not wait to be put through and, when Martin rang him back, he was 'not available'. Bad news was travelling fast in the City that had proved so lucrative.

That problems often came in threes was confirmed when, on opening the last letter from the morning's post, he found that his business account, which usually bumped along the credit / debit demarcation line was now well into the red. With the loss of that morning's business, it would not be long before his overdraft limit was reached.

This situation would be exacerbated when the expenses from the ill-fated Swiss trip hit the account. Because of the police intervention he had not been able to start, let alone finish the assignment. No client was going to pay in that situation. The final cost had arrived that morning in the shape of an invoice for the repairs to and return of the Porsche.

A damage limitation exercise where remaining London clients were concerned was necessary – as would be the liquidation of some assets to support the business. It did not take much to financially unsettle a small company. Ewen would have to work alone for a day or two.

The first good news of the day than came in a telephone call from that very man. "Hi Martin – I'm in!" There was more than a hint of excitement in Ewen's voice, going 'undercover' had got his adrenalin going – with memories of Northern Ireland! "I had a drink with Neil Fisher last night, the club is shut on a Sunday. He asked a lot of questions then whether I'd be interested in joining the door team. This morning he rang to say that he'd cleared it with management. I start on Thursday."

"Thank goodness, Ewen. I was starting to think that our little exercise had been a wasted effort."

Recent news now clouded Martin's judgement. "I know that I told you not to rush things if we got on the inside but there has been a change resulting in greater urgency. I'm going to try and get some special gear to you. Ring me back in an hour's time."

Martin's next call was to Tony Drew who, to his relief, agreed to deliver a range of 'bugging' gear to Ewen without delay. Not only that but he would spend time instructing Ewen on the installation of the equipment.

"God bless you Tony; I owe you!"

"Don't know about the first one, but the second will cost you." Behind the brusque manner was genuine concern.

An hour later Ewen rang again as arranged and, in addition to relaying the arrangements with Tony Drew, Martin also provided greater detail of the events that had led to the assignment. He perhaps said more than he had intended. Ewen left the telephone to prepare for his meeting with Tony Drew in a much more sober frame of mind. Suddenly this job had assumed a different complexion. For the first time he knew of Eileen's death and a little of the anguish in Martin's heart.

6.25 p.m. Southampton

"Bill! Good to see you."

"Hello Marty; how are you?"

They shook hands as Martin said, "What'll you have – the usual?"

Bill nodded and Martin turned to the bar to order a pint of best bitter for one of the few people that he regarded as a real friend. Bill Creighton took stock of Martins' appearance. He felt concern knowing the pressure that Wild had been under.

Settling back in a quiet corner, Bill answered Martin's usual questions about wife and family and immediately felt at a loss. With Eileen's death there was now no one to ask about in Martin's. The two had met only briefly while Martin was being 'looked at' by DCI Potter. Bill had expressed his grief but now could not help saying again "Marty, I'm terribly sorry. I know that there is nothing that anyone can say or do to help, but you know where we are."

Bill later described to his wife the pain in Martin's eyes which was followed by "…a look that made me glad not to be the opposition." The eyes had narrowed and darkened. To Bill, they seemed to go from the smiling green that had greeted him to that of a cold glacial lake in winter. When Martin spoke his voice had flattened, losing lightness.

"There's only one thing that matters to me now Bill. I want to see the bastards who did this locked up – permanently!"

"We don't seem to be any closer at the moment, Marty. I wish to Christ I could give you some good news on that score."

"Bill, I've started doing my own digging as you know and I'll feed information back to you as it seems appropriate, but I do need any help that you can give me. Having said that I don't want to put you in a difficult position."

"Sod the position, Marty, I know that you'll use your head about your sources. Whatever I know is yours. The problem is that I'm seeing only a part of the enquiry and from next week it will be even less. I'm out of the office and onto an Interview Unit."

"Damn! I was hoping to keep a feel for the overall situation through you."

For some time they discussed the progress of the investigation and the change in opinion and emphasis where Martin's suspected involvement was concerned. Bill's update on the death in Marseilles of Henri Tabarde and the Interpol info, and on the activities that had apparently led to it, answered a number of questions in Martin's mind. The fact that police thinking now was that Eileen's death and the attempts on his life were down to a simple case of one mistaken identity brought a belated sense of relief.

Twenty minutes later Bill said, "Come on. I know that you won't stop the night but Susan has dinner ready. She hasn't seen you for months. I'll get an earwigging if I don't take you home tonight. She's cooked for three."

After dinner the two men talked quietly in the lounge whilst Susan made coffee. She gave them time knowing that Martin needed Bill on his own, perhaps to talk through some of the trauma, but also to soak up all of the information and gossip that he could.

Finally Bill said, "Marty, about the question of sources, there's one that you might consider – though I'm not sure whether you would or how you could approach if you decided to."

"Bill, I'll look at any source for information on this one."

"None of the other lads on the Squad are likely to help you, You don't have the `previous' with them and Potter's feelings about you are too well known. However, all of Potter's work goes to one typist who has been seconded from the Headquarters 'pool'. Do you remember Ellie May Thomas? The West Indian girl who had the hots for you when you were in CID."

Martin grinned at Bill's overstatement of the relationship. "Who could forget Ellie May? Don't tell me she's working for Potter!" The memories came flooding back. A slim petite and very attractive eighteen year old who had been the only coloured girl employed in the Civic Centre police station at that time. Christened 'La Derrière' by one appreciative detective, Ellie May had been the recipient of the usual attentions that a pretty girl experiences. The colour of her skin was an added attraction to some. One man in particular persisted although his advances were not welcomed by the shy girl.

Martin happened to be walking past the canteen door one morning when he heard a commotion and on looking in witnessed a scene which was fairly common before racial and sexual attitudes grew teeth. His immediate action had perhaps been too effective, especially when the somewhat elevated position of the other man – a civilian employee – was considered. The inevitable result was a suspension from duty for one month whilst an internal enquiry progressed. The resultant 'canteen gossip' included suggestions that the men had been fighting for the girl's favours. Martin's subsequent reinstatement without punishment did nothing to quell the rumours.

For her part, Ellie May's gratitude to the young policeman, cautious at first, strengthened as she realised that there were no ulterior motives behind his actions that day. The tall curly haired detective with steady eyes and a ready smile on his scarred face was easy to talk to. There were no clumsy passes; he treated her with a respect that she did not always receive from others.

During the months that followed, their friendship grew. With his persuasion Ellie May took evening classes, achieving high standards in shorthand. Eventually she was promoted from her original job of copy typing and became very much in demand by those senior officers able to call upon the services of a shorthand typist rather than place their cassettes in the queue at the typing pool. Ellie May enjoyed the improved status that went with this jockeying for her services. With Martin in the wings to turn to for advice, her problems socially were less as well. The police service gossip inevitably made the mistaken assumption that the couple were 'an item'.

This did not worry Martin who had a regular succession of girlfriends. His single status gave him a degree of latitude envied by his married colleagues. The obvious attachment of a young and attractive girl was, in many respects, a benefit, especially in that odd male field where apparent sexual success equates with a certain social standing. Martin contradicted any suggestions that Ellie May had 'joined his stable' but the gossip of the day said that 'he protesteth too much'.

"It strikes me that your girlfriend of years ago might be in a position to help you now, if too much water hasn't passed under the bridge."

"Bill, of all the people that I might ask for help this is the one person that I'd least like to. She had a difficult time when I knew her at the Civic. She worked hard and did well. I would hate to do anything now which would adversely affect her position."

"She's had a difficult time since, Marty. She is now Ellie May Layton. She married a year or so after you left. A no-good Jamaican. They split quite quickly, but it wasn't easy, so I hear."

"Anybody that I might have known?"

"I wouldn't think so. First name is Erroll. He's had a conviction for ABH and a second for drink driving, both in the last year or so."

"Perhaps I'll have a word with Ellie, see how the land lies. I'll have to be careful."

As Susan arrived with the coffee Martin said, "Any other bright ideas, Bill?"

"There is just one which might or might not be of value to you. I don't know how much you know of the nightclub angle that you're looking at but a few weeks ago we had an arson at a club in town and I met a guy who troubleshoots for the company that owns it. He's ex-job, was Hampshire but left in the '70s. He gave me his card." Bill slid a business card across the table. "I doubt whether you would have met him when you were serving, before your time in Central I expect."

Martin shook his head. "Can't say that I remember the name."

"Well, as I said, he's now working for this big leisure organisation. He's got a lot of experience and a lot of contacts in the nightclub industry. He was useful to us on the arson. It's just possible that a chat with him might help you."

"Many thanks, Bill, I'll give him a ring. While we're talking about contact names and numbers, can you get me any of the French ones that were involved in the Marseilles job?"

"I'll see what I can do. Will have to be this week. Remember, I'm out on the Interview Teams next week. It'll not be so easy then."

9.40 p.m. Glasgow

Ewen Handsford was not his usual relaxed and happy self. It was dark and dirty in the roof space. The stink of the club below, stale beer and tobacco, mixed badly with the grime of the years. It was hot and he was sweating slightly as he peered about.

Quiet, intelligent and resourceful, he made a point of planning whenever he could and of calculating the risks before acting. His army career had centred upon the Parachute Regiment with two years in the SAS. The structured service life had paled and an offer from Robert Hardy to utilise his specialisations in the commercial world was attractive. He was feeling his way cautiously but enjoying the freedom.

Ewen swore under his breath as the rafter creaked. He was feeling his way in a quite literal sense now. He hadn't planned to be in this position at this time. Martin's original instructions had been to take his time establishing himself at the club, to get to know the staff and the layout before making a move. That had changed in their last conversation and he was now aware of greater urgency. This job was personal to Martin, not for some commercial client. He suspected that the financial position was a touch critical. There was not a large corporate budget to support the work, thus less time to achieve the objectives.

The principal of these was information gathering. His insertion into the club scene had to exploit every opportunity. Martin had emphasised the likely areas and these did not include questioning staff. Casual conversations might yield the odd snippet but what Martin wanted were the private conversations between management.

Another rafter creaked alarmingly under his weight. He swore softly again. The building was old and he hoped that Fisher was still out of earshot. They had met for a drink at Fisher's local watering hole a short distance from the club. Ewen was due to start on the door team shortly and, when Fisher said that he needed to spend time at the club that evening, Ewen suggested that he could be shown the premises so that he would already know the exits, panic buttons and general layout before starting duty. Fisher was pleased to find enthusiasm and agreed. On arrival they did a tour and then Fisher left Ewen to familiarise himself with the building and the monitoring system which directed 'bouncers' to trouble spots.

The opportunity was too good to miss. His newly acquired knowledge and bugging equipment was waiting to be used!

He had quite quickly found that there was a Staff Room immediately over the Manager's office. Whilst the public areas were reasonably smart, when you stepped through a door marked 'Private' things changed totally. Alterations made over the years resulted in a plethora of stud walls and partitions. These areas did not produce the money so no money had been spent on them. The neglect was obvious.

In the Staff Room, with a copy of the Fire Regulations on the table in case Fisher appeared, Ewen investigated an old bookcase standing against one wall and, on moving it a few inches, found a gap in the skirting showing a narrow pattern of daylight from the room below. Dialling the Manager's number on the in-house phone resulted in a ringing from the room below. Confirmation!

A quick check on Fisher's whereabouts. No problem. The door to the Manager's office was secured by a simple rim latch with a shallow rebate. Out came a credit card and in seconds Ewen was standing on the other side of the door. High on the wall behind the Manager's desk was a ventilator. It was the right size and shape to match the patch of illumination seen behind the bookcase in the room above. A slip of paper from the waste basket, folded and pushed through the ventilator took seconds. A check on the desk drawers and a large safe in the corner confirmed that they were all locked, so back to the Staff Room. Using a small mirror and a pencil torch, he could see the piece of paper sticking through the ventilator. Lady Luck was smiling!

From his pocket came a miniature 'bug' provided by Tony Drew for just such an opportunity. The tiny device was a crystal controlled receiver/transmitter in a black plastic housing measuring just 3cm square by 1.5cm thick. Attached to it by press stud connectors was a PP3 battery which would provide power for ten days. Opposite the battery was a thin length of black plastic covered wire, exactly half a metre long, the bug's aerial. Using Sellotape and string, it was the work of a few minutes to suspend the bug by its aerial through the gap and opposite the ventilator. With the bookcase back in position nothing could be seen.

Half of the job done. Checking again on Fisher, he hurried to his car and collected a small radio receiver/recorder. The bug would collect speech over a distance of 8 metres and transmit it for up to 400 metres under ideal conditions. The radio was built to receive on 'airband' and had VOX operation. Its recorder was modified to run at half speed, ensuring that a longplay tape would hold two and a half hours of speech.

In the hall outside of the Staff Room was a ceiling trap with the dust of ages surrounding it. Time to take a chance! A chair, a push and an athletic heave saw Ewen standing on the rafters, surrounded by boxes and the detritus of years. There were a dozen hiding places for the radio and he chose one which would provide easy access when the time came to change tapes

Tuesday 26th May 1992
5.25 p.m. Southampton

The trickle of shoppers entering MFI's furniture showroom in Villiers Road took little notice of the man slouched in the passenger seat of a black Porsche. It is an odd fact that, whilst the driver of an exotic car may excite curiosity, their passengers are largely ignored. The public has its priorities! Additionally, the man seemed to be engrossed in his newspaper and little could be seen of his face.

Villiers Road is a side street off of Shirley Road. On one side is the MFI car park whilst opposite is the rear entrance to Shirley Police Station and staff car park. From the Porsche, Martin had a clear view of the car park entrance. It was almost five thirty and he was hoping to intercept Ellie May.

For the last few minutes his attention had been divided between the entrance and a good looking black man who had arrived on foot from Shirley Road and was now leaning against the wall. Suddenly the man straightened and hurried into the car park. For a few seconds he was out of Martin's sight but then reappeared shouting and banging on the roof of an old red Ford Fiesta that was leaving the car park. The car turned right and accelerated with a squeal of tyres and, as it shot past Martin, he recognised Ellie May at the wheel.

Galvanised into action, he heaved himself towards the driver's seat, swearing as the gearstick slid neatly up his trouser leg, but was out of the car park whilst the Fiesta was still in sight. Following, he waited until Ellie May stopped for a red traffic light at the junction of Millbrook Road, then pulled into the inner lane, stopping to lean out and tap the Ford's nearside window. Ellie May's head jerked around and, as she recognised him, the nervous stare changed to surprise and then a delighted smile. He pointed to the forecourt of the garage opposite and she nodded, understanding.

Parked, Martin got out of the car, with Ellie already hurrying towards him. He held out his arms, smiling and suddenly she was running, laughing and reaching out. With his arms around the small, slim frame, he felt her shaking and thought she was still laughing, then realised that she was crying. He rubbed her back through the thin summer dress, suddenly conscious that this was the first close female contact that he had had since Eileen – and it felt good, almost as though it was a step towards normal life, despite the tears.

"Who was the guy shouting at you?"

"That was Erroll, my husband, shortly to be my ex-husband." She recovered quickly, her shoulders no longer shaking, the last tears trickling down her face. "I'm sorry, Marty, but he has been getting more and more difficult. He phoned me at the office today and when he got to me in the car park, it was too much. When you tapped on the window I thought it was him again."

Martin smiled and said, "Just like old times."

Ellie smiled, perhaps wistfully "My knight in shining armour, again?" Then "I missed you when you left – and now you've got problems yourself." Deep brown eyes searched his. "I'm working for Mr Potter and I know that he thinks you're mixed up with wrong people. What's happening Marty?"

"What are you doing now – right this minute?" To change the subject.

"Going home to defrost my dinner."

"Will Erroll be there?"

"No, we split a long time ago. He still lives in the flat that we had. Mr Potter pulled some strings for me – I think because he wanted me on this job – and I've got a council maisonette now."

"You're not defrosting your dinner tonight then, you're coming out for a meal with me."

Martin followed Ellie May back to her place in an estate of mixed council and private housing on the outskirts of the city and waited in the lounge whilst she showered and changed. When she rejoined him he said, "Hey, I can't take you to a pub like that!" For a moment she was not sure, then saw the teasing approval in his eyes and giggled. Time dropped away. Suddenly they were back in the happier days of his time at the Civic Centre, but with an Ellie May who had altered, was now a different woman – in appearance at least.

She had changed into a 'little black dress' which clung to a figure which seemed, to Martin, much more curvaceous than he remembered. The chocolate skin at the neck and shoulders was flawless and as she did a pirouette for his appreciative eyes. He realised how much the slim, petite, nineteen-year-old of five years ago had matured. She was an attractive – no, a very attractive – young woman, whose curves seemed endless. As she walked in front of him to the door, for the first time in many weeks he found his eyes lingering on those very feminine attractions endowed by her ancestry, the movement of a delightfully prominent and mobile derrière above slim and shapely legs. For the second time since meeting her he felt his senses quicken. He checked himself mentally. Ellie May was not Eileen.

At a quiet table in an Oxford Street Brasserie they ate, drank and talked of days gone by, people they had known, of Ellie May's failed marriage, of Martin's love affair with Eileen and then, naturally, of the investigation.

"I've typed all the statements and Potter's reports. Have you really no idea what made someone put a bomb under your car, Martin?"

Martin sat quietly for a few moments and then, "No. I haven't Ellie and, as I'm sure you've guessed, our meeting today was not an accident. I'm trying to find out the reasons, hopefully who was behind it. I've people of my own working on it and a friend in CID is updating me on police thinking, but I need more. I wondered if you would be prepared to help? I don't want you to give me an answer now unless it is a straight 'No'. If there is any chance that it might be a 'Yes', then I want you to think about it seriously for at least a couple of days. I don't want you to risk your position for me, unless you are absolutely sure that you wish to help."

Deep brown eyes studied him for several seconds, a slim hand slid across the table to rest on his.

"You can ask me in a couple of days Marty, but the answer will be the same. It's 'Yes', of course I will, but I'll have to be careful. I'll still need a job when this is all over and you have gone your way again."

Martin thought that there was a note of sadness in the last sentence, but the eyes did not confirm it.

"Ellie, thank you, but I'll ask the question again before I ask anything else of you and you must consider longer and be prepared to change your mind if you do have second thoughts. We would be very careful and that means that we should not meet openly again, but we can fix that easily."

This time there was no doubt in Martin's mind that the little smile on Ellie's lips was a sad one. He wondered whether the sadness was to do with her situation or his — or then whether it was deeper even than their recent histories.

Martin paid the bill and, as they got up to leave and he followed her through the tables towards the door, he automatically scanned the room. No one that he knew, but the realisation of a changed Ellie May was emphasized. There was hardly a head in the place that did not turn to look at the young woman. He overtook to hold the door open and, despite the fact that they had spent the last two hours opposite each other, he was struck by the changes that five years had made. The warm brown eyes above high cheekbones were the same, the black curly hair was cut closer and styled a little, but there was an indefinable difference and, as they walked to the car he wondered about it.

The naive girl had been replaced by a mature young woman who had learnt to deal with a life which was not all easy. He felt pleased — privileged — to know that their ease with each other and the trust built up in an earlier life was still there.

"Are you tired?" he asked.

"No," and with a cheeky smile, "Are you taking me clubbing?'

Martin laughed "No, but I thought I might take you for a drive in the forest."

She looked sideways at him but, before she could phrase a reply, he said,

"I want to show you where we can meet with safety and how to make sure that you are not followed."

'Why are you worried about me being followed?'

'Well apart from the Potters of this world, you also have a husband who is obviously not at all happy. As I said earlier, we must be very careful if you do decide to help."

Friday 29th May 1992
11.00 a.m. Southampton

"That's about it." Martin leant back in his chair with a sense of relief and then called, "Angie, could we have some more coffee?"

John Mann, sitting opposite, said, "Coffee, is that the best that you can do?"

Smiling at the memory of John's inevitable production of a bottle when at his office, Martin called out, "Cancel that Angie!" and made for a filing cabinet labelled "V to Z", which would cater for his visitor.

During the previous four days, he had been in touch with the more important clients and had spent time with Angie to ensure that the routines of business were observed. John was an old friend in a similar Bristol based business, with whom he had an excellent working relationship and who would deal with those contracts that Martin knew needed specific action. Easing the cork from the bottle he slid a handful of files across the desk.

"These will fill you in on the detail of the jobs that we discussed. If you could be in touch with Angie on a daily basis so that I can get an update when I phone in, it would be most appreciated."

Resulting from his meeting with the bank manager, he had arranged to cash some bonds which would cover the immediate requirements. He had also agreed to place his beloved boat on the market, which, hopefully, would look after the midterm situation. As for the long term, that was not now a consideration. The important thing was to have sufficient cash to cover his investigation into Eileen's death and the more personal threats to himself.

As Martin was pouring the drinks, Angie called out, "I have Ewen on the line."

Since Ewen's insertion into the door team he had done well. Martin was receiving tapes from the concealed bug. They had not yet produced anything of interest but were providing valuable background into the workings of Lowland Leisure. Now Ewen had another worry.

"Martin, the bug's been in place a week or so now. Tony told me that the battery life would be about ten days and I haven't had a chance to change it."

"Do what you can, Ewen. It's Sod's Law that if we miss a day that will be the one that matters, but don't take any chances. Remember to collect what you can from the main man's rubbish bin. Send me anything of interest."

"You'll be getting a pile of stuff from the bins, Martin. I've been up to my elbows in Big Mac cartons for the last week."

"All useful experience in investigation!" Martin chuckled.

"Got to go," with a click on the line.

"Did you get anything of use from that guy – the ex job trouble shooter or whatever he is – that Bill knows? The one who's in the nightclub world?" from John.

"I'm due to meet with Bill this lunchtime," said Martin. "I couldn't get to first base with the guy himself, but Bill's spoken with him again and I'm hoping that he's got something for me. Have you got time to join us?"

"No, I've got to get back to Bristol. Got a business to run there as well. Give Bill my regards."

12.45 p.m.

Martin's knowledge of Lowland Leisure was substantially improved when he met Bill Creighton later that day. In a quiet corner of a favourite pub, he provided Martin with the results of his probing into the nightclub industry that neither knew much of. It was quickly apparent that Lowland Leisure were seen as an unusual group. Some thought that this was due to their headquarters being in Scotland, but Martin had other ideas.

"Apparently it is normal for people to move about in the industry, from one club or company to another. There's little of that with them." From Bill.

"Couldn't that be due to good wages or working conditions?"

"Their wages are said to be no better than others and the working conditions worse. Lowland have a longer cycle between club renovations and, when they do them, they are known for the low budgets that they set. Specialist contractors to the industry tend to avoid them. The designers and suppliers can't get the profit margins that they need and they don't like doing work that reflects badly on their image. Also, according to this guy, Lowlands directors are not nice people to work for. All of this makes management more difficult."

"What sort of guy is your informant, Bill?"

"Oh, I would say very reliable. He did twenty-five in 'the job' and he's been at exec level for one of the biggest organisations in the industry for some years."

To Martin, the omens were that Lowland Leisure were not going to be an easy company to dig into. He had no idea how right he was.

3.30 p.m. Glasgow

"That new laddie Neil started on his team, Ewen somebody or other. Whas he from?"

The question, from his head cleaner, to Andrew McAinsh, the manager of Shadows, went unheeded for a moment as McAinsh completed an entry in the book on his desk.

McAinsh was a thin, almost gaunt, man in his early forties. His complexion was sallow and his hair dark. On his face he sported a growth which couldn't make up its mind whether it was a two-day beard or an attempt at designer stubble. His eyes were very dark brown and his voice flat. He rarely showed emotion.

"Why d'you want to know?"

"He's no like a doorman. He's here with Neil when he dos'na have to be. He stays behind when he could be away."

"Neil knows him, says he all right."

"He does more than his job. The other day he was clearing rubbish bags." The voice was aggrieved. This was someone trespassing on his turf. "I hav'na had to clear your bin for a week."

The fingers busily scribbling into a book slowed to a stop. McAinsh looked up. "Say that again."

"Y'know ah do the offices while t'others bumper the floor and clean the Hall. Well fur the las' week there's been little to tak from your bin in this office – and Alice has seen him carrin' thu black rubbish bags out o' the back door."

"Where does he take them?"

"I dinne know. Alice saw him."

Neil McAinsh sat very still staring straight ahead. Then slowly, "OK. OK…I'll have a word."

8.35 p.m.

As various members of staff were gathering at Shadows for their night's work, Ewen noticed a stranger enter the premises from the side door and go straight to the management offices. No one spoke to him as he went through the club.

"Who's that?" he asked of another doorman.

"Oh, that's Liam, he works for the boss."

"I've not seen him before. How long has he worked here?"

"No, not here. He works for the big boss, Mr Mabbett. Drives him around sometimes, does jobs for him, not Andy."

They were sitting in the staff room with two other door supervisors, drinking coffee and waiting for the rest of the door team to arrive.

"You want to steer clear of him." This from a third member of the team, sitting at a table reading a comic.

"Why's that?"

"He's a hard man and he's said to have some heavy friends."

The gossip continued. The door team were all big men, Ewen was the smallest and was regarded with some curiosity and a little amusement by the others. His apparent friendship with the head doorman, Neil Fisher, and the comments made by Neil that Ewen could "Look after himself" had ensured that he was accepted. He now sat and listened as these men, who would have been regarded themselves as heavies by ordinary folk, spoke about the man Liam with the sort of respect normally reserved for the best of their own number; even a touch more, he thought.

He was just about to direct another question, hopefully to turn the discussion into greater specifics of why and where, when Neil Fisher came in with the roster of the night's duties. On hearing the subject of the conversation he cut it short, saying, "He's nothing to do with us."

9.05 p.m.

Andrew McAinsh rang a number that was not listed in the telephone directory. When Dermott Mabbett picked up the handset in his house at Kilchatten Bay, he listened for some time.

"How long's this man been working for you?"

"A matter of a few days."

"Is he on tonight?"

"Yes, he's here now."

"What address has he given?"

Then, making a note, "You've got Liam at the club tonight. Have him look at this guy Handsford straight away. No, on second thoughts, get Liam to ring me here. You're not to speak to anyone until you hear from me. Get onto Gordon though and tell him to ring me here. If he doesn't answer his car phone within the next half hour, come back to me yourself."

Mabbett waited a few minutes and then the phone rang.

"Liam, have a look at a room used by one of our doormen, it's at this address." He read the address given by McAinsh. "Guy by the name of Ewen Handsford, put into the team by Andrew on the recommendation of Neil. He's not one of us, just a bouncer. He's been poking his nose around, might have been looking through Andrew's office and such. See what you can find in his room. Phone me back as soon as you've done that."

Within thirty minutes the phone rang again and this time it was Gordon Wilson. Without pausing for preliminaries, Mabbett said, "I'm having Liam take a look at a guy by the name of Ewen Handsford. He's a new doorman at Glasgow. Does the name mean anything to you?"

"No."

"Right. This guy Handsford is in the club working tonight, so Liam is going through his room. We may need to move fast on this one. Stay close to this phone for the next hour."

Within another half hour the phone rang again. This time it was Liam Mahoney. Mabbett listened with his face tightening. Then "Tell me again what it says on the ID, exactly." Then, "And what's that address?"

He thought for a few seconds and then said, "Liam, we're going to have to deal with this – tonight! Get over to the club and sniff around, see what else you can find out. Tell Andy I'll be over before midnight and I'll see you then."

He put the phone down and immediately dialled another number. "Gordon, I've heard from Liam. He got in and had a look around. He found an ID with this guy's photo on it. He works for some security company."

"I didn't know anything about this."

"I know you didn't!" impatiently. Andrew took him on – on Neil Fisher's recommendation! There's also some envelopes addressed to a security company with an office down your way. I'll give you the details later to check out, but we need to deal with this end tonight. I want you on the first flight up here. Let me know what time you get in. I'll have you picked up at the airport and brought here. No, on second thoughts, we'll meet at the club, that'll be quicker."

Mabbett was lucky with the ferry to the mainland and traffic into Glasgow was light for a Friday. He made good time and walked into Andrew McAinsh's office at a few minutes before eleven. Mahoney was waiting for him. "Liam, tell me about this ID in Handsford's room."

Mahoney repeated what he had seen, but with greater detail.

"And what do you make of the envelopes?"

"There were half a dozen of them. I brought you one back." He slid a large brown padded envelope across the desk.

Mabbett turned it around to study the address.

"Do we know anything about these people?"

"I made a couple of phone calls. The security company is an ex army bunch, they specialise in body guarding – Close Escort in the jargon."

"Bodyguarding! Close Escort! What does that mean to us?"

"Can't say, though it's possible that they do other work as well."

"One thing's for sure, we can't afford to have these sort of people sniffing around our operation, no matter what their reasons are."

"Want him 'gone over'? See if we can sweat some answers out?"

Mabbett was silent for a few seconds then, "No, he's not been in the club long enough to have picked up much, if anything. This should be quick and clean. Just get rid of him, sit back and see what that shakes out. If he's with anyone else, it'll rattle their cage. All we need to do is have clean hands. You see to it, but not on the premises. Somewhere outside, perhaps some punters that he's upset getting their own back. I'll speak to Andrew and set a story up for the Pigs."

As they discussed the implications of Ewen's employment, the last of the life in the battery of the bug behind the ventilation panel transmitted their conversation to the tape unit in the roof space. The club was in full swing. The thin partition walls reverberating to the beat from the amplifiers, the disc jockey earning his crust and the thousand or so youngsters stamping their approval. With a single "listening device", the noise and vibration might well have rendered the installation useless, but Tony Drew's equipment was sophisticated and his installation advice to Ewen specific and unusual, designed to counter the problems inherent in 'bugging' a noisy office. He had supplied two bugs. Both were crystal controlled and manufactured specifically for use in noisy conditions. The second bug, on a slightly different frequency, had been placed by Ewen in the main club room and the equipment supplied would anti-phase the two signals through a sophisticated processor, eliminating the background noise from the club and leaving the recorded conversation clear until the battery eventually failed.

Mahoney slipped quietly out of the office, minutes before Andrew McAinsh arrived in response to Mabbett's call on the internal system. Mabbett leant back in McAinsh's chair, the other man feeling the usual frisson of concern – even fear – generated by the look in the cold dark eyes.

"I'm not at all happy with this situation, Andy," Mabbett growled. "Handsford's here on the say so of Fisher. If you've any doubts at all about Fisher, you're to say now. If you're wrong about the man – and he is YOUR man – then tomorrow will be too late."

"I've na doubts about Neil. I've known him too many years and he's up to his neck with us in the business. The Handsford guy came out of the blue and did Neil a favour. Neil was set up and did'na see it."

"We're making arrangements to recover the situation, Andy. It would be handy if there was a reference in your diary – the one that you keep for the official visits – that you've had to warn him about his attitude to the customers. He put someone out, treated them roughly. You had to reprimand him. Say it was through one of the fire exits. No one else there, you're the only witness. You got that? Get it in the book now for earlier this evening. Now let's talk about Neil."

10.30 p.m.

In the roof space, sweating again with the heat, Ewen was spending his break recovering the tape from the hidden machine. He was as unaware of its content as he was of the fact that the bug's battery was dying at that very moment. He was very aware that he needed to get back to the staff room quickly, and that he should get rid of the tape before the close of business. There was sometimes a management search of staff as they left the premises.

Saturday 30th May 1992
12.20 a.m. Glasgow

The early morning darkness was warm, close. Too much so for the less enthusiastic 'clubbers'. The queue at Shadows had disappeared just after midnight. At its height, an hour before, it had straggled from the front doors, along the street and around the corner of the building. Youngsters, mostly from eighteen to twenty but some as young as fifteen, had chattered, laughed and shuffled forward to pay their £2 admission. There was an air of suppressed excitement; of young people about to 'party'. Testosterone fuelled fists crushed empty drinks cans into crumpled parcels, stuffing them into crevices in the walls, lodging them in the gaps in the railings or merely tossing them into the road to join the resident rubbish. The impression of partying was heightened by the girls. Glittery colourful dresses, most so abbreviated that they left little to the imagination, vied with cropped tops, 'boob tubes' or lycra to fulfil the '90s' maxim "If you've got it, flaunt it!"

Some, at the back of the queue – the more discreet or streetwise – whilst drinking from their cans had slipped a little blue pill, the Ecstasy tablet, the dance drug, into their mouths between drinks. Most clubs in Glasgow searched for drugs on entry. Taking the 'E' outside ensured that the high of energy and adrenaline would be achieved inside, without risk of loss. One or two would take more than one pill during the course of the night without heed of the possible effects. There were those who preferred older style drugs and secreted 'Wraps', 'Tabs' or 'Speed' about their person for later use. The 'Hash' crowd took a chance that the marijuana laced 'Smokes' would be missed within the cigarette packets that they carried.

Some of the youngsters intended financing their night out by selling spare 'E's or other substances. A few were more ambitious and dealt in drugs as a regular income. These very often relied upon girlfriends to hide the tablets where the door supervisors could not search.

Ewen had been on a rapid learning curve since joining the door team. For the first two nights he had been paired with an older member of the team who, according to Fisher, "knew the ropes".

"Knowing the ropes" proved to be enlightening. Ewen had encountered drug use before, during his army career, but not to the extent that he saw now. It seemed that the youth culture frequenting Glasgow's nightclubs had little respect for their own or other bodies. Ewen wondered how anyone could be so unconcerned about the various substances that they swallowed, smoked or injected. It was obvious that they had no knowledge of the composition of the pills and powders or the likely effects when they took, on trust, substances which could well have been 'knocked up' in any back street kitchen or third world laboratory from base materials of dubious quality where hygiene was the last consideration.

His mentor impressed upon him the wisdom of keeping an eye on 'E' users.

"You can tell them easily enough, they're on the go all the time, can't keep still. Have this silly grin on their faces like it's fixed there. They take 'E's so they can dance all night, like at Raves. They drink soft stuff mostly, Colas and such. If they don't drink enough they can pass out, then we have a real problem. It's like heatstroke. Doesn't happen very often, but it can be bad when it does."

"What happens then?"

"Get an ambulance and, if they're lucky they might live!"

Ewen learnt a lot during the two evenings of tuition but had the feeling that there was much under the surface and not being said. Tonight he was on his own for the first time and determined to fill some gaps. In particular he was curious about the activities of Denis.

Denis was not an employee, but seemed to be a customer with a particular relationship where door supervisors were concerned. Ewen had noticed that on two occasions, after speaking with bouncers, they would disappear into the toilets to be preceded out a few minutes later by a customer who looked either angry or frightened. Ewen queried this with Neil Fisher, who paused then said, "Denis is a regular. He helps the door team out by fingering customers who might be a problem. He gets the occasional drink. You're not to worry about him."

Now, relieved from his front of house job and on his way to a position inside the club, Ewen saw the sleek black hair and expensively tanned features of Denis in conversation with two bouncers, whose job seemed to be supervising activities on the stairs leading to a balcony. Their heads were close together, the conversation animated with a final gesture towards the balcony. They separated, the bouncers mounting the stairs two at a time.

It was difficult to see detail in the darkness. The whirling, flashing lights of the disco, red, green, blue, yellow and white did not help. By the time that Ewen, with raised voice, "Staff coming through!" had threaded his way across the floor, the bouncers had disappeared. At the top of the stairs he peered along the almost empty balcony, a dark area with two or three shabby couches and a disused bar position. The area was relatively empty, a contrast to the bobbing, jerking, swaying throng below.

On one of the couches were a couple engaged in fairly heavy petting. Beyond them were the two bouncers, with a young man up against the wall and a girl, perhaps his girlfriend, being pushed away by the pair. Ewen made for the pair on the couch, pulling the youth's hand away from its centre of activity beneath the girl's short skirt.

"That's enough of that. Save it for somewhere private!"

Making his way to the bouncers, he saw that the youth against the wall was being searched. As he reached them the nearest turned and said, "What're you doing here?"

"Oh, I had a complaint from a girl on the stairs about that couple. Think she was pissed off, her boyfriend is more interested in the tart that he's with than he is with her." He lied smoothly and then, "Want any help with these two?"

The second bouncer snorted with laughter and was about to say something when his partner said, "No, we're dealing with this. You can get back to your front door."

"Is that a packet kicked under the couch?" he queried as he turned away.

Both doormen bent, one retrieving an empty cigarette packet. As they did so Ewen saw that the one holding the youth had small white packets in one hand, which he slipped into his pocket. The youth cried out, "Hey, that's my..."

He was silenced by a cuff from the lead bouncer "Shut your mouth!"

Ewen had seen enough. Raising a hand in a half salute, he turned and made for the stairs. Back in the foyer he found Fisher and said, "Neil, I've left my flask in the car. OK to go and get it?"

"You and your flask. I'm beginning to wonder whether it's only coffee. OK, but don't be too long, Jimmy's due a break after you."

"Back in a moment."

Under Ewen's bomber jacket was the envelope destined for Martin. It contained the last tape recovered from the roof space recorder but needed addressing. He slipped into a toilet and, keeping the boltless door closed with one foot, hastily scribbled a note and added the address. With time pressing, once out of sight of the club's door supervisors, he broke into a trot and reached the postbox round the corner some two hundred yards from the club.

Just then the club's internal phone rang and McAinsh asked for Neil Fisher. "Where's your new man, Handsford?"

"Just popped round the corner to his car. Back in a minute. Why?"

"No matter, Neil. Come up to the office straight away, will you."

Fisher mounted the stairs from 'front of house' and, as he did so, Liam Mahoney slipped out of the building, using a rear fire exit.

Parcel posted, Ewen started back at a more leisurely pace but, on reaching the club's side entrance, found the figure of Liam Mahoney standing, hands in the pockets of a long coat and cigarette drooping from his mouth, staring up at windows which, in a former life, had illuminated the balcony where Ewen had recently been.

As Ewen approached, slowing to speak and with a warning bell sounding in his mind, Mahoney turned towards him.

"We've got a problem up there," he said, gesturing upwards and now facing Ewen. The pale cold features of the hard boned face were emotionless and Ewen glanced up as he came to a stop. In that moment, from the corner of his eye, he was aware of a sudden swift movement from Mahoney and he started to turn sideways on, in an automatic protective stance.

It was too late. The blow smashed into his belly with sickening force. In that first gasping second of surprise and hurt, Ewen thought that it was just a heavy punch then, as the fist drew back for a second strike, he saw the gleam of a blade streaked with blood in the man's fist. Before he could grasp the full significance, the second blow came and this time there was the knowledge – the silent horror of alien cold steel piercing his intestines, the awful agony as skin, muscle and tissue were sliced apart.

In the next moment the shock hit him. Suddenly there was no strength in his knees and he stumbled forward, almost falling. He felt an unbelieving horror and a single strangled word – half shout – came from his lips. It might have been "No" but it was an indecipherable croak.

The blade was still in his belly, the second blow higher up than the first. He felt the brutal twist of the wrist below his sternum and knew again, as though in a nightmare, the horror of his injury. As the blade was wrenched out there was another long drawn tortured spasm.

He could no longer stand upright. He could not stop himself. With hands clasped to his stomach, he fell forward onto his knees. A despairing groan was the only other sound as he hung in a conscious world which was slowly blackening. He fought against the blackness, willing himself to live. Beneath his clasped hands, the severed artery pumped blood into the abdominal cavity and his body's systems started to close down in the trauma of anaphylactic shock. As the blackness crept in, he toppled sideways and lay with his knees drawn up, hands grasping ineffectually at his violated bleeding gut.

As the blood oozed out, so did life. He was not aware of the stained fingers which sought and found the diminishing beat in the carotid artery at the side of his throat. All that was left of conscious thought was the fight to stay awake, to beat the sudden weak tiredness that was seeping into his mind, to grapple with the awful searing pain that lay beneath his clasped hands, just beneath the heart whose feverish pace was now slowing.

3.40 a.m.

The harsh double trill of the phone woke Martin from a deep sleep. He fumbled in the dark, knocking the handset to the floor, then had to search for the light switch, eventually finding it halfway down the flex of the bedside lamp. His sleep had been very deep and the different layout of the small flat, his new base, confused him in his waking moments. With the phone to his ear, he apologised to the caller, thinking belatedly that he had no need to do so at this hour of the night – or morning – whenever!

The voice was Scottish with a broad Glaswegian accent.

"Is that a Mr Wild?"

"Yes, who's this?"

"Detective Constable Cantrill, Govan CID. Sorry to disturb you at this time of night. Do you know a Ewen Handsford?"

"Yes. What's the problem?"

"What's your relationship with Mr Handsford?"

Abruptly Martin was awake – and wary. That particular question from a police source often meant that the enquiry was critical.

"Ewen works for me." Mind getting into gear, seeking the right answers.

A brief pause, he could hear the murmur of conversation through a hand over the mouthpiece but couldn't catch the words.

Then, "Mr Wild. Mr Handsford has been injured and we would like to speak to you. In the meantime, can you tell me where I can get hold of his wife or family?"

Martin realised that, in his befuddled state, he might have said the wrong thing. Ewen was supposed to be working for the nightclub, not him. Ewen's cover – if he still needed one – was now blown as far as the police were concerned. If their enquiry – whatever it was – led them to Shadows, there would be major problems.

"How badly injured is Ewen?"

The direct question was avoided. Another pause and more murmured conversation, then, "He's at the Southern General Hospital. We don't have an address for Mr Handsford, he's no identification on him. Where does he live?"

Thinking furiously, his brain now in gear. Concern for Ewen tempered by the need to buy time, to find out more of the circumstances before saying too much.

"I don't have his home address here. He's not married. His parents live just north of Glasgow, in the Trossachs area, near Callander. How did you get my phone number?"

"It was on a slip of paper in Mr Handsford's diary. What is your address, Mr Wild?"

Martin gave the address of the flat that he had moved into only the day before, thinking that his bags were still mostly packed. He could move out quickly if necessary.

"I'll go to the hospital now."

"You'll not be able to see Mr Handsford. We have somebody with him just now. If you'll put some clothes on, we would like a word here with you first."

"I'll be with you in half an hour or so."

Putting the phone down, he thought for a moment and, picking it up again, dialled Directory Enquiries, asking the number of the hospital. He rang the number and asked for Admissions.

"Glasgow CID here,' he said. "You have one of our men there with a Ewen Handsford. Can you tell me which ward they are on?"

"I'll transfer you to the Mortuary."

He replaced the receiver mechanically and sat for several minutes staring into space.

5.45 a.m.

The roads were damp and deserted when Martin eventually left the police station. He hurried the Porsche towards the nightclub, driving automatically, responding to the stimuli of red traffic- lights and other headlights without conscious thought. For the second time in less than a month he would attend a funeral, would look into the faces of grieving family and feel his own personal anguish heightened by a sense of guilt. As with Eileen, it was because of him that Ewen had died. He knew that he would be haunted by concern for the young man's family and friends, by the sight of another polished wooden box, by the thought of how it must have been in those last few moments in a Glasgow back street. He had not known Ewen long but there had been a strengthening bond as the days had gone by. A sense of more than comradeship. Instinctively he had recognised the same values in Ewen as drove him and already, despite employment by proxy, loyalty had been growing.

There was not the confusion this time. There was no doubt about the orchestrators of this death. Whilst the Glasgow CID were looking at a wider spectrum, which ranged from a mugging gone wrong to a grudge attack, on his way to the police station Martin had slipped into Ewen's lodgings. The room had been ransacked. The covers were off the bed, the few contents of the chest of drawers and the wardrobe in a heap on the floor and Ewen's briefcase was open on a chair. It contained the remainder of the bugging gear, together with a supply of batteries and envelopes addressed to Martin, some to the hotel where he had been staying before moving to the flat and some to his office address in Hampshire.

Martin closed the case and took it with him. To leave it with contents in place in an obviously ransacked room would have generated awkward questions from the police when they eventually got there. He was going to have his share of those anyway, judging by the recent interrogation at the police station.

His next stop was the car park at the rear of the nightclub. Police activities were centred upon the backstreet where the murder had taken place and the club itself was now deserted. Ewen's car was still there and, finding the doors locked, Martin wasted no time. A jemmy made short work of one door lock and then the boot. He quickly searched the car, taking any items which might have a bearing on the work that Ewen had been doing. A black dustbin liner, which contained what he guessed to be the rubbish from the nightclub office, cardboard cartons, screwed up papers, a small wooden box and separate pieces of wood, were quickly transferred from Ewen's boot to the Porsche. He didn't stop to examine them, leaving that job for the relative security of his room.

Tomorrow he was required to identify the body and then meet with the officer in charge of the murder enquiry, rather than the detective who had dealt with the immediate death scene. Martin needed to know all that he could about Ewen's last hours before that time.

9.30 a.m. Winchester

Some nine hours later and four hundred miles to the south, the police leading the hunt for Eileen's killer gathered in Detective Chief Superintendent Lawson's office for the Saturday morning de-brief. This meeting was for the more senior officers involved and was designed to evaluate progress during the past week, identify options for the week to come and prepare for the Monday morning meeting, at which all officers involved and available would attend a 'Case Meeting' at Shirley Police Station.

Ray Lawson looked around the table. DCI Potter's face was grim. The Detective Inspector from Special Branch was talking quietly to the Chief Inspector from the Anti-Terrorist Unit. Only the Detective Superintendent from the Metropolitan Police, who represented Interpol at the meeting, looked relaxed. This latter was a newcomer to the gathering, due to the 'French Connection' which had materialised in the form of a very dead Monsieur Henri Tabarde.

Lawson knew the reason for Potters' grimness. There had been little progress on the British side of the enquiry. Scene of Crime and Forensic examination of Eileen Padgett's murder had confirmed that the bomb placed under the Citroen was of a type favoured by the IRA but there was no indication as yet of who had been responsible.

The French on the other hand, with bodies in the Mercedes to follow up and Tabarde's crusade against drug traffickers as a motive, had moved forward. They had located the gite used prior to the ambush and had narrowed the enquiry to a known French drug cartel. There had not been arrests as yet, but that possibility did not seem to be too far off.

"Perhaps we can start, gentlemen, by DCI Potter updating us on progress in the Padgett murder since our meeting last week." Lawson brought the meeting to order and Potter rose to his feet without any sign of enthusiasm.

Monday 1st June 1992 11.10 a.m.

The large padded envelope arrived by the second post. Martin collected it from the flat's communal box on his return from a third visit to the police station. His identification of Ewen's body on Sunday had been followed by a lengthy interview and then statement taking. Today he had been required to return and answer further questions by a canny and, he thought, disbelieving Scottish detective.

The envelope, with Martin's new address in Ewen's handwriting, contained not only the usual tape recovered from the recorder hidden in the roof, but also documents that Ewen had retrieved from McAinsh's rubbish bin. There was a note which read:-

> Martin, I have other larger items from the rubbish for you in my car. I also now have direct evidence that bouncers are shaking down punters in the club for drugs and then keeping them – to recycle as we thought?

Martin slipped the tape into the portable unit that he carried in his case. It started normally with conversation between a flat, unemotional voice addressed by others as "Andy" and who, he thought, had to be Andrew McAinsh and various other visitors to the office. As the tape ran on with conversations about the routines of running the club, the speech became less clear, being broken and fading as though the power was running out. Then came a discussion, the content of which was unmistakable, given the history which he now had. It was a conversation between McAinsh and a man with a broad Glaswegian accent.

"…laddie that Neil started on his team, Ewen…whas he from?"

"…you want to…"

"…no like a doorman…with Neil when…stays behind when…away."

"Neil knows…all right."

"…more than he his…clearing rubbish bags. I havna…your bin for a week."

The conversation went on and Martin, with the heart deadening happenings of the previous day still so clear in his mind, could anticipate the content of the next item that mattered on the tape. It followed conversations between McAinsh and employees which were about the routines of the business. It was one end of a telephone conversation between McAinsh and Dermott Mabbett. McAinsh detailed the employment of Ewen on Neil Fisher's recommendation and followed this with the information given him by the cleaner. There were then periods of silence when he was obviously listening to Mabbett. During these he spoke only to answer questions and to give the address of Ewen's room.

After more inconsequential conversations with employees about bar prices and staff rosters, there was the sound of a door opening and closing, furniture being moved and then a new voice, a hard, impatient, authoritative voice. Martin guessed it to be Mabbett.

"Liam, glad you…let's see…"

The transmission from the bug was now much worse, the gaps in the conversation longer and the speech very blurred. The little that he could hear was confirmation to Martin of that of which he was already certain.

An Irish voice, a flat monotone, the accent not very pronounced. 'They're down in…perhaps Gordon will…"

Then Mabbett "…deal with this situation first…Handsford's on tonight…I want you to…make sure it's finished…talking to anyone."

A question from the Irish voice that Martin could not catch.

Mabbett again "we'll cover that. You…take another."

The sound of doors closing and then Mabbett's voice. "… you seen Andy?" A pause and "Tell him…his office."

"Come in…take…Andy"

"… a drink… a large Malt… bottle you keep in your…" There was an edge to the voice. It was not only asking for a drink.

"…how do you know… Macallan?" The tone was aggrieved and surprised.

"I make it…everything worth knowing…as you…by now." The hard voice had a hint of satisfaction. "Liam's going to look after this Handsford…you to…" and there it finished. The remainder of the tape was blank, the bug's battery had finally given up.

Looking at the crumbled documentation, one envelope was of particular interest. It had been typed on a word processor and then scrapped because the address block was misaligned. It was addressed to Dermott Mabbett at Kilchatten House, Rothesay, Isle of Bute. Martin's heart leapt. At last the leader of the pack's lair was known.

Turning to the polythene bag from the boot of Ewen's car, Martin found amongst the rubbish a crumpled sheet of A4 from an internal directory that listed Shadows' nightclubs in Glasgow, Newcastle, Birmingham, Cardiff, Bristol and Southampton. Some telephone numbers and management names had been altered. It was a list that had been updated and then discarded. "So now we know the extent of your organisation," thought Martin. It was much larger than he had thought and emphasised the size of the man's activities across the country. "Must concentrate on Glasgow, that is the main club."

Thoughtfully he repacked his bags and sought out the landlord on the floor below.

"I'm going to be away for a couple of days. Would you look after any post that comes. I'm expecting a package that I'll need to pick up personally. I'll ring you to see if it's arrived."

Driving to his previous hotel, he was lucky. There was no space in the street at the front, so he parked at the side of the building. Walking towards the entrance, he saw the meeting of two people outside of the hotel, one of whom he knew. He slipped into a newspaper kiosk to watch. The man that he recognised was Neil Fisher whom he had last seen during the service station set up, when Fisher had been 'rescued'. The second was a tall, lean, hard featured man with a pale sallow complexion and dark hair. He was wearing a long black leather coat, belted at the waist and was walking away from the hotel. Fisher had double parked his car and was dodging across the street calling out to the first man. Martin heard the name called out. It was "Liam" but he could not hear the brief conversation that followed as they stood together on the pavement.

Abruptly they turned together and went back to Fisher's car, the lean man Liam getting into the passenger seat to be driven off by Fisher.

"And now I know what your man looks like," breathed Martin.

At the hotel Martin was greeted by the receptionist. "You've just missed your friend, Mr Wild."

"Who was that?"

"A tall gentleman called and asked for you. You must have almost passed in the street. I told him that you had checked out and he asked if we had a forwarding address."

"Was he wearing a long black leather coat?"

"Yes. He asked whether you were expected to return."

"Thanks," said Martin. "I'll get in touch with him myself. Is there any post for me?"

There was not and Martin arranged for the hotel to hold any that arrived pending his return.

Within another two minutes he was back in the Porsche and hurrying it towards the A8 and the Rothesay ferry at Skelmorlie.

At Greenock he paused briefly to fill with petrol and do some shopping. He purchased a dark green Barbour jacket, a soft tweed trilby and a high powered telescope complete with tripod, as used by bird watchers, and a fishing outfit. Also a map covering the Isle of Bute area.

At seven o'clock that evening, the middle aged couple who ran the small hotel on the shore of Kilchatten Bay provided Martin with both a meal and a room for a stay "...of a few days."

After dinner casual conversation in the bar, prompted by Martin, centred upon the locality, the sea birds likely to be found in the area and the availability of the hotel owner's outboard engined dory to visit the rocky headland on the seaward side of the bay.

As darkness fell, Martin excused himself from the handful of drinkers in the bar to "… take a constitutional before turning in." Inevitably the walk led him past the high hedges of Kilchatten House and up a track which, in turn, gave onto the hillside overlooking the house and the bay.

After a short wait he was rewarded by the sight of a car swinging off the narrow road which bordered the bay, to stop facing the gates of Kilchatten House.

Security lighting clicked on and the car was revealed as a dark coloured Jaguar XJS coupé.

The pause was brief, the gates swinging open without any apparent action by the car driver. The car disappeared from view to park at the front of the house.

For another two minutes Martin stayed in position. The rear of the house remained in darkness apart from a ground floor room, which had been illuminated all along.

On his way back to the hotel, Martin could see a blaze of light from a first-floor room, which had a commanding view of the bay. Doubtless Mabbett's room.

10.00 p.m.

As Martin tried to sleep in the hotel room, the Glasgow CID team investigating the death of Ewen Handsford were meeting at Govan police station. Detective Constable Cantrill and other investigating officers were reporting the result of their day's activities to the Detective Chief Inspector leading the enquiry. He was reading from a statement made by Martin.

"…our information indicated that the girl might have left home to be with her boyfriend, believed to work at the premises as a barman…"

In making a statement to the police, Martin had felt that it would be unwise to tell the truth about Ewen's employment at the nightclub, so he lifted a scenario from a dormant Missing Person case that was on his files, and said that Ewen was working for him to try and trace a teenage girl for her parents.

Statements taken from Neil Fisher and Andrew McAinsh, dovetailed neatly. Fisher and McAinsh told of Ewen "knocking back" – refusing admission to – a group of drunks who were trying to get into the club earlier on the night that he died. They hazarded the guess that Ewen had the misfortune to encounter them again in the dark side street as he went for his flask. Poor descriptions were given to the police, with the comment that Ewen was new to the game and that he had acted unwisely in leaving the premises on his own shortly after such an incident.

"DC Cantrill, what d'you make of this man Wild? It seems odd to me that a private investigator from Hampshire would spend time and money on a missing person case up here when he already has a man working here on it?"

"Aye, I agree sorr, but we could'na shake him. Robbie had him in thu twice an there was na difference at the end."

"What paperwork did he have on this girl that they were supposed to be looking for?"

"None at all sorr. Said that Handsford had that but we could'na find any."

"And what's this about Handsford's car being done?"

"That's queer again. The door and the boot had been forced."

A second detective joined in. "We were considering the possibility that Handsford interrupted whoever was doing his car, was chased and knifed by them. We're getting a lot of car crime from that area, mainly druggies looking to steal car radios to get the readies for a fix."

"So we have three options then. He was attacked by a person or group that he had upset in the club, it was a straightforward mugging gone wrong or he disturbed a car thief?"

'We hav'na traced anyone at the club who might be the missing girl or her boyfriend," from Cantrill.

"We'll consider that a fourth option, but not a strong one."

The Glasgow CID were set on a wrong path and it would take some time for them to pick up a different scent. To Martin, the consideration was that Mabbett and company were not alerted to his presence and the interest in Eileen's death nearly four weeks earlier.

10.24 p.m. Southampton

At the Civic Centre police station, a worried Scene of Crime officer, taking advantage of the overtime option offered by the Padgett murder enquiry, was debating with himself whether to report a missing item from the Murder Log – or to say nothing. The Scene of Crime photographs that he had been working on clearly showed a small cylindrical object, rather like a shortened pencil, lying amongst other debris in the gutter at Parksyde Avenue. The problem was that the "pencil" was neither in the evidence bags nor were there prints of it amongst the photographs of the more "interesting" individual items that would have been taken subsequently in the Photographic Department.

With a sigh of exasperation, he pulled the Exhibit Log towards him and made a note about the missing item. If it was a pencil, as the photograph suggested, some other helpful sod had probably sharpened it and stuck it behind his ear! It was too short to stir the tea with.

Tuesday 2nd June 1992
8.50 a.m. Kilchatten

The early morning sun was obscured by a high layer of thin cirrus, the forerunner to an unseasonable Atlantic "Low" which, in a few hours, would bring an end to what had been almost a month of fine weather.

The only noise on the calm silvery sea was the lapping of small wavelets trapped beneath the Dory's trihedral hull. From the gently rocking boat, anchored fifty metres off the seaward headland at Kilchatten Bay, Martin had a clear view of the house occupied by Dermott Mabbett. The whole of the front and one end elevation, together with most of the front garden and approach road, were clearly visible.

His distance off allowed him to see over the tall shielding hedge, which separated the garden from the road. The previous afternoon he had taken a number of photographs from the hillside above the house. Today he intended to complete the exercise from the loch.

He had been anchored, apparently fishing, since before 7 a.m. It was now nearly nine and the light was sufficient to produce good prints.

From the fishing bag he took a 35mm Canon camera with a telescopic lens. He took a couple of shots showing the house set into the surrounding hillside and then two of the house and garden in close-up.

Re-starting the outboard motor, he hauled in the anchor and pottered slowly to a position across the bay, which provided a view of the other end of the house. Anchoring again, he took two further close-ups of the opposite end elevation.

Martin was just debating the value of further time spent watching from this position when a figure appeared from the rear of the house. It was a man with a large dog on a lead.

From his first position Martin had used his binoculars safe in the knowledge that, with the sun rising behind him, there was no danger of light reflecting off the lens. His new position was a different matter and he would have to use the glasses with care.

As he was wondering whether the dog walker was Mabbett, that question was answered. The curtains covering a first-floor bedroom were suddenly drawn back. The doors onto the bedroom's balcony opened and a man, in what appeared at this distance to be a dressing gown, stepped from the bedroom.

For perhaps half a minute the man stood there and Martin risked a quick glance through the glasses. Then he stepped back into the bedroom only to reappear with what appeared to be a tripod. Martin guessed that the binoculars, which it probably carried, would be large.

Busying himself with the short fibreglass spinning rod, Martin hoped that the impression of a serious angler, intent only on what the loch held, would he strong enough to ensure that there were no detailed enquiries at the hotel, should there be a follow-up on the SSR number on the side of the boat. From under the brim of his hat, he saw that the distant figure spent some two or three minutes peering into the binoculars, before walking to the edge of the balcony and speaking to the dog walker below. The latter turned again and released what looked like an Alsatian from its lead.

It interested Martin that the dog did not run around cocking its leg against every available tree but, in a period of some fifteen minutes, with its handler close behind, methodically quartered the whole of garden, searching the shrubbery thoroughly.

4.00 p.m.

"This guy is going to be very difficult to get close to, Tony. He lives in a small lochside community in an isolated village where every stranger sticks out like a sore thumb. His house is surrounded by tall hedges, no other buildings close at hand. Between the hedges and the house there are flat lawns which a rabbit couldn't cross without being seen." Martin was speaking on the telephone from his Glasgow hotel to Tony Drew, with photographs spread out before him, enlarged courtesy of a one hour processing service.

"What about staff, Martin? Is he on his own or are there others with him?"

"He has one man with a dog, who does a check of the garden but I haven't seen anyone else yet. Problem is that I'm not going to be able to hang around the area much longer without showing out. I'm wondering about the possibility of a 'tap' on his phone line?"

"Do the lines feed into the house overhead?"

"It's a bit odd, Tony. There's one telegraph pole at the side perimeter of the garden and that has wires leading from it to under the eaves of the house. It looks as though they may be underground up to that point though."

"You said this place is on the edge of a loch, Martin, then that's the reason. In the sixties, the Telecom people had to re-route lines where the road ran beside a coastline or similar expanse of water. It was for environmental purposes. If you look closely at other properties on that road I'll bet that you'll find just one pole by each, with the cabling coming out of the ground and running up the pole to a junction box."

"I don't have to look for a DP on the ground then?"

"No, the lines will disperse from the box on the pole."

"I'll lay a bet that he has a fax and perhaps a computer in the house," said Martin.

"If that's so then you're not going to be able to do this job yourself."

Martin's experience in communications was limited. Tony had taught him a certain amount during their work together when sweeping client premises to de-bug them. Identifying the correct line from a bundle within a casing, intercepting the line successfully and ensuring that there was no risk of weather or other problems drawing attention to the intercept, was a skilled job; especially in the middle of the night!

"Hear what you say about sticking out like a sore thumb but I'd better look at this one."

"OK, Tony, but we'll meet and go over the photos. We'll talk the whole thing through before you get involved. I can't afford to lose any more mates."

Despite the flippancy, Tony could hear the seriousness in Martin's voice. This would not be one of their routine jobs where the only consideration was out-thinking the opposition who had planted the bug. If they were discovered at work by these people the consequences would be serious. The death of Eileen might be thought unlucky, but Ewen's was another matter and, from what he had been told, very professionally done.

6.50 p.m.

The two cars passed each other in a flurry of spray on the road between Rothesay and Kilchatten, Martin in the Porsche was returning to the hotel from Glasgow, the XJS was heading in the opposite direction from Kilchatten towards Rothesay.

Martin cursed, waited for a second vehicle to follow the Jaguar and then braked hard and 'U' turned in a convenient gateway to accelerate after them.

Although the glimpse had been momentary the car and colour were right, there couldn't be another similar XJS on Bute, surely?

The lorry that had been following the Jaguar came into sight and was quickly overtaken. Anxious to close with his quarry, Martin was driving too fast for the wet conditions. At the bottom of a slope the steering lightened as the car hit shallow standing water. Aquaplaning at 80 mph on a narrow road brought him back to sensibility and he reduced speed.

Now he was on the coastal part of the road with the speed limit signs for Rothesay coming up. Then relief. As the road straightened after Bogany Point he saw the rear lights of the Jaguar in front – and only just in the nick of time. The car was slowing rapidly, brake lights now joining the rear lights and then the amber left-hand turn indicator.

Martin slowed as he passed the hotel. It was a large building with a car park in front and, in better weather, a view over Rothesay Bay. Turning at the next side road, he drove slowly back to the hotel, swinging into the entrance as though approaching from the town centre.

The Jaguar was parked close to the hotel entrance and a man and a woman, upper halves hidden behind a large umbrella, were going towards the doors. As they reached the shelter of the doorway, the man holding the umbrella furled it, pushed the door open and walked through, turning to momentarily hold one half of the double door open for his companion.

Martin recognised the face only previously seen at a distance through binoculars. The principal distinguishing mark was a 'Mexican' moustache, the ends drooping in what had been a fashion during the 1980s, but was now unusual. For the brief instant that the door was held open, Martin saw that Mabbett was tall with dark hair brushed back from a long face. The raincoat hid his build but from the way that he moved, Martin knew that he was looking at a man who did not carry too much weight.

Parking the car, Martin thought for a few minutes, took the Firth of Clyde Ordnance Survey map from the door pocket and then retrieved Tony Drew's 'camera' from the bag where it lived. With head bent against the drizzle, he ran to the door that Mabbett and his companion had gone through.

Inside the Victorian building he found a reception area with typically high ceiling. There was no sign of Mabbett or his companion and he guessed that they must have gone straight into a bar to the right of the main entrance doors.

The only other person in sight was a receptionist behind a counter on the left of the area, intent on the inevitable computer screen. She looked up briefly but Martin ignored her, heading for the door to the bar.

On the other side he found a smallish room with half a dozen people in it. Mabbett was standing at the bar waiting to be served and Martin walked to a position where he had another person, a short heavily built man with a drinker's nose, between them. He leant on the counter, also waiting whilst the bartender served this man.

As Mabbett was ordering a glass of white wine and a large malt whisky, the door to the 'Ladies' opened and he was joined by a brown-haired, vivacious woman in her mid-thirties. It was the companion that Mabbett had walked in with.

Now without the raincoat and at close quarters, Martin was able to take stock of the man. He judged Mabbett to be about forty years of age and was impressed with the urbanity of the man and his clothing, as he listened to the three-way conversation between the bartender and the couple. It was apparent that Mabbett was known to the bartender, whose manner was substantially more deferential than to his previous customer. Mabbett's dark suit was of an expensive cloth and well cut; the dark hair was groomed and swept back from a left parting; the moustache not too large and well trimmed. As he and his companion turned away to the doors of a restaurant, which lay beyond the bar, Martin again noted the smooth movement of the body beneath the clothing. Whatever he did in the nightclub world, he evidently kept himself fit!

As he ordered a drink, Martin asked whether it was necessary to book a table in the restaurant, which was already half full despite the early hour. He could see that Mabbett and the woman were seated in a corner close to the large window which faced over the bay. A few minutes later the Head Waiter arrived at his elbow with a menu.

"I'm half expecting a friend to arrive, could you seat me at a table for two in the window where I can see the car park?"

"Certainly, sir. Will you take your table now or shall I leave you with the menu?"

Martin elected to finish his drink whilst he studied the menu. Ten minutes later he followed the head waiter to a table only a few feet from that occupied by Mabbett and his companion. If anything, it was too close, too easily inspected by the subject, whose hard interrogative eyes had immediately swivelled in his direction as he sat in the chair held out for him by the head waiter.

Casually Martin placed his opened and folded Ordnance Survey map on the table to the left of the place setting and the 35mm camera with its long lens on top of that. The lens was not pointed in the direction of the next table and Martin noted that Mabbett's eyes were on the camera for some seconds before looking again briefly at Martin. To Martin's relief he then turned his attention to his female companion and took up the conversation that Martin's arrival had interrupted.

Martin sat studying the wine list handed to him. He had placed his order for food and now quickly selected a half bottle of Muscadet to accompany it.

With the wine waiter despatched, he was able, for the first time, to study both Mabbett and his companion in detail. At close quarters, he could see that Mabbett was probably older than he had first thought; perhaps closer to fifty than forty, the dark hair was just starting to recede and the strongly boned face a little on the fleshy side. He wondered if the dark hair was dyed. The face was hard, authoritative, used to giving orders – and being obeyed. Both the face and the hands were expensively tanned whilst gold glinted from a large ring on the right hand's little finger and from a heavy bracelet on that wrist.

The woman was younger, perhaps mid thirties but not much more. The hair was brown and curly but expensively done whilst the pale coloured lightweight sweater and tartan skirt had not come from a high street shop. She wore a necklace of green stones, which matched the green in her tartan and she had rings on the fingers of both hands. The fingers of her right hand continually and unconsciously twisted rings on the fingers of her left hand.

They were now talking animatedly together but in low tones which were inaudible from Martin's position. To Martin, Mabbett's comments and replies, though delivered quietly to his companion, were made in a manner which, visually at least, indicated that he expected no alternative view. From time to time Mabbett's gaze returned to Martin, but now without interest; another tourist was his probable assumption.

The wine waiter returned with the bottle of Muscadet and Martin ordered a bottle of mineral water to go with it. The placement of the bottles on the table gave him the opportunity to adjust the angle of the camera without touching it, by casually moving the map that it rested on. The lens now pointed directly at the occupants of the next table; the adjustment had gone unnoticed.

He occupied himself by studying the map and making notes on a small pad. He was conscious again of the eyes on him, but took no notice, deliberately, concentrating on the map and his notes until Mabbett again turned his full attention to his companion.

Martin's chosen seat meant that he had the window to his left with no other tables on that side. He was not sitting directly foursquare to the table, but slightly away at an angle as he looked at the map. With the waiter gone for the moment he slipped his hand into the left pocket of his jacket and then raised that hand to his left ear. Had there been anyone watching from his left, they might have seen that now there was a thin wire leading from that pocket to a very small earpiece. Had he had the time to prepare for this situation, the wire would have been visible for a few inches between the collar of his shirt and the ear, but the few moments that he had spent in the Gents had not been enough to do the job as thoroughly as he would have liked.

Martin fiddled casually with the map, adjusting the angle of the long lens by minute degrees. At first all that he got was silence broken by rustlings and static and then, quite suddenly and quite clearly, he heard the voice of the man that he was watching. The miniature rifle mike – for that was what the camera really was – worked, confirming all of the promises made by Tony Drew when he had left it with Martin after the ill-fated Swiss trip. The tiny transceiver within the camera's body was picked up by another receiver in his jacket pocket and that, in turn, was connected to the earpiece. It had been Tony Drew's intention to complete the outfit with a receiver and tape unit combined, but circumstances – in the form of a portly Detective Chief Inspector – had interrupted development. Martin had to make do with what he had.

Carefully watching the movements of the waiters as they moved around the room, he prepared to slip the earpiece out of sight if one should come his way, Martin was able to eavesdrop on the conversation between Mabbett and the woman, although he could only hear one side of it. The microphone's angle of reception was too narrow to pick up both people at that distance. It was only when Mabbett sat fairly still that Martin could hear him clearly. When he leant forward to pick up the cruet and when he bent sideways to rescue a dropped serviette, the reception was lost. Nevertheless, in the five minutes before the arrival of his soup and in the fifteen minutes before the plate of sea bass came, Martin was able to garner the background of the meeting.

'Ann' had flown up from Heathrow; the weather down south was just as bad as Glasgow. He knew that she had been so looking forward to seeing him again, his time in "The States" had been busy; he had phoned hadn't he? Who was the new occupant of the flat next to hers? On and on with the conversation of two people who were meeting again after an absence.

It was after the waiter had cleared away the main course and Martin had refused anything other than a pot of coffee that things became interesting.

"No, that's not possible. Gordon and I are on business. We'll be gone only a day or so."

Then, "No, we'll drive ourselves. Liam has gone back to Ireland for a few days."

"...not possible." A pause and then, "I'll tell you what though, I'm arranging for 'Spirit' to be at St Malo – probably...three or four days. Why don't you join us there? Fly from Heathrow to Dinan. That's only a taxi ride to Dinard...could pick you up there."

Although Martin could not hear them, the questions put to Mabbett were obviously a plea. They had met with a firm rebuff, until the St Malo offer, when the woman's face lightened and she spoke animatedly for several seconds.

"Why don't you stop with Gordon's wife at Cadnam? They have... you could talk her into flying over with you."

At that moment Martin felt, rather than saw, a movement to his right. A waiter was approaching. He slipped the earpiece into his pocket, but the man was signalled by Mabbett, who asked for his bill, then rose and, followed by the woman, walked from the restaurant into the small bar.

Martin sat back and relaxed with a small glow of satisfaction. Tony's device had worked. He now knew some specifics about the man and his movements. Coupled with the tape and message from Ewen, the jigsaw was coming together. Was it now time to speak again with Bill Creighton? No, he would dig a bit deeper. Tony was on his way north and that visit might result in an even fuller picture.

Martin ordered a coffee and his bill. He would not follow the couple further that night. He guessed that he knew their next destination and the road to Kilchatten was too quiet to follow another car without risk of being spotted.

Wednesday 3rd June 1992
2.55 p.m. Kilchatten

Tony Drew cursed quietly as he slipped on the short wet turf of the hillside. A fine Scottish drizzle had saturated the ground earlier in the day and the sheep trail of a footpath that he was following was still treacherous. The situation was not improved by a shortness of breath, a legacy of too many hours in the workshop and not enough exercise. Aching legs told him that the rucksack on his back, now seeming to weigh twice what it did half an hour ago, deserved a rest as well. With sweat trickling he swung it from his shoulders with a grunt of relief.

As he stopped his black Scottie dog, getting on in years now and a trifle overweight, stopped too and gazed back at him. Scottie wasn't used to this either, as the lolling tongue suggested, but was enjoying it more.

It had seemed a good idea at the time, as these things do. Scottie would provide 'cover' making his presence on the hillside innocent. Now he was not so sure. Tired of waiting, the little dog barked impatiently, as it had on each stop to catch breath. Sighing, Tony hefted the rucksack onto his back and continued the climb.

Ten minutes later he crested the hill and saw in the middle foreground the house which had to be Mabbett's and, some half a mile beyond it, the row of smaller dwellings lining the road which followed the shoreline. At the end of the road was a larger building, which would be the hotel that Martin was using. Beyond the glint of the damp roofs was the greater gleam of the loch. It was just as described in their telephone conversation of the previous evening.

Heaving the rucksack to the ground, he took his waterproof jacket off and, on sitting down on it, saw with relief that his act of sitting satisfied Scottie, who came back and settled by his side, panting and eyeing him expectantly. From the rucksack he took a plastic bowl and a bottle of water. Scottie wagged his tail as they shared a cool drink. Digging deeper, he unearthed a small pair of binoculars and, using these, examined the surroundings of the house minutely. As Martin had said, there was absolutely no cover that would hide a closer inspection on foot. Having confirmed the detail in his mind, he turned to his principal interest, the telegraph pole and an area of low gorse and heather that surrounded it.

For several minutes he continued using the glasses and making notes on a pad. Then, with Scottie once more up and impatient, he took care to follow what was apparently a casual route down the hill, walking past the telegraph pole. In so doing he memorized the number of paces and the direction from the base of the pole to the largest clump of furze.

Half an hour later he had regained his car and was en route to the Glasgow hotel, which was his base for the next day or so and where Martin was to join him later. He wondered how Martin had got on with the Glasgow CID, who had 'requested his presence' on the previous day.

4.25 p.m.

At that precise moment Detective Sergeant Macgregor and Detective Constable Cantrill were debating the import of information which, following the interview with Martin, they now had from the Southampton police. Their routine background check of the name and address given had resulted in a long and interesting conversation with a certain Detective Chief Inspector Potter. There was no doubt at all that high level negotiations would be required to decide whether Hampshire or Strathclyde had the next go at Wild!

5.15 p.m.

In his office at Shirley police station DCI Potter was already on the phone to his boss. "You're not going to believe this Ray. Our friend Wild is now mixed up in a death in Glasgow! A guy that he was employing to do an investigation there was stabbed outside a nightclub."

"When was this?"

Potter went on to give all the details that he had and then said, 'I'm waiting for a fax from Glasgow with more information, but it may be necessary to send someone up there to have a look at the situation, to see whether there's any possible connection with our job."

6.10 p.m.

Martin tapped on the door of 110. A gruff voice answered, "Who is it?"

"MW TD." The simple code was answered by the door opening to reveal a shirt-sleeved Tony Drew with screwdriver in hand. Behind him on the bed was an open toolcase and on the obligatory chest of drawers, a scattering of small electronic components and a plastic box of the type used to store foodstuffs. Martin identified a crystal controlled miniature transmitter, drycell battery packs and the type of small soldering iron used by serious modellers.

"How's it going?"

"Nearly done. Just have to finish off the internal connections and then seal the lid in place. The recorder will give us about three hours of speech. I've modified it to run at half speed."

"It's a voice activated unit?" Martin's question was really not necessary and Tony's look said as much. "It's just that we were losing part of the first word on the last Vox unit that we used, which was a bloody nuisance. Is there any way that we can overcome that?"

"Can't be helped, although you should lose a fraction less with this model. It's more sophisticated – and more expensive – as you'll see when you get the invoice." Tony grinned and settled down to complete the work.

"Did you get the climbing gear?" asked Tony. "You'll not be able to shin up that pole without getting some splinters in your arse."

It was Martin's turn to grin, he guessed that it was a Tony windup and that they would do the intercept at or below ground level but he played along. "Yes, but they didn't have spiked boots in my size elevens. I hope you can get an eight on? The belt's going to be a tight fit too!" He ducked as the lid of the plastic box sailed towards his head.

By eight in the evening the gear was ready but Martin judged it to be too early to get onto the hillside. With time in hand, they broke their journey to Kilchatten to put away a dish of one of Tony's favourite curries, and reached the lay-by, where they were going to leave the car, by eleven. It was a dark and damp night, any moon hidden by the heavy overcast that had brought the rain earlier in the day.

"I hope this bloody car's still here when we get back," said Tony.

"There's hardly anyone about at this time of night in Kilchatten," said Martin. "If it's seen, then they'll probably think it's a courting couple and although they're curious about strangers, I don't think the local population are the sort that would poke their noses into that sort of situation."

"You should have told me earlier. I'd have knocked up a rocking machine to improve the appearance. A tape recorder inside with a few Ooohs and Aaahs—would've done the trick."

Hoisting the rucksacks to their backs, they started up the hillside, wet bracken clutching at their feet and tangles of gorse threatening to bring them down.

In the darkness, it took twice as long to reach the ridge above the house, despite Martin using an image intensifier, enabling him to see the main features of their path and to identify landmarks that he had memorised from the previous visit. Muttered curses reached his ears as Tony stumbled to a halt behind him. For several minutes he checked the house surroundings, and the lane leading to it, before they moved again.

The last stretch, from the top of the hill to the tall hedge bordering Mabbett's garden, was completed slowly and quietly. Sweating, they collapsed at the base of the pole with a lighted window of Mabbett's house only a few metres away. There was no movement from that direction. No dog barked and they sat still for several minutes, listening whilst they regained their breath.

Undoing his rucksack, Martin took out several items which, to deaden sound, were separately wrapped in pieces of torn up blanket. One of them was a shortened lawn edging tool, whose blade had been sharpened before they left. With a length of cord he traced a path to the clump of gorse identified by Tony earlier in the day and then started to cut a line through the turf to a depth of two or three inches.

Meanwhile Tony was working at the base of the pole, on his knees with a large blanket over him and a headtorch illuminating the metal conduit covering the telecom wires running up the pole. He had taken off the top covering of turf at the base of the pole with a large knife and small spade to expose the conduit for several inches below ground level.

Martin knew that he had drawn the short straw when he reached the gorse bush. Despite leather gardening gloves and an anorak which did up at the cuff, there was no doubt that the gorse was getting its revenge for being disturbed. It took twenty minutes during which there were regular painful injections before the sealed plastic box, now spray painted a dead gorse brown, was positioned to his satisfaction. He now knew why Tony had elected to have the final terminals on the end of two metres of cable exiting through a weather resistant plug on the side of the box. Tony would be able to do the final connection at a safe distance from the gorse.

Two hours later, with a misty rain starting to fall again, the job was complete. Tony had successfully intercepted the phone wires, although the use of special sealants to avoid damp affecting the transmission had prevented the replacement of the metal conduit. As that area was now beneath the replaced turf, that was not a problem. They had carefully eased up the line of turf and buried the cabling to the plastic box connectors, replacing it and treading the sod back into place. All being well, the next three hours of telephone conversation on Mabbett's ex-directory line would he recorded by the 'tape in a box'.

Martin's only concern was that, for the immediate future, he was destined to have a nightly fight with the gorse bush when he changed tapes.

By the occasional appearance of the part moon from behind broken clouds, Martin could see the pale ribbon of the sheep trail winding ahead through the bracken. He moved carefully, quietly, standing still when the moonlight illuminated the terrain, moving as the clouds cut out the light. The extreme care was probably unnecessary. He had seen no one at all on his previous visits and didn't expect to now, despite the improved conditions. The weather on Thursday and Friday had continued wet. Saturday the rain showers stopped and, by Sunday, there was sunshine in the afternoon. Tonight the hillside, or at least this path across it, was well known to Martin and had dried out, ensuring that the pilgrimage to change the tapes was easier and, again, uneventful.

Martin was concerned. His time at the hotel as a declared bird watcher and walker was approaching the end of the week's holiday that he had originally booked. For three days there had been no sign of his target, no communication of note to or from the house. The occasional domestic call was handled by a man, who was probably the employee whom Martin had seen from the boat on that first day. It seemed that, in Mabbett's absence, he dealt with all of the domestic routines apart from cleaning. A woman, who arrived each weekday at about 10 a.m., didn't appear on the tape at all and was apparently a 'daily' rather than a secretary. Martin could extend the 'holiday' by a few days but more than that was sure to arouse the sort of local interest that he did not want.

Tony had intercepted two pairs of wires that he identified as the 'voice lines'. Martin wondered briefly whether they had been the right ones but, that night, his confidence in Tony's abilities was confirmed when he got back to the hotel and replayed the 'Sunday' tapes in his room. Suddenly there was a lot of activity. A dozen calls made and half a dozen received, all by Mabbett. The man had obviously been away and was now back.

Most of the calls were to or from people who, Martin guessed, worked for Mabbett in the club world. Three calls were of interest. He had no problem putting names to two of them.

The first of these was to Andrew McAinsh, the manager of the Glasgow club where Ewen had worked. "Andy what's the score with the little matter that was dealt with last week?"

'We've had the 'Busies' in and out all week. They've taken statements from the lads who were on that night and had several down the station looking at photos. On Saturday they had people on the door, talking to the punters as they came in. The same night Liddell, who's the local detective in charge, came in with an English detective. I wondered about that. That's about it."

"Play it cool, Andy. You know nothing about it. The man just worked for you. Keep an eye on the lads and, if any seem to be singled out, more than one interview or asked to visit the Bride a second time, then let me know."

The second call was from Gordon Wilson. "DM, I've got a possible for the transportation that we were talking about."

"Where are they based?"

"Just outside Portsmouth, family business, two brothers and a wife who manages the admin. They work from home with a parking lot leased from a garage. They have two lorries and use Le Havre as their French port."

"What's their business?"

"You name it and they'll do it. They have a refrigerated unit which they use for a contract to move frozen meats to Germany and then meat products to Spain. They return with loads of fresh veg from Spain. Now they've been hit by the BSE business and don't have a load to Germany although they still have to go there for their load to Spain. Their latest problem is that they've been caught by customs with red diesel in a hidden tank and a package of 'jeans' that a French driver 'liberated' from one of his jobs and sold on to them."

"What makes them right for us?"

"Customs are doing them for the diesel and the police are likely to charge them with receiving stolen goods. All small stuff, but costing them. They're already well into the red at the bank and now their second vehicle is off the road in France with a hefty repair bill pending. They've been running on a prayer for some time and, with the likely fine for the custom's job, will be out of business unless they can find some cash quickly."

"OK, so they're prepared to chance their arm for us but that still doesn't mean that they've got the bottle to carry for us."

"The clincher for me is that my man knows the elder brother, has done time with him when he was put away for a 'blagging' some six years ago and reckons him to be a hard one. I've got someone else checking the English side a bit further but we need to have a look at their contacts on the other side of the Channel."

"Gordon, I'm due to meet the French people in a few days. I'd intended spending a day or two with Ann on the boat at St Malo but I can cut that short. If you're willing to give them a try, let's keep it at arm's length and have someone do a trip with them in the next week to find out some more about that side. Why don't the two of you come over, join us on *Spirit* at Dinard. We could talk the French side of the operation over then."

"They come back through Rennes normally...that's where their vehicle is off the road just now. St Malo is close and might be just right for setting things up."

"OK, I'll firm up my movements and the meeting over there and let you know when. You set someone up to get closer to these people and we'll look at the Rennes area as a possible transfer point. One thing though, I want to keep this from the French side that I'm seeing. Remember that we're looking elsewhere for future supplies. I'll ring you again tomorrow late p.m. OK?"

The conversation finished with Wilson and Mabbett arranging a precise time to speak.

"Well, Mister Potter, here's a present for you. If you can't set up a suitable operation with this info, you're not worth your rank," Martin murmured to himself. He remembered the conversation that he had listened to in the hotel restaurant on the previous Tuesday. He had not been able to pick up all of it, but it had sounded at the time as though Mabbett and the woman were arranging a jolly. Now it seemed that business would be on the agenda as well.

The third call was made by Mabbett to an international line but the voice that answered was very English – with a touch of an east London accent. "Jimmy, how are you?"

"Dermott! Twice in one week after months without a word. You must want something!"

"Something for both of us perhaps. When are you free for a meet?"

"If it's over here, then I'm free this weekend."

"Can't make it that soon. What about the week after?"

"Got some people with me then for a couple of days. Not sure which ones."

"I'll give you a ring next week to confirm then."

"OK. I'll wait to hear from you. And bring me a bottle of that special Malt of yours."

Martin replayed the tape and then sat back in the chair marshalling the information that he now had, fitting it into place with that supplied in the reports and tapes produced by Ewen and the background passed on by Bill's nightclub contact. In the initial enquiries after Eileen's funeral, he had organised company searches to obtain year end accounts and details of the night club directors. These had shown a profitable estate of clubs and a very small and tight management. Before his death, Ewen had discussed with Martin the activities of the door team and their hangers-on. Both had agreed that the door supervisors were almost certainly involved in re-cycling the drugs that they seized from customers on the doors and in the toilets and dark corners of the Glasgow club. Martin wondered about the Frenchman Tabarde, details of whose death Bill Creighton had passed onto him. That indicated Marseilles connection, an area notorious for drugs and with a strong French Mafia influence. The speed and violence associated with Ewen's death indicated something much more than local re-cycling of seized drugs. This new information pointed to organised smuggling on a large scale, tying in the death of the French politician and everything since.

Rousing into action, he slipped the tape into a padded envelope and addressed it to Tony Drew. Tony would put it on the oscilloscope and find out the telephone numbers rung. Hopefully the next tape would have Mabbett booking flights. If he could get details of where and when this meeting and the next one that Mabbett had discussed were, then there might be confirmation of other prime movers. Martin wanted to be sure that he knew all who were responsible for the deaths of Eileen and Ewen.

It would soon be time to impart more of the information that he now had to the police, but he preferred to do that when he had something positive to offer them rather than circumstantial evidence and supposition. The last meeting with Potter still rankled. It would be nice to jolt the man out of his suspicion and prejudices.

Martin decided that he would pay another visit to collect the next tape, book a flight to Heathrow for Tuesday and then get an update from Bill Creighton. Before leaving Glasgow he could pay a casual call to the CID and see whether there was anything fresh in their investigation of Ewen Handsford's death. He could also phone Ellie May and arrange to see her again. Perhaps she might then have some more information on Potter's teams' activities.

At the thought of seeing Ellie May again, Martin surprised himself by feeling a frisson of anticipation. The memory of endless curves in a little black dress was provoking and he smiled at himself as he turned out the bedroom light. It was a reaction that had been absent for many weeks.

He would not have smiled had he known the content of a meeting then happening in Andrew McAinsh's office.

11.40 p.m.

"So, how are things in the big bad world outside?" McAinsh's question was addressed to a thirty-something burly, ginger haired man who had been shown to his office by Neil Fisher. "I heard you'd left the Busies just ahead of a big shiny axe!"

Ginger looked discomforted. "They had nothing on me, just a complaint or two. You're bound to upset people when you're doing that sort of job. Anyway, I needed a change."

McAinsh's sallow face showed the disbelief that he felt. The night world of Glasgow knew Cameron as a quick tempered plain clothes policeman who, it was said, was not averse to planting some "smack" or a tablet or two if he wanted to justify an arrest. There were those who said that he added to his salary at times by the sale of drugs seized. This allegation was thought by many to be the reason for his sudden departure from the police family halfway through his service.

"Well, you're too quick with your fists to join my team on the door." The jibe of an ex-policeman working as a bouncer went home and Cameron flushed an angry red but restrained himself.

"You know better than that, Andy. I dropped in because I thought I might have something of interest for your boss. That's what I'm doing now." He slid a white business card across the table, which told the world that Gerald Cameron was now a private investigator.

McAinsh grinned mirthlessly. "From a blue suit to a dirty mac, eh?" He was enjoying taking the man down. Previous encounters had been in Cameron's favour.

"I thought that you and Dermott Mabbett would be interested in who put the man Handsford in your path, but if you've nothing but shitty jokes to share, then I've got better things to do." Cameron got to his feet and made for the door.

The smile left Andrew McAinsh's face. "Hold on a minute!" Cameron paused at the door and looked back. "What do you know of Handsford? You've been out of the police for months, long before he came to work here."

"I've still got my friends and I keep my nose to the ground. If you were as good with your checks as you are with your tongue, you'd not be wondering where the man came from or what he was doing as part of your team."

McAinsh sat still for a moment, then said quietly, "We got off on the wrong foot, Gerald. Sit down and have a drink." He reached for the bottle in his drawer.

Cameron stood at the door to make the point that the choice was his, his face showing anger. His drinking session the previous evening with a police "civvy" had not yielded as much information as he would have wished, but he didn't want McAinsh to know that. If he was going to get anything out of Mabbett, then he'd be better off playing the fish a little longer and McAinsh had given him that opportunity.

"Tell you what, Andy. If Dermott Mabbett is interested, I'll do the background checks on your employees in future, for a fee of course! And I'll throw in what I know of Handsford when I get the first payment. But tell him not to wait too long, it's not only the local CID that are interested in your little operation now!"

McAinsh remembered the English detective with Liddell. "And what's that going to cost us, if Dermott says yes?"

"Let's start with your present team. You've got what? A dozen men at least. Let's say £200 per man. I'll give you a job lot price, £2,000 for the lot, as an introductory package." It was Cameron's turn to grin, as he left the room.

Wednesday 10th June 1992
12.50 p.m. Southampton

"I have a bit of a situation, Bill."

Greetings over, Martin lost no time in getting to the urgent part of the reason for their meeting. Bill Creighton and he were sitting in a quiet corner of the comfortable Regents Park Hotel in Southampton, only yards from the spot where Martin had intercepted Ellie May a couple of weeks before.

"You always worry me when you say that you have a 'situation'," said Bill with a grin. "I seem to remember that usually means you've what others would call a major problem."

"Could be," Martin grinned back. "This time it could be terminal, unless I'm very careful."

The smile left Bill Creighton's face. "You'd better fill me in."

"The opposition know about me at last. It was bound to happen sooner or later, but it's sooner than I'd hoped. I've had an intercept on the main man's phone and on the last tape that I picked up there was a conversation with one of his managers. This guy has a contact with an ex-copper in Glasgow who, in turn has his own friends in that force. They now know that Ewen was working for me. They had a man visit the hotel that I've been using."

"Shit, Marty, you're going to have to drop out of sight or get yourself some protection." Bill's concern was very obvious and real.

"Don't worry, Bill. That's all in hand. Before I do though, I need to update you guys, talk to Potter again, or do I give you what I've got? I think it's time for me to duck out, leave it all to you 'professionals'. Martin grinned as he teased. "But the thing is how much do you want to be dealt in, or do I leave you out altogether?"

"Leave me out altogether, Marty. I'm not one of Potter's favourites and he'd leave me off the team if he knew that we'd been meeting behind his back."

Martin had anticipated Bill reaction and considered the possibilities beforehand. "In that case, let's try to put you into a stronger position. If you've got information about one of the villains that I'm going to talk to him about, you could drop that on his desk after I've seen him, as though it's independent. With any luck, he'll tell you to check the man out and bring you more into the centre of things."

Martin talked for some minutes about Gordon Wilson, giving Bill all of the information that he had on the man and filling him in on the detail of his investigation since they had last met.

"The last time that you dropped out of sight, no one saw or heard from you for three months. How do I get in touch if we need to speak, Marty?"

Martin grinned at Bill's exaggeration. "I'm not dropping that far out of sight. Use my mobile or my pager number. You'd better know that I'm in touch with Ellie May as well, although not publicly. And thanks for that suggestion."

"Any good?" Bill's smile and double meaning were not lost on Martin but he ignored it.

"We're meeting later. She's got things for me to look at. I'll phone Potter today for a meet. If I'm going to make myself scarce then I've arrangements to make as quickly as possible."

8.30 p.m.

The small white hulled yacht, tethered by its mooring to fore and aft buoys, moved gently with the current. It was a Scandinavian-designed Folkboat. A minor classic now some thirty years old with teak planking and oak frames. The boat had been Martin's pride and joy for the last three years, bought with the first serious money that he had earned after leaving the police. Although now up for sale, she was still his hideaway and, since the loss of Eileen's flat, his home when in the Southampton area. It was a quiet refuge from the world that he now inhabited. It was the only place where he was able to fully relax.

To the southwest of his mooring, the last rays of the sun tinged the outline of Hengistbury Head with gold. The promontory of elevated land sheltered Christchurch harbour and the river Avon, where the boat was moored next to tall reeds lining the west bank. Beyond the headland, the late evening sky and summer cumulus were turning a darker red, providing a beautiful and dramatic backdrop to the winding river.

Truly Fair's cabin was warm and comfortable. With the forehatch open, the cooler evening air was just noticeable. Freshly washed crockery stood upright in a drainer on the sink and an almost empty bottle of Chablis was on the cabin table, which was folded so that the boat's occupants could recline at ease on opposite sides of the cabin.

Martin was stretched on the port berth, reading steadily through a pile of paperwork. Ellie May was curled on the opposite berth, glass in hand and a photograph album on her knees, feeling surprisingly relaxed. When Martin had pointed the boat out to her a week or so ago at the end of their first evening together, she had felt uneasy about meeting him there. Never having been on a small boat and aware that she would have to sit in an even smaller one to be rowed out to it, had not encouraged her.

On this evening, they had met at a car park by the Christchurch Council offices, where she left her car. Martin then driving her in his, turning back to the roundabout that she had just passed and then doing a slow circuit of Christchurch, collecting a Chinese meal on the way and deliberately 'doubling' another roundabout to make sure that they had not been followed.

They had eaten in *Truly Fair*'s cockpit, stretched on comfortable cushions and enjoying the warmth of the summer evening. Ellie May's forebodings had quickly changed to interest as she investigated the small boat. She was curious about life in such cramped conditions and marvelled at the clever use of limited space.

Using the main cabin as his living area, Martin had converted the small forecabin to a wardrobe and storage area with hanging space over one of the bunks for his suits and shirts. The opposite bunk in the forecabin carried a 'Harry Tate' construction of reinforced cardboard filing boxes, which still gave access to the storage areas beneath the bunk. The main cabin was unchanged apart from the fact that his usual library of nautical almanacs, tide tables and charts on the shelf behind his bunk had been replaced by an overflow of business paper work. The boat's normal VHF radio was now supplemented by a mobile cellphone sitting in a modified car kit, which was wired to the boat's batteries and an antenna at the masthead. In the first year of ownership, he had replaced the old cockpit cover with a custom-made cockpit tent, which converted in a few minutes to a sun canopy or could be demounted completely. The boat was now very comfortable for one person, or very cosy for two.

Ellie May's conversion from hesitancy to interest had pleased him. She had clambered about the interior asking innumerable questions. Also she had dressed sensibly for the occasion with a black short-sleeved jumper and tight matching ski pants to replace the 'little black dress' of their previous outing. Sensible perhaps, but the new outfit did even less to hide her curves than the previous one. Martin found himself distracted from the real reason for their meeting until, that is, she produced from a large shoulder bag a thick file of documents.

They had finished their meal and retired to the cabin by then. Martin washing the plates whilst she dried.

"Now, you must forget about me for a little while and read this. I cannot leave it with you. I'll have to return it tonight before I go home."

"Won't they wonder what you're doing, going into the office so late?"

"Yes, but it will be easier to answer that question than it would be to find a reason for getting in before the Early Turn man tomorrow morning. He starts at six! Part of his job is to add a daily summary of the Squad's activities during the previous twenty-four hours. He does that separately but he may want to look at the file to check previous entries or something. The file does not have much detail. It's like a summary of the whole job with just some appendices giving detail of particular things of interest. It's Mr Potter's bible in some ways. He uses it every day."

Martin sat down to read. "Ellie, you've taken a big chance for me. Thank you."

"It'll give you an overview Martin and I may be able to 'borrow' more detailed stuff if you can point out to me what you're interested in."

It took Martin the best part of an hour to leaf through the file, pausing every so often to make his own notes. He spent several minutes studying one particular photograph in one of the first appendices. It was of individual items that had been found in Parkside Avenue after the bomb blast. One of them appeared to be a short length of pencil, just over two inches long. It was dark blue and, by using a magnifying glass, Martin could see what looked like "ows" in lower case with stars, all in silver. The rest of the inscription was missing, the pencil having been cut short. The cut end of the pencil was much too blunt to have been fashioned for use as a writing instrument.

Martin was certain that he had seen a similar pencil before and, after some thought, remembered that during one of their meetings, Ewen had been using one. Ewen's, however, had been a complete pencil with the name Shadows Disco in silver surrounded by silver stars all on a dark blue background. According to Ewen, the pencils were routinely used in the box office and staff room at the Glasgow nightclub. They were an item which had been part of a Club promotion. Suddenly he remembered the plastic rubbish bag full of debris from the night club offices, recovered from Ewen's car after his death. There had been a similar length of blue pencil in that, also cut short though not with writing on it.

"Ellie, could you see whether there are any enlargements of this photo or whether there is any mention of it elsewhere in the investigation?"

"I'll try, Martin."

"And there's mention here of a nurse returning home from the General Hospital. She found a motorcycle parked outside the entrance to her flat and made a statement about it. Do you think you could get a copy of that statement for me to look at?'

"That should be easier than the photograph," Ellie May said.

"Would you like a coffee before I take you back to your car?"

"No, but I'd like to use your 'littlest room', if I can work all of the pump handles and levers that you showed me and don't flood the boat."

Martin showed her again how to flush the sea toilet and then made a coffee for himself as he listened with a smile to the giggles and bumps coming, from the confined space.

He called out, "On a boat you don't call it the 'littlest room' or the loo, not even the toilet. It's known as the 'Heads'."

Ellie May appeared from within the tiny compartment and giggled again. "That's not a very appropriate name in my case. I didn't bump my head, but I did keep bumping my too big bottom!"

Martin laughed. "Don't knock it, Ellie May, that's one of your most attractive features. In fact I've debated in the past whether or not I should call you 'La Derrière'.

'What does "derrière" mean?"

"It's French for rear."

She gave him a cheeky grin and said, "One of the girls in the typing pool used to say that you were always watching my bottom."

They were very close together in the confined space. "Thank you very much for bringing the papers, and your derrière, onto my boat tonight. The papers were very interesting, when I could concentrate on them!"

"Ooh! What stopped you concentrating?" She gazed innocently up into his eyes, a little smile twitching the corners of her mouth.

"The sight of your delightful derrière bobbing about the boat," Martin whispered as he bent and gently kissed her very full lips.

Moments later against his mouth she murmured, "You don't know how many times I've wanted you to do this." For moments that seemed to stand still he was lost in a new world, a world bounded by the softness, the fullness, of her lips. Like many men, he had gazed at West Indian and African women and wondered about that particular difference from their European counterparts. Now he knew, and in knowing, was transported to a deeper sensual world which threatened to engulf him and delay actions which he knew were essential.

His hands slid down her waist, to more prominent curves.

"And you don't know how often I've wanted to do this," he said as he caressed her. "But now you are a married woman!"

"Not for much longer."

With difficulty Martin fought the urge to continue this sudden change in relationship. He wanted very much to enter this new world but there were other priorities, some of which could make a difference where life itself was concerned. There was always another time, he hoped!

Finally, by the shoulders now, he held her away. "I've too much to do tonight. I must take you ashore."

"That's what you say with your lips," she whispered "but it's not what the rest of you is saying." She leant back from the waist and moved her pelvis suggestively.

Abruptly, in his memory another face was before him. A very different face with fair curly hair and blue eyes, a face from his previous world, which already seemed so long ago. It confirmed his decision.

"Ellie May, if you decide to risk an affair, please, I would love first refusal." Unusually for Martin, his words were clumsy. The situation and the priorities had thrown him. Carefully now he said, "But tonight I really have things to do which are important and cannot wait until the morning. Things which may make it possible for us to be together again under much better circumstances."

He turned her around and, picking up her bag, moved her towards the steps leading into the cockpit. At the bottom she stopped and, leaning forward to gasp the handrails, she deliberately pushed her bottom back into his crotch and did a little gyration with it.

"Just to let you know what you're missing, mister."

"God, Ellie May, I know what I'm missing! You've no idea how difficult it is for me to do this, or not do that!"

9.10 p.m.

Warmth and good will were singularly missing in the conversation taking place just then in the big house at Kilchatten some four hundred miles to the north. Anger was not a thing that Dermott Mabbett was afraid to show, and it was obvious now.

"So, Liam, you see how it is. This man that you followed, the wrong man, and whose girlfriend you killed, by mistake, the man who put Ewen Handsford into the Club, who you had to deal with just a little while ago, is an ex policeman and some kind of private detective into the bargain. It's difficult seeing how you could have made a bigger balls-up if you'd tried! We now have not only the Glasgow police looking at us but also detectives from England travelling to Scotland to find out more! And all at a time when we are changing our market. This will cost us, on top of what we're losing from the punters that we can't sell to whilst the police are thick on the ground in Glasgow."

The lean hard face of Liam Mahoney gave nothing away. There was no attempt at self-justification or excuse. "You want me to make the man disappear?" The Belfast accent was unemotional. He might have been discussing a change of plan for a Saturday night 'crack'.

"What we do not want is for the police to think that there is yet another connection to us. We don't know what this Wild person knows of us, or has told the police. From the questions being asked by the Plainclothes at the club, and what our own man has heard, it's not much yet. The one thing that you've been good at so far is hiding yourself. No one has connected you with the two jobs."

"I've asked Gordon to dig around the Southampton end of this as

132

discreetly as he can, see if he can find Wild's base. I want you to go to this address. It's a cottage in the New Forest at a place called Beaulieu Road Station. It's well off the beaten track and you'll have to look after yourself there. The nearest town is Lyndhurst. There's no phone at the cottage and I don't want you to use a mobile or the phone at the farm next door that owns the cottage. You'll have to phone Gordon on a daily basis. Use a kiosk. When he has some information, we'll discuss how you handle it. We need to do something quickly but carefully. Wild must appear to be an accident!"

"What's my cover for the people at the farm? Do they know us?"

"It's a man on his own. He doesn't know of 'us' but he knows Gordon. He's an antique merchant that we use through Gordon, so steer clear of that. You'd better invent some serious illness that you're recovering from. Doctor has told you to convalesce. He lets the cottage to holidaymakers so shouldn't be too nosey but try and avoid contact all the same. Speak with Gordon about the name that you'll use and let me know as soon as you're down there."

9.30 p.m. Christchurch

The ebb tide was starting to run in earnest as Martin released the bow rope, nudged the engine into gear and cleared the mooring. It was going to be tight. The brown water of the estuary was sliding towards the sea quickly now. It would take him half an hour to reach The Run at Mudeford and that was at least half an hour later than he would have preferred. Christchurch Harbour was only navigable for very shallow draught boats at anything after half tide and his boat needed more water than most local ones to float in. The fin keel made it a very safe boat in bad weather but it was a liability in shallow waters.

Darkness was coming on, which did not make things any easier, but that was also the opportunity to disappear sea ward and let the night and the Solent swallow him up, away from the eyes of his enemies. Not to run and hide, but to gain an advantage.

As the boat gathered momentum, he blessed the half moon that was now his only source of light. The sunset was long gone and, as Martin strained his eyes for the channel markers, it was the moonlight reflected from the ripples that threw them into silhouette. One by one they were sighted and passed, Grimbury Marsh, Wickhams Marsh, Blackberry Point. Then the jetty which served the local ferry taking people to the long thin peninsular of land that formed the sea ward side of Christchurch Harbour and ended at the Black House and The Run.

Martin now had the lights of the Haven House Inn on Mudeford Quay to steer for. As he passed the last buoy, he could feel the boat picking up speed. All of the water from Christchurch Harbour was channelled through The Run and, at this state of tide, was moving at over six knots, which was faster than *Truly Fair* could either sail or motor. He was committed to staying with the channel of water which, in daylight, required care but, in the dark, was a swirling, rocking sleigh ride with very little control.

The lights from the Inn and the car park beyond slid past quickly. Now out of the shelter of Hengistbury Head, the movement of the little boat was affected by waves. Earlier in the day there had been a brisk southwesterly wind. The wind had died an hour before with the sunset but the wave formation, breaking against the quay only to be thrown back in a confusion, was still enough to add another dimension to *Truly Fair*'s passage through The Run.

Standing in the cockpit, with the tiller in his right hand, balancing against the irregular movement, Martin continually corrected the course as the boat was thrown this way and that. A late night fisherman on the quay hastily reeled in his line and shouted something as the little boat appeared unexpectedly out of the dark. Martin couldn't hear but raised a hand in apology. By then they were approaching the end of the car park, with the two green channel lights marking the last of The Run.

The boat slowed slightly as the force of the water lessened but Martin remained tense. These were the critical moments. They were approaching Christchurch Bar. Beneath the boat's keel the river had deposited gravel and silt beds. The level of what was now the sea floor was rising. Martin knew that there could only be inches of water between his keel and the sea bed. The underwater shingle banks were altered by winter storms each year and, although there were channel buoys, they were not lit and, in any case, were only an indication of the channel's general direction. Local sailors took care to find the exact channel in the early weeks of the season, always in daylight and always with a rising tide. Due to events Martin had not used his boat or had an opportunity to check out this year's changes. Here he was, in the dark, with a falling tide and enough speed through the water to put his boat high and dry if she went seriously "onto the putty".

For several minutes *Truly Fair* continued smoothly through the water. Martin altered course, searching desperately for a sight of the outermost channel buoys. The moon again came to his aid. There was the outer mark, he was still in the channel, just! Another correction to centre the boat and he was starting to relax when *Truly Fair* slowed abruptly, leant over to port and he heard the sound of gravel beneath the keel. Quickly he put the tiller over and opened the engine's throttle to full power. Now the force of water from The Run which had been a danger, became his helper. With the push of the river on her starboard side and the extra power from the engine the little boat continued its forward motion, the keel dragging off of the gravel bank and into deeper water, the new course curving away from the hidden danger and towards the open sea.

For five minutes Martin continued seaward into deepening water then, switching his navigation lights off, he altered course to due east. With a watchful eye on the depth sounder, he followed the coast towards Hurst Castle and the narrow entrance to the Solent. At that moment the ebbing tide was pouring westward through the gap between Hurst Point and Fort Albert on the Isle of Wight. This heavy tide caused a weak circular back current which followed the coast. Martin used this local knowledge to gain a little speed over the ground. An hour later he sighted North Head Buoy marking the channel between the shore and the dreaded Shingles, a mid-channel series of drying banks, which had caused many boats to perish over the years. Here he was losing the help of the reverse current. The ebb tide through the narrows was still too strong for his boat's small engine, so he put the helm over and the engine into neutral, dropping the anchor to wait for the tide to lessen.

With the boat settling back onto its anchor chain and the kettle on for a cup of coffee, Martin used his mobile phone to ring Bill Creighton.

"Sorry to ring you so late. I hope I haven't dug you out of your pit."

"Just in time, Martin, we were about to go."

"What shift are you on tomorrow?"

"Lates, why? Do you need something?"

"I could do with a lift, if that's at all possible."

'I'd promised to take Suz shopping but, as it's you, I expect we'll be forgiven.'

"No need. If the pair of you pick me up in the car park on Lymington Quay at about ten-thirty, I'll buy you a coffee at The Bluebird and lunch at the Christchurch Sailing Club. In between, Suzanne can do her shopping in Lymington, or at Sainsbury's in Christchurch if she prefers. How's that?"

"You're on, Marty."

Two pots of coffee later, *Truly Fair* putputted past the red and white navigation lights of Hurst Castle. An hour after that, Martin left the flashing red of Jack in the Basket to port as he entered Lymington River. Half an hour later the boat was secured to a visitor's mooring off Lymington Quay with the prospect of several hours' quiet sleep and a good sailing breakfast before meeting Bill.

Thursday 11th June 1992
11 30 a.m. Southampton

"Morning Chief Inspector, how are things?"

Potter grunted in reply, indicated a chair and said, "We've made some progress. We're working with the French police, there are foreign connections. Understand that you've some information for me. I'll have to ask you to be quick. Only have twenty minutes to spare."

Martin smiled and relaxed in the chair. "Of course. As you now know, the initial incident stemmed from a mistake. Eileen's death was due to an attempt on the life of a Monsieur Henri Tabarde, who was later murdered in Marseilles. He was shot in the head and dumped in his car in the harbour..."

"How do you know all this?" The demand was aggressive, the eyes surprised and angry.

"You forget that I've been working abroad for some time now. I've my own friends in the Sûreté and elsewhere." Martin lied smoothly. "I've been to France myself, and also to Glasgow where, as you know, I've had an operative working. What you may not know are the names and details of the people who were behind the murder of Eileen and Ewen and are currently engaged in the importation and distribution of Ecstasy and other prohibited drugs through a string of nightclubs. As you haven't much time, I'll leave this with you."

Martin slid several sheets of paper, photographs and a mini cassette across the table.

"The voices in the second conversation on the tape are those of Dermott Mabbett and Gordon Wilson, whose details you will find here." He tapped the sheets of closely typed paper. The name of the boat that they will be aboard tomorrow is *Spirit of Ecstasy,* cheeky beggar isn't he? She's moored in Beaucette Harbour on the north coast of Guernsey at the moment. The fourth conversation on the tape is to a telephone number in Spain. I've listed the number at the foot of the page. I don't know whose it is but, from the conversation, I'd guess he is one of our expat criminals who has joined the 'Costa crime set'. The photographs are of Dermott Mabbett's house at Kilchatten on the Isle of Bute. Happy hunting!"

"How did you get?... Where is this tape from?... Sit down!" Potter spluttered as Martin rose and moved towards the door.

"I 'acquired' the tape in Scotland, quite expensive and highly illegal, I'm sure. No use to you as evidence, I know, but confirms what I've told you in the paperwork."

"Come back here, God dammit," as Martin opened the door.

"Read the document and listen to the tape. When you have more than twenty minutes we can talk again. I hope to have something more for you in a day or so." Martin closed the door quietly, smiled and winked at a curious face peering round the door of the next room. He walked, unescorted, back to the front office. There he handed his visitor badge to a surprised civilian employee, who was holding a telephone aloft.

"Mr Potter says to hold onto you. You're not to leave the building."

"You tell the Chief Inspector to have a nice day and I'll call him tomorrow."

12.30 p.m.

An hour later, Martin was relaxing in the bar of the Beaulieu Road Hotel, a cool glass in one hand and the local tourist guide from the Information Centre at Lyndhurst in the other. He knew that the hotel was full, which suited his purpose and, with information from the police Antique Dealers Squad, courtesy of Bill Creighton, he now also knew that a particular dealer owned a nearby farm. It would be too much of a coincidence for there to be two antique dealers with farms in the immediate vicinity. This one had to be the dealer that Mabbett had referred to in his telephone conversation.

"If you haven't any accommodation yourself, is there anywhere local that I might find a room?"

"There are several hotels in Lyndhurst and a couple just off of the road before you get there." This from the man who had served him, a large individual with Brewers Goitre and what appeared to be a gammy leg.

"I'd prefer to stay in this immediate vicinity. Is there nowhere within walking distance of your restaurant?"

"You could try David Watson. He has a farm less than half a mile from here, but he only has the one cottage that he lets and at this time of the year it's probably already booked."

"How do I find Mr Watson's farm?"

The directions took him across the road from the pub and down a rough track which led through pine trees into a small valley. Hidden behind a thick belt of mixed woodland was a low built farm with two large barns and, off to one side, a timber bungalow.

As Martin approached the farmhouse, a chain rattled and a large rough-haired dog suddenly appeared, growling and then barking. The door of the farmhouse opened before Martin reached it and a sandy-haired man stepped out.

"Good afternoon. Sorry to disturb your dog. I'm after using your cottage." Martin's soft Irish brogue was nothing like that which he had heard on the telephone, but it was the best that he could do and he hoped that Watson had not yet spoken directly with Mahoney.

"You must be Gordon's friend. He told me to expect you tonight, but you're a little early." Watson advanced, hand outstretched.

Martin seized the opportunity. "Oh, he phoned ahead, did he? That was nice of him. Is that the place over there?" He nodded toward the bungalow.

"Yes. I'll get the key. Where's your car?"

"I had a drink at the pub and walked here. It's nice to stretch the legs after a drive."

Watson went back into the farm and reappeared after a few moments with a large old-fashioned key. He led the way towards the bungalow and, as they went in, said, "Gordon told me that you had been ill. Nothing too serious I hope?"

Martin swiftly took in the layout out of the large room, which obviously took up most of the small building's ground floor. He noted the small wood framed windows, without locks, and the large old bolts inside the front door. There was no sign of an alarm system.

Not wishing to push his luck or confirm suspicion, he said, "I didn't tell the landlord that I was ill. Never been better."

Watson stopped in his tracks at the door which, Martin anticipated, led to a kitchen. "I'm talking about Gordon, not the landlord of the pub."

"When you said Gordon, I thought that you meant the landlord. I've just been asking where I could get accommodation. His place is full."

Watson and Martin faced one another. "Who sent you here?" Watson asked quietly.

"The landlord of the pub, as I said. You do have accommodation, don't you?"

"Yes, but it's taken. I have a visitor arriving, this evening. I thought that you were he."

"Oh, that's a shame. This would have suited me fine. Is your visitor staying long?"

"What part of Ireland are you from?" Watson ignored Martin's question.

"The south, near Kinsale. But that's a long time ago. I've been all over since those days. Why do you ask?"

"You've not much of an accent left," Watson said. "Give me your name and phone number and I'll let you know when the cottage is free."

"Not to worry," said Martin. "Your visitor is obviously going to be here some time and I must be on my way in a few days. Sorry that we had a misunderstanding. Perhaps next time."

As he walked back along the track, Martin was conscious of Watson's eyes following him. When he reached the pub he bought another drink and sat outside in the sun, wondering how he was going to watch for Mahoney's arrival without showing it and how he was going to get in close without arousing the four-legged foot soldier.

For ten minutes or so he sat in the sun and cogitated. Then, with a plan forming in his mind based upon the memory of the bomb under the Porsche and Ellie May's domestic troubles, he got to his feet and abandoned his watching post outside the pub. Back in the car he dialled the number of Shirley Police Station and asked for Ellie May by name, refusing to give his own, saying it was a personal call. Her slightly husky voice came on the line.

"Who is this?"

"Ellie, I haven't given my name. I hope there is not a problem getting you on the phone by saying it's a personal matter. Call me Jim, just in case."

"It's no problem, I'm on my own just now. Mr Potter's out and the others are in the canteen. It's lunch time. Where does 'Jim' come from?"

"My second name is James, but I don't use it unless there's a purpose. Ellie, when we first met you told me that you had been to see the doctor because of the problems and that he had prescribed some pills for you."

"Yes, they were Valium to make me sleep, but I didn't take them."

"Do you still have them?"

"Yes, they're at home."

"Excellent. May I have them?"

"Mart… Jim, you know what you said the last time that we were together, about giving you first refusal?"

"Yes."

"I'm taking you up on that, and you're not having Valium beforehand!" Her voice sounded even huskier.

Softly, "Sweet Ellie May, can you collect the pills from home then drive back to the police station for about eight this evening and park your car there? Walk up Shirley Avenue opposite, as though you're going to the post box outside the Post Office, and then continue walking. I'll be parked further up the Avenue. The pills are not for me, I promise."

"Do I need my ski pants and flat shoes?"

"No. But you can pack a toothbrush if you like!"

Martin spent the next hour making phone calls and shopping. As he made his purchases, he thought about Ellie May and the relationship that was developing. Ellie was not Eileen. There were no thoughts of the long term, a permanent situation. When he had first known her, his actions on her behalf had been protective. Her youthfulness, her colour, her diminutive size had all made her appear vulnerable. Their friendship had developed to almost an older brother and younger sister relationship though, grinning to himself, he wondered whether perhaps she had viewed it more as a father-daughter situation. But now she had grown up and the difference in their ages seemed less important. Certainly he had no wish to hurt her in any way and he found himself having second thoughts about the evening to come. What did she really feel for him? The look in her eyes and the tone of her voice indicated an affection over and above the sexual chemistry, which was not just obvious but blatant between them. He hope that was the extent of Ellie's feelings though, uneasily, he guessed there might be more.

Shopping completed, Martin reached the Southampton Motor Auction in time to catch the last of the modern cars being offered that day. A quick look at what was left, followed by ten minutes in the sales hall, and he was the owner of a dark blue Ford Escort which looked in good condition despite the high mileage declared. Bill Creighton arrived half an hour later and, between them, they ferried the Escort to Winn Road off The Avenue, where an old friend had a garage. Martin had arranged to use the garage for a few days, although he personally thought it might be a few weeks.

8.05 p.m.

Reversing her car into a spare slot behind the police station, Ellie May sat for a few moments checking her face and hair in the mirror, thinking of the evening with Martin. She was excited! She felt slightly breathless at the thought of the hours to come. Martin had been a special person in her life all those years ago. Not a lover then. But in the last year or so of that relationship, a potential one in her mind. Then his sister had died and he had left 'the job' to become divorced from the police life and personalities, whilst he built his business. She had heard of him from time to time and seen him on a couple of occasions but her own life had gone on. There was her first serious boyfriend, a white man in his mid-twenties. They became lovers and she now found herself comparing him to Martin, not at all favourably. It had not been a successful relationship and they had parted after some months. Then she had met her present husband, a Jamaican with a reputation as a ladies' man. He was good looking with a dominant personality. He had quickly won her over. She thought that her influence would alter him but, once married, she quickly realized that his life style and reputation meant more to him than she did. There was a procession of other 'ladies' and increasing reluctance on his part to observe the norms of married life.

Now Martin was back, but she was not sure for how long. His re-appearance had been opportune, again providing support when she most needed it, and a diversion from the grim life that marriage had turned into. She now hoped that, even if he did leave again, there would be more to their relationship this time. Tonight was the culmination of these latest hopes and feelings. She felt confidence in a way that her previous lover and present husband had never imparted. Whatever happened tonight, she knew instinctively that Martin would be good for her. Her limited experience with men had not proved very satisfactory and she wondered what it would be like with him.

A last look in the mirror and she slipped out of the driving seat, locked the door and, holding her short jacket protectively across her breast, hurried towards the side gate and Shirley Avenue.

8.15 p.m.

Parked in the Porsche, facing away from the police station, Martin saw the petite figure of Ellie May in his rearview mirror. She carried a large shoulder bag. Her other hand was clutching her jacket to her. He reached across the inside of the car and released the passenger door. Ellie May sat on the seat of the low slung car and, swinging her legs into the footwell, reached towards him. White teeth gleamed in a welcoming smile. There was warmth in the brown eyes, a flush beneath the dark honey of her cheeks. Their lips met in a lingering 'hello' kiss.

Still kissing and with slim brown fingers caressing the back of his neck, Martin felt immediate arousal. Instead of reaching for the door pull, his hand disappeared inside the open front of the short jacket that she was wearing. The contact made through thin silky material was a firm rounded breast and prominent nipple, quite obviously free and unsupported beneath the dress.

"Oh, Ellie!" as his hand lingered, exploring, fingertips caressing.

Abruptly he straightened up, pulled the door closed, turned the ignition key and, as the engine caught, slid into first gear to accelerate with a squeal of protest from the rear tyres.

"Put your seatbelt on," he ordered.

"And prepare for take off," she giggled.

Martin grinned and headed for Winchester Road, where he turned south.

"Where are we going?"

"I've booked a room at the Coach House Motel at Ferndown," he told her. We should be well out of the area where you're known."

"Marty, would you please slow down. Driving fast makes me nervous. Besides I'm already breathless."

He glanced at her and saw that she was holding hard to the grab handle and obediently eased his foot off the accelerator. "Letting my eagerness take over." He reached and squeezed her other hand.

141

As Martin and Ellie May headed west on the A35, a Citroen ZX saloon turned off of the forest road opposite the Beaulieu Road Hotel and slowly followed the rough track to the farm that Martin had visited earlier. The car stopped in front of the bungalow and Liam Mahoney got out to be met by David Watson.

Again Watson held out his hand saying, "Mr Mahoney, I'm sure."

"How're you sure?"

"You're the second person to arrive for accommodation today. I thought the last one was you and I was wrong. I phoned Gordon Wilson and he described you quite accurately so that there would be no more mistakes. He was concerned about the first man. He thought it was odd. Said to tell you about it."

8 35 p.m.

At the Coach House Motel, Martin drove straight into the rear parking area and left Ellie May in the car whilst he booked in and collected their room key. Returning to the car, he lifted a large soft bag from the rear seats, held his hand out to Ellie and led her up the external staircase to their numbered room.

Inside, she crossed the room looking about her as he set the bag down. She turned towards him and he said, "Ellie, would you like a drink or are you hungry? There's a reasonable pub next door. They do food."

She had slipped the jacket from her shoulders and, as she walked back towards him, a mischievous little smile appeared when she saw the direction of his gaze. She deliberately strutted the last few paces, the thin silky material emphasising the jiggle that drew his eyes.

"Yes, I'm hungry, Marty, but not for food," slipping into his arms.

They kissed gently and then again, more urgently. Breaking after a few seconds he said, "I've something for you." Reaching into the soft bag at his feet he produced a package, prettily gift wrapped. She tore the wrappings off as he busied himself with a bottle of cold champagne, also from the bag.

"Oh, Marty!" with obvious delight, holding the cream silk and lace shortie nightdress up to her chin and then giggling as she found the tiniest of silk panties that went with it.

Then, in a husky voice, "I guess you like looking at pretty packages." And scampered into the bathroom.

Martin uncorked the bottle, cursed as he dropped one of the two glasses brought with it, breaking the stem from the bowl. Ellie May had not reappeared so he slipped off his top clothes, poured a glass of champagne and tried, unsuccessfully, to relax on the large double bed. The door to the bathroom opened and Ellie May stepped out.

"We're going to have to share…" Martin's voice trailed away as an absolute vision walked towards the bed, stopped in the centre of the room, did a pirouette and waited, hands clasped in front and eyes demurely downcast. Thin shoulder straps held the frothy concoction in place on wide smooth brown shoulders. Dark nipples extended the silk bodice. Below a lacy hem, slim brown legs seemed to go on and on, whilst at the top of them a tiny triangle of silk was just visible, not quite hiding the dark curls beneath.

"Ellie May, you look fantastic!"

"I can see that I'm pleasing my Lord and Master," she murmured, eyeing his briefs.

She ran to the side of the bed and, as he reached for her, rolled into his arms. Showering her face with kisses, he slipped his hand beneath the silk nightie to her naked breasts. He found himself breathless as his hand moved from one to the other caressing, but hampered by the nightie caught under her.

"Do you want it off?"

"Sweet Ellie, the whole point of buying it was the pleasure of taking it off!" She sat up and pulled the nightie over her head then, as he said, "Don't move!" held that position, her arms raised, chin tilted upwards, perfect breasts poised, stubby dark nipples erect, on a wide chest that tapered to a slim waist where the tiny panties only served to emphasise the sweep of her hips, the sensuous bulge at the junction of smooth brown thighs. She lowered her arms to lay at his side again. Martin slid his right hand slowly up the length of her thigh, from knee to the tiny panties, marvelling at the skin's satiny smoothness. His fingers confirmed what his eyes had suggested; the silky vee was warmly damp. As her legs fell apart for him, with the lightest of fingertips, he traced outlines beneath the tightly drawn material. She closed her eyes and shuddered. His hands went to the waistband of her panties and she lifted her hips as he started to ease them down. It was difficult. Full, deeply curved cheeks, coupled with the swell of her hips, resisted removal. He guessed now why it had taken her so long in the bathroom.

She giggled in her husky way and said, "That's the problem with my 'too big' bottom."

"You know what I think about your gorgeous derrière, so don't expect me to agree."

As the panties slipped over her ankles, he raised himself, removing his briefs to kneel between her legs.

"Marty, may I see you?"

"Of course," and, still kneeling, he moved to straddle her waist.

She raised on elbows, then murmured "You're a big man!"

Moving back between long slim legs he paused for a moment, taking in the erotic contrast in colour. Coffee and cream came to mind. He saw the little pulse beating at her throat, the tremble of nipples as she settled, the neat mass of tight curls and, as he leant forward to kiss again the full lips, the firm pectoral muscles, the soft breasts, her dimpled belly, he inhaled expensive perfume and the scent of an aroused woman. His lips and tongue sought and found satiny skin, exciting folds and secret places. Ellie breathed deeply, raggedly her hips bucking gently.

"He leant forward, lips and tongue caressing the slim neck and tiny ears, then whispering, "All the better to love you with!"

"Oh....you…you....please!"

Kneeling upright again, he lifted with hands beneath the curve of her buttocks, supporting them on his thighs. Ellie tensed in anticipation of his weight on her diminutive frame, as had been her experience, but it did not come. He remained kneeling and then moved her right hand down to guide. He moved gently, seeing her eyes widen and then close as her lips parted in an intake of breath She responded and, as their passion grew, Martin knew an intensity of sensation which threatened to overwhelm.

"Ellie, lay still for a moment, I want to last for you!"

Again surprise, her experience had been brief acts of selfish lovemaking by men intent upon their own gratification. Expectantly she waited, knowing now that this was special, that this man who had always been – to her – different from other men in the conventions of life, was again different, but in such a delightful way.

Seconds passed as he regained control and the tempo of their lust resumed. Ellie May gloried in the depth, the fullness of their union. Minutes passed and she surrendered to the sensual rhythm of their passion. She had reached the level that she had previously known and expected no more.

"You come, Marty, don't wait for me."

"There's no hurry, sweet Ellie. We have all night."

The note of resignation in her voice spoke of previous disappointments. Martin brought skilful fingertips into play and was soon rewarded with her responses. A new height of ecstasy filled her. It was as if an erotic charge was building, centred on his fingers and that part of her body. It built and built; sensations only previously implied took over. Her body arched and stiffened. Then she cried out in a little voice which trailed away. He felt convulsive shudders diminish to uncontrolled twitches as tears trickled from the corners of her eyes.

As he leant to kiss away the wetness she whispered, "Oh Marty, Marty, that was wonderful." Then with concern, "But you didn't come at all, did you?"

"I became a Tantric years ago…" and, on seeing the puzzlement in her eyes "…I'll tell you about it one day, but that's not important, you did and it was wonderful that you did it so beautifully!"

"Tell you a secret."

"Yes?"

"That's the first time for me"

"The first time that you climaxed?"

"Yes."

"Oh, you poor darling! Why?"

"I don't know, I never have. Perhaps it's because my man has never lasted for me. But I'm not a 'poor darling' any longer!"

*

Later they showered together, soaping each other. He marvelled again as, now wet, her skin seemed to change colour, becoming much darker. Inevitably the soapy slippery curves beneath his hands had their effect. She giggled as, bending to retrieve the soap she felt him hardening again, against the cleft of her bottom.

"No, I couldn't again, not so soon. It's been a long time, and you're a big man!" She turned to face him and, standing on tiptoes, pulled his head down to kiss him on the lips. Leaning back and looking questioningly into his eyes, she slid slowly down his wet body until she was on one knee, still looking up at him. He said nothing but breathed out quickly as her head went down and he felt first her tongue, searching, caressing and then the soft, full lips encircling. Minutes later it was his turn to twine fingers in tight curls as she refused to release him, his turn to groan deep in his chest, shudder and, with head thrown back, face contorted, to cry out.

Even later still, curled in his lap in the big bed, with his arms around her, still with the sweetly salty taste of him on her tongue, Ellie May felt relaxed, safe, happy. But also a little sad. There were memories of her Caribbean childhood with its poverty. Her parentage had included a man of mixed race, hence the milk chocolate coloured skin, but also the taunts that went with racism, even in her home island. Arrival in England brought no relief in that respect. The so called tolerant society was tolerant on its own terms. Hard work at school resulted in a safe job and it was partly due to Martin that she had improved her status in the work place. Marriage to one of her own colour had been a disaster instead of the delirious whirl that she had anticipated.

It was only now, with this man, in this protected position, with muscular thighs beneath her legs, strong arms around her chest and his warm breath on her neck that, for the first time, she had known the real ecstasy of love making. As she drifted into sleep, she smiled a sad smile and determined to make the most of the present. For he would leave again, as he had before. Though he was gentle, kind and passionate, he was also at times distant and in a world of his own, which she knew that she could not enter. Instinctively she knew that the feelings that he had for her, though considerate and generous, were not as he had had for Eileen, the white lover of his recent past. She wriggled her bottom into him, deriving sensuous pleasure as sleep enveloped her. Her last conscious thought was that there was still the morning together, and who knew after that?

Friday 12th June 1992
10.10 a.m. The Channel Isles

The islands appeared through the haze one by one, first the elongated shape of Alderney, visible behind the wing, out of the starboard windows, then on the port side the more triangular shape of Guernsey, whilst Jersey was a low line on the horizon beyond. From one thousand feet, the off-lying reefs around Herm and Sark could be seen in the clear blue water with occasional white triangles of sail or feathery white wakes from power boats making an early start to the weekend.

The British Airways jet banked to port, lined up the runway, landed smoothly and taxied to the small terminal building at Guernsey Airport. It was on time. The Channel Island skies were blue. Barry would he waiting with his BMW to chauffeur them to the boat, which would be spick and span, ready for its owner to step aboard. Dermott Mabbett enjoyed the trappings of wealth and especially the fact that such wealth brought with it the personal attention of people who benefited from it. It was at times like this that Dermott Mabbett was nice to know and his greeting to the short, heavily muscled man who waited for them in the terminal building was jovial.

"Hello Barry. I see that you've laid on the sunshine for us again!"

"Good morning, Mr Mabbett, Mrs Hadley. I think you brought it with you. We had mist first thing." The steady blue eyes that regarded Mabbett and Ann Hadley gave nothing away. He was a quiet watchful man whose business was boats, nothing else.

"Everything OK on *Spirit*?"

"Yes, the boat's fine. We've gone right through her, checked everything and fueled her up. She's ready to go when you are."

"What about the provisions?"

"I've got one of the lads finishing your list off now. Should all be on board by the time that we get there."

The drive to Beaucette Yacht Harbour was slow on the island's narrow roads, but within half an hour they were down on the wooden pontoons that provided floating parking lots for the dozens of yachts and small boats. The sheltered harbour was within what had been an old quarry, before someone had the bright idea of blasting an opening through to the nearby sea and forming what now, on first sight, might be thought to be a natural feature.

The *Spirit of Ecstasy* was a forty-five foot Nelson motor cruiser, powered by twin Cummins diesel engines. She could maintain twenty knots in almost any sea conditions short of a full gale. The hull which the boat was based on was identical with pilot boats and 'go anywhere' work boats, which relied on their sea keeping abilities to do a job of work under the most arduous conditions. Fitted out by Seaward Marine, a small local company with a big reputation, she had cost Mabbett a quarter of a million sterling some three years previously.

Much of the money, routed from his nightclubs, but not through the Company books, had ended up in a Channel Islands bank account with a Channel Islands Charter Company as the apparent beneficiary. The company had a managing director and a secretary as required by law. They were local people with no apparent contact outside the island. In the three years since the boat had been launched, she had been chartered on half a dozen occasions, just enough to cover the running costs. All other sailings had been under Mabbett's control and purely for his pleasure or business.

As always, when he reached the boat he paused to stand and admire the classic dark blue hull and white superstructure. Doing so gave his ego a polish, with the knowledge that this was all his, and had cost him virtually nothing where legally gained wealth was concerned. The boat's name, in gold lettering on stained teak, was apt and, once again, brought a mirthless grin to a face that was handsome on the outside but hid an exceedingly ugly soul.

11.45 a.m.

Some two hundred miles to the north, in Bristol Royal Infirmary, Friday the 12th June was much the same as any other to Pauline and Ron Emery. They had 'enjoyed' a night of broken sleep, risen early, avoided breakfast, driven to the hospital and sat for what was now a routine period by the bedside of their only son. Jason, at sixteen years of age was a tall, good-looking boy, outgoing and friendly with a circle of other boys and girls from ordinary families. He was doing well towards his 'A' levels and was popular with his teachers.

His life and theirs had changed totally in the previous week when he had been found amid the empty drink cans, fast food wrappers and other street detritus of our environmentally enlightened age. He had collapsed outside a fire escape door of the Bristol nightclub, operated by Lowland Leisure, that he and his friends sometimes frequented. Thrown out by bouncers acting as door supervisors, who did nothing to help. It was at first thought that he was drunk but police attention quickly turned to concern. The ambulance delivered him to Casualty where, after tests, he was diagnosed as an 'Ecstasy' case. One of the occasional but increasing number who react badly to a drug whose manufacture was frequently of dubious quality, whose distribution and supply were illegal and whose after effects, as in his case, could be catastrophic. His body temperature had gone out of control, he went quickly from semi-conscious to coma and his internal organs were now giving up one by one.

The mass of drips, pipes and needles invading his body. The monitoring by a battery of sophisticated instruments. The continuous attentions of highly qualified medical staff. The presence and prayers of his parents were all to no avail.

As the twin diesels on *Spirit of Ecstasy* roared into life, settling into an even beat, the overloaded heart of Jason Emery, a young innocent, whose only fault was to succumb to the peer pressure of friends, faltered and gave up. The high-pitched call of the intensive care monitors was echoed by a similar cry from Pauline as she collapsed into her husband's arms. The rush of medics with their crash trolleys was to no avail. Another young person had contributed to Dermott Mabbett's sailing pleasures.

3.50 p.m. Christchurch

Neither Gordon Wilson nor Liam Mahoney were happy. They had spent the best part of the day searching boat yards, marinas and river banks on the Avon and Stour rivers at Christchurch, with not a smell of the small white-hulled sailing boat named *Truly Fair*. Wilson's source had been positive. Martin Wild had a boat on a river mooring just below the sailing club, which he had slept on regularly over the last month or so. He had been seen rowing to and from the boat on occasions, though he had not sailed it from the mooring in recent weeks. Liam Mahoney was not impressed with the results of their efforts so far and that fact was very evident.

In the late afternoon, after Mahoney had boarded the local ferry to broaden the search and check out boats further downstream, Wilson spoke again with his informant, who had no explanation other than that the boat must have left in the last two days. At a short-tempered meeting in the Priory Café, they decided that if they couldn't find the boat, Mahoney would have to start staking out Wild's office. The information in this respect was even less optimistic as only Wild's secretary was there regularly. Wild himself visited rarely now. The office was, in fact, only a pair of rooms in a shared suite, which was vacated every night. Wild was proving to be an elusive character and Wilson couldn't afford to be too open in the search. He would have to leave it to Mahoney who was using a different identity and was adept at vanishing, at short notice, when necessary.

11.30 p.m. The New Forest

It took Martin twenty-five minutes to cover the fifty or so yards. He started, cautiously, from the edge of the wood surrounding the farm at Beaulieu Road, and ended up at a position just inside the treeline, close to the wooden bungalow. His quiet navigation through the dark of the undergrowth and trees had been aided by a low light monocular, an expensive piece of kit bought for his security business but with thoughts of night-time sailing also in mind. Now it was earning its keep in a manner not anticipated.

Outside the bungalow, a car was parked close to the front door. It had to be that belonging to Mahoney. Martin's approach had been slow and careful to avoid disturbing the furry monster. The dog was not visible and he wondered whether his extreme care had been necessary. Perhaps the owner had the dog in the house where, although it was nearly midnight, the lights were still on in the kitchen, as well as the main ground floor rooms.

Kneeling at the base of a large tree, Martin extracted from opposing pockets a catapult and a plastic bag. From the bag he took what looked like a small ball of meat. It was fillet steak, carefully sewn up and with one of Ellie May's Valium pills inside. Placing it in the sling of the catapult, he took careful aim and launched the steak and Valium sandwich towards the kennel. The immediate reward was a commotion of barking and rattling as the brindle-haired monster exited the kennel to the full extent of its chain. It stood straining at its leash and looking directly towards him, barking ferociously.

Martin froze in the undergrowth, hidden he hoped by the bulk of the tree, and taken aback by the result of the catapult's soft thwack on releasing the missile. The door to the cottage opened and sandy-haired Watson appeared, calling out to the dog to be quiet. Next the lights came on in the bungalow, the door opened and a lean male figure appeared, naked above the waist and with trousers still being zipped up.

This man was in silhouette, features not visible, but Martin felt a curious crawling sensation on the nape of his neck when a hard voice called out questioning the noise. With the strong Irish accent, it had to be Mahoney.

"Not to worry, it's probably deer that he heard. We get a lot of them after dark. I'll take him for a walk round shortly. That will scare them away for the rest of the night."

Both men disappeared back into their respective doorways, although the door to the main house was left open, as though the walking of the dog was imminent.

Martin had the premonition that this little expedition was on the verge of disaster. He was torn between two desires. To feed the hairy brute with the remaining medicine balls or to turn and run from what appeared to be an aggressive animal with a large mouth full of pointed teeth. It probably weighed a hell of a lot when launched at one's throat. The prospect of imminent exposure to the dog on being released from its chains made his planned actions urgent. Quickly now he produced more steak and Valium balls and proceeded to aim them one by one at the ground in front of the kennel. The dog barked first in his direction and then at the bushes behind his kennel. Martin adjusted the trajectory, suspecting that his second and third bombs had gone beyond the aiming point. He was rewarded with the dog's attention being immediately drawn to the front of the kennel and then some sniffing at the ground interposed with barking. In the light and at that distance it was impossible to see whether the dog had eaten the sandwich but Martin felt certain that he had scored at least two more "area hits" before he ran out of ammunition.

Quickly but quietly he moved back through the trees and was about twenty metres into thicker cover when he heard a door open and close and the Irish voice speaking. He could no longer hear the words but, through a gap, could see that both men were now dressed. It was evident that the search was going to be quicker and more thorough than he wanted. If he moved more quickly himself, there was a great risk that the noise would almost certainly attract the attention of the dog, Valium or no.

Through the monocular, he could see that, some ten metres further on, there was a ditch which he had crossed on a convenient fallen tree during his way in. He remembered that, another ten metres along the far bank of the ditch, there was a tall old Scots Pine, whose roots had lost their hold on the disturbed ground and which was leaning at an angle against another tree.

As quietly and quickly as possible, he made his way to the ditch and then down into the water. A few inches of muddy liquid covered a foot of boot-sucking loose mud and dead leaves. The next ten metres were difficult. The mud clung and water gurgled softly but eventually he was at the foot of the pine.

Voices were now approaching from the direction of the farm and the light of a torch played on the ground. Reaching up he grasped the first branches of the pine and hauled himself out of the ditch and into the lower limbs of the tree. He was just congratulating himself when a branch that he was using to get even higher, cracked under his weight. It didn't give but the voices stopped and the dog which had been quiet, barked and then growled as it was shushed.

For a space of several seconds there was silence and then the noise of feet and bodies pushing through the surrounding bushes with the beam from the torch getting stronger.

Martin froze trying to control the ragged breath that his exertions had caused. For several seconds the sounds became louder until he anticipated that the searchers were only a few metres away. There was another pause and then voices again.

The hard Irish brogue, "Will you not let that dog go?"

"No, I tell you if he scents a deer he will be gone for the rest of the night."

Snuffling noises and the sound of leaves being tossed brought a mental picture to Martin's mind and he forced himself to be still and combat the desire to climb frantically higher.

"It's as dark as a peat bog in here," the Irish voice said.

"There can only be animals about," from Watson. "No one could have moved through these trees and over that ditch without a torch and we would have seen that."

The conversation ceased as they moved again, with the torch sweeping the ground around them. Martin remained motionless, thankful of his black clothing and balaclava. The voices moved to his right, altered course again and seemed to be following the bank bordering the ditch away from him.

Three minutes later, he could still hear distant noises but they were getting fainter. Moving carefully, he climbed even higher in the tree until he reached a point where it was leaning against its neighbour. Here he made himself as comfortable as he could and settled down to wait.

At 2 a.m. he climbed stiffly out of the pine and again quietly made his way towards the farm bungalow. All lights were now out. On the edge of the clearing he catapulted a small stone against the wood of the dog kennel. No response. He stood absolutely still for ten minutes. There was no sound other than an owl calling and night-time rustlings in the undergrowth.

On his stomach he moved slowly and silently from the dark shelter of the tree belt across the mossy grass to the parked car. The bonnet was towards the bungalow. Keeping it between himself and the building, he wriggled towards the rear and pulled himself under the boot area. Above him was the spare wheel suspended from its mounting.

"Now this is very convenient, Mr Mahoney," he muttered.

For several minutes, he worked with a small package, tape and a knife to complete his objective before wriggling back into the tree line, to disappear amongst the shadows.

Saturday 13th June 1992
11.15 a.m. Shirley Police Station

"A lot of the information that you left with me checks out." It hurt Potter to say so. He would much rather have received information from another source, any other source Martin thought. "But there's not much we can use as evidence."

"I'm aware of that, that's the reason I'm now stepping backwards. I don't want to muddy the water for your team any more than I've done already. Have you found Mabbett and Wilson?"

"We've confirmed that Mabbett's boat left Guernsey yesterday. Unfortunately we don't know where for. Wilson and his wife are still at Cadnam, but information from the local area officer is that papers have been cancelled, milk deliveries stopped, that sort of thing, so it looks as though they are leaving as well."

"According to the tape that I gave you, they will be joining Mabbett at Dinard, on the opposite side of the Rance estuary to St Malo tomorrow. That's where Mabbett is headed now I should think," said Martin. "The good news is that I can tell you where Liam Mahoney is at this moment and, if you're prepared to indulge me just a little, you might get a 'situation' that's useful to you."

Potter hesitated only a moment. "What do you want?"

"Mahoney is staying at Blackwood Farm near the Beaulieu Road Hotel but not under his own name. He's using a bungalow at the farm as a base while he's looking for me. He using a Citroen ZX saloon. Here's the registration number." Martin pushed a sheet across the table which contained details of the vehicle and a sketch map. "You'll see on the sketch that the B3056 is a straight road on both sides of Beaulieu Road Station for a couple of miles, then there are bends. "What I would suggest is that, tomorrow morning, you put a traffic check beyond the bend at Calverley Farm on the Beaulieu road, a routine stop and check job. When Mahoney appears, give his car a good going over. You may well find things of interest to you that will give you the opportunity to pull him in for questioning. If you'll take my advice, you'd better have an armed response unit nearby."

"What makes you think that's necessary? How do we know that he will take that route?"

"The indications in there..." Martin nodded towards the cassette on the desk, "are that Mahoney is Mabbett's axeman, responsible for both Eileen's and Ewen's deaths. My guess is that he could well be armed and that road at Beaulieu is a lonely spot. Leave the route to me. If I'm wrong about that, you'll still be able to pick him up at the farm. You'll need to have at least one of your murder team there. If it's someone who knows his local contact Gordon Wilson, that might be helpful. Wilson is Mahoney's controller whilst he's in this area."

Potter looked undecided and Martin knew what was going through his mind. To obtain permission to mount an armed roadblock meant that he would have to extend his neck a little. Potter had made a career out of not exposing himself to censure. Additionally, the cost of that manpower and of divorcing people from his own team would bring a frown to the faces of those whose job it was to prune budgets.

"Look," Martin said, "you already know that most of what I've given you checks out and you'll find that the remainder will as well. If I've been right so far, why should I suddenly be wrong now? If you can pin this man down whilst his boss is out of the country, you'll have an opportunity which may not present itself again. Just think what the forensic boys might find to tie him in to your job and possibly the Glasgow one! If you can pick him up and hold him for a couple of days without Mabbett knowing, then you've the opportunity of perhaps bagging two or three of these bastards!"

"OK," said Potter. "I'll see what we can do."

"I'll get onto my end of this and make sure that Mahoney takes the Beaulieu Road."

As Martin was escorted from Potter's office, the latter lifted the telephone and spoke with his Admin. Officer on the Murder Team.

"Locate Bill Creighton for me and ask him to get on the phone ASAP."

Twenty minutes later the Detective Chief Inspector was speaking, with Martin's friend.

"Bill, you were providing information about Gordon Wilson at the briefing the other day. How well do you know his friends and acquaintances?"

A suitably advised Detective Constable Creighton proceeded to detail a number of people, one of whom happened to be an antique dealer who occupied the farm at Beaulieu Road. Within a matter of seconds he was instructed to attend the Chief Inspector's office without delay.

1.10 p.m.

A breathless Ellie May jointed Martin in the Porsche halfway up Shirley Avenue, to be whisked away for a lunchtime sandwich.

"I only have thirty minutes, Marty. Potter is pressing all his buttons today. What did you say to him this morning?"

"Don't worry about that, Ellie. More importantly, I need you to do me a favour around five this afternoon. Is that possible?"

'What is it? I'll probably be leaving work then."

Martin told her what he needed and arranged to meet her again at a few minutes after five. He then made a telephone call.

"Is that the Buckler's Hard Harbour Master's office?"

"Yes."

"Can you find room for a twenty-five footer tonight?"

The answer was in the affirmative and Martin gave details of his boat with no intention of doing what he was stating. "I might be late arriving, what number mooring should I look for?"

5.05 p.m.

The telephone rang in Gordon Wilson's farmhouse at Cadnam. Wilson was out and his wife answered it.

"Mr Wilson, please." The voice was husky, female and with a trace of an accent, which sounded foreign.

Rachel Wilson knew her husband's proclivities and was immediately curious. "He's not in. Who wants him?"

There was silence for a few seconds and she wondered if a hand had been put over the mouthpiece, then, "We're just closing the office. Would you give him a message please. He was enquiring in Christchurch about a particular boat the other day. Would you tell him that we've heard that *Truly Fair* is expected at Bucklers Hard on the Beaulieu late tonight."

The caller rang off before Wilson's wife could speak again.

Twenty minutes later, Wilson arrived home and she told him of the call. He frowned. "Who was the call from?"

"Didn't give me time to ask. It was just after five. It sounded like an office girl who couldn't get away quickly enough."

"We didn't talk to any offices. Suppose it could have been the Sailing Club. We spoke to a couple of people there."

He thought for a few seconds, shrugged his shoulders and went into his office to use the private line.

"Liam, I've just been told that Wild's boat is due at a place called Bucklers Hard at some time tonight. That's a small harbour on the Beaulieu River between Beaulieu and the coast. The office there will be closed by now and Rachel and I leave first thing tomorrow to join DM. I don't know how whoever it was knew to contact me or got my phone number. Check it out but tread carefully. You'll have to contact DM on the boat at Dinard if there's anything immediate, and he will phone you back in the usual way. Make a point of phoning him at about this time tomorrow for an update." Wilson gave Mahoney directions to the small marina at Bucklers Hard and again urged caution.

11.10 p.m. Glasgow

Shadows front of house was just starting to warm up when Andrew McAinsh was summoned from his usual early evening position on the front door to take a call from Dermott Mabbett. The call was a routine of checking the business, how busy the club was, promotions offered, opposition activity, visits by the police and the dozens of other points of information that are normally monitored by a nightclub owner who knows how to stay ahead of the game.

When immediate business was out of the way, McAinsh said, "I've had our friend Cameron in tonight. He's been making himself useful again. This Martin Wild has been on the phone to Glasgow CID. Seems he's coming up to Handsford's funeral on Monday. It's being held at Callander, where Handsford's family are. He's also got a description of the man. Cameron told his police mate that he was looking for contacts for his security business."

"Damn, and I've got Liam looking for the man down south. I can't contact him until tomorrow afternoon and that's too tight for him to get back to Scotland."

Silence for some seconds and then, "Andy, get in touch with Mick Docherty. You'll probably find him at the place he uses in Finnieston. If you've got a problem, ask Neil Fisher to speak with his lads, but only do that as a last resort. It you can find him, see whether he might be for it. Go to 20k if necessary."

"DM – he's a dangerous man. I wouldna want to trust him with a job like this."

"Leave that worry to me, Andy. Give him half on account and we'll have Liam back with us when he arrives to collect the rest!"

*

As this conversation was taking place, Martin Wild's mobile rang. As usual with mobiles, the timing was bad. He hesitated, debating whether to ignore it.

Ellie May whispered, "If you stop for that damned thing I'll turn my back on you." Her eyes glinted wickedly in the light from the bedside lamp.

He smiled down at her and, reaching with a long arm, was just able to pull the trousers that the phone was belted to, within reach.

"Wild."

"Marty, sorry to ring so late. Hope I haven't disturbed you?" He recognised John Mann's voice.

"Your timing's bloody awful as usual, John." Martin moved gently to keep the fire glowing.

"I've just been watching the late news. Thought you would want to know.

You remember Ron Emery? He and his wife were at the exhibition that we went to last year. He was working with handicapped children and you had a long chat with him about a sailing dinghy that he was building for his son. You sent the youngster a compass or something."

Martin remembered the young couple whom John had known through their joint interests. He had a clearer impression of the son, whom he had met very briefly. A handsome, bright and active lad, full of enthusiasm for the sea and boats. He had given John an old but serviceable hand bearing compass to pass on to…what was his name? Jason. That was the boy's name.

"Yes, John, I remember." Ellie May stirred impatiently.

"It's on the local news. Jason died in the BRI yesterday. He'd taken Ecstasy at the Bristol Shadows club."

Martin was silent, then, "What a damned waste." He felt himself shrink in more senses than one. "John, add my name to your card or flowers will you? I'll square up when we meet."

"Just thought you'd want to know, Marty."

"Yes. Thanks John." He pressed the Finish button.

"What is it, Marty?" as he moved to lay beside her.

He told her quietly and lay thinking of a youthful life ended, just as Susan's had, five years ago.

Sunday 14th June 1992
9.50 a.m. Beaulieu, Hampshire

Liam Mahoney stood to one side of his hire car, where the officer had led him. Hands in trouser pockets, cigarette drooping from a corner of the mouth, pose casual. The eyes, narrowed against the early morning sun, were watchful, but he wasn't worried. The car hadn't been used for anything, it was clean. These English Pigs doing roadside checks on a Sunday morning. Had they nothing better to do?

"And where were you going in such a hurry on a Sunday, Mr Dunhill?"

"No hurry. Out for a drive. I'm on holiday. Thought I'd have a look around before it got too busy with the other visitors."

The one talking to him was a uniformed sergeant. A constable was working his way around the Citroen, looking at the tax disc, checking tread depth, feeling the play in the road wheels and steering.

There were two police cars parked on the verge a few yards away. One was a van, which he assumed was that driven by the two who were with him. The second was a saloon, which contained three men. He could see that the two in the front were in uniform but the car bore no police markings.

Why were these three still in their car and not out stopping the other, occasional, passing traffic? Gossiping, he thought. Out here to do a job but too lazy to stay on their feet. Why didn't they stop pissballing about? He felt anger growing inside him. He had his own priorities, which didn't include a stop check by the police. The last thing that he wanted, today of all days, was interest by the English Pigs.

"You say you don't have your driving licence on you, Mr Dunhill. We'll need to have it produced within five days. Where would suit you best?"

As he was considering the question, the man sitting in the rear seat of the saloon opened the door and got out. Mahoney, stiffened and then forced himself to relax. The man was short for a policeman but stocky, and he was in plain clothes! Suddenly Mahoney was less at ease. Why a plainclothes man and why an unmarked car at a stop and check? Another movement from the car caught his eye. The front passenger side door was just open – had been all along, he realized. He saw now that the policeman on that side of the car, which was blind to him, was in fact sitting sideways, probably with his feet out of the door.

What Mahoney could not see was that the officer was cradling a Heckler & Koch carbine across his knees, with his thumb on the safety. The briefing that morning had emphasised that this stop and check would be specific to one car and person and that the driver of the car was suspected of murder and might well be armed. Their 'Plan A' covered the possibility that the man might at some stage produce a weapon. In which case, the uniform sergeant – the only one near him – was to throw himself to the ground, away from Mahoney. The armed officer would simply stand and cover the "target" with the very efficient and accurate Heckler & Koch, whilst the driver would provide back up with his Browning 9mm, which was between his knees on the seat.

Bill Creighton walked to the constable, who was just straightening up from the last of the road wheels, and said, "Have a look at the spare as well, Andy."

The constable nodded, went to the driver's seat, removed the ignition key, opened the boot and started lowering the spare wheel, suspended in a bracket beneath the car. He wound the bracket down and slid the wheel out with a heave and a grunt.

Bill Creighton took one look, wheeled and walked to Mahoney and the sergeant. As he reached them, he nodded to the sergeant who, immediately joined Bill in "Plan B". He seized Mahoney's nearest arm whilst Bill took the other. The armed officer came out of the police car like a jack in the box, his weapon levelled across the roof of the vehicle. His body was shielded by it. The driver slid out of his seat with the Browning pistol levelled.

"On the ground!" ordered Bill as they forced a cursing Mahoney downwards. Ankles kicked apart and arms outstretched, he was thoroughly searched before being lifted to his feet and walked to the rear of the car.

Incredulously he stared at the spare wheel, or rather at the slightly misshapen stick of what looked like an odd-coloured plasticine, wrapped in remnants of brown coloured paper with black writing on it, strapped to the top rim of the wheel with black tape.

"Perhaps you would like to tell us what that is?" Bill asked softly.

"You fuckin' bastards. You're stitching me," snarled Mahoney, body taut, bent cigarette still in his mouth and the pale face now with an angry red spot on each cheekbone.

"You saw us take the wheel out. The tape is right around the wheel and that would have taken several minutes to do. You know that we didn't put it there, Mr Dunhill. No, I think that you should accompany us to the police station to, as they say, help us with our enquiries, don't you? You are of course not required…" and Bill Creighton administered the obligatory caution smoothly, and with a satisfied smile.

10.00 a.m.

As Mahoney's head was being pushed down, none too gently, to enter the police car, a BAC146 jet climbed away from Southampton, Eastleigh airport.

Inside the plane were Gordon Wilson and his wife, bound for Jersey where they would change aircraft to the small Hawker Siddeley 148 used on the Jersey to Dinan route.

Sitting two seats behind was a medium-sized man with prematurely greying hair wearing a lightweight linen suit. He closed his eyes shortly after take-off and appeared to doze. Two seats further back was another man, who studiously avoided looking at the Wilsons. They did not know it, but they had company. Whilst they were en route, they would be watched by this pair and another couple, one male and one female, who would replace the original pair. The second pair were not police but from Her Majesty's Customs and Excise, now working with Potter's murder enquiry team, being very much interested in the anticipated importation of 'suspect substances'.

11.05 a.m. Rennes, France

The office was large, impressive and brightly lit by windows, which occupied most of one wall. A second wall was lined with bookshelves, a third with maps of the police district, whilst the fourth had, in addition to the door through which they had entered, a large display cabinet filled with trophies. The room was on the top floor of the police station off the Rue Guillaudot in the French town of Rennes. A senior Agent de Police was in deep conversation with an English policeman. Inspector Dempsey had a degree in French Language and a penchant for dropping the odd French phrase when in the hearing of his peers. This had ensured that his name came to the fore when interaction was required between the Hampshire 'boys in blue' and their French counterparts. He had been appointed Liaison Officer to the murder team when it became obvious that there was a cross-channel connection. The members of the team now in France were less confident of his abilities, having spent time watching the growing expression of exasperation on the face of the Agent de Police.

Potter, on the other hand, was full of cheer. He had just received a telephone call from Bill Creighton and was actually smiling. An event reported at a later date by another of the team and met with disbelief by those who knew their Detective Chief Inspector.

Arrangements were being made for the arrival of the Wilsons and their escort at the small airport just outside Dinan and for observations on the Wilson/Mabbett party to be coordinated between the English and French authorities.

To Potter's surprise, the French chief of police was being remarkably co-operative, content to allow the British police and French customs men to call the tune where the 'obs exercise' was concerned. He only insisted that each of the observation teams be accompanied by a middle-ranking French plainclothes Agent de Police to ensure that, as Inspector Dempsey interpreted it, his responsibilities are properly addressed, that any action is correct and sanctioned and that he has a complete report of all that occurs.

From the French point of view, this was an ongoing investigation into two British murders by nationals in Britain with, almost as an aside, the possibility that at some future date there might be the transportation of drugs within his jurisdiction. If and when that became a fact, then his officers or the French customs might have occasion to take a more active interest. In the meantime, these supposedly efficient English policemen were doing all the work so "Bon Chance".

Potter was feeling very confident. The news from Bill Creighton was excellent. Mahoney had been arrested for being in possession of suspected explosives, which gave ample reason to hold him whilst the forensic lads did their work. As predicted by Martin, and the content of the tapes he had provided, Mabbett and Wilson were respectively at, and travelling to St Malo. Handled properly, this situation might clear up the Glasgow murder as well as the Hampshire job and net a drug running team into the bargain. Potter remembered Ray Lawson's brevity and obvious disappointment at the last briefing and the Chief Constable's words during their initial meeting. With luck, he might shine sufficiently brightly to warrant consideration when the next round of promotions came up. Everyone badly wanted a 'result' in the Padgett case.

6.30 p.m. Scotland

As the various elements for good and bad busied themselves on the French side of the Channel, and Bill Creighton tried in vain to extract something – anything – from Liam Mahoney, Martin, with Robert Hardy, was en route to Callander in Scotland.

Usually their infrequent meetings were accompanied by easy conversation and casual banter. But there was none of that. The funeral and the feeling of responsibility for a death, which neither of them had anticipated, ensured lengthy silences and short replies.

As they took their seats in the British Airways Heathrow to Glasgow shuttle, Martin would have been even less at ease had he known the conversation that was then taking place between Andrew McAinsh, in the Glasgow nightclub and a short, heavily built, thickset man with pale blue eyes, a pasty complexion and very bad breath.

"Mick, Mr Mabbett wanted to talk with you, but he's out of the country just now. He wondered whether you would do a little job for him?"

"I've bin away mes'sel fur a wee while; jes' got bail las' Friday. What's it tha' he's wantin' then?" Mad Mick's voice was casual but his eyes were all over the office.

McAinsh, as uncomfortable as he always was in Michael Docherty's presence, hadn't wanted to make this meeting. The less that he saw of this particular man, the better. Mad Mick was a Govan "hard man" and a feared figure in local criminal circles. It was said by some, who were well-placed to know, that he was pathologically violent and totally unpredictable. Why Mabbett was considering using him, he couldn't understand. Now he had to make the offer and he was not at all sure of its effect on the man on the opposite side of the desk.

"We have someone who has been bothering us. We need him taking care of. Mr Mabbett thought you might be interested."

"Yur boss already has his mon fur that. Why wouldna he use him?"

"He's away doing another job for us. This one's not far from your patch and it needs looking after tomorrow. There's no time for Liam to get back, even if he had finished where he is."

"What's it worth?"

"Five."

Mad Mick glowered and got to his feet. "I dinna work for peanuts," he said unpleasantly.

"We're talking five grand, not five hundred."

He sat down again. "Who is it? Mus be a big mon fur five grand."

"No, he's not. Just a Sassanach who's poked his nose in where it's not wanted."

"Yuh want 'im in thu hospital?"

"We'd prefer him on a slab."

"Fur five grand – yuh mus be jockin'!"

"Mick, it's an easy one. There's no connection. The Busies wouldn't know where to start. You're not with us, it's not close to home and you're not connected to the Sassanach!"

"It's still no' enough."

For several minutes the two argued over the price of a life as they might a secondhand car, before coming to an agreement which pleased both, although they were careful not to show it. To Mad Mick the offer was opportune. There were witnesses to be dealt with in the case pending against him and a handful of money gave him an alternative approach to his usual one. His present GBH problem had been witnessed, not all of those present might be amenable to threats but cash was different. McAinsh, on the other hand, was getting the job done for considerably less than Mabbett had suggested and that would please his boss.

"Your man's name is Martin Wild. He's going to be at Callander Church for a funeral at 2 p.m. tomorrow. He'll probably be on his own." McAinsh proceeded to give an accurate description of Martin which, with the remainder of the information, had come from Cameron's police contact. The police "civvy" had thought that he was just doing a favour for an old colleague, who was trying to make contacts with others in the security business.

"It's likely that he'll stop overnight, although we're not sure of that. Half now, the other half when the job's done." He pushed an envelope over the desk top.

Monday 15th June 1992
2.00 p.m. Callander, Scotland

This time it was raining, not heavily, but the sort of spotting and occasional light drizzle that made you wonder whether you needed an umbrella or not. Neither Martin nor Robert Hardy had one, so they turned up the collars of their raincoats and ignored the dampness.

To them both it was a grey day in every way. Robert had wanted to see the club, the area, which his man had been working in. Useless though the exercise was, Martin understood his motives and spent the morning quietly driving Robert around. The grey Glasgow streets were depressing. The rain had started almost as soon as they stepped into the hire car and had not stopped since.

To Martin, this second funeral brought a mood that he had not experienced before. Not the shock and confusion that had followed Eileen's death, but a sombre guilt. Whilst the act that had taken Eileen from him could be rationalized as criminally accidental, he had put Ewen into the firing line. He was responsible more directly for the young man's death. He himself had been operating at a distance, in relative safety. Even the obvious fact that it had needed a younger person to infiltrate the organization, operate in the disco world, failed to assuage his guilt.

Inside, the small chapel was crowded. How had Ewen been this popular without those that he worked with knowing it, wondered Robert? Then, listening to the whispered conversations around, he realised that it was not the man himself, but Ewen's father who had drawn this number of people to the service. His father and the circumstances of the death. There were not many sons of a respected Provost who died violently in the small hours of the morning, whose death was the subject of a police murder investigation and whose burial was of interest to both the police and the press.

The chapel was tiny and, viewed close up, in a neglected state. It was positioned on a small peninsular of land which jutted into the ruffled waters of Loch Achray, a few miles south west of Callander. Robert and Martin wondered together why such a prominent person as Provost Hansford had not chosen the much larger church in the centre of Callander and whether the form of Ewen's death had influenced the choice of this remote and neglected building. It wasn't until the service had finished and they were all grouped around the freshly dug grave that Martin noticed older headstones with the Handsford name upon them. This must be a family burial ground covering many generations.

As the first handfuls of earth covered the coffin, Martin and Robert joined the queue of mourners waiting to speak with Ewen's parents, to express their sympathy and, in Martin's case, his desperate sorrow that Ewen had died when working for him. The warmth that had comforted Martin when speaking to Eileen's parents at her funeral was not present in Alderman Handsford's response. There was desperate hurt and, upon realising who he was speaking to, anger in the eyes and voice.

"My son was not working in what I would term a respectable or proper business. If he had used the brains that God gave him, he would not have been where he was that night. The pair of you carry a weight of guilt that I cannot help you with."

"It was Ewen's choice that he worked for my organisation," Robert interposed gently. "We do a great deal of good for people who have problems that are not of their own making."

"So you may say, but that is no consolation to either his weeping mother here or myself."

"Mr Handsford," Martin said, "perhaps I should not tell you this and I would ask you to respect the confidence, but it may be of some consolation for you and your wife to know that at this moment the police are arresting a number of men who have been involved in the importation of drugs and the death of innocent people. Ewen was largely responsible in obtaining the information that has led to those arrests. His work for Robert should not he decried."

Handsford's eyes registered surprise and his mouth opened but, before he could say anything, his wife a small gentle woman with eyes which, when not red-rimmed, would have mirrored those of her son, said, "Alex, there is a lot that Ewen did that he could not tell us about. Perhaps we should not be so hard on these gentlemen – and especially on the memory of our son."

As they left the churchyard, with Martin feeling even more depressed, he noticed a squat, heavily built man with almost shaven ginger hair standing to one side of the gateway. He was dressed in a none-too-clean fawn mac and looked out of place. His manner was more of a watcher than a mourner or participant. Martin turned as they reached their car and saw that the man was now in conversation with the priest who had carried out the service. He noticed that they were both looking in the general direction of the car that he and Robert were entering.

A comment from Robert drew his attention away from the man, whom he put down as a member of the press or a plainclothes policeman. In conversation with Detective Constable Cantrill, who he had seen at the start of the service, he had learnt that there were two Glasgow CID men at the funeral. Perhaps that was the second one.

As Robert and Martin left the chapel parking area, having to queue for a few minutes in the line of cars entering the narrow winding road, a very angry Mad Mick hurled himself into the passenger seat of a black Ford Scorpio, driven by a lean man in an even dirtier raincoat.

"Not only the wrong fuckin' church, but he's not alone," he was muttering to himself. "Wassat?" the driver said.

"Never you mind. Jus' get on thu tail of tha' blue Vauxhall Cavalier tha turnin' out o' thu gates jus' now."

The majority of the cars leaving the chapel were turning right onto the road back to Callander but Martin had turned left where the queue was much shorter, intent upon finding a pub or hotel where Robert and he could have a drink and a sandwich before catching their afternoon flight south.

The narrow winding road followed the loch and, after a short distance, they came across what seemed to be the conversion of a huge old hotel, built to resemble a castle. To the right of the road was the original building with magnificent spired turrets looking out across the loch. To the left were large excavations, portacabins and a building site. Martin slowed and pulled into the side so that he would not obstruct a black Ford Scorpio which had appeared in his near view mirror as he slowed to study the large noticeboards. These proclaimed that this was to be "Tigh Mor Trossachs", the future home of an organisation called the Holiday Property Bond.

As he idled past the building site, he realised that the Scorpio had pulled into the side of the road behind. Martin gave it no more thought and accelerated away. About half a mile further on they found another hotel but, on turning into the forecourt, saw coaches parked, indicating a busy bar and dining room.

"Let's head back towards Callander," suggested Robert. "There were a couple of likely looking pubs on this side of the town."

Martin circled the car park and, as he approached the entrance again, saw the black Scorpio driving in. In the passenger seat of the Scorpio was the ginger-haired man from the funeral.

"Looks as though the CID are looking for a nosebag as well," observed Martin. "Would have thought they'd have teamed up with local lads, wherever their regular boozer is."

Some ten minutes later they were standing in the bar of a comfortable small hotel with glasses in their hands, awaiting a plate of sandwiches ordered by Martin. On looking out of the window to the car park at the side of the building he saw, at the far end of a row of cars, a black Ford Scorpio. Thoughtfully Martin placed his glass on the bar and, murmuring to Robert, "Just going to the loo," walked to the door. In the hotel foyer talking into the handset of the pay phone was the rear view of a dirty fawn mac topped by a gingery close shaved head. Standing a few feet away, gazing out of the door, was Dirty Mac Two.

Martin made way back to the bar. "No time for explanations, Robert. We'll not wait for the sandwiches. Go out through the garden door here and straight to the car. Pick me up at the car park entrance." Martin slipped the bolts of the door and pushed it open for Robert.

As Robert made his way to their car, Martin ran, doubled over and stooping behind the line of parked cars, until he reached the Scorpio. With that car between him and the hotel windows, he quickly removed a dustcap from a wheel and jammed the valve down with a discarded matchstick. With the tyre deflating rapidly, he rejoined Robert in the hire car and said, "Sandwiches at the airport as soon as you like, Robert." There was no sign of the pair of dirty macs as they drove off.

At the airport, Martin made a phone call to Glasgow CID. DC Cantrill had not yet returned from the funeral but a colleague confirmed that the two plainclothes men were travelling in a white Vauxhall Astra.

"Well, Robert. They were not policemen and I'm not prepared to accept coincidences where this lot are concerned. Let's see if we can get onto an earlier shuttle, get you back to London and out of the firing line. I'll check with Potter and, if all has gone well with that end of the investigation, I'll drop out of sight until this is all sorted and Mabbett and Co are locked up."

They were lucky with the change of flight and, in just over an hour, were in the air heading for Heathrow.

7.30 p.m.

Back in Glasgow, an angry telephone call was taking place between Mad Mick and Andrew McAinsh. Mick felt that he had been given bum information. McAinsh was glad there was a telephone line between them and not just a desk. Putting down the receiver, he thought for a couple of moments before telephoning Dermott Mabbett's numbers in St Malo only to be frustrated again. There was no response to either the mobile or the boat's VHF set.

Had he tried Wilson's mobile number, he would have found it engaged for Wilson, Mabbett and their respective partners were in the plush surroundings of the Dinard Yacht Club, enjoying a pre-dinner drink. Wilson was tying up the final details of an exchange due to take place in two days' time. The caller was Chris Targett, the 'harder' of the two brothers who ran the haulage company that Mabbett intended using as part of his new supply route.

"There were no problems, Mr Wilson. We got your package OK and your friend got his as arranged."

"When do we see you then?"

"All being well, we'll be with you late on Wednesday."

"Good. Give me an update when you're an hour or so away. I've got another package for you to deliver, so you can make another run straight away."

Pressing the finish button, he returned to the table from the terrace where he had taken the call. Mabbett raised an eyebrow at him. Wilson nodded, "All OK."

Ann Hadleigh said, "Don't you two ever leave business behind?"

Wilson's wife laughed shortly, "Never!"

Mabbett smiled and, signalling the white-gloved waiter, said, "Another day, another dollar. We businessmen don't have the luxury of a rich auntie to pay the bills."

Wednesday 17th June 1992
10.45 p.m. Dinard, France

Gordon Wilson left the bright lights and comfort of *Ecstasy*'s cabin for the damp pitch dark of her deck. External lights were not on. Neither he nor Mabbett were keen to advertise their activities on this particular evening.

"You'll have to give me a few seconds," he said quietly. "Can't see a damned thing."

"There was a grunt of acknowledgement as Mabbett paused just behind him, also waiting for his eyes to become accustomed to the dark.

The lights of St Malo in the distance, and Dinard nearer at hand, oriented Wilson and he groped his way towards the side of the boat that was nearer the latter, locating the waiting tender by the irregular beat of its idling two-stroke.

A short angled boarding ladder had been rigged and, as he reached *Ecstasy*'s rail, he called out quietly, "All ready, Jock?" There was no reply but he swung his leg over to clamber down into the small inflatable.

Jock, the motor yacht's skipper and a longtime employee of Mabbett, was waiting, steadying the tender against the bottom of the ladder. Having found a seat in the unsteady little boat, Wilson reached up to take a large rectangular package that Mabbett was now lowering over the side. The package was wrapped in black plastic and securely sealed, making it quite waterproof. Wilson braced his feet against the sides of the tender and cradled the package on his knees as Jock caught the mooring rope dropped by Mabbett and then opened the outboard's throttle.

The trip to the Dinard club jetty was uncomfortable. Despite the sheltered position in the harbour, there was a short chop on the water and Wilson, whose idea of sailing was lounging in the sun on the upholstery of something not less than forty foot long with a cold drink in hand, was pleased to step onto dry land. Waiting for Jock to secure the dinghy, he reflected on the recent discussion with Mabbett and the job that he now had to do.

The package contained an oil painting, which, with two other old masters, had been "liberated" some months before from a West Country mansion. The burglary had been quick and professional, occurring in the evening whilst the occupants were attending a well publicised social event in aid of prison reform and improved conditions for long term inmates. The owners of the paintings would not have been amused had they known that the leader of the raiding party had been released from his long-term sojourn only a matter of week before. The elaborate alarm systems at their country house had been avoided by a careful and informed approach, using a ladder taken from a nearby outbuilding to enter through a first floor window. Only those pictures that were out of range of the movement detectors, which ostensibly covered the room, had been taken. The detectors had, in the interests of a cost effective system, concentrated on covering the centre of the room and its doorway approaches, where most of the other more valuable and vulnerable items were positioned. The CID officer's muttered "You get what you pay for" went down like a lead balloon.

The three pictures stolen were chosen quite specifically from a shopping list provided by the underworld "receiver", an antique dealer friend of Wilson. It was known that they would be of particular interest to a certain East German contact of the receiver who, in turn, would pass them on to a private collector in one of the eastern bloc countries. As the Communist state crumbled, and the workers drew in their belts, there were many ex Soviet Union entrepreneurs with a desire for status to accompany the success of their new free market businesses.

This particular picture, valued at a mere £800,000, would not be paid for in cash, but in designer drugs, the current favourite being MDMA, better known in the western world as Ecstasy or, to the club goers "E". Criminal values meant that a picture worth nearly £1 million would change hands for drugs with a 'wholesale' value of less than £10,000. These in turn would increase in price as they covered the return journey and, when inflated for sale in the clubs, discos and raves of the British youth culture scene, would exceed that of the oil paintings original value – and untaxed of course.

"Where did you leave the car?" The question from Wilson was abrupt. "I don't want to carry this further than I have to."

"I'll pick it up from the club car park and meet youse' at the end o' the jetty." The reply was brief. Jock was not noted for communication skills.

Wilson was not unduly worried about this trip, just being careful. Mabbett had telephoned ahead to the Secretary of the Dinard Club and been given clearance to moor Spirit of Ecstasy to one of the club's visitor buoys. His stated destination on the customs form completed before leaving Guernsey was the Port du Plaisance at St Malo. They had arrived at Dinard in the late evening and, at first light, would drop the visitor mooring and continue into St Malo. If customs bothered with a search then, which would be very unusual, they would find only normal ships stores and equipment. No old masters.

As Wilson waited at the car park end of the jetty, he did not notice a sudden stirring in a nearby car. Then the hire car, left at the yacht club earlier by Jock, drew up beside him and he settled the picture in the rear floorspace and himself in the front passenger seat.

"Take the Dinan road out of here, the 766," he directed.

Again, neither of them noticed the dark blue Peugeot saloon, which pulled out from the shadow of the yacht club to follow at a discreet distance.

Some twenty minutes later, just south of the little village of Pleslin, Wilson directed Jock off the narrow D road onto an even smaller side road which gave access to a diminutive industrial estate. The streets of Pleslin had been almost deserted, the industrial units totally so. The buildings were of grey brick, there was no street lighting. The only illumination was the reflected lights of vehicles using the nearby Dinan by pass.

"Turn the car round. I'm going for a wander," said Wilson. He took a small torch and checked around the various buildings, ensuring that they had the place to themselves.

A hundred yards past the turning into the industrial estate, the Peugeot was now stationary with its nose in the entrance to a remote farmhouse. It contained three men. The driver, Jean, was a plainclothes police officer from "la police judiciaire", the equivalent of the British CID. He was accompanied by André, an investigator from the French customs. The third was the English liaison officer, Inspector Colin Dempsey, on loan from Detective Chief Inspector Porter's Murder Squad. An animated conversation was taking place, with some language difficulties, despite Colin Dempsey's much vaunted abilities in conversational French!

Spirit of Ecstasy had failed to appear at the St Malo marina, where customs had expected it and could not be found in any of the other "Basins". Following a hurried search for it by both police and customs, the boat had been traced at the Dinard Club's moorings only two hours before. The French police were now busily diverting the covert cars and officers tasked with the observation exercise from St Malo to Dinard. This present car with its three occupants had been a stopgap until the proper surveillance team was in position. Before they had arrived, Wilson and Jock had appeared with the package.

The three personnel in the Peugeot were now arguing the merits of whether to stay put with their limited view of the industrial estate, or to attempt an approach on foot to better observe activities. They had been forced to continue past the narrow entry road to the estate when Wilson's car turned off. To have followed would have meant certain detection. Now the argument was settled when their radio call to the Rennes 'control' was answered with an instruction to stay at a distance until further instructions, but not to lose the "bandits Anglais".

11.15 p.m.

Some fifteen miles away, the ten-wheeler driven by the Targett brothers, was holding a steady sixty as it travelled north on the Route National 137. Both were tired having, that day, driven in turns from just north of the Spanish border to Rennes. They were now on the last leg before their rendezvous with Wilson, which was just off their usual route.

"Where's the turn off? Which junction is it?" from the younger of the two, who was at the wheel.

"The next one. We slip left onto the 176, cross the Rance and take the first slip the other side of the bridge at Plouer-sur-Rance. We go the opposite way to Plouer, to a place called Pleslin, turn left in the centre on the D766 and then look for a railway bridge just through a village called La Biotière. On the right is a small industrial estate just before the bridge. They should he waiting there. We're ten minutes early."

11.25 p.m.

The lights of the approaching artic brought life to the now silent police car. Jean, the French policeman, picked up his handset to inform control at Rennes. Colin Dempsey opened his door saying, "I'm going to take a look, wait here."

"Non, non," from André. "It is better that I go. If the car leaves before I get back, follow it and pick me up later – or get someone else to."

Jean cursed and shrugged his shoulders, still waiting for a reaction from Rennes control. When that came half a minute later, the artic was already parking up, with its lights off, whilst André was up to his knees in brambles on the edge of the field bordering the industrial unit. He was trying to move silently but not succeeding.

Standing between the lorry and the hire car, Wilson handed over the package and confirmed the arrangements already made. They were short and simple. The package was not to be opened but would be handed to the same German contact as on the previous handover, a man named Karl. As before, he would introduce himself to them at their lorry. Again this would take place in the car park of a certain well known but none too salubrious transport hotel, which was close to the border crossing that they normally used on their return trips from Germany. He would take the package and in turn would hand them a locked briefcase, which was to be transported unopened to their Portsmouth base. That would be collected from there, by arrangement, after their return. At that time, they would receive £5,000 in used notes. Any deviation from the instructions would cancel the payment but not a subsequent "visitation". The brothers remembered the hulking size and intimidating attitude of the group that had accompanied Wilson on the last meeting and the younger one shivered.

Within another two minutes, the meeting was over and Wilson was back in the passenger seat with the briefcase collected from the Targett brothers, whilst Jock accelerated out of the side road back towards Dinard.

Jean cursed yet again, started the police car and, not daring to switch on headlights, creased the offside wing on the gate post of the driveway as he attempted to turn quickly. Colin whistled a little tune as he listened to yet more Gallic expletives. The tune was a corruption of an old English music hall melody but "Mr Porter" had been altered to "Mr Potter" with, since the expedition to France, the addition of some caustic lyrics now known to most of the Murder Squad lads, but fortunately unintelligible to their host, in the gendarmerie.

The noise of the lorry's diesel engine drowned the low cry of "Merde" as André, turning to hurry back to the police car, tripped in the brambles and fell headlong. Regaining his feet, he saw the reversing lights of the Peugeot go out as it completed its reverse away from the now drunken driveway post. It accelerated after Wilson's disappearing car, which was some fifty metres down the Dinard road. As he regained the driveway himself, André was forced to leap into the shadow of a hedge as the artic pulled out of the industrial estate, now with its headlights on. In so doing. André found a ditch running with "farmyard" mud, which was much deeper than the smart town shoes that were his normal footwear. Instead of taking the route back to the main road, as André had expected, the driver was heading for an alternative intersection, which had access roads onto the N176 but not off it.

This last action, as well as completely destroying André's sang-froid, provided the only positive piece of information gathered by the three officers that night, the registration number of the lorry.

11.30 p.m. Cross Channel Ferry

As the good guys in plain clothes acted out their charade on the mainland in France, Martin Wild lay sleepless in his cabin between Poole and Cherbourg. Initially it had seemed like a re-enactment of the last trip that he had made. The Porsche was in the car deck, his immediate destination was France. There the similarity ended. Life had changed totally with the loss of the only person that he had met whom he wished to spend his life with. Eileen's death had been the forerunner of events which had led to his present position with little left of his previous life. Added to that, there was black guilt at the loss of Ewen. Memories of the distraught faces of two sets of parents did not help.

That morning, he had signed the bill of sale for his much loved boat, cash now being an urgent requirement to cover costs. With all bills paid, he was left with a couple of thousand pounds in the bank and his Porsche.

The business was still afloat but a shadow of its former self, with two of the larger clients lost, again due to events since Eileen's death.

With the case against Mabbett and company in the hands of the authorities, and with the threats against him still evident until the police took action, it seemed sensible to drop out of sight and this is what he was doing. The French roads could swallow him up and perhaps a visit to Monsieur Tabarde's widow might help close a period from which he needed to move on. After that, who knew? He was conscious of the age gap where Ellie May was concerned. In any case his feelings for her were not as for Eileen. Deciding that there was no point in trying to plan a future with so many uncertainties, he tried, yet again, to sleep.

Part Two

'An eye for an eye'

Monday 27th July 1992
3.30 p.m. Vitrolle, Provence, France

The wrought iron gate to "La Maison Vue Vitrolle" was firmly closed as Martin slowed the Porsche at the entrance to the gravelled drive. Then he saw the white post with a communication module at driver's height, but on the wrong side for his right hand drive position. Walking around the car he turned to face a camera inside the gate and pressed the buzzer. A male voice with the thick local patois of the Provençal, queried who the caller was.

"Bonjour Monsieur. Est ce que je peux vous aider?"

"Monsieur Martin Wild a retrouver Madame Marie Tabarde."

"Entrez s'il vous plait."

The gate swung slowly open as Martin reentered the Porsche and, driving in, took care not to disturb the carefully levelled surface of a drive where each pebble seemed graded to match the next. It curved past manicured lawns and well tended borders that spoke of a gardener and much care, to a large open gravelled area in front of the house.

For a moment he sat in the car, taking in the imposing facade and shaded patio. The house was on two main floors with small windows in the roof, lighting a third tier of rooms. To the right were garages and outbuildings. Beyond these, in a sunny spot on the edge of the lawn, was a swimming pool with white chairs and a table. On the left corner of the house's facade a tall turreted spire, semicircular at first floor level, rose above the roofline, providing first floor windows on that corner of the house with extensive views over the lawns and garden.

The house and gardens were enclosed by a border of tall hedges and trees which ensured privacy.

There was a movement behind the curtains of this first floor turret window and he wondered if it was the master bedroom, with Madame Tabarde curious about or preparing for her visitor.

He had spent the previous six weeks driving through France, stopping where the mood took him to spend a night or two. In the Loire he had visited a Monsieur Huet who, from a tiny tree encircled house, produced Martin's favourite Vouvray. In Burgundy he had paused in Chambertain and Musigny to try the latest vintages.,

Tired of solo wine tasting, he reconsidered the second reason for following that particular route; the thought of continuing through the Rhone Valley to Provence. There was then the possibility of meeting with Madame Tabarde, the intended murder of whose husband had brought him into the spiral of violence which had cost them both so dear. He was not sure why he wished to meet with her as, apart from their linked losses, there was no reason. But he was curious, had time to spare and felt that perhaps a meeting would help him to move on from the trauma and loss of Eileen. In any case he anticipated that, within a few days, he would hear when the committal dates were to be for Mabbett and company, news of whose arrest had been passed to him by Bill Creighton.

At Lyon he had contacted a member of the International Police Association, that worldwide grouping which acted as a social platform for serving and retired police officers. Through them he had been put in touch with another officer at Marseilles, who knew the prominent family and was prepared to try and arrange an introduction. Martin's subsequent telephone conversation with Marie Thérèse Tabarde was cautious on her part but had resulted in agreement that they should meet this afternoon.

The door opened in response to pressure on the bell and an older man wearing, to Martin's hidden amusement, a very formal waistcoat but no tie, bade him enter the tall cool reception area. He was led to an expensively furnished lounge and, almost immediately, was followed by a tall, slim woman with striking deep brown eyes and a light olive complexion beneath black hair piled high on her head.

"Monsieur Wild, I am pleased to see you. Would you care for a drink – tea perhaps?"

Martin was surprised by the excellent English, so much better than his fractured French – and the voice, low, well modulated and very attractive, especially with the French accent.

"Madame Tabarde, that would be nice. Thank you."

She issued instructions in French to the waiting servant and gestured to a deep settee, sitting herself in an armchair opposite. Martin was struck by the poise and elegance of the woman. The lightest of makeup had been carefully applied to a face which was oval in shape, with a strong nose and chin. Mascara lengthened the eyelashes and lipstick emphasised the curve of her mouth. These were the only obvious additions to a skin which appeared soft and unblemished. Around her long neck was a gold necklace which, at the front, formed a scroll of words that he could not read. The summer dress was simply cut but looked expensive. Long slim brown legs, crossed at the ankles, were bare. She wore high heeled shoes of expensive latticed leather. Gold and diamonds flashed on the fingers of hands that were clasped in her lap.

"My apologies for being direct, but you have come out of your way to see me?"

"No, Madame, I have been visiting acquaintances in the Loire, then Burgundy and the Rhone vineyards. It was only a small deviation to your house from the road to Cannes where I have another visit to make."

"You are a wine connoisseur?"

"More an enthusiast than a connoisseur." Martin smiled.

A tap on the door was followed by a middle-aged woman who bustled in with a trolley bearing a fine bone china tea service and an assortment of biscuits. A few words, again in French, and the woman left. Madame Tabarde busied herself pouring tea and offering biscuits.

Martin said, "I'm sure that you are curious about my reason for wishing to see you, but I felt it natural, as I was so close, to call and offer my sympathy over your loss and ask whether you know – or even wish to know – of the events that occurred in England prior to your husband's death, but which were connected to it?"

"You are very kind Monsieur Wild. I understand that you lost a loved one as well. Yes I would like to hear all that you know."

Talking quietly and unemotionally, Martin told of the explosion that had killed Eileen and sketched in the background of the investigation that had cost Ewen his life. He detailed the English criminals and their contacts with the drug trade, the police action and anticipated outcome of the court hearing now pending.

When he had finished, Marie Tabarde sat still for some moments, staring out of the window. "So you lost a good friend as well as your fiancée?"

"I knew and loved Eileen for such a short time," Martin said quietly. "I think it must be much worse to lose the partner of many years, the father of your children."

He thought that he saw tears in the corners of the brown eyes that continued to gaze out of the window to sunlit lawns, but the voice was strong and controlled. "We do not always appreciate that which we have until we lose it. I take strength in my children now; do you have anyone to turn to?"

Again Martin was surprised, but at the directness of the question, then said, "I lost both of my parents in an air accident when I was at school. I lost my twin sister to the drugs trade some five years ago. But I am fortunate to have good friends."

The deep brown eyes regarding him had widened as he spoke. "Oh, I am so very sorry. My question was thoughtless, but you must feel very strongly about the drugs barons. Now I perhaps understand why you involved yourself in this dangerous business rather than leaving the investigation to the authorities."

As Martin drank his tea they talked about the effect that hard and soft drugs were having on their respective communities. The woman continued to surprise Martin, her knowledge of certain aspects of crime and drugs was more than he expected. She asked a number of pertinent questions and commented knowledgeably on certain drugs.

There then seemed to be a natural break and Martin murmured the conventional, "I should be on my way." They both rose and Martin's sense of sympathy and joint loss caused him to, almost unconsciously, make a half step towards her, but he stopped immediately as she took a pace backwards.

"Thank you, Monsieur Wild, for your kindness in coming to see me. I hope that you find happiness again, soon."

She pressed a bell by the fireplace, the door opened immediately and the woman who had brought the tea appeared. Marie Tabarde issued a quick instruction and the servant disappeared, only to reappear as they shook hands at the front door. She had an ornate wine bottle in her hands which she gave to Madame Tabarde, who presented it to Martin.

"We have – or rather had our own small vineyard. This is a bottle from the last vintage that Henri supervised. He was proud of it. It has a good name in Provence. I am sure that you will enjoy it."

Martin thanked her and left, promising to let her know the result of the trial. He drove slowly and thoughtfully back to the main road. He had gone to meet Marie Thérèse Tabarde without any preconceived thoughts and now found himself fascinated by the widow. Her apparent strength and poise at a time when she must be emotionally damaged impressed him. He found her very attractive but, remembering what had seemed like an unspoken rejection in the half pace backwards, he mentally shrugged his shoulders. Up to that point, in the last half of their conversation, there had seemed to be a strange chemistry developing. A mutual awareness, an anticipation of words not yet spoken. But, with a wry smile. He had been wrong before.

*

Marie Tabarde perched on the wide windowsill of her bedrooms turret window, a glass of wine in one hand and a small package in the other. She gazed reflectively after Martin's Porsche as the gates closed behind it. She wondered about this man who had walked into her life – and wondered about her own feelings. Her guard had been up on his arrival, consciously so – and for many good reasons. But within twenty minutes she had found herself warming to him. Surprised, she had checked, deliberately looking away from pale green eyes in a scarred face, to the gardens and lawns that Henri had loved, seeking a balance to her feelings.

That was the trouble, she decided. In some ways Martin reminded her of her husband. Not physically, Henri had been a little shorter, heavier, with dark hair, brown eyes and a furrowed brow. No, it was the direct gaze, the quiet voice, the calm manner. The feeling, of reliability. Suddenly, despite the warm day, not knowing why, she shivered. Standing, she looked from the wine glass in one hand to the package in the other, then walked to her bedside table throwing the small package into the drawer, drained the wine glass and, leaving the room, tried to dismiss the Englishman from her mind. In the garden, with gloves, basket and secateurs she collected flowers, but still the green eyes with their glint of humour at some inconsequential remark appeared before her. The tall muscular figure, moving with a fluidity that Henry had lacked, remained in her thoughts. She heard the telephone ring and turned thankfully towards this diversion but, as she did so, remembered Martin's promise to contact her again when he had further news of the trial.

Turning towards the coast, Martin headed for a small town in the hope of finding accommodation before reaching the expensive route along the Riviera. He was lucky and, after dropping his case, telephoned Bill Creighton. Bill's wife answered and, on realising it was Martin, her voice became subdued. The news that she had was a shock and he had to ask her to repeat what she had said.

"What happened, Bill?"

"Sit down, Marty. It's a long story."

Martin sat with a weary sigh. The drive up to the channel port had taken two days and that had been followed by a night crossing on a crowded boat with only a reclining seat. All of the cabins were booked. He had slept badly and then driven straight to Bill's place, arriving as Suzanne was preparing breakfast.

Bill came back from the kitchen with two coffees.

"Let's take it from the beginning," he said. "Remember the stub of pencil that you ID'd from the Soco photo, blue with silver writing on it – the pencil that would have tied Mabbett's Glasgow club into the Parksyde crime scene. It can't be found! It's disappeared! It's in the photos all right, but missing from the evidence bag. All the other debris from the road is there. That's the only item missing."

"The number on the bike that was given by the girl who lives farther along Parksyde – remember the statement from the nurse – belongs to a different motorbike owned by a guy in Norwich. He's eventually come up with a cast iron alibi, which includes the bike. There's no doubt that Mahoney – if he's the man as we all think – was using false plates. We got a bike and rider on a service station CCTV at Redbridge but the quality's bloody awful and the guy kept his helmet on. Can't even be sure of the make of the bike, but it's only got one exhaust, whereas the Norwich bike has two. The bike was evidently heading west but we've had no joy from Dorset, Bristol and Avon or the other likely areas in that direction."

"The explosive found on the Renault...by the way, you were right about the spare wheel, how did you know?...Anyway, it's not the same as that used in Parksyde Avenue. The car was hired and we can't tie what it was carrying into Mahoney. Nothing on his clothes, nothing in his luggage, nothing on him."

"Interestingly, we did come up with another of those blue pencils. It was in his case. Also, now that we've fingerprinted him, we can tie him into one of your cassettes from Ewen Handsford's room at the Glasgow hotel that they turned over. But the tapes were found by the Glasgow police in the Manager's office at the club. The manager says that they were just found in the staff room and taken into his office. Ewen worked there, used the staff room and without an admission from somebody, we can't prove that they weren't left there by him."

"That brings us to the people. Mabbett's clever and has distanced himself from the operation. Says he's just the owner of the clubs and leaves everything to his minions. We know from the tapes that this isn't so but we can't use the tapes. They're illegal and are frightening the pants off of Potter. I'm surprised that he still has them!"

"Wilson's scared but has been carefully coached. He's much more scared of Mabbett than he is of us. They each have their own brief and won't say a word without him nodding his head. If we we're going to get anything from the main players, it was Wilson. But we didn't!"

"Mahoney's the obvious hardman. Got no previous convictions but is known to Special Branch, had connections with the IRA in the late eighties. Fell out with someone there and moved to the mainland. Was thought at one time to be still involved but they now think that he's too well known to be used as a sleeper and, in any case, there's a suggestion that the IRA no longer trust him themselves. Seems there's a suggestion of a drug habit. He's been working for Mabbett since '89, does all of his dirty stuff is the opinion. But he's the most difficult of all, just will not open his mouth. He has the same brief as Mabbett, but doesn't need him. Keeps absolutely stum."

"Then there are the Targett brothers. Run the haulage firm that Mabbett and company had just started to use. Chris, the elder brother, has form. Quite a list, armed robbery, GBH, handling, you name it. Another hard man and not prepared to talk without his brief – same one as Wilson, nodding his head, and not much then. Younger one is a different kettle of fish. Initially we got a statement from him, which told the story of the drugs side and implicated Wilson. Would you believe that, two days later, he withdrew his statement saying that he might have been mistaken, it was dark, wasn't Wilson that they met after all. We think his wife, who runs the admin side of the business, had a visit. There's no doubt that both he and his wife are frightened to death and that's got to be down to Mabbett."

"We've still got the brothers inside and will be able to make some charges stick there. They were handling stolen paintings. Thought is that they were destined for East Germany in payment for drugs. We haven't heard the result of the investigation out there yet."

"Finally, there's an embarrassment from the Glasgow end of this. They had information from one of the club staff which looked as if it was going to tie Mahoney to Ewen leaving the club on the night he was knifed. A WDC was present at the interview and took some notes which are relevant. She then added some notes of her own to the file after they had finished talking to him. The second lot were not considered relevant and were not sent to the other side for disclosure. Now the whole interview has been thrown out cos her second set were not included in the disclosure. CPS are saying we haven't got a chance. Potter's in the dark and murky with Lawson and once again you are off Potter's Christmas card list."

Martin had listened without interrupting and now the two men sat in silence. In Martin's mind the realization was that, once again, his faith in the law had been misplaced. The precepts that had been drilled into him by his parents, reinforced later at Sherborne, Sandhurst and the police, would once more fail. That the people who had murdered Eileen and Ewen would walk away from their crimes without punishment. The devastating loss and subsequent rage that he had felt immediately after Eileen's death had been replaced by a disciplined anger. An anger that had fuelled the activity of his investigation and had helped him come to terms with the situation. But that anger, though not used up, had been based upon the anticipation of a successful conclusion to the case.

Suddenly, his mind's eye was in the public mortuary at Southampton all those years before. The sheet covering the body was drawn back to reveal the cold white features of his sister's face. Beautiful Susie, spirited and fun loving with everything to live for. Then dead and awaiting the pathologist's knife – with the knowledge that drugs had played their part in her death.

Now, in fast forward, he revisited Parksyde Avenue, his imagination seeing again the pitiful remnants that would have been Eileen. He'd been spared the act of identification but, in traumatic days and sleepless nights, tortured visualization of the blast had left its mark in his mind. His previous life had provided the experience and knowledge of such scenes ensuring that, when otherwise unoccupied, and especially during the long lonely nights that followed, the pictures that played in his head of the beautiful woman and lover that he knew, were pushed aside and lost to the imagined destruction in the Citroen. A criminal mistake perhaps, but again the drugs trade.

And then there was Ewen. Required once more to identify the body, this time in a cold Scottish mortuary. Easier in some respects as he had not been so close and Ewen was a man who had lived a life which knew danger. But much more difficult in others. The strong sense of personal responsibility and, later, the devastated parents. This time the direct link to a drugs trade that was concerned only with greed and paid no heed to the suffering it caused.

How many more innocents like Jason Emery would die whilst the law ran around in circles, it's hands tied behind its back by a society that placed ever increasing demands where proof of crime was concerned without, it seemed, doing anything constructive to root out the evil which flourished in the back streets of its cities? Young people introduced to chemical euphoria whilst still at school, later seasoned in the drug-fuelled nightclubs, discos and raves.

Bill interrupted his thoughts. "Potter moved too quickly, that's obvious now, but hindsight is a wonderful thing and there's nothing that we can do about that. What I'm more concerned about now is you. Mabbett and Wilson are out today and there's every chance that they will want to shut you up. What will you do?"

Martin sat quietly for a few seconds. When he looked up his eyes were dark and his face seemed pale beneath it's tan. 'I've lost Eileen and Ewen to those bastards, Bill. I've also lost my home and many of the things that I've worked for over the last few years. I'm not going to walk away from this!"

Martin stopped talking abruptly, realising where his thoughts and words were taking him. He could no longer share this anger. Bill was a close friend but also a copper. It would be very wrong, even unwise, to put him in a position where the strongest of loyalties would be strained. He was now truly on his own. He would have to avoid Ellie May as well, and that could prove equally difficult in a different way. He sat for a few more seconds then got to his feet.

"Bill, I'm going to have to think this through myself. I'll drop out of sight for a couple of days and call you again when I've got my head around it."

He went into the kitchen where Suzanne was clattering pans, put his arms around her and gave her a kiss on the cheek saying "Sorry, Suz, I've got to go."

"Can't you stop for breakfast, Marty? It won't be long."

"No, my dear. I'd love to but not this time."

Turning, he took Bill's outstretched hand in both of his saying, "Bill, must get away. I'll call you soon." He was out of the door before the couple had grasped the significance. Neither could put into words what they felt, but both knew that this was not a normal "see you later". The cuddle, the added handshake, the speed of departure, all were different from the usual casual warmth of Martin's goodbyes.

Firing up the Porsche, he sat for a few moments, consciously pushing down the new anger, saving it for later. He had to assess his immediate requirements. His few remaining possessions had been put into store when the boat was sold. He had been living out of a suitcase from the time that he had left England to visit the South of France and Madame Tabarde. To have a permanent base now might be more of a liability than an asset. He had been considering a mobile home as a temporary measure but now shelved that idea. First stop before "dropping out of sight" must be a camping shop. Thankfully it was summer!

11.25 a.m.
Winchester, England

The Wessex Hotel in Winchester seemed like a slightly up market country club to Dermott Mabbett. It had been Gordon Wilson's suggestion as a suitable meeting point. They had both been due for release and Mabbett was first through the procedures. Now he was passing the time waiting for Wilson with a mobile phone in one hand and a celebratory glass of champagne in the other. He wondered when Liam would get out. He needed to talk to him urgently but, for some reason, there was a delay.

This had been a close call; too close for comfort. Thank Christ he had always been careful; but must do even better next time – there was bound to be a next time! Got to separate myself even more. Don't know yet what might still come out from this present investigation. Can they use the evidence again or did the dropping of the case knock that on the head? Must speak with that expensive bastard of a barrister. They're all sharks when it came to money and totally patronising in dealings with clients.

Then he saw Wilson walk past reception and he called out to him.

"You're pushing the boat out, DM!" from Wilson, eyeing the bottle of Krug sitting in the ice bucket.

It had been a quite deliberate gesture on Mabbett's part when he reached the hotel. Despite his reluctance to part with money to others, he always indulged himself and six weeks away from the little luxuries of life demanded an appropriate gesture. He had walked into the hotel, booked their best bedroom, ordered the Krug and phoned Ann to join him there for coffee and – he anticipated – some much needed "exercise", all within three minutes of arrival.

Pouring champagne into a second glass, Mabbett replied, "Yes, but I'm worth it!" and grinned wolfishly.

Wilson took a long drink from the glass, half emptying it. "God, that's good!" and wondered to himself about the grin. Mabbett smiled rarely and, when he grinned like that, it was inevitably bad news for someone.

"We need a council of war, Gordon. I've got Ann joining me here today but I want you to get hold of Liam as soon as he is out, then the pair of you get to Kilchatten as soon as."

"When is he due out?"

"Today I hope. I got a message to him that we were meeting here. I'll leave you to sort that out. Make sure he doesn't slip off to the Emerald Isle without seeing you."

Turning, he saw the back of Ann Hadleigh's curly head walking toward the lounge and he rose, topped up Wilson's glass and, taking the bottle, moved to follow her. "Phone me on the mobile this evening and let me know what time you'll both be arriving. I want you together, mind."

Ann Hadleigh was dressed in a smart brown two piece suit and crisp white blouse. She had an expensive leather bag over one shoulder. The nylon covered legs were muscular rather than shapely and the brown leather brogues, matching the handbag in colour, seemed appropriately "county." She was standing in the doorway looking around the lounge as he came up behind her.

Had Martin been present, he would have recognised the woman who had dined with Mabbett in the hotel in Scotland and on whom he had been unable to get any sort of line.

"Ann...!"

She turned to him: "Dermott!"

There was no embrace, no affectionate greeting. Rather an intense meeting of eyes. The smiles had an eagerness rather than warmth. He waggled the bottle of champagne.

"Drink?"

"Too early for that," she said. "I'd rather have tea."

He raised his hand to a waitress and followed Ann to a table on a side of the room which was unoccupied.

"How was it? Pretty awful?"

"That's the first and last time," he said.

She raised eyebrows which, had they not been carefully plucked, would have been heavy. The hazel eyes beneath were mocking – but also excited. "That's confidence! I always understood that once that lot had their hooks into you, they never let go. Are you being watched now?"

She looked around the room, concern mixed with excitement again.

He smiled grimly. "No, I'm not." Then to change the subject, "What have you been doing whilst I've been away?"

"Oh, working mainly." It was his turn to raise eyebrows. "I've had a couple of big stories to cover, not enough researchers and some delicate decisions to make. She continued talking about inconsequentials as the waitress brought tea and a plate of biscuits. He listened quietly as she spoke of high profile media meetings, the difficulties imposed by the increasing requirement for political correctness in television broadcasting and the boring business/ social round.

As always, she adopted a "holier than thou" mantle in their conversation and he wondered, as he had frequently before, what it was precisely that drew this woman to him, like a moth to a flame. He knew that her view of him was as a moneyed wheel within the leisure industry. He was sure that she had accepted his explanations that the recent incarceration had been the result of allowing lower echelons of his organisation too much freedom. But here she was, back again almost before the prison gates had closed. He knew that he excited her and he guessed that, like a lot of well bred women – especially those with the freedom of divorce and children flown the nest – a handsome rogue, especially a wealthy one, was more than a little attractive. He was tempted to tell her that no one involved in the media could afford the luxury of a "holier than thou" attitude but, in deference to his own appetites he kept his mouth shut, just for the present. He would not have been happy had he known the dismissive reference made about him by the only friend that Ann had confided in. To her husband the friend had described Mabbett as "…Ann's bit of rough."

A natural break in the conversation and she said, "And what are you doing now?"

"Back to Kilchatten as soon as possible but, before that – I do have a room booked here."

The eyes opposite brightened and he grinned inwardly, wondering what the waitress setting tables nearby would think of this well dressed, beautifully groomed, impeccably spoken, county lady, if she could lip read.

"Why have you kept me here, drinking tea with no knickers on, when you've a room waiting?"

Inside the room they embraced immediately, urgently and, as their breathing quickened, tore at each other's clothes, leaving a haphazard trail of strewn garments to the bedside. There were no preliminaries. As the very dominant male, he forced himself upon her without a pause to find whether she was ready. She was anyway – always was at their meetings. As usual she protested and gasped about "…being ravished…". The very words seemed an aphrodisiac to her as, gasping in his ear, clutching, bucking against him, she repeated them. Again – despite the animal urgency within, a detached part of his mind wondered about a woman who left her underclothes off to meet a man and then revelled in pseudo rape.

He knew very well what it was that attracted him. The availability, the eager availability, of a well born and glamorous "County" woman. A woman far removed from his modest upbringing in a dusty and none too clean secondhand shop. He'd plucked from a top drawer and, in the throes of lust, could treat his prize casually, almost with disdain. And she came back for more, again and again!

Five minutes later they lay side by side on the bed, as usual, silently satisfied.

Then "It's a good job that I was called a way when we were at St Malo. I don't know what my neighbours would have thought if I'd been arrested too."

"Probably 'just deserts', depending upon whether they were prompted by jealousy, if your friend or by grievance, if one of the many who have been injured by the media," he murmured.

She lifted herself on an elbow, carefully groomed hair now awry, naked slightly pendulous breasts swinging, frowning at him, as usual unsettled by this man who quite obviously had little concern for, as she saw it, her position. Seeking words to protest she did not have time; he rolled abruptly off the bed and made for the bathroom.

"I've some urgent business so I'll have to leave you," he said.

"I've a meeting myself late afternoon. Will we have dinner here tonight?"

"No," he said. The past half hour had satisfied the hunger. Instead of staying for lunch and perhaps the night as he had intended other priorities were at the forefront and he was impatient to engage them. "I'll get the evening flight to Glasgow. I'll ring you when I've dealt with this other business."

Downstairs in the bar he found Gordon Wilson talking with Liam Mahoney.

"Liam, how goes it? Any problems inside?"

Mahoney shook his head. "Your man had the moss from the blarney stone on his lips."

"Gordon, I've had second thoughts. You'll want to pop home for a wee while, but I need you up at Kilchatten tomorrow night as I said. Liam and I will go on tonight. There are some loose ends to be tied off quickly, then we have to sort out this 'Wild card' that we've been dealt."

Ten minutes later, with Wilson on his way and Mahoney booking flights, he saw Ann stepping out of the lift. He went to her "Sorry, I have to rush. I'll have more time shortly. We can make up for St Malo then."

The hazel eyes were angry but the voice was level and cool. "No problem. See you around."

With a sudden thought, he went to the Reception desk. "Dermott Mabbett. I booked a room with you an hour or so ago. I'm afraid plans have changed and I no longer need to stay the night."

"That's all right, Mr Mabbett. We'll tear up your credit card slip."

"I paid cash, not credit," he said pleasantly.

The girl checked the register and then counted out £110 in notes from the cash drawer. Mabbett pocketed the money with added satisfaction. Ann had truly been a "freebie" this time.

12.45 p.m.

Ann Hadleigh stepped out of the Wessex Hotel and, collecting her car from the covered parking space opposite to Reception, turned left to make her way up West Hill to the afternoon appointment. As she passed the huge grey structure of the Police Headquarters building, set back in its own grounds just before the prison that Mabbett had been released from, a meeting at the Police HQ was just coming to an end.

In Ray Lawson's office on the fourth floor, a debriefing had taken place between Lawson and Potter. One was undoubtedly angry, the other subdued. Having dealt with the few successes and many failures of the Padgett murder enquiry, Lawson then said "And what about Wild? He seems to have dropped out of your logs some six weeks ago. What's happened to him?"

"Last heard of holidaying on the continent. He was living aboard his boat before that, but I believe that he sold it before leaving the country. Still using the boat yard at Christchurch as a mailing address. Doesn't seem to be active in his business any longer so the short answer is that his whereabouts are unknown."

"I was with a friend the other night who is in touch with people who know Wild. It seems that this business has hit him harder than most will have realised. I'm told that he would only have sold that boat as a last resort. It meant a lot to him. It's said that he needed the money to pay off debts caused by his work on the Eileen Padgett enquiry. Thing is that Mabbett and friends, who are released from Winchester today, may well be looking to even the score. Perhaps we should be concerned for him?" Lawson's voice was gentle now but interrogative. His dark eyes intent upon Potter.

The Detective Chief Inspector looked uncomfortable. "The Glasgow CID said that they thought a leak from their end had marked his card, but I don't see what we can do if we don't know where the man is."

"Do you not think that it's up to us to have maintained contact with Wild?" Lawson's voice was harder now and Potter shifted uncomfortably in his seat, knowing what was coming. "He was the object of criminal attacks, a principal witness, if you like. He came to us with information. Surely he should have been treated in such a way that his cooperation would have been guaranteed?"

"He was a difficult man to pin down, Ray." Potter's voice was placatory. "He wouldn't accept advice, walked out of meetings, had no regular address or contact point."

"Perhaps he felt that he wasn't welcome," drily from Lawson, now sitting back in his chair. "But it'll not look good on the record of this investigation if he becomes the final casualty. I would suggest that you at least make every effort that you can to locate him and talk. We cannot afford him protection unless there's a known threat, but we should at least have it on record that suitable advice has been offered."

"I'll get onto it straight away."

Ray Lawson remained at his desk as Potter left, his thoughts on Wild. He had known him as a young detective years before. Had recognised the innate goodness and honesty of the man, not always a frequent characteristic in an operational detective. He had admired the courage shown when, during an undercover exercise Martin had risked injury in ensuring the safety of others. He had tried to dissuade him from leaving the police after his sister's death, when the police investigation failed to produce the result that Martin wanted. Now other tragedies had struck and Lawson wondered how Martin was dealing with a world which seemed intent on heaping trouble upon troubles.

12.55 p.m.
Bristol, England

The brakes on the Ford Escort felt spongy and the well used engine smelt of oil, as Martin pulled up outside John Mann's secluded detached house on the outskirts of Bristol. He was in the car that he'd purchased at the Southampton Motor Auction. The more easily recognisable Porsche was now stowed away in the garage that the Escort had occupied.

John greeted him at the door in a casual shirt and linen shorts. "Ah, the wanderer returns. Come on in, there's a cold beer waiting for you out back."

John led the way through the house with Martin pausing to greet his wife in the kitchen. Joan Mann was a dark attractive woman in her late thirties. "Put your bag in the usual bedroom, Marty. Lunch in about thirty minutes, you two."

The centrepiece on the rear lawn, in the shade of a tree, was a garden table and chairs with three place settings already arranged and glasses of beer frosting in the midday sun. Martin's telephone call an hour earlier to set up a meeting with John had brought an immediate invitation to lunch and to stay the night, which he had gladly accepted.

"Not good news?" said John as he flopped in one of the chairs raising his glass in a salutation.

"No. Those bastards are out today, according to Bill Creighton."

"How is dear old Bill?" Did he have anything of use for you?"

"Only a warning to stay on my tippy toes if I want to one day draw a pension."

"I wondered about that. Anything that my lads can do?"

Martin smiled his appreciation. John's "lads" were a tough bunch from a local boxing club, who formed a nucleus for the more "demanding" of the commercial guarding operations that were part of John's business.

"Nice of you to offer, but with the greatest or respect to your 'lads', I think that Mabbett and company are in a different league."

190

John nodded acceptance and his eyes were serious as he said, "What will you do? You know that you're welcome to stop here as long as you like, but these mafiosi are not likely to go away because you've dropped out of sight for a few weeks."

Martin smiled gently but didn't reply immediately. Then "You're absolutely right John and I'm going to have to give this some careful consideration. I've been thinking about things on the way here. Apart from the moral or legal stuff, as you say, there's the question of self-preservation. I don't see Mabbett and company forgetting about me."

"But Marty, they're a group, a gang with plenty of money and a network of contacts. Can't the police provide you with protection – a safe house – whilst they rebuild the case?"

'Reading between the lines offered by my police contacts, I don't see much chance of them rebuilding the case." A pause and "You know, while I was in France, I paid a visit to the widow of the Frenchman, Tabarde, whom they murdered in Marseilles. There's a grieving wife, two children without a father and a mother who's lost her son there. In Scotland there are two sets of parents who have lost a daughter and a son each. Across the country there are probably dozens of other parents, wives, husbands, partners and children who have lost loved ones, had their lives blighted, by these and other similar 'Mafiosi' as you call them. They've taken, either directly or indirectly, just about everything that meant anything to me. It really started with Susie back in '87, though that wasn't down to their particular group. Then Eileen, then Ewen, now the boat and, despite the best efforts of friends," Martin raised his glass to John "now the business as well. There are three differences between the previous victims and me, John. I've got no one else to worry about now. They've left me no options and, finally, they've given me just cause!"

There was a pause as he dwelt in his mind on the anger that had led to murderous thoughts when talking with Bill Creighton some hours before. He now felt with increasing certainty that he was on the point of "crossing over" the legal and moral parameters by which he had always lived. He was not sure what he would do, or how he would do it, but he was not about to roll over or run, and that left just one course.

He said quietly "You're the only one that I can say this to. It's almost as if I've been building up to this all of my adult life. Sherborne School, mum and dad dying so suddenly; the army did their very special bit; the police experience, Susie's death; Eileen and Ewen's murders; young Jason Emery; this business that I've done too well at, according to my dear friend, DCI Potter. In some ways, it's as though the decks have been cleared. In other ways, it's been a very good learning curve."

John sat quietly for some moments, studying a man whom he knew well. A man who was honest to the point of embarrassment, principled and, until now, law abiding. But also a man who, he knew, derided half measures and had a history of sticking his neck out when other, perhaps wiser people, took a rain check.

Martin was leaning back in his chair, quite relaxed, his eyes on white clouds seen through the green leaves over their heads. John, listening to his words, felt an air of disbelief, of thinking the impossible. Then he saw the eyes in the scarred face opposite, eyes which minutes before had been a smiling pale green were now dark, icy cold and expressionless.

In all the years of their association, he had not seen Martin like this and, draining his glass, got to his feet. "Time for a bottle of that special plonk that you gave me," he said, returning a few minutes later with a burgundy shaped bottle, which bore the legend "Chambolle Musigny" and the name "Domain Comte George de Vogue" on its label.

Martin laughed, the green eyes pale again. "Have you still got that?" Some years before he had entrusted John with the collection of a case of the wine from Avery's cellars in Bristol. Customers had been limited to one case each from a small but fabulous vintage and the scarce wine had been expensive.

When they met weeks later, Martin had enquired about his wine. John had said, casually, "Oh that. We had a bit of a celebration in the CID office and saw it off. But, don't worry, I'll get you a decent case of red from the off licence." Martin's face had been a picture but the twinkle in John's eyes gave the game away. They laughed together and Martin opened the case that John then produced and handed him a bottle to keep for a special occasion. Neither of them had anticipated that the occasion would have such sombre overtones.

John set about removing the capsule and cork whilst Martin tilted his head back again, enjoying the warmth of the sun on his face. Again his thoughts drifted back to the feelings that he had experienced whilst driving between Southampton and Bristol that morning. The drive had been on auto pilot. His mental processes seemingly on a different level, divorced from the practicalities and routines of life. The rage that had followed Eileen's death, dissipated to some extent by the activity of the investigation, had returned, but in a different guise. It was now deeper, calculating cold, corrosive! A phrase remembered from the classrooms of his days at Sherborne came back. "Revenge, a dish that tastes better cold." He smiled sardonically at himself. Could he really be thinking of exacting personal vengeance for the loved lives that had been wasted? Could he really step over a boundary which his very style of life and upbringing had put in place?

He wondered what Mabbett and Co were doing now picturing the urbane figure with its strong features and drooping moustache. A good-looking man but, behind the façade, he now knew there to be a cold, calculating mind bent on personal pleasures and profit, dealing mercilessly with those who got in his way. He thought of Wilson, larger physically but weaker mentally. Nevertheless, a man who had followed his leader's code was just as responsible for the horrors of the last few weeks. And then there was the lean, cold Mahoney. A man devoid of a soul? Only a foot soldier, but probably more dangerous than his master, killing without compunction, without hesitation, enemies and innocent alike.

The cork came out of the bottle with a soft "plop", bringing him back to the sunlit very English garden, and John pouring ruby coloured wine into three glasses. Martin picked his up and swirled the liquid around the half-filled glass. Noting the broad band of brownish red around the edges of the wine he said "You may have kept this too long, John." Then, inhaling the bouquet deeply and sipping appreciatively "No, it's still with us, but not with a long life ahead."

Putting the glass on the table and with an apologetic grin "And that brings me to the main reason for calling on you at short notice." Martin slid a white envelope onto the table by the wine glass. "In case anything happens to me, I've jotted down some last wishes and wondered whether you'd be good enough to tidy things up. It's been witnessed etcetera so there shouldn't be any problems."

John's face had lost its usual relaxed smile. He said, "Of course, Marty, but you're not going to…"

Martin interrupted him. "No, Jonno, I'm not going to take any unnecessary chances but not having a base any longer means that I need a collation point somewhere. I've lumbered you by leaving your name and address with my solicitors. That brings me to Bill Creighton. He's helped a lot in sorting this job out but I can't continue meeting or talking to him now. The way things are going, it's too dangerous for him in the job. If you've no objection, I'll give him your "ExD" number, saying that you'll take messages for me. He might feel that he knows you well enough to feed me scraps via you. I hope so anyway."

"No problem, Marty. Just remember to keep your mobile switched on."

They smiled together, somewhat sombrely, jointly remembering mobile phone calls that had interrupted life's little pleasures.

As usual, a refusal on John's part to accept anything other than the positive side of life, coupled with Joan's food and a glass or two of favourite wine, ensured that Martin's evening was pleasurable in the circumstances.

He went to bed in their spare room, anticipating his usual ability to sleep soundly, ready for an early start on his journey north. He was wrong, waking in the middle of the night with nightmares in which Eileen appeared, whole again and supported by a bloodied Ewen. She was crying out for his help, but he was unable to approach her, being buried to his waist in a thick, slippery Irish bog, through which his limbs could only push slowly and from which there arose a stench which turned his stomach. Rising, he crept into the bathroom for a drink and his towel to dry the sweat from his body. He slept again, only to sink into the same nightmare, but this time swimming against a black tide, again unable to reach the couple, whose pleading arms were extended to him. Dawn was breaking as he awoke yet again and he gave up the struggle, lying awake in the pale light through floral curtains, thinking his thoughts, weighing options, reaching decisions.

The roll call of dead loved ones, friends, called out to him, reminding without doubt that his name was on a list that now bore theirs. He knew the odds but they counted little in the new scheme of things. Previously he had "disappeared" but running for cover took money, which he now had little of. In any case, that action had been based upon the supposition of a successful criminal trial, murderers brought to book. The police and the CPS would require much more in the way of evidence before they took action a second time. That was if they could. With a certainty born of bitter experience, staring sightlessly at strengthening sunlight on the curtains, he came to the, for him, inevitable conclusion.

He could not accept that these "Mafiosi" had the right to continue to live and kill at will. Society's protectors had failed. It was down to him to do what he could. He knew that he might, very probably would, lose his life in the doing, but felt a growing consolation in the thought of action, direct action, of some sort, almost any sort.

Slipping out of the house, he retrieved his maps of the Isle of Bute from the car, and studied them until John appeared with a morning cup of tea.

Saturday 1st August 1992
8.30 a.m. Scotland

The murmur of voices woke him. For a few seconds Martin was totally disorientated. The sleeping bag, subdued daylight filtering through the walls of a small tent and then the Scottish dialect outside, brought it all back. Friday had been a long day and the well worn Ford more than a little different from his normal transport. Finding the campsite had been the easy bit. Wrestling with an unfamiliar tent in gathering darkness was the final straw. He was surprised the tent was still upright.

A glance at his watch and he saw that it was just after eight thirty. A quick visit to the shower block was called for. Breakfast on an unfamiliar camping stove was another adventure, though not as difficult as the tent. He was just finishing bacon and eggs when the neighbours, whose conversation had woken him, appeared from their caravan on a nearby pitch.

Cheery greetings and a brief conversation established that Martin was taking a few days holiday to fish the nearby loch. "Kilchatten" rods and hat on the back shelf of the Escort corroborated the story. Behind the casual conversation and promise to "…bring you back a trout…" was, to Martin, the knowledge that his "fishing" was going to be a grimmer business than he had ever contemplated undertaking. During the daylong drive to the site, he had thought long and hard. He was not sure of the effect that it might have on him, but now considered only the "how" and not the "why". If the community was incapable of doing justice, then it would be exacted the "jungle way", an eye for an eye; a tooth for a tooth.

The elderly Scottish couple, left Martin to his second cup of coffee, remarking to each other how nice it was to meet a young man with such a cheery outlook and innocent pursuits. But behind the facade was black determination for vengeance which, had the three men at the centre of Martin's thoughts been aware, might well have spoiled their breakfast.

As it was, Dermott Mabbett and Gordon Wilson were just then tucking in some twenty five miles to the west at Kilchatten and awaiting a telephone call from Liam Mahoney to confirm that Mad Mick would return the unearned £5,000 within the week – or else.

"Now let's see what we can find out about Wild." Mabbett lifted the handset and set about contacting various people who might have knowledge of Martin's whereabouts.

2.30 p.m.

It was early afternoon before Martin reached Kilchatten. Leaving the car in a convenient lay-by, he set out for what he hoped would be seen by any curious locals as a casual walk. Nothing seemed to have changed as he viewed the familiar hillside through binoculars. He thought it unwise to approach the area of scrub where the "bug in a box" had been left all those weeks before. Reaching a higher curve of the hillside, he found a comfortable root under a solitary tree and contented himself with a distant view of the house. He was rewarded within half an hour by the arrival of a car. Though too far away to see the detail, he was confident that the driver was a man and that there were no passengers. For the next half hour there was no further movement and Martin took a different route back to his car, thinking to return after dark and investigate the recording gear. If it was still there and intact, he could check out the tape that had remained in it and perhaps try using it again. In the meantime, with nothing else planned, he would park up at a convenient point on the road between the house and the nearest hamlet of Kingarth. There was just a chance that a departing car might lead to something of value.

4.10 p.m.

Inside the house there was no delay. Mabbett barely waited for Mahoney to get in the door, let alone find a chair before barking, "And what's happened with Mad Mick, Liam? Has he returned the money?"

"No, but it's promised within the week."

"Or?"

"He knows better than not to deliver."

"Right. Then let's throw him a bone. Tell him he can keep a thousand of it, but for that he's to pay a visit to the Glasgow Club every night that its open. Not to go in but to keep a watch on who's outside from eleven to one every night. If Wild appears, then he can pick up where he left off. If it's anyone else that he's not sure of, then we want to know straight away."

In answer to the raised eyebrows he said, "I've been talking to people this morning and Wild came back from France as soon as he heard the news. It's thought that he's in Hampshire but no one knows where. I think that he may take up where he left off and we can thank him for our weeks in Winchester. So I'm not hanging around waiting to see what he's doing. We'll find him, and quickly. I want Gordon back down south pulling in all the favours that he has. If Wild's in that area, we want to know. I've got Cameron sniffing around his old police connections so, if he comes this way and makes contact with the Glasgow Busies, we should know. Liam, I want you to spend time inside the Glasgow club when we're operating but stay close here during the day. If there's a sighting we have to move fast, faster than we have in the past. He's been beating us to the punch so far!"

"Do you want me in the house, DM?" from Mahoney.

"No. You're in the cottage as usual, but I want you near a phone at all times and to check with me in any case every morning before you go anywhere."

"Now have you any bright ideas?" The hard eyes swept from Mahoney to Wilson and back again.

"What about the other clubs?" from Wilson. "He could decide to look at them."

"He's never shown any interest in the other clubs and I don't want to advertise our concerns too widely to the other Managers."

Then to Mahoney "Gordon and I have some things to talk over before he goes south. You'll want to put some food in the cottage. Why don't you do that, then come back here in time to take him to Glasgow for the six o'clock shuttle."

To Wilson as Mahoney left the room, "Gordon, I want you to collect 'Spirit' from St Malo. The brief tells me that Customs there are prepared to release her now that the case has collapsed. They're holding the Targett's lorry but the boat's costing them too much in harbour dues, I expect. In any case they haven't enough on us to hold her."

"Can't Jock take her back? I'm not a sailor!"

"That's the point, Gordon, I don't want her taken straight back. You'll leave as though you're taking her to Guernsey, but instead you'll go to Barfleur. There you'll hand over one of the remaining paintings, with instructions about the contact, to Chris Targett, who's looking around for another lorry. You'll have to organise this with him. You'll come straight out again on the same tide and back to Cherbourg. It's only a half hour away. You'll wait in the marina there until you get the word on where to collect the goods that I'm buying, mainly 'E's, Crack and some Smack. Then it's cross Channel and we are in business again."

Wilson started to protest. It was too soon, the police or customs would be watching, it was too dangerous. He was cut off in mid flow by Mabbett.

Impatiently, "That's the very point, man. They'll never expect us to move so quickly! It's the last thing that either the police or the customs would expect."

He went on to explain that the younger of the Targett brothers had taken the rap for the charge of dealing in stolen goods. With no previous convictions, he'd been given a slap on the wrist, a fine, which Mabbett had paid. The older brother, on being released, still wanted "in"; was impressed with the way that the main movers had walked out of Winchester and had looked after him. He was prepared to act as courier if Mabbett bought them a replacement vehicle for the one seized by French customs, and a suitable "transportation fee" of course.

For the next half hour they talked the action through, with Wilson still trying, ineffectually, to move himself away from the sharp end of the business. Mabbett would hear nothing of it. Their trade of 'goods' through the clubs had been hit hard with the loss of the last shipment. All that the business had had in the way of the hidden margin for the past six weeks was what the "bouncers" and club management had managed to extract from punters and recycle.

This was peanuts. They needed to be back in the main supply chain. It was time for Wilson to earn the very good "bonuses" that he had been taking for the last few years.

4.35 p.m.

For his observation spot, Martin had chosen a gravelled drive facing the handful of cottages that formed the hamlet of Kingarth. It was on the left side of the road travelling from Kilchatten and led to one isolated cottage, which seemed unoccupied. All windows were shut and curtains drawn on a warm sunny afternoon. He had been parked in the side road for only some twenty minutes when a car approached from Kilchatten. To Martin's surprise, instead of passing, the car slowed and swung into the drive in which he was parked. Lifting the newspaper from his lap, he lowered his head but was conscious that the car slowed even more and its driver stared hard as he bumped slowly past, up to the cottage behind.

In his mirror, Martin saw the driver of the other car get out by the cottage gate. The tall lean figure confirmed the sideways glance that he had made as the car passed. It was Liam Mahoney!

Mahoney stood for moment and then started towards Martin's parked car. Before he had covered more than a few yards, Martin had the Escort's engine running, was in gear and moving off. In his mirror, Martin could see that Mahoney was now running, and with one hand tucked inside his jacket. Ignoring the possibility of other cars passing, Martin swung onto the road, accelerating away towards Rothesay debating his immediate movements. He had been surprised by Mahoney, was on an island with only ferries to carry him away. At either of the ferry points there was bound to be a delay before he could board and the ferry sailed. He was unarmed, whereas he was quite sure that Mahoney would not be. Mahoney would either be following now as quickly as possible, or on the 'phone to others of Mabbett's crew. What to do?

Martin drove hard in the direction of Rothesay. Any confrontation with

Mahoney had to be on his terms, not Mahoney's. He ran the various options through his mind until a plan formed. Then, still with an empty road in his rear view mirror, he swung off, taking a secondary route across a hill and into the small streets at the back of the town. He looked for and found an area where a number of cars were parked around guest houses and small hotels and slotted the Escort in amongst them. Taking his hand luggage he made enquiries and eventually found a hotel which could provide a room overlooking the parking area. Using a false name, he booked in and settled down to rest, prepare the radio transmit and receive equipment that he had brought with him and to keep one eye on the parked car.

The evening passed slowly and he left the room only once to purchase fast food and a couple of cans of drink. By midnight, the normally quiet area was very quiet indeed and Martin slipped out of the hotel with no one aware of his departure.

Sunday 2nd August 1992
12.30 a.m. Kilchatten, Scotland

There was not a glimmer of light from any of the Kingarth Cottages. In the darkness outside the headlamps' beam, Martin saw that the track which led from the road to Mahoney's darkened cottage was empty. He guessed that the hunt was still on for him. He hoped they would give up before dawn.

Cutting the engine on the Escort, he stepped out of the car. Taking the detonator and receiver that he had just spent ten minutes wiring up, he opened a plastic package which contained the remaining stick of Semtex from the two that he had removed from the Porsche. The thin surgical rubber gloves on his hands made his movements slightly clumsy as he checked the connections on the equipment, pushed the detonator into the Semtex and slid the package under the Escort's seat. He then walked quietly away to settle down behind the garden wall of a cottage on the opposite side of the road. There was a convenient hedge behind the wall and he was completely out of sight unless someone leant over the wall with a torch. It was perhaps a long shot, but long shots were the only ones in his armoury at that moment.

The dark hours passed with little local movement and Martin, curled up under the hedge, shivered and wished that he had brought the sleeping bag as well. To his surprise, he felt calm, despite being on the point of an action which, a few days ago, would have been totally alien. He wondered about that and, not liking the premise that he was perhaps no better in some respects than the enemy, he deliberately shifted his thoughts to what he should do in the event of a no show.

2.35 a.m.

He need not have wondered. The headlights of a car appeared from the direction of Rothesay. It slowed and turned into the drive then braked abruptly, close to the parked Escort. Martin raised his night glass and waited. There was no movement for several seconds, then the driver's door opened and a man stepped out. He moved quietly around the Escort, peering in, then walked towards the cottage, taking his time and moving from the cover of bushes to trees and then the hedge which bordered the garden. Avoiding the gate, he disappeared from sight through a gap to one side of the building.

Seconds dragged by and became minutes. Each minute seemed to take an age, but the wrist watch told him that only eight minutes had passed before the figure appeared again. This time it moved quickly towards the Escort and, reaching it, placed a hand on the bonnet then shone a torch into the interior. It moved around the car, the torch playing over the body panels and then the ground as the man lowered himself and checked underneath.

Martin found himself holding his breath, conscious that his heart was racing. He wondered still whether he could do what was in his mind and what he had prepared for. He knew that he could still change his mind. He need not throw the switch now in his left hand. Then he thought of Eileen and Ewen. Thought of Madame Tabard and her children. Thought of young Jason Emery. Then he remembered the impassive, emotionless face that he had watched in court during the remand hearing, and knew that he was about to take a life, given not a chance but half a chance.

The figure stood, moved around the car to the passenger's side and Martin heard the sound of glass shattering, although the door had not been locked. "Clever bastard" he whispered to himself. Through the monocular, he could see the figure clearing glass from the shattered window, then it leant in and the torch searched the inside of the door panels. The beam suddenly swung up and the figure reached up. The interior light of the Escort came on. Now Martin could see clearly. It was Mahoney. There was no doubt in his mind and, with no hesitation, he thumbed the switch in his left hand, lowering his head as the explosion shattered the quiet of the Scottish night.

The shock wave hit him, despite the protection of the wall. Debris rained around, pattering, through the bushes, rattling against the walls of the cottage. Looking up, he saw a smoking wreck where the car had been with flames flickering small beneath the shell and a pall of smoke just visible, darkening the night sky above.

"Die, you bastard, die, die!" he muttered beneath his breath and, to his surprise, he felt a sudden savage exultation.

Getting to his feet, he forced stiff legs that did not wish to function into a trot, running past the row of cottages where lights were coming on and voices could now be heard. By the time that the first door opened, he had passed the last cottage on his side of the road and was opposite a house which faced the beach on his left. The door opened and, blessing the absence of street lighting, he dropped to the ground as the occupant walked to the road and called out questioningly to others who were now gathering. As this man walked to join them, Martin slipped down onto the sand and shingle of the beach, walking parallel with the road and the shoreline. In the distance, opposite the hotel where he had stayed before, he could just make out the pale shape of the dory that he had used previously, swinging on her moorings. He breathed a sigh of relief, settling into a cleft in the rocks which was hidden from the road.

For the best part of another hour he lay and listened to the noise of various vehicles arriving and departing. First two tones and blue lights. Then there was a pause with only an occasional engine starting and vehicle leaving.

The cold from the rocks crept into his buttocks, back and shoulders. His mind, which had been racing, slowed and he waited with an almost detached curiosity for the horror of what he had done to envelope him. He waited for the first pangs of conscience, the twinges of guilt, at the very least he expected unease. It did not come. Instead there was a coldness and a sadness, an indefinable sadness. Not for the man he had killed, more for himself. A selfish sadness, creeping like a dark fog from the smoke of the explosion to envelope him in a strange feeling of loss. He had stepped through a door, a one way door. There was no going back, no return to what had been. He sensed that for now and forever, wherever he was, there would be a dark cloud, not far away, at the back of his mind.

Mentally he replayed the moment of the explosion. He had not seen the actual event; his head had been down, sheltering, but he could see again the black pall of smoke against the night sky. Instead of guilt, he found himself considering the effects in much the way that he had been trained both in the army and the police. The petrol tank had not caught so there had been no fire. That meant plenty of forensic. He had not thought that far when he set the trap. The traces of explosive from this stick of Semtex would match the first stick, which he had placed on the spare wheel of Mahoney's Renault and which the Hampshire Police now had. No problem there except that Bill might wonder again about Martin, knowing where to direct the police search of the vehicle. His fingerprints and clothing traces would be expected on the wrecked Ford anyway. The only item which might jar in a good forensic examination were the striations on the door glass broken by Mahoney. They would show that the glass had been broken from the outside, not a likely event if someone were setting a trap for him, as he hoped the police would believe.

The noise of yet another car starting up and driving away brought him back to the present. He stood up, stretched stiff joints and looked out to sea. The dory moored in the bay was now swinging in a different direction. The tide had turned, it was starting to run north, which was what he had been waiting for. Slipping off his outer clothes, he made a tight bundle, strapping it with the belt from his trousers. With only underpants on, he stepped into the cold waters and, holding the bundle above his face, began quietly swimming, on his back, to the dory. Despite the time of year, the water was very cold. And he was conscious that he could not stay in it too long.

Reaching the boat, he pushed the dry top clothes under the boat's cover onto the stern seat. Cold was eating into him now and he began to wonder whether he would find the energy to heave himself out of the water.

Swimming to the bow, he sought the mooring rope and then the small buoy that held that rope when the boat was off its mooring.

He could no longer feel his fingers, his muscles felt leaden. The cold, the long swim, the hours of waiting before that and very little food during the previous twelve hours. These all compounded now to weaken him. Struggling with the weed covered rope, he tried but failed to put a bight into it to provide a foothold onto the boat's bow.

Desperately now, he swam back to the stern, feeling for the thin cord holding the cover in place. With strength ebbing, he found a slip knot, which had been tied to undo easily and release the cover. With that loosened, he was able to pull a section of the cover's retaining rope down. Holding on with both hands, he got one foot into it, transferred his grip to the boat's hull and, with the last of his strength, hauled himself onto the cover which, with its retaining rope loosened, collapsed under his weight.

For several minutes he lay motionless, breathing ragged, as he regained strength. Then, stripping off the underpants and using his dry shirt as a towel, he rubbed himself down, struggled into his top clothes and, with warmth gradually seeping back, fumbled the cover off of the boat and dropped the mooring buoy over the side.

Freed from its mooring, the boat drifted on the back current until the main tide caught it. Then, moving first east and then north, it drifted away from the shoreline. Still he waited, until sure that he was out of earshot of those still working near the beach at Kingarth. With the boat now north of Bruchag Point, he investigated the motor and fuel tank. Tonight was his lucky night. He could forget about the unwieldy sculling oar that lived in the bottom of the boat. There was fuel in the tank. Releasing the air vent, he closed the choke and opened the throttle slightly then pulled sharply on the recoil starter. On the third attempt the engine spluttered and died. On the fifth attempt it caught and, easing in the choke, he opened the throttle and headed north for Rothesay Harbour.

The first light of dawn was turning the dark eastern sky into a pearly glow as he eased the boat alongside the harbour jetty. Replacing the covers, he made sure that it was secure and set off at a fast walk through the deserted streets. In half an hour, he was back in his room, taking a hot shower. Minutes later he dropped straight into an exhausted sleep.

6.30 a.m.

The telephone roused both Mabbett and Wilson from easy chairs. They were fully dressed, had been all night, awaiting another call from Liam Mahoney. The first call had been half an hour after he had left their afternoon meeting.

He had reported the presence of a Ford Escort outside the cottage with, he thought, Martin Wild in the driving seat. Mabbett's instructions had been terse and to the point. For the rest of the afternoon, the evening and into the night, searches of the island had been organised, but without result. Then, just before three in the morning, they received another call from Mahoney, stating that the Escort had reappeared outside the cottage, though with no one in it. Nothing further had been heard and it was with more than a little confusion that he now listened to the voice of a police officer telling him that there had been an explosion, that the cottage was damaged, that a motor car had been destroyed and that a body needed identification.

Police scene of crime tape barred entry to the approach drive at the cottage and an officer sitting in one of the small local police cars stopped Mabbett as he swung the Jaguar off the road.

The shattered shell of the Escort was partially, hidden behind a canvas screen. Floodlights, imported by the police forensic team during the night, were still illuminating the scene, although no one appeared to be working on the car at that moment.

Upon Mabbett giving his name, the officer used his personal radio and, presently, two men in plain clothes came out of the cottage. The taller of the two said, "Mr Mabbett?

"Yes."

"I'm Detective Inspector Erskine. I understand that this is your property?" He nodded to the cottage.

"Yes, I own it, although don't live here. An employee, Liam Mahoney, uses it. He should be here."

"Could you describe Mr Mahoney?"

Mabbett gave a brief description and the two CID linen exchanged glances.

"When did you last see Mr Mahoney?"

"Last evening."

Would you know what Mr Mahoney was wearing last night?"

Mabbett supplied a description of what Mahoney had on.

"Mr Mabbett. We are rather afraid that your employee may have died in the explosion which wrecked that car. We need someone to identify a body. Do you think that you could do that from clothing and personal possessions – or are there any relatives living locally?"

Mabbett was silent for a moment, not trusting himself to speak, taken aback that these policemen should think Mahoney dead, when he had expected Wild to be the victim.

Now, carefully, "Liam does not have relatives in this country. I'm not sure of his connections in Ireland, which was his home. Perhaps, as his employer, I can help."

The Detective Inspector said, "I'm afraid it won't be a straightforward identification. As I said, we can show you some clothing and personal effects. There was not much left of the face. He must have been right over the bomb…the explosion, when it occurred."

"Bomb! You mean that this car was wrecked by a bomb!"

"Perhaps I should not have said that. We're not absolutely sure yet so I would be obliged if you would keep that remark to yourself for the time being."

"What makes you think that it was Liam? That's not his car," from Mabbett, still not believing what he was hearing.

"The build and clothing that you described are similar, but we'll need positive identification."

Arrangements were made for Mabbett to attend the Rothesay Mortuary later that afternoon and, grim faced, he left the scene to return to Kilchatten House.

1.30 p.m.

The desk man in the small police station at Rothesay seemed mildly surprised when Martin reported that his Ford Escort was missing from its overnight parking space.

"We dinna have many car thefts on the island. Are you sure that you looked in the right place?" He had met silly Sassenachs before. Turn them round twice and they're lost.

Martin assured him that he had looked most carefully and was quite sure that the car had been taken. It was not until the man started taking details that the air of slight disbelief disappeared.

"The registration number, Sorr?"

Upon being told it, the pen creeping across the paper slowed and stopped. A second's hesitation and then he walked to a nearby VDU screen, tapped a couple of keys, waited for the screen to change and, without a word, picked up a telephone. "I've a Mr Wild in the office, the owner of…" and he gave a description of Martin's car.

All casualness was now gone and walking quickly to a side door, he opened it, went through to reappear at a second door on Martin's side of the counter. The door had the words Interview Room on it.

"Perhaps you'd wait here, Mr Wild. An officer will be with you shortly."

In the following half hour, Martin described a holiday in Scotland, fishing and bird watching, which had ended with the disappearance of the Ford

Escort. He thought that the story had been accepted, until another, and obviously more senior plain clothes man walked into the room. Martin was then taken to another room on the first floor of the building, where the senior officer read his statement, flicked the switch of an interview recorder, stated his name as Detective Inspector Erskine, gave the name of the other officer present and asked Martin to state his name and address "for the record".

"Now, Mr Wild, before you are asked to sign this statement, perhaps you would like to think again. I've just had a conversation with an Officer from Hampshire where you once, served. He has told us about your previous efforts to help in murder enquiries in that Force area and up here in Glasgow. He was quite complimentary, but it's obvious that you're not here for the fishing!"

With an effort, Martin smiled, paused and said "I was hoping not to get too involved this time. I really know nothing of value. I arrived on the Island yesterday with the intention of having a look around. As I came off the ferry, I saw one of the people who had been arrested during the previous enquiry. I didn't hang around. I didn't think I'd been seen, so found a hotel and spent the rest of the day getting some sleep and then eating and having a drink."

"How do you explain your car being at Kilchatten?"

"I parked it outside the hotel. When I next went to it, it was gone so I came in here to report it as stolen."

"How did you get about on Saturday?"

"I walked, getting to know the town. I can only think that the car was stolen during the night. From the reaction of your Officer when I gave him the index number, and your own interest now – I presume it must have been used in a serious crime of some sort."

For the next half hour, Martin answered detailed questions, going over and over the same ground. He knew the game and kept his story simple until Inspector Erskine told him of the explosion and the death.

Martin looked shocked. "I guess I've been very lucky then. Presumably the car would have reappeared where I left it and something nasty would have happened to me?"

Erskine made no reply but picked up a telephone. "Is McNeil from Soco in the building?"

Waiting for a reply, he said to Martin, "You'd have no objection if our specialist runs some tests on your clothing and skin, would you?"

"No problem at all." Martin thought of the rubber gloves and the clothing now disposed of, hoping that there was nothing new in the police armoury since his days in Soco.

Then followed an hour of questioning, checking the statement. The name of the campsite that Martin had stayed at, descriptions of the couple that Martin had met and the site's manager. The officer was especially interested in the purchase of the Ford Escort and the reason for Martin's return to Bute. It was only after telephone calls had confirmed a large element of the statement's content and the Soco tests had proved negative that he was allowed to leave.

He was warned that he should stay in touch with the investigating officer, supply any new address and inform the police if he was about to leave the area. To his relief they did not "Police Bail" him and appeared, from their comments, to accept his story.

Fortunately also, the Dory from Kilchatten still lay undiscovered at Rothesay pier and, being a Sunday, the CID office at Southampton which received the Rothesay enquiry was short staffed. By the time that the Southampton office man had read the fax that followed his telephone conversation with Erskine, realised its import, found Potter in the middle of a Sunday round of golf and then contacted the Rothesay police, it was too late. Martin was out of the station and Potter's input of little use.

As a diversion, Martin telephoned the Bookings office at Glasgow Airport to reserve a seat on the BA shuttle to Heathrow. He then took a taxi to the Bothwell Services at the top end of the M74. Luck was with him and within twenty minutes he had a ride southbound on a haulage lorry with a promise to buy dinner for the driver en route to London.

He kept his word to Detective Inspector Erskine by leaving a telephone message at the Rothesay desk and giving the address of the Christchurch Sailing Club as a contact point!

For the following two days the enquiry into Liam Mahoney's death progressed little apart from forensic confirmation of the cause and fingerprint evidence from the RUC to confirm the identity. Then, almost simultaneously the Harbour Master at Rothesay informed the police of the strange dory and its owner reported its loss. Suddenly Martin was again of extreme interest to the police for, under the aft seat of the boat was found a pair of sodden men's briefs with a laundry tag in the waistband which, upon investigation, pointed the police in his direction. Once more both the criminal fraternity and the law enforcers were looking for him, but now with increased urgency.

Tuesday 4th August 1992
10.50 a.m. Bristol

Joan Mann had opened the door to find a weary Martin Wild leaning against the wall outside. She said to John when he got back later "Marty's sleeping in the spare room." It was more intuition than perception that made her add "He looks different, seems changed somehow."

"I expect he's just tired."

"No, it's more than that, I'm sure. I can't put my finger on it, but he seems different, quieter, not so free and easy. I haven't seen him smile properly since he arrived."

"Give him a chance Joan. He's been in bed most of that time, hasn't he?"

"But you know Marty. That lopsided smile's his trademark!"

An hour later movement from their guest room brought Joan to the kitchen where a pot of coffee was soon brewing. She heard Martin speak to John as he headed for the bathroom.

Another twenty minutes and the two men were drinking fresh coffee in the room that John used as an office when at home, whilst Joan prepared a late breakfast for Martin.

"God, that tastes good," said Martin as he sat back in the chair.

"You still look tired, Marty, despite sleeping for half a day."

"Yes, but a hundred per cent better than I was a few hours ago." Dozing in the cab of the lorry between Glasgow and London, then again on the coach that he had taken from Victoria to Southampton. Some broken sleep in the reclined seat of the Porsche en route to Bristol. None of that had properly refreshed him. The morning in John's guest room had been the first true sleep in two days and, although it had lasted only a few hours, he felt revitalised.

"So what have you been up to?"

Martin outlined the events of the past few days, sticking to the story given to the police and omitting his own part in Mahoney's death.

When John questioned the cause of the explosion, Martin shrugged his shoulders and said. "I suggested to the police that perhaps the car was being boobytrapped ready for my return but I'm not sure that they took that seriously."

He was careful not to put John in a position where any subsequent questioning by the police might require him to lie, although he noted the quizzical look in John's eyes as he avoided direct answers to certain questions and merely smiled at some comments. John would draw his own conclusions and Martin knew that they wouldn't be far wrong. John was a wise old bird and would understand the reasons for his evasiveness. They had known each other for a long time, had worked together, sometimes in fraught situations and, perhaps most importantly, came from a similar background with common experience. Either would have done all that they could for the other, but both knew the value of "need to know". In this case Martin was sure that his caution was essential for John's sake.

"Is there anything that's happened that I should know about, that I can help with?" was John's final question.

Martin thought for a moment and then said, "No, if any chickens come home to roost and I need an egg collected, I'll let you know."

They both grinned though Martin's effort seemed somewhat forced and John suddenly remembered his wife's words. Martin had changed. In some indefinable way he was different from the old friend and trusted companion, who had shared lunch with them less than a week ago. John felt a sadness, wondering whether that which had happened in the last few days had altered Martin in a significant way. A level of casual good humour was missing and there seemed a veneer of hardness, a wariness that was alien to the personality that he had enjoyed for so many years.

"What do you intend doing now?" he asked.

"Well, sticking with the chicken metaphor, the foxes will be sniffing around the coop in Hampshire as well as Scotland, so I'll see whether I can continue laying a false scent for them. They haven't been all that clever so far. My only real problem is that the "gamekeepers" may also be wondering about me again by now. I can't expect them to prowl around without tying me in in some way or another."

"You take care. Don't get too cocksure."

"You know what they say about a moving target."

With that, Martin got to his feet. "Thanks for the rest and refuelling stopover, John. I'll collect a few essentials from that trunk that I left with you, but then I must be on my way – wherever it is!"

"Stay in touch, Marty. Anything I can do, just ask."

Martin raided the large travelling trunk that he had left with John before his last trip to France, said his goodbyes and thanked Joan for the bacon sarni thrust into his hand for later.

John walked out to the Porsche with him and, as Martin was just about to move off, the carphone rang. It was Bill Creighton.

"Martin, I've been dialling this number all morning."

"Sorry, Bill, what is it?"

"I've just heard from one of our French contacts at St Malo. They've released that bloody boat of Mabbett's. The skipper that he employs, Jock somebody, is back there already. Thought you'd like to know."

"Many thanks, Bill. Any other news?"

"No, but what's this I've been hearing about Liam Mahoney? Potter was on the phone to the Rothesay lads for half an hour."

Martin gave Bill the Wild version of Mahoney's death, as he had to John.

"Well I haven't spoken with you, Marty, cos they're bound to be looking for you again. Better stay out of sight unless you want another session with the CID up north."

Martin put down the phone and looked at John, who was leaning in the window listening to Martin's end of the conversation. "Guess that makes up my mind for me, Johnno," he said cheerfully. "La Belle France once again. I'll send you a postcard!"

10.15 p.m.
Cadnam, New Forest

Gordon Wilson was in a foul mood. Mabbett was moving fast and Wilson was a man who liked to take his time and think things through. He wasn't being given the chance. In the six days since they had walked out of Winchester, he had flown to Scotland with the man, argued unsuccessfully against another early drugs run, helped organise the searches for Martin Wild on the Isle of Bute, ferried the more trusted "bouncers" from the mainland to Rothesay and back to do that, sat with Mabbett whilst they waited the long hours before news of Mahoney's death, and then stood apart as Mabbett vented his anger after his visits to the police and the mortuary.

Now he was at home for only the second time in seven weeks just to pick up fresh clothing before leaving to join Jock on that blasted boat. That was half the trouble. The weather was not good and the thought of a rough trip in a small boat around a coast that he knew to be dangerous added to his concern. And then there was Chris Targett, the haulier. He didn't want to trust the man but was going to have to. Mabbett had forced him into a situation where he, Wilson, had organised the Targett family into the operation and was the only person with whom they had direct contact. Since their arrival on the scene, things had gone wrong and the way that the elder brother had walked out of the "handling" charge made Wilson wonder. He had checked them out himself but, again, had not had time to double check and get to know them as he would have preferred.

Now there were new instructions, new information from Mabbett. Some guy, that he did not know and had never heard of down in Spain, was apparently organising the German / French side of the deal for Mabbett. He guessed it to be one of Mabbett's expat Costa criminal friends but, not knowing the detail made him nervous. In the back of Wilson's car was the second of the three paintings stolen from the country house and which he had just collected from Watson at Beaulieu Road in the Forest. It was in a frame with another painting over the top of it. The paperwork for export of the visible painting was legit, but it was another risk that he would have preferred not to take so soon after his holiday in Winchester.

With a final check over his baggage, he shouted at the dogs as they got in the way, kissed his wife and left in the Mercedes. He hoped to Christ that this car wasn't on some police list somewhere, but he had no time to organise an alternative. He had to be on the night ferry in an hour. The rear tyres spun gravel as he went up the drive and he barely stopped as he hit the road. He cursed again as he had to slow and hoot Forest ponies out of the way then he was off, heading for a rough English Channel with still no proper sleep and not much appetite. God damn this man Wild, things had been fine and dandy before he came along. Then his thoughts went to the reason why Wild had "come along" and the shattered body that had been Liam Mahoney came to mind. He shivered suddenly. Mabbett had better deal with Wild pretty quickly, the man was dangerous and had disappeared again. Perhaps there was a good side to putting up with a rough channel and Jock and that damned boat.

Sturminster Marshall, Dorset

Some twenty miles away, a black Porsche was carving a discreet path through the traffic on the A350 leading to Poole. Martin was not in a hurry, but it was a winding country road that he enjoyed and concentrating on driving helped relax him. A ticket was waiting at the Brittany Ferry office. The bookings girl had been very cooperative despite the poor connection from his car phone. He had time to spare.

As Gordon Wilson drove onto the car ferry, Martin pulled the Porsche up beside the ticket office. A few minutes later and he was amongst the cars going up the ferry's ramp. As Wilson opened his cabin door, Martin was approaching the Information Desk to enquire about availability. There was no problem and he dropped his travel bag in the cabin before joining the queue at the ship's restaurant.

With due deference to the weather conditions – blowing half a gale from the southwest – Gordon Wilson decided to pick up some duty frees rather than food. He would wait and see how he felt when the boat sailed.

An hour later, with the lights of the English coast now out of sight, Martin sat at a window table enjoying the last of a half bottle of Muscadet and moonlight through ragged clouds, glinting off white-topped crests. Although the ferry was crowded, there were some empty tables in the restaurant.

In his cabin, Gordon Wilson lay on his back, eyes shut and hands clasped across his beer belly, hoping that the porpoising, screwing motion of the boat would not get any worse. He was on the borderline and thankful that he had his own toilet.

Wednesday 5th August 1992
7.15 a.m. St Malo, France

The black cavern of the ferry's car deck was noisy and fume filled. Martin eased the clutch on the Porsche as the cars in front of him moved again. His thoughts were on an early stop for breakfast, until the queue that he was in came to the unloading ramp where other cars were slotting in from the right. The driver of a white Mercedes saloon two cars in front looked over his left shoulder checking his gap was available – and breakfast was forgotten!

Martin recognised the profile first and, checking memory banks that were just waking up, remembered that Gordon Wilson's car was a white Mercedes. Then the registration number was visible and that confirmed it.

"Well, who would have guessed? Thank you Lady Luck!" Martin murmured.

The Porsche would stand out like a sore thumb in a wary driver's mirror, so Martin eased off and allowed another car to slot in ahead. As he cleared the ramp, he moved to the right, allowing another car to take a space. If the Mercedes headed for the countryside, there would be difficulty following him but, to his relief, Wilson drove slowly to a different part of the port area.

Martin need not have worried. Gordon Wilson was recovering from sea sickness, concentrating on driving on the right hand side of the road and also attempting to follow directions given to him over the telephone by Jock, the skipper, to the customs berth where *Spirit of Ecstasy* lay. He did not once see the squat shape of the Porsche three or four cars back in his rearview mirror.

As they turned into another part of the dock area, Martin lost the cover of other traffic, and was forced to drop back even further, approaching each change of direction with caution in case Wilson had stopped. His care was rewarded when the Mercedes came to a halt where the white superstructure of *Spirit* was just visible above the quayside. Quickly turning into a side road, he left the car and ran back to peer around the corner at the distant scene. Wilson was standing on the quay with cupped hands to his mouth. Martin could not hear, but presently another figure appeared, clambering into sight from a ladder, which evidently gave access to the boat.

After a few minutes conversation, Wilson took a bag and a large flat package from the boot of the Mercedes, handed them to the other figure and disappeared down the ladder. The other man then dropped the bag, for Wilson to catch? Then, lying flat out on the quayside, he carefully lowered the flat package.

He then walked to Wilson's Mercedes, got into the driving seat and started the engine. Martin ducked back as the reversing lights came on and, as the

Mercedes circled the quayside, ran back to the Porsche. He guessed that Wilson was not going anywhere. The new driver was either going to park the car, or was off on an errand. If the latter, it might be useful to know where.

Martin followed at a distance for the best part of a mile when, just outside the dock area, the Mercedes pulled up at a ship's chandler. Martin drove past and parked some yards beyond another vehicle. The driver of the Mercedes hurried into the chandler's. He was gone several minutes and Martin left his car to peer through the glass door. There seemed to be some difficulty.

Martin did not know the driver of the Mercedes, so walked in and stood quietly waiting. The pair were not getting very far. The man from the boat was a Scot and his accent put him at a disadvantage when speaking to the Frenchman behind the counter, who obviously had little, if any, English. Martin presently said in English, "Can I help you? I speak a little French."

The man swung round, frustration written all over his features. "Aye. Can ye tell thus mon that I need a chart of Barfleur Harbour and approaches?"

Martin translated the requirement and said, "Nice little harbour. Been there before?"

"No. We've charts up to Cherbourg but nothing further east."

"Best time to approach is two hours before high water." Martin said. "The off lying rocks are a bit dodgy. How much do you draw?"

"Five feet to be safe."

"You'll have plenty of water to half tide but moor with care as the harbour dries."

The Scotsman swore. "That's all I need!"

"If you're staying over a tide, try and lay against the harbour wall to starboard as you enter. You'll see fishing boats there," offered Martin.

"Thanks, but we should be in and out on the one tide." He took the chart being proffered, paid for it, thanked Martin and was gone.

Martin purchased a local Tide Table and left the shop as the Mercedes drove away. "Useful. I'll take a look at you in Barfleur, then decide about Gordon bloody Wilson!"

3.10 p.m. Barfleur, France

The wind from the west had moderated and moved around to the north east, but was still strong enough to whip up wavelets in the harbour and scatter nylon twine from the fishermen's nets on the quay. Barfleur was an attractive sight to the few holidaying visitors walking the dockside. The fresh breeze ensured that more were sitting at cafe tables inside than out. The wind's change of direction brought it straight into the harbour mouth and, Martin knew, would have put it right on the nose of *Spirit of Ecstasy* as she headed north along the Cotentin Peninsular towards Barfleur – that was if she was headed there on this day.

"They'll have had a rough passage," he mused, as he sat in the window looking out over the harbour.

From the tide tables that he had bought and the distance of about one hundred nautical miles that his Michelin map told him lay between St Malo and Barfleur, Martin had reckoned it would take the boat some five hours in good conditions to make the trip. At St Malo, he had found a position which gave him a view of the customs berth and started a watching brief from 10 am that morning, six hours before high water. Sure enough, at a quarter past ten, a figure appeared, working around the boat. Ten minutes later, a second figure joined the first and Martin had then seen a puff of dark exhaust as the cold diesels came to life. At a few minutes after ten thirty, the mooring lines were slipped and 'Spirit" moved out from the Quay.

Martin left his position and drove to the promenade overlooking the harbour entrance. There he parked on the cobbled pavement in front of The Casino. From this point he had watched the boat leave the harbour and, rolling and pitching in the broken waves south of the Ile de Cezembre, turn north east towards the Iles Chausey.

"He's going to take the inside passage, east of the Minquiers," thought Martin. "That will give him some shelter from this sea," and with thoughts of the vast scattering of rocks and reefs in a dangerous tidal area. "Hope he knows his navigational marks."

Leaving St Malo, Martin had a good run, despite the holiday traffic, and was at Barfleur just after one thirty. His luck held and a comfortable hotel close to the inland end of the harbour had a room free. Even better, he found a bar with a view, towards the sea. Now he waited and hoped that his assumptions from the conversation with Jock had been correct and that the weather had not been too much for the boat's crew. He wasn't worried about their comfort, just their "availability!"

That thought brought another consideration to mind. In Martin's revised plans Wilson was fair game, but what about "Skipper Jock"? It was conceivable, though not very likely, that he was innocent of the group's activities where drugs were concerned. To Martin, there was a total distinction between being involved in "normal" smuggling and the supply of drugs to the naïve world of club-going youngsters. Unless he found to the contrary, any plans made for Wilson must avoid injury to Jock. That might make things difficult.

For almost another hour he sat there musing and with growing concern at the non-appearance of the boat. Then, around the sea wall guarding the harbour from the waves, came the dark blue hull of *Spirit*, now salt stained and with her white superstructure wet to the deckhouse windows. She slowed to a standstill in the centre of the small harbour and a single figure appeared from the wheelhouse to fasten fenders on her port side and prepare fore and aft mooring lines.

Where was Wilson? The man that Martin watched through his binoculars was almost certainly the skipper. Despite the less than figure hugging sailing jacket and hood, worn against the cold breeze funnelling through the harbour, he could see that he was smaller and leaner than Wilson and was moving about the deck with the almost leisurely but assured air of a practised seaman.

Fenders and ropes in place, the figure stood for a moment staring at the fishing boats lying alongside the quay and then returned to the wheelhouse. The boat turned in her own length and moved ahead, then astern and finally almost sideways to occupy a space between two trawlers, which was not more than twenty metres in length.

"Well done," murmured Martin to himself, "but I bet you've got a bow thruster to help."

The single figure then walked aft, picked up the stern mooring line and, with an easy accurate motion, threw it onto the quay. Walking to the bow, he picked up that line and then climbed the ladder with it looped over his shoulder. Within a few seconds the boat was secured and Martin watched as additional breast lines were put in place.

Still no sign of Wilson as the figure disappeared down below.

Martin was now in a quandary. He could not risk approaching the quay in broad daylight for fear of being recognised and thus interrupting whatever their purpose was. On the other hand, he badly needed to get a better idea of the reason for the visit to Barfleur. He need not have worried about being seen, for there was now no activity on the boat and it was not until some minutes past six when, once again, a figure appeared.

This time it was Wilson. Even at that distance, the beer belly and grey lock of hair were visible as, dressed in a sweater and jeans, he stood at the rail, looking around.

The tide had now turned and was well on its way out. The nearer part of the harbour to Martin was drying with mud visible around the edges and boats settling at odd angles as water disappeared. It was obvious that, despite Jock's remarks in the Chandlers about leaving on the same tide, there had been a change of plan.

The evening shadows were reducing visibility as Martin made up his mind. He returned to the parked Porsche and, selecting some items from the two equipment cases that he carried in the car, put them in to a shoulder bag.

On the quay he saw that Wilson had disappeared but, before long, the two men came up from *Spirit's* cabin, climbed the dock ladder and made for the few bright lights of Barfleur. Martin followed on foot at a discreet distance and said "Yes!" as they disappeared into a restaurant. He waited a few minutes, then walked past on the other side of the road. They were sitting at a table studying menus.

Quickly now he made his way back to the boat and, in the gathering darkness, climbed the ladder down to the deck. The cabin doors were locked, so was the forward hatch. No problem, he had anticipated that and crossed the deck over the saloon area to where there was a Dorade box ventilator. Unscrewing it to its fullest extension, he was able to insert a very small miniature transceiver and suspend it inside by taping the aerial to the rim that went through the deck. He then screwed the ventilator down again, into the closed position.

If the boat were in a sea way there might be a slight tapping noise as it swung, but it was unlikely that the saloon would be occupied at sea by either of the two on board. Logically they would be in the wheelhouse which was several feet away. In any case, even if he only got their conversation that night, it would be worth the effort.

He was just about to run a check with the small receiver that was also in the bag, when he heard voices and footsteps approaching the berth. They had not stopped to eat at the restaurant. Quickly he slid off the saloon roof onto the side deck and, stooping, ran aft where he leant over and dropped the bag onto the teak boarding platform that jutted out from the boat's stern. The platform was just above the waterline and in a couple of seconds he had followed it. As Jock turned his back to climb down the ladder, Martin was stretched horizontally in the angle where the platform met the transom. He wouldn't be seen unless someone looked directly over the stern or walked along the quay.

No one did. The two men entered the boat and Martin lay still as the hull rocked gently to their movements. He could hear the murmur of voices but not what was being said. Out came the receiver from the bag together with a pair of earphones. Plug in, switch on and press the preset that he had tuned to the transmitter's frequency. Praise the Lord, voices. Not too clear but enough to understand most of what was being said.

Wilson's voice: "Glad that Targett…late arriving…enough of that weather."

Jock: "This wind'll be easing now. By the time that…arrives and we get away, the sea will have dropped."

The conversation centred on the rough trip and Wilson's lack of appetite after seasickness. Then further references to Chris Targett. Jock's speech was much clearer to Martin than Wilson's and he guessed that the Skipper was closer to the vent.

After some minutes, the conversation turned to personalities within the organisation and it was obvious to Martin that Jock did not know many of the clubland team. It was equally obvious that Wilson wasn't keen to talk about the others very much. He turned the conversation back to Jock, asking him how long he had known "DM".

"Oh, we go way back...always looked after his boats, right from...to Kilchatten. That was...came up, wasn't it?"

Wilson gave an affirmative and Jock said, "I heard you were...from the Busies."

"Who said?"

"Oh, the lads that worked in the cottage."

The boat rocked again as there was movement in the saloon and the conversation turned to Chris Targett again.

Jock: "Isn't it time he was here?"

Wilson: "He said between ten and eleven."

"I'll get the package up into the wheelhouse."

With another arrival imminent, Martin's position on the boarding platform would be too risky. He could listen to the bug's broadcast from anywhere within a couple of hundred yards, but how to move? There was no way now that he could climb back onto the deck without rocking the boat and risking detection. It seemed there was only one way out of it. He took off his windcheater, rolled it into a tight ball, and pushed it into the shoulder bag. Next the shoes and trousers. With the bag zipped up, he slid his legs gently over the side and into the dark cold water.

"This is getting to be a habit that I don't need!"

Turning, he took his weight on his arms, extended them and then lowered slowly and almost silently into the water. His legs floated up beneath the platform and suddenly encountered a thin length of cord. Cord or rope of any description is normally kept well away from a boat's propellers. Curious, he investigated to find a second, similar length a metre or so away. They were both black in colour, were secured to the stainless steel struts that supported the platform and disappeared under the water towards the rudders or propellers. He could not imagine what they were for but had to dismiss further consideration in the circumstances.

On his back in the water, he took the bag from the platform and, holding it above his face, gently fanned his feet, heading towards a gap between two fishing boats moored side by side astern of *Spirit*.

The water smelled of oil and fish and, as he climbed out onto a slipway beyond the boats, the wind felt colder than ever. Stripping off the wet clothes in the darkness of a seawall, he once again used his shirt to dry as best he could and then put on his jacket, trousers and shoes, the only dry clothing that he now had. The wet stuff was rolled up and put into an empty fish basket on the quay for recovery later if possible. He couldn't put that on the precious electronic equipment in his bag.

Once more respectable, though damned cold, he made his way along the quay. He found that, in the ten minutes or so that he had taken to get away from *Spirit*, a large articulated lorry had arrived and was standing silent and driverless on the quay parking area.

About a hundred metres from the boat was a dark shop doorway and, ignoring the cold, he sat back in it to switch on the receiver again. There were three voices this time. The new voice was English and with an accent which was familiar to Martin, a Hampshire accent perhaps.

Wilson: "…here then, about this time…no later. How will that suit…Jock?"

Jock: "Ay, we can be here but we'll no get away until midday. The tide'll be two hours later than now."

There was more conversation which Martin could not properly hear. Were they moving away from the bug's position?

The new voice: "I'll be away then. Give me a hand up the wall with this."

The conversation faded completely and a minute later a figure appeared climbing from the ladder to turn and reach down for a large package. It looked to be the one that Martin had seen taken onto the boat at St Malo.

The man walked to the artic, climbed aboard, started up and drove off.

The receiver came to life again and Martin's guess that two hours of tidal difference meant three days for the lorry to reappear was confirmed when he heard Wilson say, "We'll get…to Cherbourg and lay up…Saturday, Jock. How long will that take?'

"We're only an hour away."

"That's the best news today. I'm off to my bunk then."

Martin shivered, suddenly very cold. He put away the receiver, got to his feet and made for the hotel and a bath. He hoped no one would get within smelling distance on the way.

Friday 7th August 1992
9.30 a.m. Cherbourg, France

"So that's how it's done!"

Sitting in the cramped cabin of a little Beneteau motor cruiser, with the receiver's earphones clamped to his head, Martin listened to a conversation taking place in the saloon of *Spirit*, some fifty metres away.

The previous day he had watched as the blue and white boat slipped out of Barfleur and, some two hours later, had located her again on the Visitor's Moorings at the Cherbourg Marina. An enquiry of the dockmaster had provided the address of a local company that hired out small motor boats. Within a few hours he was one of dozens of leisure sailors entering the Port du Plaisance to moor on the wooden pontoons, which formed the extensive marina.

Once secured alongside, a quick radio check revealed that the bug in the ventilator was still in place and working. Not only that, the reception was better. Perhaps the light swell in Barfleur harbour had influenced the transmission from the bug, which was hanging by its aerial. Here in Cherbourg Marina there was little water movement at all. Whatever the reason, he could hear clearly now without the infuriating gaps. The limited conversation monitored on the first evening had revealed little of value. Today was a different matter, as the discussion between the two men centred upon their rendezvous at Barfleur the following evening.

There had been references to the return of Chris Targett and the transfer of "…the gear." And then from Wilson, "Where's your wet suit? I haven't seen it this trip. You'll need it tonight."

"It's in the locker forrard. I'll not need it until tomorrow night."

"I'd prefer that we get the containers in place after dark tonight. We can check them for leaks at Barfleur then."

"We could be seen here, Mon," from Jock with a note of protest.

"That's not likely if we do it late. Anyway, you could be clearing a line from around the props or something like that."

"At that time of night!"

"Yes. It's safer here and I want to make sure that everything's tight and together. We haven't used them before and I want to check the locators while we've still got time to sort any problems." Wilson was definite and Jock capitulated.

As Martin listened,, the pieces dropped into place. He visualised again the thin cords at the stern of *Spirit* that his legs had contacted when going for his unplanned midnight dip in Barfleur. No boat would normally rig cordage beneath a boarding platform. It was too close to the propellers and a line around those could put a boat out of action. But, if you were wishing to hide containers and yet have them positioned to be easily disposable, fitting them below the boarding platform and waterline would be ideal.

"That's what they must be for," he breathed to himself. The voices on the receiver faded away with the sound of the saloon door being opened and closed. Martin grappled with the new information, seeking what options this might offer. He knew the time and location of the transfer and he now knew where the drugs would be carried. The more that he thought about it, the more possibilities he could see. Perhaps it was time to deal the "boys in blue" in again. He had not intended following that route again but it would provide insurance should his own, more deadly and certainly more problematic, plans fail.

It was time to do some shopping.

1.35 p.m.
Shirley, Southampton

Some four hours later, Detective Chief Inspector Potter received a telephone call during a meeting in his office.

"Said I was not to be interrupted!" he snapped.

"DC Creighton said you would want to be for this one, Sir. It's Martin Wild. Says it's urgent.'"

The two officers with Potter saw him stiffen, then "Put him on."

"Afternoon, Chief Inspector."

"Martin, where are you? The Glasgow Police want another word with you to clear up some queries on this sudden death on their patch. Explosions seem to follow you around." Ironically.

"No matter where I am, it's where I'm going to be that should be of interest to you."

"Yes?"

"Our friend Mabbett has organised another shipment of drugs. I think they may be landing in your area Saturday night, early hours of Sunday. "Thought you might like to have another crack at him."

Potter's emotions were mixed. The call was out of the blue. He had thought that Wild was on the continent. He certainly would like to redress the embarrassment of the last episode with Mabbett and company but, equally, he could not afford to fail again. Time to share responsibility!

"I'll need more than a telephone call to set this up. Just a minute."

Covering the mouthpiece, he said to the others present "We'll finish this later. Ask Bill Creighton to come up, he's in the office downstairs."

At the end of ten minutes' conversation, Martin had given Potter enough facts to check and, subject to satisfaction and necessary authorisations being obtained, had agreement that the police, and hopefully the customs, would set up an operation following further information from him.

Potter spent the next hour talking to Detective Chief Superintendant Lawson and, with that man's agreement, to the Customs Liaison and Intelligence branches. The section DS and Bill Creighton set about locating the personnel and putting together teams to cover the police side of the operation.

By the late evening it was coming together. There was to be no French involvement at all. The police Air Support Unit would be on standby from first light. The Hampshire police launch *Ashburton* would be stationed in Alum Bay just inside The Needles at the western end of the Isle of Wight. A naval patrol boat with a police team on board would be on standby in the area of the Nab, just off the eastern point of the Isle of Wight. Tactical Firearms Units would be on both craft. A fast Customs cutter was being recalled from other duties but there was no guarantee that it could refuel and be on station in the time available.

Potter was satisfied that, if Mabbett's boat intended making for the Hampshire shoreline, they stood more than a reasonable chance of intercepting it. Dorset Police to the west and Sussex Police to the east were aware of the operation and were putting their own contingency plans in place should the boat end up in their respective patches. His conversation with Wild had anticipated provision of final details from that man and, more importantly, that he would ensure the evidence was available when the boat was intercepted.

That aspect of the exercise was the most worrying to Potter. If things went wrong again, his renowned ability to duck and dive would be tested to the full. It was also occupying Martin's thoughts at just that moment.

10.45 p.m.
Cherbourg, France

The wetsuit was not as good a fit as his own and he could have done with a little more weight on the belt, but at least he was better equipped for the cold of Cherbourg's harbour than he had been at both Kilchatten and Barfleur. Martin had slipped over the side of the Beneteau as soon as it was dark enough to hide his movements and had been in the water under a pontoon by an unoccupied boat for the past forty minutes. Despite the suit, he was cold and hoped that Wilson and company would not wait too long before starting the preparations that he had heard discussed earlier in the day

Twenty metres away, the stern of *Spirit of Ecstasy* was easily visible in the pontoon lighting and Martin knew that, with the assistance of the "night glass", he would be able to see whatever activity took place on the stern of the boat as though he were standing two metres away rather than twenty.

He didn't have any longer to wait. The lights in the boat's saloon went out and then illumination appeared in the stern cabin. Martin expected this to be the Master Cabin on the boat, usually occupied by the owner when he was on board. During previous periods of watching, that cabin had remained in darkness, the saloon and forward cabins being the only ones used by Wilson and Jock.

Removing the waterproof pouch from his belt, he held it above water level and unscrewed the two fasteners which, with double folds of heavy plastic and precisely manufactured strips of a stiffer plastic, provided the sealing effect. With care he extracted the monocular and, on placing it to his eye, could clearly see the detail of *Spirit's* stern.

The light inside the cabin was moving and, as he watched, a new rectangle of torchlight appeared below the cabin portholes. It was about 50 cm square and right in the centre of the transom.

"It's an escape hatch!" Martin breathed.

As he watched, the torchlight went out and a figure slid through the hatch to crouch on the boarding platform. It spent some seconds there, apparently working on the wooden slats of the platform and then, through the hatch, was handed a dark package or container. As the figure turned, Martin caught the glint of reflected light from goggles around a wetsuit hood. Holding the container with one hand, the figure turned again, slipped into the water to disappear under the platform.

For several minutes small ripples spread out from the stern of the boat as the figure worked out of Martin's sight. Then it reappeared and was handed a second similar container from within the escape hatch. Again it disappeared for some minutes to reappear without the container. This time the figure pulled itself up the boarding steps from the water to the platform, stripped off the wet suit and disappeared back through the hatch.

"Well, that was neat and took very little time," Martin muttered to himself, slipping the optic back into its pouch and tightening the screws.

He waited another twenty minutes and was just about to set out to examine *Spirit's* new stern gear when the saloon lights went out, the cabin door opened and the two occupants stepped from the boat onto the pontoon to walk away towards the marina's shoreward lights.

"Perhaps the nosebag calls opportunely," Martin muttered. He waited for a further five minutes and, with no sign of the two returning, took a deep breath and duck-dived quietly beneath the surface, swimming the twenty metres with little effort, to come up under *Spirit's* stern.

By the light of the torch strapped to one arm, he found two identical flat containers secured to the boat by the cords discovered at Barfleur. They were about 18" by 15" and 8" thick and were held flat to the lower surface of the boat's hull under the transom by the tension or the cords. With the point of his diving knife, he scratched the surface to find that the lower section appeared to be a lead casting. The centre and largest section was of a grey plastic, painted over and, when tapped with the knife's handle, seemed to be hollow. The upper part was again of plastic but of a different sort and, he thought, not hollow. There was what appeared to be a short aerial projecting from the top of each container.

The cords came up from the rudder stock, passed through holes in the lead bottom of the container, over the outside of the plastic and through another hole at the top, to tie off on the tubular stainless steel supports of the platform. The whole apparatus was painted black, matching the antifouling of the boat's hull below the waterline. It would be difficult to spot with the boat stationary and virtually impossible when the boat was moving, as the stern would sink lower in the water when under power and especially so at speed.

"What a neat arrangement," Martin muttered, "and I bet that the locators they spoke about are acoustic or ultrasonic transponders, enabling them to be found after they've been dropped from the boat. That way, they could be transferred from one boat to another without the boats actually meeting or, if the Customs were about, they could be ditched and still found later."

Martin was now starting to feel very cold, despite the insulation of the wetsuit. It was time to back off and make some plans. Perhaps he could arrange a "double whammy".

Saturday 8th August 1992
10.45 a.m. Cherbourg, France

Cherbourg harbour was a busy place on a sunny weekend in August. Whilst commercial shipping movements were few, there was a myriad of small pleasure boats, both sail and motor, which passed to and fro in the harbour and its approaches.

Apart from being one of the larger motor yachts out that day, there was nothing to attract attention to *Spirit of Ecstasy* as she cleared the piers enclosing the Petite Rade and, with a white bone of water at her bow, made for the Passe de L'Est, the eastern exit from the Grand Rade or main harbour. With Ile Pelee abeam, Skipper Jock altered course for the La Pierre Noire buoy, which marked the outermost of the underwater rocks jutting almost two miles out from Cap Levi. They had plenty of time and he intended taking the "outside" route to Barfleur rather than the rockhopping inshore passage with its continuous critical pilotage, which would have saved both time and diesel.

As *Spirit* disappeared beyond the old fort on Pelee, Martin slipped into the driving seat of the Porsche, also with Barfleur as a destination. He knew that the next few hours were going to be difficult and almost certainly dangerous. A lot of what he and the police wanted would depend upon circumstances which were not yet known and a large degree of good fortune would he involved as well.

"They say you make your own luck in this world," he murmured as he gunned the Porsche out of Cherbourg onto the road past the local airport and towards Barfleur. "So let's see how true that is."

11.25 a.m.
Winchester, England

In Winchester, DCI Potter stepped into the lift at Police Headquarters. He was on his way to a meeting with Ray Lawson. The Detective Superintendant wanted a briefing on the arrangements in place as a result of Martin's latest information. Potter was not surprised Lawson was taking a lot of interest in this case. Neither he nor the Chief had liked the loss of Eileen Padgett or the subsequent red faces in court!

1.30 p.m.
Glasgow, Scotland

Two hours after the police meeting at Winchester, another main player was on the road far to the north. To Dermott Mabbett it was essential that on this particular day and night he should be very much in evidence, following the routines that any normal hard working night club owner observed. His decision to be even more careful than his previous wary self and avoid another "Winchester experience" deemed that a high profile presence in and around the Glasgow clubs would be wise. His normal routine on those days that he made an appearance was to spend time with management during the day and, in the evening, pay a visit or two to some of the "opposition". This time he would ensure that a number of his competitors in the disco scene were aware of his "innocent" activities and for good measure he would be accompanied by Andrew McAinsh and one the heavier bouncers. That would raise an eyebrow or two – and stick in people's minds.

Wilson would be at the sharp end. It was time for him to earn his hidden commissions. The man had had a soft run over the last few years,

2.50 p.m.
Barfleur, France

Martin finished the last of his coffee in the restaurant at Barfleur. He had not felt like eating but had made himself sit down to a typically extended French lunch. He did not know when the next opportunity to refuel properly would come and couldn't afford to run out of energy later.

He was just paying his bill when a large articulated lorry cruised slowly past towards the harbour. He recognised it instantly. It was the same vehicle that had figured in the after dark transfer on the previous Wednesday night. The first part of the jigsaw was in place!

The parking area on the quayside was very full when he got there. There was no sign of the lorry. Martin guessed that the driver had taken one look at the crowds of tourists and weekenders and continued on to find somewhere less busy. There wouldn't be a transfer in daylight, he felt sure. Nevertheless, when a gap appeared at the inland end of the quay, he slipped the Porsche into it and settled down to wait and watch.

5.35 p.m.

Gordon Wilson glanced at his gold Rolex as Jock brought *Spirit* to a standstill in the centre of Barfleur's small harbour. He wondered where Targett would park and then which side Jock would want mooring ropes and fenders out on, so he stepped into the wheelhouse to ask.

"Starboard side to," was Jock's monosyllabic answer to his query and, during the next few minutes, as he busied himself about the deck and Jock manoeuvred the boat alongside one of the fishing boats, neither of them noticed the quiet departure of the black Porsche to a less conspicuous position in a side street..

Martin, with a large soft bag in his hand, left the car to find a space on the quayside where he settled down and put together a collapsible fishing rod. He also slipped what appeared to be headphones from a Walkman radio over his ears. Inside the bag was the receiver, tuned to the frequency of the bug that he had placed in the boat's ventilator. For several minutes he fiddled with the set, but couldn't get a thing – not even static. Perhaps it had become dislodged or the aerial had become detached, or the battering that it must have received during the trip from Barfleur to Cherbourg had caused it to fail. Whatever!

"Down to eyeballs mark one and intuition, I guess," he said to himself.

He hadn't long to wait – and no intuition was required. As the crew of *Spirit* made her fast to a large fishing boat, a figure detached itself from the people walking the quayside, to drop onto the fishing boat's deck and cross to *Spirit* where, without any preamble, it stepped aboard and stood in the cockpit aft of the wheelhouse, whilst the final ropes were secured.

Wilson then joined the figure and the pair disappeared out of Martin's view, into the saloon.

Again Martin tried the radio receiver, hoping against hope for a crackle and the murmur of voices. Nothing. Deal in the intuition again.

Ten minutes later, Wilson and the newcomer climbed up the quayside, leaving Jock on board. Martin debated whether to follow them, but the distance was too great to get into position without hurrying and that might have drawn attention. He elected to wait and, nearly half an hour later, was rewarded by the sight of the two returning, each carrying a small holdall. These were passed to Jock as they boarded the boat and all three disappeared into the saloon once more.

Twenty minutes later the third man left empty handed.

Time passed, evening came and, as people strolling the quayside thinned, Martin considered his position. If his assumptions were correct, the drugs were now on board and, at some stage before the boat left, probably after dark, they would be transferred to the transom containers via the aft cabin.

The difficulty that he and the police/customs reception committee faced was that they could be dumped at any time after that, by the crew releasing the transom cords. That was what he had to prevent if the operation was to be successful. And that meant waiting until the transfer to the containers was complete. He hoped that the crew would follow the routine of their last visit by going into Barfleur for food after they had made the transfer. That would give him the time that he needed. He was prepared, with the wet suit on under a pair of trousers and an old windcheater. Now all he needed was the transfer and the opportunity. In the meantime, perhaps a change of position would bring some life into the radio receiver.

Reeling in the fishing line, he walked the length of the quay, past *Spirit* to where a short sea wall and large rocks dominated the entrance to the harbour.

From this angle he had a clear view of the boat's stern and her now empty wheelhouse, but the radio was still silent. He felt sure that the sight of a lone fisherman by the harbour entrance would blend with the surroundings. He was also sure that, with the tide now approaching low water, Jock would have to wait until day light to leave the harbour. By then the tide would be getting towards high water and the buoyed channel clearly visible. What he did not know was when the containers were to be filled, though he felt that the positioning of the boat, with only the harbour entrance astern and thus no view from the quay or town, was deliberate. Darkness fell and, sure enough, two figures appeared from the saloon and made immediately for the town centre. Now the problem would be that, if they left the transfer until the dark hours, there would be very little opportunity to "get at" the gear. It was essential that the containers were "got at" before the boat was under way. A change of plan was needed.

Martin knew a little of the layout of the Nelson range of motor yachts. He also anticipated that Mabbett's cabin would only be used to access the escape hatch. The behaviour of Wilson and Jock during the time that he had been watching their movements was to occupy the saloon, the forward cabins and the wheelhouse. He guessed that Mabbett's cabin was sacrosanct, apart from the essential access to the transom.

With the two now out of sight, Martin made his way back to the quayside and, waiting for a moment when there was no one in the immediate vicinity, dropped onto the fishing boat's deck, thence onto *Spirit*, quickly checking the cabin doors, then the escape hatch. No go. All were secure.

From the open area aft of the wheelhouse, he could see that the forward hatch over the saloon was slightly open, normally the case on a boat left temporarily in harbour, but that would give access only to the forward accommodation and the saloon, not the aft cabin which was separated from the rest of the boat by the centre cockpit.

"Ah, but wait," he breathed. A possibility suddenly occurred and he quickly made his way forward. The hatch over the saloon was secured by two internal pivoting arms which, in turn, were held in place by a thumbscrew on each. With these loosened, Martin was able to open the hatch and drop through into the saloon.

Using his torch, he examined the floor and found the recessed thumb loops on the hinged panels, which lifted to give access to the small engine room. Dropping into that area, which was at stooping height for him, he made his way towards the stern of the boat between the two diesels. There, to his relief, he found what he was looking for, a watertight hatch, an internal escape hatch that would lead further aft, into the owner's cabin, he guessed, probably into a wardrobe or hanging locker.

The hatch was secured by two large pivoting levers, which released easily. He had been right! The other side of the hatch was a wardrobe filled with sailing clothes and shore-going gear on coat hangers and in polythene suit bags.

Pushing these aside, he found the double-leafed door, one side of which was bolted on the inside and the other secured only by a spring-loaded catch. He released the bolt, pushed the door and stepped into Mabbett's cabin.

The steps leading down to the cabin from the deck were to his left and, beyond them to a door to the en suite "heads". Facing the stern, to the right was a large bunk and a second similar one was to the left. Between the two bunks was a dressing table with an opening cupboard over it. Opening this, he found it to be, as expected, empty. There was only the interior of the transom escape hatch, again secured by two large pivoting levers.

Returning to the wardrobe, he placed a couple of suits on the floor as cushions, shut the doors and made himself comfortable inside the small compartment. He left the engine room escape hatch open, leaving the option of two hiding places. He guessed that both men would work together and he thus stood a chance of wriggling into the engine room when they came to the cabin or into the wardrobe if Jock followed normal practise or checking the engines before putting to sea.

An hour later voices and movement of the boat indicated a return of the crew. Martin poked his legs through the engine room hatch, waited until the voices moved from the saloon and he heard a key unlocking the aft cabin door, and then slid into the engine room, closing the hatch gently after him.

For the best part of forty minutes there was the murmur of voices, the sound of objects being moved. Through the hull of the boat, upon which he was lying, he heard the disturbance of water. Finally there was some further noise from the cabin and then the sound of doors closing and the voices moved to over his head, in the saloon.

Quietly he shuffled back through the hatch into the wardrobe, closing the hatch behind him. The voices continued for another half hour, with the just audible clink of bottles or glasses and then silence. He waited for another thirty minutes before going back through the hatch from where he could hear the sound of snoring.

"Hope that's both of them!"

Opening the wardrobe, he moved quietly into the aft cabin, opened the cupboard and released the levers securing the watertight transom hatch. The night air was cool as he pushed it carefully open. There was little visible outside. Stars were shining but the moon was behind a bank of cloud. Most of the light from the quay side was blanked out by the bulk of the much larger fishing boat. There was minimal reflected light. Jock had chosen his position well.

Wriggling through the hatch, Martin slid over the boarding platform into the water. He moved slowly and smoothly to reduce movement of the hull and ripples in the water. Sliding under the rear of the boat, he found the twin cords running up from the containers to the teak slats of the platform. Previously they had been individually knotted to the slats. Now he found that they passed through them and were linked by a single strand of dark cord, which formed a tight loop.

"Just one knife cut of that through the escape hatch and they're gone," muttered Martin.

He regained the platform and took a reel of thin but strong braided nylon from the weight belt. Cutting two lengths from it, he formed a loop in one end of each and slipped back into the water. Attaching the loops in the nylon to the eyes in the top of the containers, he passed one strand over the lower ends of the stainless steel platform supports, some inches below the water's surface, whilst the second strand was secured directly between the containers.

Cutting the release rope would now leave the containers suspended from the new nylon, though the old cords should still disappear as the containers changed their position, giving the appearance, he hoped, that the release had been successful. In the event that the nylon was seen and also cut, the containers would fall away from the transom, but hopefully still be attached to the boat.

Everything was going well. Feeling confident, perhaps more so than he should, Martin stood on the platform for several minutes, waiting for water to drain out of the wetsuit. As he did so, he unscrewed the two knurled releases of the watertight pouch clipped to the weightbelt, took out his mobile and punched in the contact number that Potter had given him. He spoke quietly for a few minutes, put the phone away and slid back into the boat, securing the escape hatch. He mopped up wet footprints with one of Mabbett's hand towels and finally collapsed on the suit bags in the wardrobe.

He had committed himself. Mentally he went through the sequence of actions, past and future, looking for some way in which he could improve his chances. Nothing doing. He was tired and he was cold but, despite the latter, he curled on his side and, with the remainder of Mabbett's clothing piled over his body for warmth, drifted into a doze.

Sunday 9th August 1992
5.30 a.m. Barfleur, France

Martin was suddenly awake. Wide awake! There was the murmur of voices from the saloon. Slivers of faint daylight pierced the gloom of the locker space. He had dozed fitfully during the small hours and he checked his watch against the tide times in his head. The movement brought a reminder of the cramped space. As best he could, conscious that he would need mobility very soon, he stretched stiff muscles and aching joints. Mabbett's shore going gear didn't make a comfortable mattress.

Suddenly there was the noise of catches being operated and panels moved. Skipper Jock was doing an engine check! Holding his breath, Martin twisted around and pulled against the shut but unsecured hatch between the wardrobe back and the engine room. If Jock saw that the hatch handles were upright rather than in their normal horizontal position, he might be tempted to look further. If he did, it was all up!

"Concentrate on your engine checks, Jock!" Martin whispered to himself.

The sound of movement seemed to be around the starboard diesel, then it came closer! Now it sounded as though he was working on the port engine. Metallic sounds, a muttered curse. More sounds and then, thankfully, a grunt as he heaved himself back into the saloon. Then the sound of panels being replaced.

Martin released the escape hatch again and lay still, feeling drained. Would they come into the stern cabin?

The sudden clatter of a starter motor followed by the hard, knocking roar of a big diesel, only feet from his hiding place, made him wince but answered his question. Then, as the engines' six cylinders settled into an even roar, he knew that he had not fully appreciated the noise that he would be subject to and this was just the first engine, and not at speed. The second motor burst into life, increasing the noise still further and Martin knew that he would not be able to stand several hours of cramped confinement so close to the big diesels, especially later, when they were up to speed.

He checked through the ventilation louvres and opened the wardrobe door. Stepping into the cabin, he exercised stiff limbs, stretching the muscles, rotating the joints. His mouth tasted foul. He could do with a drink, but no chance of that for the next few hours. The door from the cabin to the open cockpit of the boat was at the top of a companion way. In the door was another louvred ventilation panel. He could not look directly out but, through the angled louvres, he could see a few feet of the cockpit decking in front of the door. The door was locked so he could sit at the top of the steps, away from the worst of the engine noise and still have time to make it to the wardrobe before anyone approaching the cabin could unlock and open the door, he hoped!

A slight rocking movement of the boat indicated that the crew were busying themselves with mooring ropes. Then an increase in engine speed from the starboard diesel told Martin that they were under way. The motion was backwards and he visualised the boat's stern moving out and swinging to port. The starboard engine note dropped momentarily and then increased again to be joined by raised revs from the port engine. Again there was a drop in engine speed followed by an increase and a surge forwards. Both engines were stabilising at steady low revs and he knew that they were leaving the harbour.

Stepping down from the companionway into the cabin, he could see Barfleur harbour receding through the stern windows. The side windows looked out onto a rocky coastline in one direction and a smooth sea in the other. To the east, the waters of the Channel sparkled with early morning sunlight. The bizarre situation of stowing away as he had and his now entrapped position brought a mirthless grin to the scarred face.

"Oh well. The worst case scenario is two to one and I've got surprise on my side."

6.10 a.m.
The Solent, England

Sergeant Frank Berry, Hampshire Police Marine Division and skipper of the fifteen-metre police boat *Ashburton* stepped through the rear doors into the aft cockpit, leaving the unusually crowded saloon to his crew, the uniform inspector and the four men of the Tactical Firearms Unit who were with them for the day, or until their "target' was located and dealt with. It was a lovely morning and, as he looked astern at *Ashburton's* foaming wake, he said his silent thank you to whoever had ordered his professional life. Here he was, being paid to operate the sort of vessel that other wealthier men worked their arses off to own.

With feet braced apart, he lit his second cigarette of the day, congratulating himself that he was kicking the habit, one behind his usual "early turn" quota by this time in the morning.

His thoughts turned to the men he had on board. Had not had much to do with the TFU lads in the past. He felt a little uneasy at the thought of an "intercept", which required an armed response team on board.

"Thought you were giving up, Frank?"

The chiding voice behind made him start. The noise of the diesels pushing *Ashburton* through the water at fifteen knots had covered the sound of the door opening. It was his number two, who looked forward to the day when this crew didn't have to put up with passive smoking.

In answer to the questioning look, he continued, "There's nothing about. I've left her on auto. Terry's taking over the helm. What's the form?"

"We'll take a look at the little hidey holes around The Needles and Hurst Spit, just so that we know what's about. Then we'll anchor in Alum Bay and wait to hear from the Air Support boys. They should be leaving about now to have a look at the French coast."

6.20 a.m.
Lee on Solent, England

At Lee on Solent's airfield, Inspector Mike Lovell, a quiet Scotsman in charge of the Hampshire Air Support Unit, was completing his briefing.

"...so to summarise, if you find this boat, you're not to repeat a pass. We don't want to let them know that there is any interest in them. That's why we're not doing a grid search. You'll fly the reciprocal headings on the various courses from Barfleur. At this time on a Sunday morning, there isn't likely to be any other Nelson type boat coming away from Barfleur. Our information is that no others have been seen in the Cherbourg area during the preceding two days, so there shouldn't be a problem. Once you spot her, stay out of sight on radar watch and let the Control Room know her heading and speed and, remember, the critical signal should be by mobile phone. That's when they're within range, which we won't be aware of directly, or by red flare. In the latter case, if we see it, and especially if it's likely to be out of sight of the marine units, we inform control immediately and close in. Any further questions?"

"I saw the Search and Rescue lads on the apron. Are they in on this, sir?"

"Yes, the helicopter will be scrambled when the target is ten nautical miles south of the island, that's if it's on a heading which will bring it into our area. There are separate arrangements with the adjoining Forces if the boat's heading is away from our area."

There were no more questions. "That's all lads. Finish our checks and let's get out there."

The crew of the aircraft rose to their feet and trooped out of the room with Mike Lovell following. In the early morning sunshine he stood for a moment watching as they went about their business. The Islander aircraft was in silhouette against the brightening sky and, with thought of the hours to he spent over the sea, he took comfort from the aircraft's twin engines.

6.25 a.m.

Off Barfleur, France

With *Spirit of Ecstasy* away from the rock encrusted coastline and up to her cruising speed of eighteen knots, Jock checked the heading and tapped in the autopilot. He watched the compass needle for a moment or two as it settled and then scanned the horizon ahead for other craft, before turning to join Wilson, who was bent over a large scale chart of Poole Bay.

"This is the Fairway Buoy. DM says between there and Studland village is a favourite mooring place for day sailors."

Wilson's manicured finger was joined on the chart by Jock's dark rimmed nail.

"Do we wait for the pick up?" he asked as he traced the contour lines.

"No. DM says that if its reasonable weather, there will be lots of boats moored at this point. Our pick up will be amongst them. We cruise slowly up to the seaward side of the moored boats and, when we've got a transit between the Fairway Buoy and the church tower at Studland drop the containers and push off. It'll look as though we changed our minds about anchoring. We go on into Poole, where we clear customs in the usual way."

"What if there's problems from the other end? What's the 'insurance' position?'

"They'll contact us. They'll use the usual radio channel and, if they want us to abort the drop, they'll tell us to keep clear of Milkmaid Bank."

"That's this drying area to the north," said Jock, his finger still on the chart.

"That's the point. No one goes there anyway."

*

Time passed slowly for Martin, just the occasional distant view of a passing vessel, until he saw a patch of cumulus cloud through the starboard windows with a low haze beneath it.

"That'll be the Isle of Wight," he murmured. "We're heading for the Needles Channel or Poole!"

As Martin turned from the porthole to return to his monitoring position at the top of the companionway steps, he heard the sound of a key in the cabin door. Two quick strides took him to the wardrobe and he was inside the open door and about to pull it to – but too late. Jock stepped into the cabin and, from the top of the companion way, stared incredulously at the rubber suited figure. For a fraction of a second he was motionless, open mouthed, then turned to shout a strident warning to Wilson, who was still in the saloon.

As Jock started down the companionway towards him, Martin bent and unclipped the diving knife from its scabbard on his right calf. The sight of eight inches of wickedly pointed and serrated stainless steel blade caused Jock to stop in his tracks and shout again, more urgently.

Wilson appeared behind him, took one look, slipped his hand beneath his jacket and produced a small automatic. Without pausing, he pointed the gun over Jock's shoulder and fired.

The shot caused Jock to cry out and, turning, grabbed at Wilson's arm, pulling it down as he squeezed the trigger a second time. "No. We need to know about him, Mon!"

Martin had felt a blinding blow to the right side of his head at the first shot. For a second everything was black, then a moment of light and distorted vision, then it turned to grey and he knew no more.

The next sensation was a roaring in his ears and a grey surrounding haze. As consciousness and vision returned, the noise in his head receded to be replaced once again by the roar of the diesels. He was in pain; the right side of his head hurt like hell and he could feel blood that had run down his face and congealed between his neck and the collar of the wetsuit. His wrists hurt and, raising his head, he found that his hands were bound above him to a vertical stanchion of the port hand bunk. Then constriction and discomfort from his ankles and he realised that they too were bound. He felt desperately weak, weak and physically sick. Putting his head down he fought to contain the nausea, fought to retain consciousness.

Minutes passed and he could hear noises, voices and occasional shouts. Wilson and Jock were searching the boat. Were there any more stowaways? Presently the door to the cabin opened and Martin deliberately kept his head down, pretending.

Jock's voice: "He's still out, mon."

"Is he?" from Wilson.

Martin tensed, half anticipating, and he was right. A foot drove into his ribs and it was all that he could do not to gasp.

"Well, we know he's on his own."

"Ay, but what's he been doing?"

"How long before we reach Poole Bay?"

"We've about half an hour to run."

"That's half an hour to find out. Get a bucket of water." For half a minute, Martin struggled to pull his brain into gear. What could he give them that might satisfy, but not warn of the net that they were heading for? Then there were steps and the shock of a bucket of cold sea water dashed into his face. He couldn't avoid an involuntary gasp this time and his head was jerked back by two sets of fingers grasping his ears as though they were to be torn off.

"Now, Mr fuckin' Wild, what have you been up to? When did you come aboard?"

Wilson's face was inches away, the pale blue eyes glaring coldly.

"Early hours…this morning," murmured Martin, pretending to be still half conscious.

"What are you doing on board?"

"…early start caught me out," Martin said in a stronger voice.

"I said, what were you doing?" snarled Wilson.

"Installing a bug," said Martin.

"What! What sort of bug? Whereabouts?' Wilson was clearly startled.

"A listening device. In the ventilator over the saloon, but I didn't have time to finish it."

"Jock, have a look," snapped Wilson and stood over Martin, staring thoughtfully at him.

"And how did you reckon to get off again?"

"Swim ashore and phone a mate with that." Martin nodded at the mobile phone that had been taken from his pouch while he had been unconscious.

"How many 'mates' do you have in this little game that you're playing?"

"Just the one."

Jock reentered the cabin. "There's something in the vent but I canny get it out. It'll have to be dismantled. Then, "What'll we do with this one?" nodding to Martin.

"Over the side with a weight if he doesn't do what we want. But that'll be in a couple of hours. We deal with the other business first. Come on, lets talk."

Wilson led the way out of the cabin with Jock following. As soon as the door closed, Martin set about the ropes that bound him. The bindings at his ankles had been done very well by someone who knew about knots. "Guess that's Jock's work." The ones around his wrists had just a little slack in them when he twisted his wrists and he was able to slide the rope down the shiny plated stanchion until it was at chest height.

The mobile phone and the diving knife were on the opposite bunk, several feet away, but he couldn't see the mini flare pack which had been tucked inside the top half of his two piece rubber suit and he thought he could feet it pressing into his ribs.

Ignoring the discomfort, he twisted and strained to maximise the very slight slack in the wrist bindings. It felt as though the skin was coming off but that didn't matter. He had his right hand twisted and reversed and he could grip the large tab by which the heavy nylon zipper of the suit was opened and closed. Inch by inch, he worked it down, his fingers slipping off and losing it every so often. He persisted. Eventually it was nearly to his lower chest.

Twisting his body now, he could get the fingers of the right hand inside, but only by an inch or so. The flare pack was still two or three inches away from his fingertips.

Resting for a moment, he considered and then, taking hold of the stanchion and using his stomach muscles he lifted his feet to the bunk and, with his lower half higher than his top half, attempted to bump his right shoulder, against the cabin floor. He repeated the exercise three times with no luck, but on the fourth attempt, he felt the pack move. On the fifth, it moved again. On the sixth, he lowered his feet to the floor and found that he could touch it with the fingers of his right hand. The minutes were passing. He felt desperate!

His wrists were on fire and he could see that the skin had ruptured in several places. There was blond seeping out from under the ropes that bound him. Again he forced himself to ignore the pain and concentrated on easing the package out until it was just visible.

Then the really difficult part began. He had to trap it with his left wrist whilst he manipulated with the fingers of his right hand, a half inch at a time. The plastic seal, then the small brass firing tube and then, most difficult of all, screwing the tube into the flare cartridge top. It was a simple apparatus but designed to be used by a person with both hands free and that meant that he was still struggling when he heard footsteps approaching.

Martin pushed the pack back inside his top, losing the first cartridge as he did so, and twisted onto his side to hide the front of his body. The door opened and Wilson came clattering down the steps. He glanced at Martin but then ignored him to open the stern locker and start releasing the escape hatch.

As he did so, the boat's engines slowed, the bow came down and *Spirit* lost speed.

With the second lever undone, Wilson opened the hatch, letting in a mist of spray and diesel exhaust. He ignored these and stuck his head through the hatch, looking down at the platform.

Apparently satisfied, he took Martin's knife from the bunk, ran his thumb along the razor sharp edge and grinned at Martin. "That'll do nicely!" He placed the knife by the hatch, closed it again but did not secure it.

Beneath the cabin floor, a steady flow of diesel oil leaving the keel fuel tank started to slow. Wilson's second shot had sliced through the cabin floor, the breather pipe and the tank itself. It was now virtually empty. Only the changed position of the boat, as she slowed and levelled, kept the fuel flowing. Within a matter of minutes, the tank would empty and that engine would stop.

In the wheelhouse, Jock was dividing his attention between the group of anchored yachts that he was now approaching and the Rescue helicopter that had just passed overhead. It disappeared behind the high point of Ballard Down and he guessed it was on its way to Swanage.

Wilson appeared behind him. "How much farther?"

"Nearly there. We're on the transit line. Another hundred yards should do it. I'll give a burst in neutral when we're ready to drop the load."

In the cabin, Martin had the flare tube on the second cartridge in the pack and again had to stop and turn onto his side as Wilson reentered the cabin.

Picking up the knife, Wilson waited and then, as the boat lost way and the two diesels revved in neutral, he stuck his head and arm out of the hatch and cut through the securing cord with a swift slice. He saw the cord fall away but, instead of disappearing out of sight as they should, the two ends streamed aft in the flow of water around the boat.

Swearing, he wriggled the top half of his body through the hatch, looking for the jam and, as he did so, the starboard engine faltered, ran unevenly and then stopped. The starter motor whirred mechanically but without success. Martin, desperately struggling to screw the brass flare tube fully into the second cartridge in its moulded container, could hear Jock swearing in the wheelhouse as he tried the starter again. Wilson swore also. He had spotted the nylon that Martin had put in place and he now wriggled completely through the hatch to try and cut that also. The hatch swung to behind him and, at last, the cartridge manipulated between Martin's bound hands started on its screw thread.

Martin heard the rattle of the anchor chain and then the boat was moving astern as Jock straightened the chain on the seabed.

The escape hatch opened and Wilson's face, red with effort, contorted with fury, appeared.

"You'll pay for this, you clever bastard."

Pointing the flare gun at the escape hatch, Martin released the spring trigger. There was a sharp crack and a burning red projectile shot through the hatch. Martin didn't know whether it hit Wilson or not but the man disappeared with a cry followed by a heavy splash. And then a sound unmistakable to a sailor, that of the remaining propeller chopping into an object as the boat continued to move astern.

In the wheelhouse, Jock was cursing as he attempted to straighten *Spirit's* rearward course. With only the one prop turning, the boat wanted to veer to port and he had to continually correct. Then, to his amazement, he saw the red flare shoot almost horizontally away from the stern, cutting a curving path out to sea before it fell into the water sending, up a plume of grey smoke.

Throwing the gear into neutral, he ran to the aft cabin, past Martin, to push open the escape hatch and peer outside.

"Where is he?" he demanded of Martin as he turned around.

"Over the side I should think."

"Where did that flare come from?"

The small brass flare tube had fallen from Martin's hands as the flare ignited and was now on the floor beneath his legs.

"What flare?"

At that moment there came the unmistakable beat of a helicopter's rotors and, mouthing obscenities, Jock returned to the deck above. To his consternation, he saw the chopper closing in towards the bow of *Spirit* and the winchman already swinging out on a strop. Why were they about to board him? The flare, of course, but they would normally have contacted by radio first and he had heard nothing on the VHF.

Then he saw it. The winchman was aiming for a body in the water, floating half submerged just off the starboard bow. It must be Wilson.

He turned to enter the wheelhouse, intent on calling the helicopter over the VHF, but then he thought of the containers and swung round to the aft cabin to check whether they had been released. As he did so, he saw approaching, with a white froth of water at her bow, the dark blue hull of *Ashburton*. He did not immediately recognise it as a police boat, but stared hard at the two kneeling figures on the bow. Then he saw that both figures had short carbinelike weapons to their shoulders, pointed in his direction.

"Oh, shit, shit, shit."

Then the amplified broadcast from *Ashburton*. "*Spirit of Ecstasy, Spirit of Ecstasy*. Armed police, armed police. Stand where you are. Stand where you are."

Ashburton heeled to port and curved in fast towards *Spirit's* hull. At the last moment, when it seemed that she must strike, the starboard diesel roared in reverse and the approaching boat's speed fell off as she came alongside. The impact was then so light that the big inflatable fenders, already in positioned on her port side, deflected only slightly.

As the boats lay together, two more armed men leapt from the aft cockpit of *Ashburton*, weapons at the ready. One covered Jock, whilst the second covered the doors leading from the saloon and aft cabin, swinging the barrel in a narrow arc between them.

Jock was aware of two more figures leaping aboard with mooring lines and then a uniformed policeman, an officer wearing a cap. "Where's the other man?"

"Just being picked up," said Jock, nodding towards the helicopter, whose crewman was now in the water with the "patient".

"And where's our man?"

"In there." Jock nodded towards the aft cabin and, two minutes later,

Martin was swearing under his breath as the police inspector did his best to cut away the wrist bindings without disturbing the bruised and broken skin.

Monday 10th August 1992
8.30 a.m. Southampton

Consciousness gradually returned, the sleep of exhaustion had been deep. The strange bed was in a hospital, a private room. The curtains around the bed were drawn back and through a glass panel in the door Martin could see people walking past every few minutes.

Memory returned as well. First the chattering roar of the helicopter ride and, with that, the shrouded figure in the opposite stretcher. A figure that had been a living person only minutes before. Not a nice person, but one who had been very much alive before an argument with a large three bladed bronze propeller. Number two was down. Again he wondered at his feelings – or lack of them.

The right side of his head was sore, very sore. He could feel bandages swathing it. His wrists were sore. Lifting them he saw that they were bandaged also. His rib cage ached and he had a foul mouth. Twisting his head gingerly, he saw a jug of water on the side table and, as he moved to reach it, there was a sharp stabbing pain in his side.

Closer than the water was a bell push on a cable and he pressed that instead.

Almost immediately a nurse appeared. He could see her through the glass panel, talking to another person out of his sight. Then she opened the door and he saw that the other person was a tall man wearing a brown windcheater and either black or very dark blue trousers. A police officer pretending not to be a police officer.

The nurse came to stand at the side of his bed. The man remained standing in the open doorway, watching the corridor as well as glancing in at Martin.

"How do you feel, Mr Wild?" From the nurse.

"Mouth like the floor of a parrot cage." He tried to grin. "Could you give me a hand up in the bed, these make it awkward." He raised the bandaged wrists.

"Of course." Bending, she supported him upwards, altering the adjustable bed head as he levered with his elbows, then poured water into a glass and handed it to him.

"Doctor will be round in a short while and this gentleman has instructions to contact a Chief Inspector Potter as soon as you feel up to seeing him."

"My compliments to Mr Potter," to the figure in the doorway, "but I'd like an hour or so to sort myself out before I start giving interviews."

The man nodded, took a radio from under his windcheater and disappeared into the corridor.

"My ribs hurt when I move. What's the score?"

"You may have a couple of cracked ribs, there's bruising under the strapping. Your wrists are more painful than damaged. You'll have to be careful while the abrasions heal. You were very lucky with the wound to your head. Half an inch closer would have given you a serious head injury. An inch would probably have killed you. As it is, you've lost several inches of skin and a little blood, but that's all. Can you remember what happened yesterday?"

"Yes, it's all there I think."

"That was the main concern. Head wounds can do funny things with the memory."

11.30 a.m.

Three hours later, DCI Potter led a little delegation into the room. There was a pleased look on his face, he was almost smiling. He was followed by Ellie May, who certainly was. She was followed by a plain clothes man carrying a large silver coloured metal case and then Bill Creighton, who looked for once decidedly unsure.

"Well, Martin, glad to see you sitting up," was the greeting from Potter as he settled in a chair by the bedside. Bill Creighton moved another chair from the wall to Potter's side for Ellie May. She immediately took a shorthand notebook from a bag as big as a briefcase and, looking at Martin, slowly closed one eye in a conspiratorial wink. The man with the silver case put it down and disappeared outside to reappear with two more chairs, then busied himself opening the case and separating it into two pieces. Martin recognised it as a Henderson portable interview recorder, playing two simultaneous tapes, one for the police, the second for the person interviewed. He wondered whether he was to be cautioned and the reason for Bill's presence, but Potter continued his small talk about Martin's condition and then said "You know Bill here, I believe?"

Before Martin could reply, Bill Creighton leant forward and said, "Yes, we go back a long time. How are you, Martin? Haven't heard from you for quite some while."

Martin relaxed. The signals had been made and received. The presence of two people who were close to him was only an operational coincidence.

Silence fell as the man with the recorder did a test for audibility and then said, "You're live when you want, Chief Inspector."

Potter went into the interview introduction for the benefit of the taped record, introducing himself, Detective Constable Creighton and Martin as the interviewed person. He omitted any mention of Ellie May and the third man. Martin relaxed even more. Potter was not looking for his scalp today.

For the next hour, Martin answered detailed questions with no great problem. He was economical with the truth when it came to firing the flare and Wilson falling back from the platform. Fortunately Potter seemed to miss the fact that the escape hatch had to be supported open and thus that Wilson would have been visible. Martin's version was simply that he had fired through an open hatch to give the agreed signal.

The interview supplied him with the answers to a number of questions that had been exercising his mind since waking. He learnt about the extent of the police and custom's operation, and was impressed. That *Spirit* had been shadowed almost from the French coast and that, whilst the French authorities were not involved this time, the English and Scottish elements in the form of the haulage company and Mabbett's various ventures were all to be the subject of further raids.

It was apparent that Wilson's death was being regarded at this stage as accidental. His head had been almost severed by the propeller, with further wounds to the chest, abdomen and legs, two of which could also have caused his death.

The skipper, Jock, was under arrest but not saying anything other than that he wanted his solicitor. The two containers, though separated from the boat's hull, were still connected by the nylon that Martin had lashed in place. They had been recovered and were being examined now, first by a naval explosives team as a precaution, but with forensic specialists waiting in the wings.

That left one question. "What about Mabbett?" said Martin.

"Not been located yet, but he will he. His boat is impounded again by Customs and, with the direct evidence of drug running that we now have – hope we have any way – there will be every reason for the courts to make an order that it be sold and the monies appropriated by the authorities. When he is located, he will be arrested and will have a lot of questions to answer. Perhaps this time we'll get lucky, though CPS will want a cast iron case before they spend more money on him."

1.30 p.m.

After the deputation had left, Martin received another visit from the doctor, who pronounced that all was progressing well and he could expect to be released in a day or so. Then, to Martin's surprise, the door opened and in walked Ellie May, this time on her own.

"Ellie! Where's the rest of the team?"

"Hello, Marty. Back at the station. I'm afraid that I was silly enough to leave my purse behind so I had to ask Mr Potter for a longer lunch break so that I could pick it up." She smiled wickedly and, taking the chair by the bedside, turned it so that when she sat down she was facing him and had her back to the door. She glanced over her shoulder, saw that the glass panel in the door was empty and leant forward, slowly and deliberately kissing him on the lips.

"How are you really, Marty?"

"Feeling better all the time!" And he was! His right hand slid between knees that were conveniently positioned only inches below the bed height. The fingertips traced little patterns on silky smooth skin. To Ellie May it was as if a gentle electric shock had started there and travelled straight to the pit of her stomach. Her eyes half closed as gentle searching fingers caressed and crept farther, now out of sight. Then the dressings were in the way and Martin patted the inside of her thigh. Obediently her legs parted, his fingers crept still further, found a loose fold of silky material, eased it aside and skimmed gently up and down.

Ellie May breathed out heavily. "Marty, Marty, where have you been?"

"I couldn't risk seeing you while sorting out this job."

"Is it sorted now?"

"Not yet. But soon, I hope."

"Don't keep me waiting too long, lover…oooh!"

1.40 p.m.
Glasgow, Scotland

There was nothing soft and gentle about the telephone call taken by 'Mad Mick' in his Govan "office" just then. The office was a room with a small billiard hall on the one side and an old fashioned bar on the other. The two main rooms were a social and "business" meeting place for those of Govan's population who were not in normal work and who still had a Scottish pound in their pockets, or the desire for one. The rooms were conveniently situated, no more than 200 yards from the "Benefit office", that government emporium designed, it seemed, to make obtaining assistance by the honest needy as difficult as possible, yet providing largesse to the aggressive and "bent" opportunists, of which Govan had an abundance.

The owner of the rooms had been "persuaded" that there was a benefit in placing one of the rooms at the disposal of a certain Mr Michael Docherty, a well known criminal headcase of the parish, whose natural paranoia was regularly boosted by an excessive intake of amphetamines and anabolic steroids; "speed, or "wraps" and "sterries" to those who supplied and used them. Mad Mick did both, which worried his landlord, whose only profit was a guarantee of protection where lesser hoodlums were concerned.

Mick had dipped into that day's "wrap" twice, the first time when he roused from a "speedstyle" night's sleep of some three hours duration and the second only twenty minutes before the critical telephone call. He was feeling confident and aggressive or he might otherwise have demurred at the suggestion put to him by a desperate, and dangerous, Dermott Mabbett.

"Mick, you've not delivered on that little deal that we had."

"Am jus waitin fo the Sassanach tu show heese nose here. He's not bin back since we chased him off last time."

"Mick, you've got five grand of mine and the job's not done. I'm going to double the ante, but I want the job done NOW, not in a month's time!"

"Hao'd ah know whur the mon is?"

"Leave that to me. Andy will bring an envelope to you tonight. There will be an address and another five grand in it. When the job's done, you get another ten grand. OK?"

"Thas twenny together…yu'll leave that tu me."

Mabbett replaced the receiver and sat looking distantly into space, then lifted the receiver again and dialled an international number.

"Jimmy, DM. How are you?"

"Better than you, I'm told Dermott. Heard you were surveying one of Her Majesty's ceilings in Winchester."

"Not for long, Jimmy. Only until the Brief got there."

"You were supposed to be coming over when we last spoke. That was a couple of months ago. So what happened? What's new?"

"Yes; that's why I'm phoning. Thought I might now make it sooner rather than later. Can you put me up?"

"Stepping out of the line of fire, Dermott? Yes, I can find a place for you. May not be with me as we've got a couple of people staying at the moment, but I can organise rooms. Will you be on your own?"

"Yes. I'll phone you the time of arrival. Probably later today."

"Someone really has got their sights on you."

"Just need a break, that's all."

He replaced the phone, angrier than ever. The telephone call on the previous day had stunned him at first. The pickup man in the dory had a grandstand view. He had waited and watched as *Spirit* arrived, was boarded by police and saw Wilson's body picked out of the water by the helicopter crew. Then the chopper's stropman had picked up a second person, but this time from Mabbett's boat. He saw *Spirit* escorted away to Poole by the police boat and had the bottle to follow and saw Jock taken off the boat in handcuffs.

Mabbett's anger had been demonic but quickly controlled. Anticipating further police action, he had left the house immediately and, as the Glasgow club was closed on a Sunday, spent the night with Andy McAinsh. He had with him the necessities of life, the safe at home had seen to that, and Andy could get him to the airport to pick up the ticket already booked in another name. The Brief would look after Jock. Andy could look after Mad Mick. Mick would look after Wild. He would look after himself. After all, how was he to know that his fellow Director, now unfortunately dead, would use his boat and involve his Skipper in drugs importation.

All the same, best to be at a distance while the present situation was sorted. What to do about Mick after Wild was dealt with though. He needed help there, Liam's kind of help. Couldn't afford to leave a man like Docherty about with that sort of knowledge. Goddamn this man Wild. He had lost his numbers one and two to him. Was it just bad luck or had he underestimated him completely. Not being sure made him angrier than ever.

With an effort he controlled his thoughts. There was one more call to be made, just as critical as the last. In his mind he ran through what he should say and the way that it should be said, then picked up the phone to dial another international number. He had to go through three connections before he was talking to the man that he wanted. He recognised the voice immediately, silky smooth with an attractive Italian accent when the conversation reverted to English. Visualising, he saw again the small, suave "businessman", who always wore a dark suit and drank innumerable cups of strong coffee. He wondered how high up the tree the man was, how close to the top. Who was the top, anyway?

He also was recognised immediately. Doubtless the touch of Glaswegian in his vowels, he thought without humour.

Introductions and minimal small talk over, he got down to business. "We've had a problem on our last run. Lost the goods and the boat, so I'm having to take a holiday for a few days. In the circumstances, we'll have to postpone the next delivery while we sort the problem out."

The Italian voice was colder. "That is very unfortunate. I hope there is no one looking in our direction?"

"Oh no, no." Mabbett was hasty in his reassurances, perhaps too hasty? More casually, "It's only a loss as far as we're concerned. No problem for anyone else. It happened over here. We were almost home." They would know all of this very soon anyway as their contacts would carry the news back to them within a matter of hours. "We lost a couple of the team but they can be replaced." Feeling the probing antennae of Italian concern, he desperately tried to keep his voice casual. "The reason for the call is just to put the next delivery on hold and to let you know that I will not be contactable for a few days."

"We can do that, but it will cost us. We've already paid for our end. If there is to be a substantial delay, we may have to negotiate a new price."

Lying now and to these people, it became even more difficult to keep his voice level and reasonable. "Oh, it won't take us long to establish a new route. Not long enough to add to your costs."

"Where will your 'holiday address' be?"

A half truth: "I'll be staying with a friend in Spain."

"Ah, the English Costa Del Crime." There was a mocking tone in the jibe, which Mabbett ignored. "I'll look forward to hearing from you in a day or so then." The phone went dead.

Mabbett paced up and down in the flat, waiting for Andy's return. He was out meeting Cameron, who would find out where Wild was. Must be lying up somewhere, injured. The helicopter had taken two off, the second had to be Wild.

1.45 p.m.
Milan, Italy

In his palatial high rise office, filled with polished furniture, leather couches and Picasso paintings from the Patron's collection, one floor down from the penthouse suite that was rarely used by "he of the hooked nose", the suave Italian in the dark suit sipped from another cup of strong black coffee, then dialled a London number. The conversation was brief and in rapid Italian.

"Toni, the Glasgow contract. Have a look at their operation as quickly as you can. They've lost the last shipment, find out how. And some of their people, find out who. We need to know the extent of the damage to them and whether there is likely to be a problem for us. See whether you can find out who their contacts are in Spain."

He provided some more information and then sat quite still, wondering whether he should trouble the Patron with this new development, then decided to await their next meeting, scheduled for the weekend, by which time Toni would be sure to have more information on the Glasgow situation.

Thursday 13th August 1992
10.45 a.m. Southampton

"How do you fancy a nice little hideaway in the country for your convalescence?"

The question, from a smiling Bill Creighton, as he arrived to collect Martin from the hospital, followed on from a conversation of the previous day, when Martin had been wondering where he should hang his hat on leaving hospital.

"Sounds good. What is it?"

"Neighbour of mine has a classy two-berth caravan which he doesn't use very much at the moment. I tapped him up last night and he's agreed to let you have it for a small consideration for the next month – as long as the tax man doesn't know."

"Whereabouts is it?"

"Chilworth Towers, just north of Southampton, off the Romsey road. It's a small touring site but John knows the owner and has an arrangement to leave his van on one of the pitches. The site isn't well known so not busy, even at this time of the year."

"Bill, you're a gem. If we can pick up some supplies this morning, we could go straight there and I'll be off your hands."

"Not quite. We can do some shopping and I'll show you where it is, but you're coming back with me. My better half is expecting us for dinner and you're stopping the night. I'll take you to Chilworth after my shift tomorrow."

10.50 a.m.

As this conversation was taking place on the second floor of the hospital, the middle aged female receptionist on the ground floor was dealing with a difficult visitor. She was curious. The short, heavily built man in a dirty, light coloured raincoat, had a broad Scottish accent and was not at all the sort normally found visiting patients who occupied private rooms. His shaven head and the gold ear ring were matched by barely hidden aggression, which lay behind the words and the pale blue eyes. As she checked her records for the name Wild but was not able to find it, he became increasingly agitated, muttering to himself and swearing, softly but not so softly that she could not hear.

The receptionist was an ex-nurse, who had left that profession several years before when blessed with a late first child. She and her husband had decided that the child came first and it was only now, at a little over forty, that she had decided the time was right to become a working mum. Had a more experienced person been on duty, they might have checked the reason for the asterisk beside the name "Mr Potter", which was against Martin's room. It was not until she had been advised in an aside by another girl that the Mr Wild enquired for was occupying a room shown as Mr Potter's and she had imparted this information to her impatient Scots visitor, that she discovered the reason for the asterisk. All enquiries for the name Wild were to be referred to the Administration Manager and, in his absence, the hospital security.

By the time that the now concerned lady had discovered that the Admin Manager was not in his office and not replying to his pager, the "Scots accent" had found the lifts and was stepping out onto the second floor. She then informed security of the situation. As Mad Mick entered the main ward, passing four smaller side wards in doing so, a security officer was on his way urgently to the same location, whilst his colleague followed the instructions posted by the hospital management to inform the police control immediately.

Mad Mick stood fuming while a much more cautious staff nurse, responsible for the main and side wards, questioned his reason for wishing to see a Mr Wild. At the same time, she signalled to one of the junior nurses to join her.

Just then a procession of a man carrying a soft bag, followed by a second man in a wheelchair being propelled by a male porter, left one of the side rooms that Mad Mick had just passed. It was a fleeting view and Mick, who was anticipating an incapacitated patient in a hospital bed, did not recognise Martin, whose head was bandaged and who was receiving the compulsory wheelchair ride to the main entrance, where Bill's CID car awaited.

The staff nurse was still playing a straight bat when the security officer arrived. The failure to obtain an answer from the nurse, coupled with the arrival of a uniform triggered an automatic reaction in Mad Mick. Before the security man knew what had hit him, he was on his back, dazed. The two nurses screamed as, with face contorted in fury, Mad Mick turned on them. For a moment he faced them, on the point of striking out, then turned and ran for the corridor finding the stairs beside the lift and racing down them.

The stairs brought him to the ground floor before Bill and Martin, whose lift had been delayed at the first floor. As they came out of the lift, Martin saw the back of a dirty, light coloured mackintosh topped by a shaven head, walk rapidly through the main doors.

"Bill! That shaven head in front. I think he may he one of Mabbett's men. Tailed me after Ewen's funeral." Then, "Take care, he's a rough one!" as Bill dropped the bags and started for the doors at a trot.

Ignoring the protestations of the porter, Martin jumped from the wheelchair, wincing with pain from his ribs, and also headed for the doors.

He got outside to see Bill, with his head through the window of the CID car, talking to the driver. The car abruptly accelerated away and did a tyre squealing U-turn to follow a black Ford Scorpio, that was disappearing towards the main gates.

Bill came back, talking into his personal radio.

"Reckon you might be right," he said. "Had a car waiting, pointing in the right direction. Took off like a bat out of hell as soon as he had his arse on the passenger seat."

Ten minutes later the CID car returned.

"Out of sight by the time that I got out of the gates. I turned right at the traffic lights, thinking he would likely head back into town, but I couldn't see him and he wasn't in the line of traffic waiting at Winchester Road. Guess he turned left towards the 271. Perhaps the motorway boys will pick him up. I heard your message passed over."

A silent party made their way towards the Sainsbury's shopping complex at Lordshill. Both had no illusions. Mabbett might have disappeared, but his team had not. Seeing Bill's serious expression, Martin said, "I've been involved in lots of contracts in the commercial world, but this is the first time that I've had the feeling that I'm the subject of one." Then with a grin, "Don't want to know what the penalty clauses are!" His attempt at light-heartedness was too close to the truth and Bill didn't smile at all.

4.20 p.m.
Estapona, Spain

Some two thousand miles to the south, Dermott Mabbett was 'relaxing' in the air-conditioned lounge of Jimmy's penthouse. The term relaxing was perhaps a misnomer in that the lean frame though sunk in a luxurious white leather settee with glass in hand, hid a tightly wound angry man, who had difficulty in keeping still. The eyes were dark, the black hair less groomed. Even the droop of the Mexican moustache seemed to bristle.

His carefully constructed business empire of nightclubs was in disarray, its continuance dependant upon Andrew McAinsh who, though good as the manager of its principal club, had no experience at handling the remaining units, which stretched across the country. His newly reorganised chain of supply for the designer drugs, which had fuelled his expensive lifestyle, had been cut off before a penny of the setting up costs had been recovered. His chief Lieutenant, Gordon Wilson, now occupied a cold slab in the police morgue. His chief "facilitator", Liam Mahoney, or what was left of him, was six feet under. His house at Kilchatten, the hideaway known only to a chosen few, was now inundated with police waving search warrants for the second time in as many months. His prized motor yacht was back at the customs quay, impounded once more and likely to be sold, adding to the loss of the shipment that she had carried.

How much of this could he keep from Jimmy, who had little time for a loser? He was now out on the balcony talking to one of his contacts about matters that he wasn't sharing. He'd appeared sympathetic about the little that had been imparted, but would be less so if the full extent of the losses were known. Had to explain a little of the situation. He needed money, immediate cash. That taken from the safe at Kilchatten would not last long. The quickest and easiest answer was to sell some of his 'Costa property', which Jimmy looked after. Jimmy would take a large slice for his efforts, but would provide an immediate "deposit", in cash.

Goddamn Mahoney for making the first mistake that had dealt this man Wild into the game. And Goddamn Wild, whom he had under estimated right from the start. No ordinary man this. He had led a charmed life so far, but that was going end!

Andy had warned him against using Mad Mick. Well, that man had failed for the second time and, knowing too much, would have to go as well. Jimmy's lads would take over, no questions asked, for the right money.

In the meantime, he would briefly show himself about and then disappear. The Busies would expect him here, where other retired or in hiding "businessmen" disappeared to. But he would slide back to his "insurance place", pick up his other identity and wait while Wild was dealt with.

Saturday 15th August 1992
9.25 a.m. Rownhams, Southampton

The sound of a car approaching and then stopping in the gravelled parking area brought Martin to his feet. The small touring van site was remarkably quiet. The exhaust of Ellie May's old Escort was not. He looked at his watch with surprise. She was an hour earlier than expected.

Stepping out of the van, he saw her standing by the open door of the car some twenty metres away, wondering which of the vans was his. He waved to attract her attention and walked forward. A curtain twitched in a neighbouring van and he was conscious of curious eyes. He grinned inwardly as Ellie May, dressed again in her figure hugging ski pants and tight black top, ran towards him, her five foot four inches exhibiting fascinating motional dynamics, which seemed out of all proportion to her modest height. She threw herself in to his arms. He wondered what was going through the mind of his neighbour, whom he had spoken with for the first time the previous evening.

"Ellie! You're early! Practically caught me in my pyjamas!"

"Ooh, what have I missed?" she murmured, kissing him on the lips.

"Well, breakfast by half an hour. We said in time for coffee." Then, as she leant back and, with a naughty smile, did a little gyration with her hips against him, said, "You'd better come into the van if you're going to wriggle like that, or my neighbour will be getting the same problem that I now have."

Taking her hand, he led the way into the small van, where she sat down whilst he started making the coffee. She looked around curiously, pursing her lips disapprovingly at the two bunks which, despite their luxuriously upholstered cushions, were obviously singles.

"You certainly seem to choose small places to live, Marty. First the little boat and now this tiny van. Where is everything?"

Martin saw the direction of her gaze, the expression and, grinning, said, "Do you mean my belongings, or the facilities?'"

"Both."

Martin gave her a guided tour in miniature and then, opening the door to the tiny shower and toilet compartment, extracted a large shaped piece of fibreglass which fitted exactly between the two bunks, turning them into a large double. Ellie May's smile said, "Cat's found the cream."

Over coffee and biscuits Martin started to catch up.

"Now, did they have any luck in tracing that shaven-headed thug from the hospital?" Martin had spent much time considering his options if Mabbett's team were still on the loose.

"Sorry, Marty. No they haven't. The 'Motorway' lads checked out the nearer service stations on the M3 and M27. 'Traffic' covered the likely areas on the other main roads, the registration number and description were circulated to all Sub Divisions within the county and our own team have been on the ground in the city centre. They were also passed to adjoining forces but we've heard nothing. Couple of sightings of similar cars, but they turned out to be wrong."

"Where is the car registered?"

"To a dealer in Glasgow, but he says that he put it into an auction months ago. Apparently the new owner has not notified the DVLC. There is a question or two to be answered by the auctioneers. Glasgow CID are looking into that."

"They could well have had help from Gordon Wilson's previous contacts in this area," said Martin. "There was that antique dealer in the Forest. Has anyone checked that out?"

"Yes, Bill's been onto that, but without a result so far. Then, with a slightly troubled look, which belied her words, "Now, do you want the good news?"

"As much as you've got, please."

"Glasgow have been looking for Mabbett, who did a disappearing trick the night before his boat was intercepted. They've found that he flew out of Glasgow the next day on a British Airways flight in a seat booked in the name of Andrew McAinsh. The flight was to Heathrow and he changed planes there, picking up a cancelled seat on a flight to Alicante. When I left work last night, they were onto the Spanish police to try and trace him."

Martin was quiet for a few moments and Ellie May reached out to run slim fingers gently around the shaven area of his head, where a plaster still covered the bullet wound.

"How is your poor head, Marty?"

He grinned. "OK. I think I'll shave it all over as soon as the plaster comes off!"

"Don't you dare! I love your hair the way it is." She ran fingers through the short fair curls on the other side and gently pulled him down for a long kiss.

And what's the news about my car?" as they broke for breath.

"Oh, Mr Potter's arranged for the French police to pick it up at Barfleur," and, teasingly, "it will be waiting for us to collect in the car pound at Cherbourg!"

"I need you to be at work on Monday, sweet Ellie, so that I can get an update on the enquiries of the Spanish police. I need to know where Mabbett is as soon as possible. Let's hope they get a result!"

The worried look was back in Ellie's eyes. She was rather hoping that they wouldn't get a result, at least not the sort that would send Martin chasing off again. He had come back into her life suddenly, unexpectedly. His arrival had been opportune where her own disastrous marriage was concerned and the real bonus was that their relationship had developed in the way that she had ended up wishing all those years before. For all sorts of reasons, she wanted him here, close at hand. The closer the better!

*

For Martin, the day was a quiet joy. After coffee they walked in the sunshine to a small lake in paddocks below the camping site, where they picnicked on cold poached salmon, salad and a bottle of chilled Pouilly Fumé. They tossed little balls of bread into the lake, amused by the race between the moorhens on the surface and the carp beneath.

Dropping the basket and empty bottle at the van and enjoying the light-hearted, light-headed effects of the Loire wine, they strolled hand in hand to investigate wandering paths through pine trees, then rough pasture and blackberry bushes. Amongst the bushes were glades covered in ferns, which made a soft bed for gentle love making under the afternoon sun.

Later, on the edges of the glade, they collected smooth brown domed Ceps and, returning to the van, Ellie May investigated the shower whilst Martin prepared a simple supper of soft fluffy omelette with the Ceps sliced delicately and joined by thin crispy French fries. Another bottle from the case of Chateau de Tracy disappeared as they ate.

After supper, they lay together watching the blue of the western sky turn to a pale pink as the sun sank. Ellie May had her toothbrush and did not need persuasion to stay the night. They sleepily made plans for a lazy Sunday at the conclusion of which, reluctantly, she would drive Martin to Portsmouth to board the overnight Cherbourg ferry. For the first time in what seemed to Martin to be a long while, he felt a degree of peace as they sank into sleep, curled together beneath the duvet, moonlight filtering through the curtains.

11.30 p.m.
Milan, Italy

That feeling of peace would have been shattered had he been able to eavesdrop on a conversation then taking place in a private room at the rear of a smart restaurant in the Via Gallarate, Milan. The main guests in their dark suits and evening dresses had left half an hour before. Now only the inner coterie sat around the broad shouldered, hooked nose man at the head of the long table.

"...so, it appears that our Glasgow contract has lost two of its more important men as well as the shipment. The main man has disappeared to

Spain and there is no one of consequence left in place to run their operation?"

The small suave man nodded his sleek black head. The questioning look that followed the questions was met with raised shoulders and hands, palms uppermost, spread wide. "Toni thinks that they may be finished. His contact says that the police have good evidence, which will result in his clubs losing their licenses. If he survives, he could still wholesale but he will not have the backup that has made him strong before."

"He was not a major customer. I am more interested in who orchestrated the action that has resulted in the elimination of his top men. You tell me that it is a man called Wild and that he is the same man who evaded the two from our Paris team, who died in the car at that time. I am curious because, if there is no attempt to take over the Glasgow operation or that territory, then we may be looking at something more serious."

Glances were exchanged around the table and one of the small group said, "What are you suggesting, Patron?"

A large, broad hand took the stem of a delicate wine glass, swirled the ruby liquid around raised the glass to the hooked nose for an appreciative sniff before draining the contents. "It occurs to me that we may have a French government agency involved. You will remember that the original target was Henri Tabarde, the French Minister whom we were forced to deal with in France, despite our plans to the contrary." The dark eyes swept to the small suave man with the glossy black hair, who shifted uncomfortably in his chair. "It is not unknown for the French to take what we may regard as unconventional action, when it suits them. You will remember the English Greenpeace boat sunk some years ago with a loss of life. Now, in this present scenario, we have an unknown Englishman, apparently with French connections, proving to be very adept when dealing with others in our line of business. Then there is the curiosity of his visit to Tabarde's widow, in whom we have our own interest. I think it is about time that we knew more of this man."

He rose to his feet and nodded to a huge hulk of a man, sitting at a side table near the doors to the main restaurant. That man also rose, putting a two way radio to his mouth.

Ignoring the front entrance that had been used by the other guests, the small group moved into a foyer off the rear street, with the hulk in the lead. He opened the door, checking that two black Mercedes saloons had drawn across the two ends of the short access road, leaving a large Mercedes limousine to slide silently to a halt outside the restaurant's rear door. The hulk stepped into the street, checking doorways on both sides, opened the rear door of the limousine, waited whilst his master shook hands, slapped backs and kissed cheeks, then closed the door after him, to step into the front passenger seat. The big car slid away, its suspension sitting low under the weight of armour plating, making way for the remaining saloons to collect their passengers.

Monday 17th August 1992
8.15 a.m. Cherbourg, France

The dual carriageway out of Cherbourg was busy so Martin left it at Valognes, taking the quieter road towards Coutance and Rennes, where he intended picking up the coastal autoroutes to head south for Spain and, hopefully, a certain 'baron' by the name of Dermott Mabbett. He had no plan of action. He couldn't have until he found the man and saw the location. The planning could start then.

At Lessay there was a sign announcing that the "Relais des Tourists" was on his left and, with the ferry company's abbreviated breakfast now some hours gone, he turned to it, finding a rural hotel cum restaurant which served hot coffee, fresh rolls, croissants and Normandy butter in generous "tranches".

Having refuelled, the coin operated telephone in the Reception caught his eye and, within minutes, he had Ellie May on the line and then Bill Creighton with an update on the Spanish scenario. The news changed his plans.

"Where are you, Marty?"

"France, Bill. Just collected the Porsche. Thank Potter for me, will you."

"Where are you going?"

Martin hesitated, not wishing to put Bill in a spot then, with what he hoped was a cheerful note in his voice "Heading south, Bill. Thought I might take a short holiday in Spain."

There was a moment's silence and then, "If I were you, I'd hang fire on that for a while. The man that you are interested in dropped out of sight almost as soon as he arrived there, only to surface a day later at a bank where we know, thanks to some unusually smart work by the Guardiare Civil, that he changed a large amount of Spanish currency into French Francs."

"Guess the visit to Spain was to pick up funds then," murmured Martin to himself. "And now French money into the bargain." Then aloud, "Any chance of further info on his movements, Bill?"

"We'll try, but I'm not optimistic so don't hold your breath. Ring me at this time tomorrow morning in case we get lucky."

Thoughtfully, Martin went back to the Porsche and sat for a few moments. Although Barfleur had been the last area that Mabbett's people had shown interest in, his own investigations had indicated that they hadn't used it before where the boat was concerned. The Cherbourg visit was quite obviously a one off, a convenient port of call. In any case, the major port was too busy, too open and with too many police and customs movements to be a safe place for drugs shipments with a small boat. It had been established by Potter's team when working with the French police during the first investigation, that Mabbett and company had used St Malo on previous occasions. He was well known at the Dinard yacht club and his people had rendezvoused at a remote trading estate near there.

Equally to the point, St Malo was just off Martin's route south to Spain, and now it was as good a place as any to await further information from Southampton and perhaps do a bit of digging himself.

Going back to the Reception he rang Bill again.

"Bill, that guy who acted as liaison for Potter with the St Malo or Rennes police, Inspector Dawson? No, Dempsey. Do you think that you could find out who he would recommend as a contact while I'm over here? Someone cooperative and with some ability in English."

"Sure. I'll see if he's on today. Let you know soon as."

9.25 a.m.

As Martin drove out of the hotel forecourt, Dermott Mabbett was boarding a flight to Paris. There, he disappeared into the "Hommes" and closed the door to the small cubicle firmly. From his flight bag he took a light weight grey windcheater, which replaced the smart blazer. This, together with the Guards type tie that he had been wearing, went into the bag. Finally he donned a pair of dark glasses and a soft fisherman's hat with a brim that pulled down all round. As he left the toilet, his walk was shambling. Rather than his normal upright stature, he had developed a slight stoop. He walked to an escalator, which took him up to the first floor of the building and immediately boarded its opposite number going down. Satisfied that no one else had followed this odd course, he made his way to the Air France "Internal Routes" desk. There, using his "insurance" name, he purchased a ticket for the small twin-engined turbo prop job which provided an internal service to the local Aerodrome de Dinard Pleurtuit, located a kilometre off the Dinard/Dinan road.

At that airport's modern terminal building, he was met by a Monsieur Berliot who, with his wife ran a small hotel near Dinan. This hotel was positioned off a winding side road between the Port of Dinan and the nearby N178 to Dinard and St Malo.

The hotel was a tall rectangular building which had once been a water mill. The fast running little stream, that had provided the power source, still splashed busily through a narrow gorge on its way to the estuary, though it bypassed the still brown waters of a mill pond, now used only by waterfowl and coypu. Beside the hotel was a second, slightly smaller building, also squarely built, which was used occasionally by a certain Mr Gordon Mallett, an Englishman who, unknown to the locals, owned both the house and the hotel. Dermott Mabbett and the Englishman were one and the same. La Moulin de St Valay had provided Mabbett with a hidden French base for the past three years.

Madame Berliot had been Maggie Campbell and had crossed paths with Mabbett in her younger years. They met again when she was struggling with her French husband's drinking problem. In Glasgow, André Berliot's preference had moved from his native red wines to whisky, with potentially disastrous results for the family. Mabbett's arrival on the scene and his apparent generosity in setting up the family to run his newly acquired property at Dinan, had been a master stroke. Maggie was the only person who knew that Mallett equalled Mabbett. She was a shrewd woman with memories of a penniless past, now two young children to feed and a husband to keep an eye on. She knew on which side her French bread was buttered.

Dermott Mabbett had been very careful in setting up this alternative to Kilchatten. Everything to do with the purchase had been through French based agents via Maggie, whilst the redecoration and furnishing had been a rehabilitation project for André Berliot. The buildings, on the surface, were slightly down market, ever so just in need of a paint job. Totally different from the immaculately restored Victorian grandeur of Kilchatten. The grounds, such as they were, could have done with the attention of a gardener. Again, nothing like the carefully tended lawns, shrubs and borders in Scotland. Even the old, left hand drive MGB sports car, which occupied an unpainted wooden garage with loose boards and poorly repaired roof, was unpolished, with rust evident in the sills and the soft top ragged in a couple of places.

It had amused Mabbett to carefully create a slightly down market home in France but there was more than mild amusement behind the intent. Totally different externally yet, within the second smaller building, similar again to Kilchatten. A place to disappear to should the need arise and, behind the typically French shutters, the house was not merely comfortable but luxurious.

The Port of Dinan, with its mini marina of pontoons and boats lining the banks of the narrow estuary, was large enough to have accepted his motor yacht, just. But the boat had never been there. It would have seemed so convenient to moor his floating home only a matter of four hundred metres from the converted mill, but that would have risked identification of Mallet as Mabbett, and that he would not risk. On those occasions that he used *Spirit* near St Malo, she was kept at the Dinard Yacht Club or the Port de Plaisance where Mr Dermott Mabbett, the wealthy Scots owner was known to those that mattered, the club officers and the harbour master. The slightly scruffy Mr Gordon Mallett, who visited occasionally at La Moulin de St Valay with his old red sports car, was a very different person.

Mabbett maintained his boating interest at Dinan with a craft that matched the MGB, a slightly scruffy but powerful speedboat occupied a berth in the marina. Its fibreglass hull could have done with a polish, the canvas cover had seen better days but, in the engine bay, beneath the oil and dirt, lurked a formidable six cylinder petrol unit giving ample speed.

And so, at a little after three-thirty on Monday afternoon, the smartly blazer-clad figure that had left Spain and who had started a metamorphosis in Paris between flights, became a casually dressed, shambling figure at Dinard Pleurtuit, greeted by a sports-jacketed, slow moving Frenchman driving a battered old Renault.

The car turned left out of the airport and left again into a deserted winding road, which led eventually to the nearby village of Pleurtuit and thence by the main road to Dinan. Had there been anyone following, their presence would have been obvious to Mabbett, now Mallett and appropriate action taken. No one did, however, and half an hour later, with a change of passport as well as clothes, he was stretched on a lounger with a glass in his hand, feeling secure and pondering his problems.

All that he had to do now was wait for a few days whilst "Jimmy's Man", one Nick Rampton, found "Mad Mick" Docherty and then Martin Wild. After that it would be a damage limitation exercise with his return home dependent upon the advices of his expensive lawyer.

4.30 p.m.
London, England

He was a grey man. Black shoes and dark tie apart, everything else seemed grey. Grey suit with a faint Prince of Wales check, grey gabardine raincoat worn loose with the belt at the back, greying hair receding at the temples. Even the face seemed a pale shade of grey, as though he had inhabited dark streets for too long. One of those people, of average height and build, who never stand out, just seem to be part of the crowd. He was the last passenger off the afternoon flight at Heathrow and, having passed through the custom's Green Lane, didn't seem in it hurry to join the throng on the public side of the Arrival's barriers.

Waiting for him in that crowd were two people, Michael Docherty and his nameless henchman. Nameless because he'd used so many aliases in his chosen career of "beating the benefit" that he often could not remember who he was today. His habit didn't help. Whether he was on uppers or downers the memory, after a decade of chemical haze, was suspect, as was his physical health now that Temazepam injections had joined his stable of stimulants. This was why he relied on Docherty who supplied the drugs, occasionally, and the instructions, regularly. He was Michael Docherty's man.

Mad Mick was not a happy hunter that day. Being away from home ground loused up his own habit. He had missed his breakfast of strong tea and a "powder". The midday fix of barbiturates had not stabilised him and he was decidedly edgy. Away from the Govan district, he was edgy anyway. Down here, hundreds of miles from Glasgow itself, his edginess had increased. Not that the people around him showed overt interest in his scowling face, impatient movements from foot to foot, place to place. The short but bulging frame, the shaven head, the earring and the dirty mac all tended to ensure that passers by walked rather more quickly and, if possible, at a distance. They did not engage in eye contact and only turned to take a second look when a safe distance away.

Mad Mick now felt he had reason to be angry. He was there to meet a guy called Rampton. Someone organised by Dermott Mabbett to help in the search for Wild. That made Rampton the opposition in Mick's business sense. Why didn't Mabbett leave him to find Wild? What was the point in offering him cash for the contract and then putting this other, unknown, on the job as well? That might mean a problem when it came to getting paid! The fact that Mick did not yet have a clue where Wild was didn't enter into his thoughts.

They waited another ten minutes and then Docherty swore and stormed off towards Enquiries, found that there were no more flights in that day and made for the car park, "Nameless" in his wake. They got back to the car and were standing on either side of it whilst Docherty fumed and debated where to go when...

"Mick Docherty I believe? I'm Nick Rampton."

Mad Mick jumped. The voice came from the shadow of a pillar and the grey man stepped forth with a soft black bag in his left hand.

"Where the fuck did you come from?"

"Thought it was rather too public in there. Followed you out." The voice was a level monotone; no inflection but with a just discernible Essex accent. "Shall we go?" He opened the rear door of the Scorpio, throwing his bag on the opposite seat.

Muttering under his breath, Docherty climbed into the front passenger seat as "Nameless" took the wheel.

"Were youse in Arrivals? We didna' see youse in tha."

Rampton ignored the question. "We have to call in at a house in Clapham first. Do you know London?"

"No, but we've got this." Mad Mick pulled a battered London A to Z from under his feet.

"You won't need that. Just head for the M4 and Central London, then take the South Circular. I'll direct you." And then, "Now tell me where this man Wild is."

As the Scorpio mingled with the M4 traffic heading east into London, Martin Wild was observing due patience with traffic clogging the narrow streets of St Malo. He remembered a Hotel Mercure on the seafront near the Casino, where he had waited previously for a sight of *Spirit of Ecstasy* leaving for Barfleur, and he made for that.

He was lucky. There had been a cancellation and the clerk accepted his thanks with an expressionless face until a 100 franc note appeared with the completed Visitor form. The dour face brightened.

"Does Monsieur require a table for dinner? We are very busy but I can speak to the Head Waiter."

Martin declined the table but said that he expected to receive some messages by either telephone or fax and asked that they be relayed to him without delay. He would be in his room all afternoon.

He didn't have long to wait. Within an hour, Bill Creighton had been in touch with the name of a French police officer who Inspector Dempsey thought might be prepared to help.

Martin rang the number that Dempsey had given and asked for Detective Jean Jibault. Again he was lucky, the officer was on duty but due to finish in a little over an hour. Martin explained a little of his interest and, to his relief, Jean accepted an offer to meet for dinner, with little hesitation.

For that hour Martin sat in his room with maps of the local area spread around him, memorising the territory, getting used to place names. He was interrupted after forty minutes by a knock on the door. It was the male receptionist with a bundle of fax paper and a hopeful look on his face. Martin rewarded him suitably and sat down to read the detailed report provided to DCI Potter by Inspector Colin Dempsey. This had been prepared by Dempsey after the earlier "liaison". The text, less names, its official origins and titles, was now copied to Martin courtesy of Ellie May. Reading between the lines of the covering note, she had serious intentions on his body in the near future.

Martin changed and went down to the bar to find that Jean Jibault was already waiting, drink in hand. In answer to Martin's apology for interrupting an evening with his family, Jean waved the concern aside, explaining quite readily that he was separated from his wife and was intrigued to meet with Martin over the "peinture drogue exchange" (paintings for drugs affair). Ruefully he explained that he continued to have an "interest". The affair lived with him. He was still filing reports on the damage done to the police car that night. Martin laughed and said that he thought only the English police were so concerned with damage to their vehicles. Martin went on to relate an incident in which he had been involved. A bond was quickly established between the two men, which a good dinner and an even better bottle of '89 Saumer Champigny strengthened.

During the meal, Martin told Jean of the events that had occurred after the French involvement and explained that, for his own personal reasons, he was continuing to "investigate" the disappearance of Dermott Mabbett. Although impressed by Martin's actions in the latest incidents when the police had intercepted *Spirit of Ecstasy* and recovered drugs and bodies, Jean looked a little dubious when Martin asked whether he could hope for some help from the French police, whether officially or not.

They parted just before midnight with Jean promising to speak with his departmental boss to investigate their interest in providing assistance. As the taxi was about to move off, Jean put his head out of the window and said, "Courage mon brave, vous n'êtes pas toute seul."

Martin wondered whether it was the bottle of good wine speaking or could he, with this assurance of some support, sleep with more confidence that night?

10.00 p.m.

In an Indian restaurant just off Lavender Hill at Clapham, the grey man, Nick Rampton, finished the last of his Chicken Madras and sat back with a sigh. The area had certainly changed since he had last visited. French and Italian restaurants in each main road, most of the old pubs gone. Arding and Hobbs the only landmark that looked now as it had two years before.

He paid his bill and walked back to the terraced house in the quiet side road that he had directed "the two idiots" to earlier in the evening. What a couple of wasters. Thick as two short planks and both on pills of some kind. Jimmy would wonder about his friend Mabbett when he heard of the calibre that the man employed. They hadn't a line on this guy Wild, not a single solitary clue. Running around in circles chasing shadows. Well, he could start work on that tomorrow. Might have to go up to Glasgow, but a few phone calls first.

Reaching the house, he let himself in. It was better now, with a couple of windows open. Not so musty, aired for the first time in weeks, he guessed. He wondered how many other "little properties" Jimmy kept available. Have to have a word with the cleaning woman tomorrow. He didn't want her squawking her mouth off about new arrivals.

Climbing the stairs to the bedroom where he had left his bag, he eyed the trapdoor to the loft, debating returning the "tools" to their hiding place in the roof space, from where he had collected them whilst the "two idiots" had waited in the car. He decided against it, belched a reminder of the curry, cleaned his teeth and started to settle down for the night.

10.40 p.m.

A half mile away, the black Scorpio saloon sat silently amongst the trees and rubbish skips in the parking area off The Avenue on Clapham Common. A circus had used this patch during the previous week and the Council had yet to complete the clearing up.

The driver of a local Area Car, returning to Lavender Hill police station, at the junction of Latchmere Road and Lavender Hill, some four hundred yards away, saw the Scorpio for the second time. It had been parked there when he had left the Station on his last call to the Windmill on the Common pub. Probably a stolen car, ditched by the thieves.

Pulling in, he stopped behind it and, being a careful man, put the registration number through to the station before getting out to check the car. His torch through the passenger side window showed two people half laying and half sitting in the front seats. The head of the driver seemed to be in the lap of the passenger. With a grin of anticipation he jerked the door open.

"Well, what sort of cocksuckers do we have?…Oh shit!"

His torch illuminated the right hand side of Michael Docherty's face. There was a thin trickle of blood, only a couple of inches long, that ran from two small neat holes in the right side of the shaven head, down the cheek behind the staring blue eye. Moving the torch to the second head, he saw two similar small holes just behind "Nameless's" left ear.

His radio hummed and the station called his number. Responding mechanically he answered and then listened as they told him that the Scorpio had been the subject of a Hampshire circulation in the previous week. It should be approached with caution.

"Control, get a Senior Officer and SOCO team here as quick as you can. I've got two stiffs, both with small calibre gunshot wounds to the head. Do you receive?"

Control was silent for a minute and then asked him to repeat his message.

"I'm not pissin' about, Arnie. I've got two bodies and I need a murder team here now, not tomorrow morning!"

Tuesday 18th August 1992
11.10 a.m. St Malo, France

The room phone rang as Martin was on the point of seeking coffee. It was Jean.

"Martin, I spoke with your Chief Inspector Potter this morning and I then met with my boss."

"Yes?"

"Your Potter was, how do you say, warm about you." Martin grinned, thinking that Potter would not like that terminology at all and then that he could not imagine Potter being "warm" about anyone. Jean continued, "Unfortunately my boss does not wish to liaise to a great degree. However, he is a man with a big belly and he has expressed an interest in meeting you. Do you understand me?"

Martin understood perfectly. "I would be delighted to meet your boss. How about lunchtime today?"

"That would be good, I think."

"Where do you suggest?"

"Do you know the restaurants that line the cobbled streets just inside the main gate from the quay to the old town, by the Hotel de France? He is a lover of seafood and the Miramar just along there on the left hand side is one of his favourites."

"I'll book a table for three for one o'clock."

Martin decided to walk the short distance to the restaurant. He wanted the table to be suitably private. On his return he was stopped in the foyer of the Mercure by the male receptionist with the 100 franc eyes.

"Monsieur Wild. There was a call for you. They would not leave a name. Then this arrived."

He held a single sheet of fax. It contained five words only and had been sent from a commercial faxing centre in Southampton. "The flight was to Paris." Martin smiled to himself. Bill was being careful.

Sitting in the hotel lounge with a coffee, he thought about the movement of Mabbett from Spain to Paris and could not help feeling hopeful. Mabbett's flight could have been to anywhere in the world, but it was not. It was to Paris and that would the nearest major airport for international flights from Spain if one were making for St Malo. From there it would be a direct train or car ride. There might even be a connection to the small airport at Dinard that he had seen on the map.

He felt a hint of excitement now and, seeking out the receptionist, put the question to him. A telephone call confirmed that there was a scheduled Paris service with two flights a day during the summer period.

1.30 p.m.

Lunch passed pleasantly. Jean eased the conversation with references to Martin's previous work in the police and on this case. His boss was a big man with an appetite to match. Whilst Martin and Jean took their time over tomato salad and langoustines followed by simple fish dish each, the big man demolished a "plateau de fruits de mer" piled high on a pyramid of three plates and then was happy to severely damage a large portion of fromage. Martin drank sparingly and noted that Jean also was careful. Nevertheless, two bottles of Muscadet disappeared between them, together with coffees and a glass or two of Calvados. Martin was impressed and wondered what Potter would have thought of the performance of his French counterpart.

It was worth it though. As they left the table to return the "complete" man to his unmarked police transport, now waiting in an adjacent "No Parking" area, he shook hands with Martin in the French manner and, for several seconds, spoke quietly to Jean, who had been about to follow him into the car.

As the car disappeared towards the big man's office, Jean said, "I am pleased to tell you that you have me for the rest of the day, if I can be of help to you. But it is unofficial and nothing must appear in my log."

"Jean, that is truly excellent." Martin went on to tell him of the Paris flight and his thoughts about the local airport.

"Why don't you take me for a ride in your most sporting motorcar and we will see what we can find out. I have a contact who works in the administration there and I also know one of the security personnel quite well. He is an ex policeman."

The following two hours failed to provide a direct sighting of anyone resembling the description of Mabbett that Martin gave to Jean. It did, however, result in a possible lead, which was supplied by the security guy. He had spoken to a man whom he had known years before when he had been a gendarme at St Malo. The man had been well known to the police as a heavy drinker, frequently being found incapable. The security man thought that he was now married and ran a small hotel near Dinan. He remembered him because of the drink history and the fact that he was driving a motorcar into the airport to pick up a passenger from the Paris flight. The man's name was André Berliot.

4.50 p.m. Southampton

"Would you like a cup of tea, Mr Potter?"

The question, from the Canteen Lady through his open office door, roused Potter from study of the autopsy report on Gordon Wilson, received that afternoon.

"Please Doreen."

He returned to his reading, going over the paragraph that worried him once again. It was nearly five p.m. and, with a resigned mutter which Doreen thought included the words "...catch him now," reached for the phone. Dialling Detective Chief Superintendent Lawson's direct line, he waited until the receiver at the other end was picked up, said to Doreen "Close the door please" and then into the mouthpiece, "Is that you, Ray?" On receiving an affirmative, "I've just received the autopsy report on Wilson, the guy who went overboard from the boat involved in that drugs intercept on the 9th. It's much as expected apart from one item, which is worrying. What appeared to be abrasions to Wilson's right temple was in fact blistering, caused by localised extreme heat and the face in that area has minute burn marks over it."

"Does the pathologist give an opinion?"

"Only factual in the report but I've spoken to him on the phone. He asked whether there was an exposed exhaust pipe at the rear of the boat. There are two but they are at water level and there is no real heat. He then said that the only other possibility was his first thought, and that is that injury was caused by the flare that was discharged by Wild. This theory is supported by the pock marking of very small burns over the rest of the face. Propellant from the flare."

There was a silence and then, with what Potter thought was a tired note in it, Ray Lawson said, "There was nothing in Wild's statement about that. You'll have to interview him again. If it can be shown that he discharged that flare deliberately at Wilson or with disregard for the consequences, then technically he could be facing a manslaughter charge – or worse."

"I know. I thought I'd better let you know before I got in touch with him."

"Where is he?"

"I had a telephone call from the French police this morning. He's with them at St Malo, looking for Mabbett. They were checking him out. He's looking for assistance."

Another silence, but not so long, then Lawson said, "The Glasgow police put the explosion down to our Irish friend attempting to booby-trap Wild's car. If they were wrong and the Irishman was a victim then Wilson's could be down to him too..."

"I know, Gov'nor, I know," and, to himself, "And I gave him a vote of confidence this morning!"

"You'd better have words with them again but, be careful, we don't want to jump the gun on this. When you speak with well...well, get him back this side of the Channel and out of harm's way. Keep me in touch."

Potter replaced the phone carefully. For the first time ever he had heard Ray Lawson at a loss for words.

He pressed an intercom button and, as his secretary appeared said "Get hold of Inspector Dempsey for me, as quickly as possible. Tell him there's an urgent need for some delicate interpretation. I'll wait here until you locate him."

5.30 p.m.
Dinan, France

Detective Jean put down the telephone and said, "He's not known at the Gendarmerie at Dinan. We'll have to have a look around ourselves. Do you know Dinan, Martin?"

"I've been there, but can't say that I know it."

"You will before the night's out!"

"I don't want to frighten Mabbett away if he is in that area."

"Don't worry. We'll be, how do you say, careful with our questions."

They started in the town centre, visiting bars with Jean casually, asking whether an André Berliot was known as they paid for their drinks. There was no mention of the police but Martin thought that Jean's manner of asking probably gave the game away, judging by the sideways looks from some of the bartenders.

Having drawn a blank in the town centre, and with evening near, they jumped into the car and moved to the port area, where there were a number of restaurants fronting the road across from the quay. At one of these Jean knew the proprietor and, immediately, there was a positive response.

"Ah yes, you mean the odd couple."

"You know him then?"

"Runs the old 'moulin' as a hotel, just along the St Valay road. Only a kilometre away. Has an English wife, pretty little thing, and a couple of kids."

"Do they have English visitors?" asked Martin.

"All sorts, but yes, there are regular English people there."

The proprietor moved off leaving the waiter to take their order. When he in turn left, Martin said, "A Frenchman with an English wife, history of drink but now doing not so badly, English visitors and now meeting a man off the Paris flight that we are interested in. Could be three coincidences, but I don't believe in more than one at a time."

"We could just knock on the door and ask whether they have accommodation for next week, or next month?"

"No, if our guesswork is right, I don't want to be seen at all. We use a Chinese expression in England, 'Softly, softly catchee monkey'. I'd rather have a quiet look from a distance tomorrow."

"I could see whether the Big Man will release me for another day," suggested Jean.

"Why not wait until we know more," said Martin. "If you are happy to twist his arm again, I'd rather it was at a time when I really need your help."

After dinner, they drove back to St Malo taking the St Valay road so that Martin would know the location of the old mill. In the dark it looked difficult. Once away from the estuary the road was a very winding secondary route; lined with trees and with only occasional houses. It went quite steeply up a hill to join the nearby main road. Martin thought that any one hanging about would stick out like a sore thumb. Perhaps it wouldn't be so easy to take a quiet look from a distance after all.

He dropped Jean and returned to the hotel. There was a note pushed under his door and he recognized the handwriting of the receptionist. It read "Please telephone Bill. Urgent."

It was nearly midnight and Martin hesitated but then rang Bill Creighton's home number.

"Martin, you haven't spoken to me, OK? But you should expect a summons to meet with Potter again very soon. The autopsy report seems to have raised some hackles. I don't know what as he's not talking about it, not prepared to! He had Dempsey over this evening and they are going to be talking to the St Malo police tomorrow morning. Reading between the lines of what I've heard, I wouldn't be surprised if you were put on a boat by them and met this side."

"Thanks, Bill. I owe you, again!"

Martin put down the receiver and stared thoughtfully into space.

Wednesday 19th August 1992
9.30 a.m. Dinard, France

"But of course, Monsieur Wild. Have your chauffeur leave the keys with the Reception if I'm not here. That will be quite in order."

Martin smiled. Having a name to drop and speaking expansively about one's chauffeur depositing one's Porsche ready for one's arrival whilst one was "…bringing the boat across…" had achieved the desired effect.

In fact Martin's desire was to find a safe home for the car, hopefully out of sight of the French or, should they arrive, the English police whilst he disappeared into the undergrowth again to check out the Moulin de St Valay. Additionally there was the grim humour of using Mabbett's name as an aid in the furtherance of the man's own downfall. Martin rather hoped that there would be the opportunity for a few words with Mabbett before the final chapter was written.

Martin had made hasty arrangements following a call from Jean a quarter of an hour earlier. The tone of his voice as he enquired of Martin's movements that day confirmed the warning given by Bill Creighton the previous night. Jean had indicated that he would like to see Martin at 10.30 on a matter of some concern. The voice had been grave. The easy air which characterised the previous day's activities was gone.

Now, throwing essentials into his bag, Martin found "100 franc note" and gave him an envelope to hand to Jean on his arrival. The note simply apologized for Martin's absence, explaining that a positive sighting of Mabbett had been made in England and that Martin was hurrying back there to pick up the trail. He didn't expect Jean to fall for it, but one never knew. If it was possible to keep a valuable contact, it would be worth the effort.

Settling his bill and assuring Reception that he would be back, he left the room phone on the bed with a notepad beside it. If one went to the trouble of shading the top sheet with soft pencil, various ferry sailing times from Cherbourg and Le Havre would be seen, having been impressed from the missing sheet above. Another little ploy that might throw the scent off, or might not!

Leaving the Porsche in a "Visitors" slot at the Yacht Club, he put a note on the windscreen with the secretary's name on it, ignored the request to leave the keys with Yacht Club Reception and set out to walk the short distance to the harbour. A water taxi took Martin out to the mooring area where visiting boats waited to pass through the Rance Barrage. This massive construction was effectively a dam across the estuary housing huge turbines that provided hydro electric power and a constant level of water upstream, which made the meandering lower Rance valley very attractive to yachtsmen.

As usual, the summer holidays had resulted in the arrival of a number of British boats, easily identified by their red ensigns, and now awaiting entry into this favoured port of call. Martin felt sure that a friendly English voice offering to pilot them through the locks of the Barrage and up to Dinan at the top end of the estuary would be welcome to at least one of the boats' skippers. This would provide a crafty method of dodging his friends from the Judiciaire.

He was right. The third boat that he approached was a nice thirty-foot sloop manned by what appeared to be a husband and wife with two youngish children. There were signs of weariness in the man's eyes and his wife looked totally washed out. The results of an overnight crossing with the inevitable concerns for the family, compounded by unfamiliar waters and difficult navigation. Martin had seen the effect before when assisting in the delivery of a friend's boat with a similar family situation. The husband asked what it would cost and, when Martin replied, "Not a thing. I'm off the ferry and joining a boat at Dinan," he and his bag were hauled aboard with alacrity.

Whilst Jean and his colleagues from the French police carefully investigated Martin's hotel room and the telephone wires between St Malo, Cherbourg, Le Havre and Southampton warmed up, Martin enjoyed a pleasant day's sailing with a thoroughly nice family. The children were well behaved. The husband, a dental surgeon from London who kept his boat at Chichester Marina, was only too pleased to "crash out" for an hour or so whilst they waited for passage through the "Barrage". His wife, much relieved by the presence of an apparently knowledgeable and competent companion, produced good hot coffee and started the preparation of a picnic lunch which, to Martin's satisfaction, included a bottle of Chablis from the boat's ice box.

The sun shone with increasing heat. The lock gates opened and they were in the first batch of boats through. The chop of the open harbour gave way to a smooth gurgle of estuary currents. Green, tree-lined banks replaced houses and Martin, helming a small sailing boat once more, listening to the chatter of children and the easy talk between husband and wife, seeing again Eileen's smiling blue eyes and blonde curls, reflected with sadness on what might have been until three months ago – and with cold anger on events then and since.

9.45 a.m.

At St Valay, Mabbett surprised André by appearing in the kitchen of the Mill, sweat stained from a morning's jogging and looking for a late breakfast. Whilst his wife prepared it, André took the battered old Peugeot and drove the few hundred yards to the Port of Dinan for supplies of bread, eggs and milk

He took the opportunity to spend a little longer away from the uncomfortably cold eyes of Mr Mallett / Mabbett. Calling into the Bar de Corsairs for a morning pastis, he chatted with the chef, who was an occasional acquaintance at a card table frequented by André. Whilst they talked, they were joined by a waiter who, new to the establishment and keen to impress a friend of the chef, imparted the news that a "flic" and an Englishman had, according to the waiter from next door, been in that restaurant the previous night, asking for André Berliot.

André shrugged, nonplussed and, thinking of his former fairly frequent meetings with the law, hesitated for at least two seconds before accepting a second pastis. At lunchtime, as he carried supplies into the kitchen of the Mill, and to distract his wife's complaints about the time he had taken, he told her of the detective and the Englishman, hinting that the presence of an Englishman might indicate interest in his wife rather than himself. Maggie went very quiet. Her husband did not share her knowledge of Mabbett's background and, within a few minutes, Maggie was standing before that man in the upstairs office cum study of the adjacent building. Mabbett's reaction was of disbelief. After the care that he had taken, it was not possible that, within a matter of hours of his arrival, there should be this sort of unwanted interest. André must return immediately to his waiter friend for more information but not a word about "Mr Mallett" being in residence.

Two hours later, having been "forced" to eat lunch at the restaurant so that he could talk to the waiter who had actually served Jean and Martin, André was standing staring aghast at a Dermott Mabbett, who was incandescent with rage. The description offered by the waiter and now passed on by André included Martin's scarred face. At this, Mabbett had erupted and, for the first time, André knew fear of the man as well as unease. Mabbett's questioning had not revealed the casual meeting between André and the airport security man. Despite several glasses of pastis and cognac, André had sufficient nous to keep his mouth shut on that subject. He thus lived to see another day!

*

As the unfortunate André scuttled from the room, the cause of Mabbett's anger was sitting at ease on the cockpit cushions whilst the yacht's owner, now recovered from his loss of sleep, shared sailing reminiscences over a second bottle of Chablis. Over lunch, they agreed to moor overnight at Plouer sur Rance, a village on the banks of the estuary, where Martin could introduce them to a good restaurant and a marine engineer who would sort out a leaking propshaft gland in the boat. Martin would occupy the forward cabin for the night and leave them at Dinan the following morning.

2.10 p.m.

"Jimmy, I hope you're in touch with your man Rampton?"

"Why's that, Dermott?"

"You'll not believe this, but Wild has turned up at...in France at a place near St Malo called Dinan." Mabbett checked himself just in time.

"So will he be staying there?"

"I reckon for a while. If you can get Rampton here quickly, we might be able to knock this business on the head."

"I've had a call from Nick. He's met with your Michael Docherty and his friend."

"And?"

"Oh, you're not to worry about them anymore."

"What does that mean?"

"It means just that, Dermott. Not to worry about them AT ALL any more. Nick wasn't very complimentary about your Mr Docherty. Thought he was a total waste of space, if I remember his words correctly."

Mabbett was silent for a moment, not liking the direction of the conversation. Then, "There was a reason for bringing him in. He's not one of my team. I didn't want to use any of my people."

"I get the impression that your 'team' is thin on the ground now, Dermott."

Mabbett felt anger growing inside and controlled it with difficulty. Forcing himself to speak levelly, he changed the topic and said, "When do you think Nick Rampton can get here?"

"He was going up to Glasgow, on the information that you gave but, if I can catch him before he leaves the flat, he'll be with you tomorrow."

"Good. Tell him to let me know where and when. Phone me on this number." Mabbett gave the number of the phone that he was on, in the building next to the Mill.

"Any sign of a buyer for my flats?"

"Too soon, Dermott, too soon."

4.50 p.m
Southampton, England

"Thought you'd be interested in this, Guv'ner."

The officer laid a Metropolitan Police circulation on Potter's desk. It carried details of a double murder on Clapham Common the previous day and looked for identification of the person whose photograph had been found amongst papers in the car which contained the two bodies. The photo was of Martin Wild and with it was the information supplied to Docherty in his search for Wild. It gave Wild's name and the various locations that he had used as bases or had been known to visit by the person who had put together the original information.

"Thanks. Anyone been in touch with the Met over this?"

"No. Thought you'd like your team to deal with it."

Potter nodded and reached for the phone. He dialled the number shown on the circulation and asked for the officer named.

"Detective Chief Inspector Potter, Hampshire. Interested in this circulation of yours on the Clapham murders. The man Wild is involved in an enquiry that we have here and others in Scotland. I'll fax you details but I wanted to know about this job that you have. Can you fill me in?"

Potter listened for some time, then gave brief details of Wild's involvement in the Eileen Padgett's murder enquiry and the deaths of Mahoney and Wilson, promising to fax fuller information later.

Dialling Detective Superintendent Lawson's direct line, he said, "Ray, glad I caught you. There's a new development that you should know about. The two Glasgow villains that were looking for Wild when he was in hospital after Wilson's death, have been found in a car at Clapham, South London, both shot in the head. The Met are looking for Wild as his details were left in the car that they were in."

"Is there a suggestion that he was involved?"

"Not directly, but it adds to our concern. He was close to the deaths of both Mahoney and Wilson. Now the Met have two more bodies!"

"Have we heard any more from the French side? Have they found him yet?"

"No, and that worries me as well. He disappears just at the moment that we want him back here. He did the same thing with the Scottish police when Mahoney's body was found. I'm beginning to wonder whether he's got a contact in the team, whether someone's marking his card for him."

"If you've got something solid in that line, then we should be talking to Internal Affairs but remember that, if they come into the job, it will almost certainly upset your team's operation."

"I've got nothing that solid, Ray. In any case, I'd prefer to handle this myself."

Friday 21st August 1992
8.30 a.m. Dinan, France

Early morning sunshine was warm in the cockpit of the moored boat. The strong coffee was wakening. Down below, children were stirring in the aft cabin. Martin could hear their voices over the sound of the kettle coming the boil, the background of gentle river gurgles and cheery distant conversation from the harbour master as the Skipper, returning from the boulangerie with an armful of French sticks, practised his French.

"You'll stop for breakfast, Martin?" The question came from the skipper's wife, rattling plates down below.

"Thank you, Audrey. Just some toast and another coffee please."

"I'm doing scrambled egg with the remains of the smoked salmon for Gordon. There's plenty. Same for you?"

"You'll not get rid of your stowaways if you feed them like this!" Martin laughed.

The remainder of the passage to Dinan had been completed in a leisurely manner the previous day and Martin had accepted the skipper's offer to have dinner ashore as a "thank you" for the pilotage and to stay another night as there was no sign of his friend's boat yet. Martin didn't enjoy misleading such a nice couple but it was very convenient, giving the whole of this day to check out the area where Mabbett had gone to ground.

As he watched the skipper step from the roadway onto the wooden pontoon of the marina, Martin saw two joggers trotting along the road by the quay. Another track suited pair had passed a few moments before and, as Martin looked for them, he saw that they had turned left into the side road which, from his previous visit with Jean, he knew led to the Mill. Five minutes earlier, a lone jogger had followed the same path. It seemed that there was a regular route for these energetic early risers that could solve an immediate problem that he had.

"Are you leaving the boat here today, Gordon?" Martin queried as the skipper climbed aboard.

"Yes, we thought we'd take the youngsters into the town on that little tourist train that they saw yesterday. Do some shopping, stay here tonight and start back down the river tomorrow."

"Would you mind if I left my bag in the cockpit to collect later in the day? I thought I'd have a wander locally whilst I'm waiting."

"No problem."

Half an hour later, wearing a track suit and a long peaked cap from his small supply of stand by clothing, Martin stepped ashore and, once out of sight of the boat, broke into a trot, following the same path as the earlier joggers.

The side road led uphill, following a narrow valley with a tumbling stream that emptied into the Rance below the marina. The land on either side was heavily wooded with trees clinging to the rock faces and only the occasional house. It was a pretty, winding road with few opportunities to divert. As it climbed higher, there was a sharp "S" bend where the road crossed to the other bank of the stream, which here foamed over rocks in a swift current. A long sweep to the right and there were two buildings that formed the Mill. Not overlooked by any other house and without a path off that might give opportunity to deviate and find a "viewing" spot.

"Chosen with care if this is your hideaway, Mr Mabbett," muttered Martin as he trotted past. "Road to the front, gorge and river below, steep hillside and trees behind and the millpond and river above. No undergrowth to give cover."

Beyond the buildings there was a long archway of metal, which bridged the valley and, Martin thought, probably carried the railway line that he remembered from the maps that he had studied previously.

There had been no sign of movement from the Mill as he trotted by and Martin resisted the temptation to look back until passing under the high girderwork of the rail bridge, the road swung abruptly left and, as he turned with it, he saw a post van pulling into the small parking area in front of the building. At that moment there was the clatter and rumble of a train overhead and, as he continued uphill, he had the thought that the railway and bridge might provide the only possible vantage points. Another hundred metres and, through the trees, he could see an embankment. Then, to his left, there was a break in the steep ditch and a gate and track, which led into a small clearing.

Climbing the gate, Martin came to the embankment and rail tracks some two hundred metres from the road. There was no one in sight and he followed the rails back towards the latticework of steel that was the start of the bridge. Once on the bridge, he came within sight of the buildings but felt it wise not to stay on the track. Below, the ground was falling away and he retraced the last few metres to scramble down the steep slope, trying to find a position with some cover which afforded a similar view to that from the bridge.

The undergrowth away from the rail track was thicker, the slope down steeper and progress became a series of downward climbs interposed with short, carefully judged slithers over grass, moss and boulders. As Martin was beginning to debate the wisdom of going on, suddenly there it was. The valley below the bridge laid out like an aerial photograph with the Mill buildings in the foreground. The only problem was the distance, which was too great to see detail.

Conscious of the bold blue of his track suit colours, Martin searched for a larger and more suitable thicket. He eventually settled on a clump of gorse a few feet further down the hillside, which also sheltered him from any possibility of being seen from the rail track. As he burrowed with care into the prickly base, he remembered the similar exercise on the Scottish hillside above Kilchatten. The reminder of Tony Drew's expletives brought a smile to his face. It seemed an age ago, but was only a few weeks. Satisfied with the prickly den, he settled down to watch, wishing that he had his binoculars with him and mentally making a list of requirements for later in the day.

Within the next half hour there were appearances by two different men and one woman at the door and in the garden of the Mill. It was impossible to identify them with the naked eye and, not being able to say for sure whether Mabbett was using the premises, Martin withdrew carefully, unwilling to waste further time. Back on the road, he followed what he thought might have been a regular jogger's path back to the Port of Dinan via roads which traversed a residential area and school before regaining the waterside.

Collecting his bag from the boat's cockpit, he found pinned to it a note giving him the anticipated timings of the family's return trip to St Malo with the overnight moorings that they might use and an offer to join them again should there be any problems with his own plans. It was a nice gesture but Martin dismissed it immediately. Even if the timing was right, it would be unthinkable to place an unsuspecting family in the sort at danger that might result from his next activities.

During the next couple of hours he stocked up on essentials and had a meal before returning to the railway track, this time with binoculars. The den in the gorse bush was improved immensely with layers of black plastic bin liners to lie on, whilst time passed more pleasantly with food and drink to hand. Martin settled down to spend the remaining daylight hours in the hope of confirming that this was the hideaway of Dermott Mabbett, the Mr Big of that part of the drugs world that he had stumbled into.

*

The man himself was not at home. Whilst Martin had been shopping in Dinan, Mabbett, driven by André, had left for St Malo to meet a passenger from the overnight ferry.

Rampton had boarded the boat as a foot passenger at Portsmouth. A taxi had taken him from the ferry terminal at St Malo to a large hotel in the cobbled square of the old town, where Mabbett now found him.

"I expected you to get here yesterday. Why didn't you fly over?"

There was a pause whilst the dark dead eyes swivelled in his direction, inspected him with what Mabbett thought was a degree of contempt and then, "The x-ray machine might have been a problem."

Another pause whilst Mabbett digested the significance. "Oh, of course. You won't need anything from me then?"

A shake of the head and, "What makes you think this man Wild is here then?"

Mabbett detailed the information from the waiter and then said, "Do you speak French?"

"Only enough to get by in places like this." He indicated the hotel.

"Well, you can borrow André. He's in the car outside. He doesn't need to know any more about this business than I've already told him. And keep him away from too much drink or you'll be having to carry him home."

"Who's André? What does he do?"

"He and his wife run the hotel where I'm staying. I've known them for some time."

"And what have you told him?"

"He knows that I want to find Wild. Nothing else."

"What does he know about me?"

"Nothing."

"Let's make sure we keep it that way." There was no expression in the voice, but Mabbett recognised the force behind it and felt a moment of anger. Liam would not have said that. But then Liam was dead.

"What if there's no sign of this Wild person?"

"If you don't get a line on him by tonight, I want you to come back to the hotel. If we don't find him, it's possible that he will find us. He's pulled a couple of strokes already and he seems to have the police here in his pocket."

*

DCI Potter and Inspector Colin Dempsey would not have agreed with that remark. They had arrived in St Malo by the same ferry but had been met by Sûreté car and whisked off to Rennes. There, the officer in charge of the Rennes/St Malo area wanted to talk in person to the British police officers who had firstly promoted cooperation with an English "enqueter civil", a private investigator, and then provided information that the same person might be involved in deaths that they were investigating. There was little "Entente Cordial" waiting for Potter and Dempsey in Rennes!

The journey and meeting had taken the morning and, by lunch time, they were en route to St Malo, now accompanied by a silent Detective Jean Jibault who, though blameless in the matter, felt that mud manufactured by "The English" was now sticking to his very well cut jacket. This was due to the ability of his boss, The Big Man with the appetite for fruits de mer, to duck and dive surprisingly well for one of that stature. Life was not fair, he concluded. There was no such thing as a free lunch, or dinner! And now he had to work with these two to try and find Martin Wild. What a pity, he had liked Wild – and the man knew his wine!

11.40 p.m.

Rampton, towing an André who oozed pastis from every pore, was met at the door of the Mill by Mabbett, who was patently glad to see him.

"Anything?"

"Not much. Couple of sightings that might be Wild, but nothing definite."

"Where were the sightings?"

"The waiter told André about Wild and the "flic". Thinks that he may have seen him in a party from a boat the previous day. That ties in with the harbourmaster, who said that an English boat arrived with a family and an extra man. The second man didn't stay with the boat, which left a day later without him."

"Is he sure about that?"

"Can't be absolutely but he refuelled the boat as they were leaving with what seemed like the complete family on deck. No reason for the odd man to have stayed below."

"What's he look like?"

"Tall with fair short hair and wearing a blue track suit when the man last saw him. That was mid morning today."

"A blue track suit…this morning."

Mabbett was silent then slowly, quietly and almost to himself "And I saw a blue figure up on the rail this morning. Thought it was a worker in blue overalls…"

He gestured to a pair of large binoculars on a tripod in the window. They were similar in every respect to the pair in the bedroom window at Kilchatten. "By the time that I'd got these on him, he'd turned and walked back along the rail, out of sight. Thought I saw some movement later just below the rail, but it didn't mean anything, just a rail worker."

"Can't do anything tonight. We'll have a look in the morning."

*

At about the same time, a weary little team was calling it a day at the police station in St Malo. They hadn't found Martin but were pleased nevertheless. They had found his black Porsche. There was now a police team lying in wait for when he returned to the car, which they anticipated might be very soon. They weren't to know that it wouldn't be soon enough.

Jean, who had suggested the Yacht Club and found the car, had mixed feelings. He guessed correctly that the reason Martin had disappeared from the hotel was due to information from England. In questioning the staff, it became apparent that there had been telephone calls and faxes which, to the inquisitive ear and eye of one Receptionist, were not "normal". To Jean, it was quickly clear that the Receptionist had been more attentive to the visitor than usual with hotel staff. This probably meant that money had changed hands. If the information was coming from English police sources, then it was either one very bent English policeman, or someone who looked on Martin as one of the "good guys". Anyway, he didn't particularly like this man Potter. He made no attempt to speak French, relied on Dempsey for that. He had no humour or sophistication, no appetite for good food and didn't even drink a glass of wine! Who said the English were becoming more civilized?

As he bade them goodnight with arrangements to meet again on the following day, he wondered whether perhaps he was due for a day or two of sick leave. It was some time since his indigestion had played up.

Saturday 22nd August 1992
5.45 a.m. Dinan, France

It had rained overnight, not heavily but a gentle shower for an hour or so, leaving the grass at the side of the rail track slippery and treacherous. In the first light of dawn, Martin took care as he returned to the rail embankment, especially on the last stretch before the gorse bush, which was steeply downhill over boulders and with a straggle of trees and other bushes clinging to the hillside.

At his den in the centre of the gorse, he arranged the black plastic bin liners, tearing three more off the roll. The first he slipped up over his feet and legs. The second he took the bottom out of, so that he could pull that one up over the first and tie it around his waist. The third he cut the two corners off, where it was sealed at the bottom,, and then took a semicircle out of the centre of the same seam. He pulled this bag down over his head so that his arms came through the corner holes. Dressed like a long black plastic tube but fairly impervious to further rain and the wet ground, he wriggled into the bottom of the gorse and took up a prone position with binoculars at the ready. Immediately he saw two people at the Mill. One was holding the door of the garage open, whilst the second reversed a red sports car out. Closing the doors, the first man jumped into the car and it drove off, turning right out of the Mill forecourt and up the hill.

Martin cursed. Two minutes too late! Who had been the driver? Had he missed Mabbett? The second man was a stranger to him. He had thought that it might be André at first but, although the height was about the same, the man's movements had been quick and neat, not at all like the slow, shambling Frenchman. The clothes too were not André, a dark grey suit or similar businesslike jacket and trousers. The early morning light had not been sufficient to see the detail of the face, even through the binoculars.

*

In the sports car as it climbed the steep hill towards the bridge, there was silence. Neither Mabbett, who was driving, nor Rampton in the passenger seat, were great on early morning conversation. The latter was, if anything, quieter than his normal terse self. He had not slept well, had not enjoyed the company of André the previous day and was not looking forward to the present expedition with Mabbett, who had this bee in his bonnet about a blue suited figure that had, in all probability, been a railway worker. Remembering André and, before that Docherty and his nameless friend, none of whom had impressed, he judged Mabbett as a second liner. Not in the same class as his boss Jimmy. He wondered what was happening in Spain, wishing he was back there. Even the routine of chasing his group of timeshare salesmen would be preferable to an early morning with this man Mabbett.

These thoughts were interrupted as they approached the junction with the main road. Mabbett slotted the car into the side, backed into field entrance and set off down the hill in the return direction. He said, "We've only passed one place where we could get off the road. We'll check that out."

Running the car down the hill, he reached the spot that Martin had used to approach the rail line, pulled in and got out to check the ground for tyre marks.

"No sign of a car having been here. Anyway, we'll have a look at the bridge."

"I'll have a look at the bridge," thought Rampton, but said nothing, following Mabbett over the fence and towards the rail track.

Following the rails to where the girders started, they moved off of the track onto the grassy slope that looked down the valley towards the Mill. Rampton's black leather city shoes had a smooth sole and he slipped on the damp slope, swearing as he regained his balance.

"Let's keep it quiet, Nick," from Mabbett.

Rampton noted with amusement that Mabbett was holding an automatic pistol in his hand. He used it to gesture that Rampton was to search through the bushes below the track.

"If it's rail workers up here, you'll have the local gendarmes round us like flies, waving that thing about."

Mabbett glowered but slipped the gun back into the trouser band, under his jacket.

Rampton's own "tools" were out of sight. They always were unless they were to be used. Lifting his feet high in a vain attempt to keep the shoes at least partially dry, he picked his way through the scattering of trees and bushes, moving round in a semicircle where the slope of the valley started to fall abruptly whilst Mabbett kept pace with him at a higher level.

The sun was now showing through a thin early morning mist and, just as he was about to retrace his steps to rejoin Mabbett at the higher level, he saw a glint of reflected light from a bush lower down the slope. Staring hard, he could make out what looked like a black plastic rubbish bag, pushed into the bottom of a gorse bush.

His first thought was that rail workers had stashed some materials or tools there, but then he realised that the slope was so steep that no self-respecting French workman would go to that sort of trouble, especially in a deserted place like this. Perhaps they had tossed a bag of rubbish down the slope, expecting it to disappear amongst the bushes, much as happened on the sides of many French roads.

Curious, he started down the slope, swearing softly as he was forced to use his hands to traverse mossy, slippery boulders, half buried in the grassy hillside. He was tempted to stop and leave the bag where it was. But now he could see it was longer than an ordinary rubbish bag.

Reaching it, he leant into the gorse bush, grasped the nearest corner and pulled. The bag came apart, the piece in his hand separating from the remainder, revealing a pair of legs in blue trousers and trainers. There was no movement. Stooping low, he looked along the line of the figure but could only see a tracksuit hood covering the head, which seemed to project out of the other end of the "sack".

It looked as though Mabbett had been right, there had been a man in blue up here. Perhaps a dead man, now wrapped up bin liners!

Standing up, he slipped a revolver from a shoulder holster and called, "Down here, Mr Mabbett. Here's your man in blue." And started to move around the bush to see the face.

The ground on the other side of the gorse bush was truly precarious. There was a foot or two of sloping wet grass before another boulder marked the edge of an even steeper drop. His smooth shoes gave no purchase at all. Hanging onto a piece of rock with his left hand he reached across and, with the hand holding the gun, used the side of that wrist to steady himself on a bare branch beyond the figure. He was directly in front of the hooded head.

He reached forward, intent on raising the head to see the face. Suddenly the "dead" man looked up and smiled crookedly from a scarred face. An arm shot out, the hand on the end of it grasping a short bladed sailor's knife with a marlin spike projecting. The spike stabbed into Rampton's throat.

The shock, the instinctive warding off reaction to push away the weapon in his throat – dropping his gun in doing so, all conspired with smooth shoes and wet grass to send him backwards over the boulder and then cartwheeling end over end down the rocky slope.

Within the first few metres he was almost in free fall, gorse and branches whipping at clothing and flesh as his outstretched hands grasped ineffectually at turf and empty air. Then, as the slope became less steep, he was bouncing from tree trunks and boulders, arms now flailing uselessly, bloodied head jerking from side to side.

As Martin watched the tumbling body disappear, Mabbett approached and called out, "What is it?" The thick gorse bush blocked his view, but the noise of the body crashing through bushes and bouncing off boulders caused him to stop.

Martin pulled himself forward, out of the gorse and over the ledge onto the lower slope that Rampton had been standing on. The fallen gun was a few feet to his right as he turned to face Mabbett. He moved sideways towards the gun finding, as Rampton had, that even with his ribbed trainers, there was little grip.

Mabbett too was moving sideways, looking for Rampton. As Martin's hand closed over the gun, Mabbett saw him, raised the automatic and fired. The shots crackled through the gorse.

The gun in Martin's hand was a snub nosed .38, a close range weapon that would have little accuracy at the thirty or so metres separating him from Mabbett. Nevertheless, he steadied the gun with both hands and squeezed off a shot as Mabbett fired again. Ducking back behind the boulder, he waited a few seconds before poking his head out again. Two more shots rang out and a bullet hit the boulder only a foot to his right, ricocheting off. Martin ducked back again and then out again thinking, "That was six. Is he out of ammo?" to see Mabbett in full flight, legs and arms working as he charged up the slope towards the rail track.

In the seconds that it took Martin to climb over the boulders and get past the gorse, Mabbett was on the rail track and running like a very fit hare. Martin reached the fence as the red MG accelerated out onto the road towards the Mill.

It took Martin the best part of five minutes to trot down the hill until he reached the building that he guessed Mabbett had made for. In front of it he paused for a second or so, regaining his breath. There was no sign of the MG, only an old Peugeot, which had been parked there all morning. A woman was standing at the door of the main building. She had her hands on her hips and, even at a distance of some thirty metres, he could see a slightly nonplussed expression on her face. He guessed her to be the English woman that Jean and he had heard of, who ran the hotel with André.

With nothing to lose, he called out in English, "Where did he go?"

Staring at him for a few moments she replied in English, but with a slight Scots brogue, "To Dinan with André, but he'll not be long."

Cautiously he approached her and, as he did so, she turned and stepped back into the house. With his hand under the track suit, on the butt of the revolver, he moved to the door, ready to dive out again. The woman was pouring coffee from a jug.

"He said you'd like a coffee while you're waiting," she said. "Do you take milk or sugar?"

Warning bells rang in Martin's head. Mabbett was thinking fast. He was being set up.

"Neither thanks."

Closing the door behind him, he stepped quietly across the room to a position just inside another open door, which led out of the kitchen to the rear of the building. From there, facing the front door, he was not immediately visible to anyone coming through from the rear rooms, but could see the front yard and road through the window.

As she turned to him with the cup of hot coffee he tensed but she merely put the cup and saucer on the table near him and said as she turned away again, "You can sit down if you like."

Now it was Martin's turn to be nonplussed. The woman looked like an ordinary housewife and was so cool. Whatever Mabbett had said to her had not made her nervous. He tried again.

"How long will he be?"

"About twenty minutes."

"Anyone else here?"

Her look was a little curious but unconcerned as she said "Yes, we have four rooms taken. There's a double free. Are you staying?"

He was now convinced that she knew nothing of the dangers. No normal woman could have maintained an unworried air and innocent conversation in such potentially violent circumstances.

Just then he heard the sound of childish voices from above and the woman called out in French hurrying "my little ones" to breakfast. In a lull between the conversation, he heard a sound from outside that, with the patter of little footsteps on the stairs, chilled his heart. The double metallic clicks of an automatic being cocked.

One swift stride took him to the woman. Taking her by the shoulders, he turned and pushed her towards the rear rooms. "Stop the children!" he whispered urgently and, turning again, towards the front door, upended the kitchen table onto its side between that door and the inner rooms.

The front door was thrust open and Mabbett was there, only his arm and head visible. The gun in his hand spat flame once, twice, three times and Martin, on his hands and knees behind a table that was quivering under the impact of bullets, shouted, "The children, the children!" The woman, on hands and knees too, was screaming. Martin, revolver in hand, did not shoot for fear of drawing return fire.

As the ringing deafness in his ears lessened, he heard the sound of running footsteps from outside and jumped to the window. Mabbett was halfway across the yard, gun in one hand and bag in the other. The MG was just drawing up, with André in the driving seat. Mabbett yanked the door open, grabbed André and pulled him out, hurled his bag into the car and, as Martin came through the front door, raised the gun and fired again.

At the sight of the gun, André threw himself to the ground and, as Mabbett drove off, with a scattering gravel and squeal of rubber, Martin turned to the woman now crying hysterically at the bottom of the stairs.

He feared the worst but found that the two round-eyed youngsters were as uninjured as their distraught mother.

"You said that he was with André."

"He said to tell you that," she sobbed. "I didn't know he had a gun. I didn't know he was going to shoot."

A white-faced André appeared at the door.

"Do you know where he is going?" demanded Martin. André dumbly shook his head. Martin reached for the telephone on a sideboard and dialled a number provided by Jean. Mabbett was mobile and he was not.

Connection made, he summarised to Jean all that had happened, gave an approximate location for the injured or dead Rampton and agreed to wait for the arrival of the police.

Two minutes later he had second thoughts and said to André, "Where are the keys to the other car, the Peugeot?"

Wordlessly André pulled open a drawer in the sideboard and handed Martin two keys on a ring.

At the bottom of the minor road, Martin turned right, driving slowly along the quayside towards the town of Dinan. His intuition had been right. Parked at an angle halfway along the quay was the red MG. Ignoring other traffic, Martin double parked beside it and leapt out in time to see a slim powerboat disappearing downriver at too high a speed for it to be anyone other than Mabbett.

Standing by the car he ran through his options. Inform the police of Mabbett's route and, if they were successful, see him maybe get a derisory prison sentence for illegal use of a handgun or, alternatively, continue the chase with darker intent. There was no argument and he started along the quay looking for a suitable boat. There was not a single vessel visible that looked to be ready for action, let alone able to compete with the swiftly disappearing powerboat.

Jumping into the borrowed car he set off for La Hisse, the next village down river, where he knew there was a lock that Mabbett would have to negotiate. Even if he missed Mabbett, there might be a boat to be begged, borrowed or stolen. He drove hard and without respect for other traffic but, by the time he had negotiated the narrow main street of La Hisse and then followed the road in a loop to a bridge which gave access to the lock, he was too late. The road leading to the bridge ran beside the estuary and he saw that Mabbett had been lucky. The lock was open and the powerboat was already creaming past at a rate which would give the local harbour authority apoplexy if they saw it.

Turning again, he set off for the next village downstream, Plouer sur Rance, where he and the family had moored overnight a few days earlier.

That had a large marina and he recalled seeing a Dock Master's launch lying alongside.

The slow winding road took him away from the estuary and he took chances. Reaching Plouer and the estuary again, he could see some distance down river. There was no sign of Mabbett's boat. Nor was there any sign of the Dock Master's launch.

Then his luck changed. Just coming into a jetty some little distance ahead was an open dory with a large outboard on the back. It was similar to the one that he had borrowed at Kilchatten all those weeks ago, but with a bigger motor.

Abandoning the car by the jetty, he jumped out and ran to the end, where the boat was just nudging alongside. He called out to the man at the helm, pointing to a nearby bollard with mooring warp already attached. The man raised his hand thumb uppermost in a "thank you". Picking up the Warp, he said in French, "Leave it to me," and jumped into the boat as the Frenchman jumped out with a cheery wave and a "Merci!" for this helpful new dock master.

The man's cheerfulness disappeared and he uttered a strangled cry as Martin dropped the warp, knocked the gears into reverse and opened the throttle. The boat shot backwards and then, with a flurry of foam as Martin knocked it into forward and opened the throttle again, surged forwards. It curved around and almost missed the pontoon. The "thwack", coupled with splinters of wood in the air and a detached rubbing strake waving in the wind, changed the cry of alarm to one of anger. But it was too late and Martin was away, heading for the main channel. As he cleared the pontoons, Mabbett's power boat appeared from up river, now travelling at a slightly more reasonable, and less noticeable speed, but one which would see him pass the entrance to the marina before Martin was there.

Settling into the seat behind the boat's wheel, Martin slid the revolver from under his jacket and checked the chambers. One spent cartridge and five live ones left. The snub nosed barrel reminded him that it was a close range weapon. With only five shots, he could not afford to get into a marksmanship contest. Steering with one hand he used a finger of the other to extract the dead cartridge. It was a long shell case, a magnum. At least that was good news. Closing the gun, he settled into the seat as the dory rocked onto the wash from Mabbett's boat, now some fifty metres ahead and just passing under the twin bridges at Port St Hubert, the narrowest part of the main estuary.

Martin had the dory's throttle wide open but he was only slowly catching the boat ahead. As they passed the village of Langrolay, he reckoned that he had made up only ten metres. Although Mabbett had slowed from his initial speed, his was a true speed boat and, at half throttle, was more than the equal of the dory, flat out.

The estuary was now at its widest and Martin was wondering where Mabbett was heading. There were two other main landing points before the Rance Barrage where the next lock was, the village of Le Minihic and la Richardais, which was a small town just above the Barrage on the Dinard side of the estuary. The alternative was that Mabbett was heading for the Barrage itself, intent upon going through the lock into the harbour and then to either Dinard or St Malo. Martin did not think that likely. It would take too much time to get through the lock and was an obvious place for the police to be, should Mabbett think that they were onto him.

Through the narrower part of the lower estuary there was nothing that Martin could do to close on the boat ahead. He was losing his chance to deal with the man where there were no witnesses. Once they got to the Barrage, whatever happened might well become very public. There were control rooms and viewing areas on the Barrage as well as the continuous stream of traffic that crossed in both directions. He had been lucky with the previous "accounts" that had been "settled". Police suspicion was not proof, but using a gun under the noses of the French Judiciaire could well result in a very different scenario.

As these thoughts were passing through Martin's mind, Mabbett, for the first time since Martin had been or the water behind him, looked over his shoulder. The sight of the speeding dory, now some thirty metres away, had an electrifying effect. He jerked around, his boat veering off course, stared hard, reached down into the boat and came back up with an automatic pistol in his hand. As he levelled the gun, Martin started swerving the dory from side to side. He saw a flash from the muzzle and then another. At the third flash the plexiglass windscreen in front of him suddenly starred and a lump flew out of the corner.

"That was a lucky shot, Mr Mabbett," murmured Martin, "or you're much better with a handgun than I am."

Mabbett turned to his front again, crouched forward and opened the throttle. The power boat's nose came up and the boat levelled out as it came onto the plane. With a deep "V" developing in the water behind, it accelerated away from the dory.

They were just passing the Pointe de Cancaval. Ahead was an open expanse of water in front of the great Barrage. In the distance, to the left, were rows of moored yachts and small craft. Beyond them, Martin knew, was the entrance to the lock, marked by three large towers, which projected out of the water. Immediately ahead was the huge concrete structure which housed the Barrage's power plant, the twenty-four great underwater turbines, each shaped like a bulb and each with four huge blades, as tall as a standing man, powered by the water from the estuary and the harbour. In the right hand end of the Barrage was a series of gates, which helped balance the inside and outside levels at certain times.

Mabbett was now heading directly for the entrance to the lock on the left hand side of the structure. When his boat was only a few metres from the first tower, he suddenly swerved to the right, crossing the buoys and floating line, which marked the "no go" area for boats.

Martin, now again some fifty metres back, altered course and cut the corner, crossing the same line to end up suddenly beside and slightly in front of Mabbett's boat.

Mabbett was bent to the right, apparently reaching for something on the floor. Martin guessed it to be the gun that had slid off the boat's seat and he picked up the only "weapon" within reach, a small grapnel attached to a coil of nylon warp, which was fastened to the dory's stern rail. As the powerboat surged past with only inches to spare, Mabbett straightened up with a short metal boathook in his hand. He raised it and brought the steel end whistling down towards Martin's head. Martin leant to the side and ducked, swinging the dory's wheel so that the two boats collided. As the shaft of the boathook struck his left shoulder, he threw the grapnel toward the departing powerboat's rail, desperate to stay with it.

The violent movements of the two boats ensured that Martin missed his target, the grapnel striking Mabbett between the shoulder blades, where it slid down to catch in the belt holding his trousers up. Martin immediately slapped the dory's gears from ahead to astern.

With a protesting screech from its gearbox, the dory plunged bow down and came to an almost dead stop. The twenty or so metres of rope attached to the grapnel ran out in one rush and the dory was jerked around as the weight came onto the stern rail where the rope had been attached. Mabbett, travelling at perhaps thirty knots, in his powerboat, came bodily out of the boat to land with a splash in its wake. The empty boat swerved to the right, smashed into the concrete wall of the Barrage, the bow rearing up, shards of broken fibreglass replacing the pointed streamlined nose.

As it settled back into the water, the heavy inboard motor and swamped cockpit guaranteeing that it would disappear within seconds, Martin sat watching the shocked and winded splashing of the man who had been responsible for so much grief and disaster. He engaged forward gear on the dory, eased the boat to where the shattered bow of the powerboat was sliding towards the surface of the water, bubbles from trapped air pockets breaking around it, and thoughtfully transferred the grapnel's rope from the dory's stern to the powerboat's buckled bow rail.

Twenty metres away in the water, Mabbett was gasping and splashing, still shocked and winded by the impact, threshing to stay afloat, the weight of the grapnel in his belt making that difficult. As Martin watched impassively, the eyes staring up at him widened as the pull of the sinking boat, now out of sight, was added to the grapnel. Mabbett was towed backwards on the surface towards the area of gurgling, swirling water marking the powerboat's grave. Then, with his mouth opening as well, he went under, pulled downwards to change from a distinguishable human being to a pale oval of face disappearing into blackness.

Watching the gurgling, slopping water, its surface now stained with fuel and oil, Martin was suddenly weary. Tired and empty. Mahoney, Wilson and now Mabbett. The trio who had been responsible for the deaths of Eileen and Ewen. All dealt with, gone. Rampton didn't count, just a foot soldier of the ungodly who had got in the way. He was too tired to wonder this time about himself, to worry at the lack of concern, lack of feeling.

Shouts from the guardrail of the Barrage above his head interrupted these thoughts, made him look up, bringing him back to his own situation. Someone was trying to attract the attention of the nearby control room, presumably to stop the turbines. In the black depths of the Rance, the great blades were turning steadily, water sucking from the upper estuary into the tide basin below. The current took hold of Mabbett's body and still threshing limbs and, as the powerboat settled on the black ooze in the depths, he was drawn inexorably toward the guard mesh protecting the turbine blades. He was pinned there with no escape. The dying body jerked its last and then was still, obscenely still, only the flow of water disturbing black hair that streamed through the mesh, the face with open mouth releasing final bubbles, shirt tail waving in the current, trousers pulled down to the knees by the weight, the pull of the grapnel, in the final struggle for life.

Above, Martin eased the dory's mistreated gearbox into forward and, ignoring more shouts from the walkway, headed for a landing point on the north bank. He grounded the boat there, secured it to a bollard and, without hurry, started away. He still felt no emotion, just a relief that, at last, he was able to walk away. The vendetta was over.

Friday 28th August 1992
9.30 a.m. Winchester, England

"So that's the situation to date, Ray." Potter's summary of the previous thirty minutes conversation with Ray Lawson was coming to a close. "Wild couldn't be charged with Rampton's death in France. He pleaded self-defence and, with the injuries to the body corroborating his story and no witnesses, there isn't a case against him. Add to that the information and cooperation that he gave the police there and they are not pushing too hard. After all, in their eyes, it's an English hitman who died."

He flipped through more pages in the file on his knee. "There's no sign of Mabbett's body, it's disappeared. They've had divers down on both sides of the Rance dam but without finding anything other than the wreck of the speedboat. They've lifted that out and the damage is as Wild said. Apparently it smashed headlong into the dam. The only conflicting evidence that they have is a statement from a witness who saw the two boats just before the impact. They were heading towards the dam. He lost sight of them as they got close in and, by the time he had run to the railings, the speedboat had hit. He says that Mabbett was in the water at least twenty metres from the boat whilst Wild says that it was only two or three metres."

"What did he see after that?"

"Well, that's the contradictory part of his story, it weakens what he says. He turned to shout to people outside the barrier control room, which was some distance away. When he turned back to look at the scene, Mabbett was just going under and he says that then Mabbett was in the position that Wild said in the first place, only two or three metres from the sinking boat. He's adamant that the body was some distance off when he first saw it but cannot explain why it was close to the boat a few seconds later."

"What about the clothing that you mentioned earlier?" from Lawson.

"The pair of trousers? Well, the trousers were not in the boat. They were snagged on a hook thing, like a small anchor. It's called a grapnel, I'm told. It was attached to the boat by a length of rope. Could have been Mabbett's, although how they would have come off – unless he took them off, they were half inside out – Lord knows. Could have been a change of clothing left in the boat. Could even have been an odd item from God knows where, floated down with the current and caught on the anchor thing by chance. Until they find the body, we won't know."

"And you say that they're not holding Wild?"

"They did at first but, as his version of events was checked out and shown to be largely accurate, they released him on what we would call 'Police Bail'. I can't pronounce their bloody term for it!"

"And you say that Mabbett had another major property in France?"

"Yes, they've searched his properties over there, the house and the hotel at Dinan. As I said, they found a large amount of Ecstasy and cocaine so they're pleased with Wild over that as well. There were passports and driving documents in both the name of Mabbett and that of Mallett, the name he was known by locally. Only the woman who ran the hotel and looked after his house knew his true identity."

"She was English, you said?"

"Well, Scots to be accurate. She'd known him from way back, but didn't know much about his operation. He separated everything very well. She was obviously shocked by the shooting. She kept on about Wild saving the kids, though Wild told the French police there was a bit of hysteria there, says he didn't do much other than turn a table over. It's her evidence as much as anything that has strengthened Wild's position. The local news over there has turned him into a bit of a hero. There was a leak from police sources and he's being regarded as an English bloody Batman by the TV and papers. Caused quite a stir what with a foreign drugs runner turning Dinan into the wild west and then crashing his boat into their beloved Barrage.

"Going back to Rampton. Have we got confirmation from the Lab's ballistic boys that this .25 automatic found strapped to Rampton's leg is the gun that killed the two in London?"

"Not yet but it's an odds-on chance in my opinion. Not many .25s about. It had been fired recently. There were five in the clip on the gun, another five in a spare clip in his pocket and twenty one cartridges in the ammo box that held twenty five in his suitcase. That looks like four used if he normally carried the gun and spare clip loaded. There were four bullet wounds on the two bodies at Clapham."

"And there's nothing logged against the second gun? The one that Wild picked up?"

"We're still waiting for the checks to be completed but there's nothing yet. One shell had been fired, there were five more in the chamber. That ties in with Wild's story that Rampton fired one shot at him, which missed, before he stuck the knife in him and he went down the hill."

"It takes some believing that a professional hitman, with a gun in his hand, would miss at point blank range."

"I agree, but it was a steep hillside, the ground was wet, he was wearing smooth shoes and, again, there are no witnesses now that Mabbett's gone. There's enough fact in Wild's story for it to be acceptable."

"And you say that Wild's disappeared again?"

"Yes. The French police were pretty pissed off to have all these 'English problems', as they put it, on their hands. Unofficially they were pleased that

Wild had sorted it out. He was released with instructions to report back in a week's time, that should be next Thursday. Hasn't been seen since. Knowing how much notice he's taken of other police requests, I'm not optimistic."

9.40 a.m.
The Loire, France

And he was right. At that very moment, Martin was finishing a late breakfast in a small farmhouse in the countryside near Tours. He had known the couple, who ran the farm with its vineyards, for some years. He had holidayed in one of their gites before and each year bought a few of their cases of Chinon. It was a quiet location with simple, low cost accommodation, which suited Martin right now as funds were again running low.

There were two gleams of gold on the financial horizon. In conversation with his host, he had found that they were short of grape pickers, which would provide him with some ready money and free bed and board over the next two or three weeks. Then, in conversation with Bill Creighton on the phone, there was an indication that a painting, an old master found wrapped up in Mabbett's rooms at Dinan, might be stolen and that there would be an insurance reward to come at some future date.

Today he felt restless in the confines of the farm. He needed some space, some peace and quiet after the events of the last week or so but also something undemanding to do. He needed to start coming to terms with "crossing over". To think a few things through and perhaps to start making plans for the future. He was fairly relaxed with the evidential side where the police were concerned. He felt sure that there was not enough to tie him into a court situation. You could bet your bottom dollar that there were a few police minds that thought otherwise.

Running through his options for the few days before the grape harvest began, he suddenly thought of Marie Thérèse Tabarde. He had promised to keep her in touch with developments. A quiet saunter down the Rhone Valley would give him time to think a few things over. Then the thought of Madame Tabarde brought back a picture of deep brown eyes and flashing white teeth set in an olive face, of black hair piled high and a slim figure. To him, she was a beautiful woman with an air of slight mystery.

Pushing his chair back, he walked into the kitchen where dishes were clattering.

"Madame, I need to use your phone. Is the box still in the drawer?"

"Oui, Monsieur, please help yourself."

Martin dialled the number that he had put in his diary. The phone rang several times and he was about to put the handset down when it was answered. He recognised Madame Tabarde's voice. She sounded a little breathless.

Speaking in English, he gave his name and apologized if the call was inconvenient. She sounded surprised. "That is quite all right. My maid is away for a few days and I was in the garden."

"I am travelling in your direction again and I wondered whether you might like an update on events, as I offered when we last met."

"That is kind, Mr Wild. When would that be?"

"Perhaps Saturday, midday?"

There was a pause and a rustling of pages and then, "I have an appointment in Salon on that day, but perhaps you would like to meet me there. It is just off the motorway that you would be travelling on to get here and I will be at the 'Mairie' in the centre of Salon from 10 a.m. to midday."

"Fine," said Martin, "I'll look for you at the entrance to the town hall at a few minutes past twelve."

He put the phone down and slid a ten-franc note into the drawer of the hall table where the phone stood.

Her voice had sounded different from their previous meeting and she had not hesitated to meet him again. He felt again the stirring of interest and curiosity that had been there, with sympathy, when they first met. She had seemed a remarkable woman, very feminine but also strong. She was also extremely attractive.

"Stop being a fool," he told himself. "She had just run in from the garden and was out of breath."

Walking back to the kitchen, he told Madame that he would be away over the weekend but back on Sunday night, ready for the "vendage" should it start Monday morning. It took ten minutes to clear his room, put his bag on the back seat of the car and set off. He drove steadily, keeping to the fast autoroutes and, by early evening, had covered the three hundred odd miles to the outskirts of Salon. A convenient and cheap "plastic" hotel appeared with a reasonable restaurant beside it.

The drive had done its job. Several hours of solo, undemanding motoring enabled him to get his head around the situation to some degree and come to some conclusions for the immediate future, if not for the mid-term. When the grape picking was over in the Loire, he would make for Bordeaux in the hope of a further week or two's work in the later harvest there. If there was nothing doing, he would go on to the coast at La Rochelle or Bayonne and try to pick up some casual work in the boat yards that serviced and stored yachts belonging to English owners. He knew a couple of names that might prove useful.

He had no wish to return to England just yet, too much had happened.

Did not look forward to the meeting of eyes where certain people were concerned. He felt sure that the more astute of his friends, though perhaps unsure, must be drawing conclusions that he knew were only too accurate. He needed some water to pass under various bridges before going back.

Saturday 29th August 1992
11.50 a.m. Salon, France

Martin left the Porsche in the Hotel de Ville's car park in Salon. By his watch he was early. Walking towards the building, intent on having a quick look inside, he saw Marie Tabarde standing by the main entrance. She was talking animatedly to a smaller blonde woman. Seeing Martin approaching, she broke of the conversation with a quick excuse to her companion and turned to greet him.

The brown eyes seemed concerned. He saw that the mascara on her lashes was a fraction too heavy, as was the carefully applied lipstick. He wondered at the over-application, different from the light makeup so skilfully applied at their last meeting.

"Mr Wild. I'm terribly sorry but there is a domestic crisis which requires me to return home immediately. I am not able to talk with you this afternoon as we planned."

"Madame Tabarde, please do not concern yourself. I'm very happy to wait until your crisis is over. I do hope that it is not a serious situation. Can I help in any way? Do you have a car with you? If not may I drive you to your home?"

The eyes smiled. "It is not a serious event, just a nuisance and will take only a little while to deal with once I'm home. I have my own car here," then with the smile reaching her lips, "much as I would enjoy a ride in your sporty little car."

"In that case, would you like me to call at your home this evening?" Martin smiled in turn, "And perhaps you would like a drive in the Porsche then – and a drink somewhere whilst we talk?"

The brown eyes regarded him seriously for a moment and then white teeth flashed a smile, a wider smile that he remembered from their last meeting. "That would be very nice indeed, Mr Wild. Shall we say seven o'clock?"

Martin spent a pleasant afternoon exploring the centre of Salon. Returning to his hotel, he showered and changed into a casual jacket before setting out for La Maison Vue Vitrolle. At exactly seven, he pulled up at the gate and, for a moment, sat in the car totally taken aback. Marie Thérèse Tabarde was walking towards him down the long drive. The black hair, piled high on her head, was totally in keeping with the long black cocktail gown that she wore and which hugged a slim waist, accentuating the wide bare shoulders and curvy hips. A diamond necklace flashed at her throat and its light was echoed by stones in the clasp of the small black evening bag which she carried.

Why the gown? He had suggested a drive and a casual drink. "Where do I take her looking like that?" he said to himself, leaning across to open the passenger door and totally forgetting, in his confusion that she had led the sort of life that would expect him to leap from the car and hold the door for her.

As she slid into the seat, he caught not only heady expensive perfume but also brandy on her breath. He sat, half turned towards her. The brown eyes seemed to be slightly unfocused and he thought, with another shock, that despite her walk on high heels, she must have had quite a lot to drink.

"Is there anywhere particular that you would like to go?"

"You said we would go for a ride. I'll leave it up to you." The voice was different. Like the eyes, it seemed unfocused, almost as though she were... and he couldn't think what would have made her voice so different. Then he could. Her French accent hid it but surely her speech was not so precise, slightly slurred. Too much alcohol? One thing was certain, she did not need more to drink. Some food to soak up what she'd drunk was the answer.

He remembered a hotel with a good but not expensive restaurant in the small town of Marignane, on the coast near the Marseilles Provence airport. Then he thought of her dress and changed his mind. There was a smarter restaurant near the harbour and they set off for that.

During the drive, he told her of the unexpected climax to the police investigation, being careful to speak in general terms and leave out his own involvement. Although she made little comment on the investigation, he found conversation with her surprisingly easy. She carried her drink well and a bonus was that the formality of their first meeting was gone. By the time that they reached his chosen restaurant, he knew that she was not only sophisticated but also a well travelled woman. Despite the two children occupying much of her time in recent years, she had lead a full social life. In addition to her native tongue, she spoke English and Italian fluently and, as their conversation progressed it became apparent that, despite the social round, she must have spent much time apart from her husband.

"Your husband was a very busy man, Madame?"

"Oh yes, especially in the last year or so. As well as his political and business life, he was still required to spend time locally on committees and so on. We did not see as much of him as we would have wished. The children were cheated by his sudden death."

When she found that Martin was a keen sailor, her own enthusiasm for boats became obvious. She loved the sea and, during their meal in the restaurant, she described sailing boats and motor yachts that her family and friends had owned and that she had sailed on before marriage to Henri Tabarde had altered her life.

In the restaurant, his use of the formal "Madame" was soon abandoned.

To his surprise, before the main course had been cleared, she insisted that he call her by the name that family and friends used, Marie Thé.

As the meal approached its conclusion, it became increasingly obvious that Marie Thé was now quite intoxicated, much more so than a brandy or two prior to his arrival and the cocktail before or wine with the meal would account for. He wondered how much she had drunk during the afternoon. When they rose to leave she swayed and bumped into a neighbouring table. He took her arm to steady her.

She seized the bill when it appeared and insisted on paying for the meal.

As he stood waiting whilst, with some difficulty, she made out a cheque, he saw that several pairs of critical, even disapproving, eyes were on them. When she had completed the transaction, he took her arm again to avoid any more embarrassing collisions with tables or the door. As they navigated the steps outside and started for the carpark, he released her arm only to find that she immediately took his hand.

He unlocked the passenger door and held it open for her. She slid in, searching for and clipping on the seat belt. As he entered his side and slid into the seat, a hand closed on his left thigh, just above the knee. Driving away from the restaurant, with perfume in his nostrils and a very attractive woman's slim fingers following the movement of thigh muscles as he operated the clutch, the inevitable happened. That which had been quietly sleeping, awoke.

They took the road out of town and Martin found himself struggling with his thoughts, very conscious of a situation that was totally unexpected but so sexually charged. Then mentally shrugging his shoulders, he dropped his left hand from the steering wheel, took her hand and slid it several inches up his thigh until it was almost touching. As he released her hand, wondering what she would do, in a movement which – in certain circumstances – would have been natural, her hand moved higher to curl over and take hold of him. He was totally taken aback. The meeting with Marie Tabarde seemed to have a pace and purpose of its own. He had seen her as a wealthy, sophisticated widow, reserved, even distant at first. And now this! How wrong can you be?

She did not release him until they reached the house. Out of the car, she took hold of him once again, unlocked the front door one handed and towed him up the stairs to the main bedroom. This was the room with the turret window where he had seen the curtain move on his first visit. It was luxuriously furnished with heavy drapes, deep chairs, a very feminine dressing table and a huge bed.

Still she said nothing. It seemed that words were superfluous. He threw off his clothes and lay on the bed watching as she undressed. Her condition made for slow progress, buttons and clips defeating normally nimble fingers.

She persisted and, as she walked about the room, making an obvious effort to put her clothing tidily away, he wondered about the earlier urgency, now apparently on hold.

The tall slim body was tanned apart from a narrow vee of paler olive pointing precisely to a neat black bush of curly hair. The small, darkly tipped breasts were slightly pendulous but jiggled delightfully as she weaved about the room, staggering and losing her balance here and there.

Eventually she climbed in beside him but, within a matter of less than a minute, long before he was ready again, either fell asleep or passed out, he was not sure which. She lay uncovered by the bedclothes and with the main lights still on. Martin waited as her breathing slowed and, after some twenty minutes, got out of bed, covered her naked figure, switched out the lights and slid back beneath the covers, murmuring "My introduction to French society!"

Sunday 30th August 1992
3.00 a.m. Vitrolles, France

He woke to a not unfamiliar situation. Darkness, a strange bed and an immediate question "Where the devil am I?" Memory returned and he stretched out his left hand, only to find that the large bed was not only strange but also empty.

Raising on an elbow, he saw her, standing in the turret window, open to the warm night air. A full moon gave gentle illumination. Her hands were on the windowsill and she was leaning forward as though looking at something outside.

He slid out of bed and, as he approached her, sleep clearing from his mind, was struck with the beauty of the scene. The gardens, with their perimeter of trees, were bathed in a pale light. Her naked figure, dark in silhouette, apart from another pale olive triangle, seemed poised, almost for flight. The shoulders were wide, the waist slim, legs slightly apart and disappearing into the darkness below the windowsill.

He stood behind her, conscious that that which had been dozing between courses was waking in anticipation, the unfulfilled reminder of unexplored menus. No dark bush, but a shadowy vertical cleft provided a natural resting place, much as an eager diner settles in his chair. His hands found curved hips and he pulled her gently back to him.

"What are you looking at?"

"I had to get up and then thought I heard something outside. I expect it is the little stripy faced animals, what do you call them in English, bodgers?

"You mean badgers. This is a bodger!" and he moved gently against her.

She made a noise almost like a cat mewing and lowered her shoulders to lean further forward and back again, pressing her cheeks against him, wriggling slightly.

"What happened last night?"

"You went to sleep."

"Ooh, I'm not asleep now," and lowered her shoulders even more, sliding her feet further apart.

He bent his knees slightly and, with one hand for himself and one for her, moved with effortless, liquid ease from the vertical cleft into a hidden, deeper world. A gentle reciprocating paradise that had her gripping the windowsill harder and harder, her breath, even at first but soon quickening and then, minutes later, gasping and ragged, until first her cry and then his helpless shuddering collapse brought them back to the moonlit bedroom.

8.15 a.m.

Hours later they woke again in a tangle of legs, bodies and bedclothes, sunlight streaming through the window that was still wide open. A clatter of cups from the ground floor brought Marie Thé swiftly out of bed. Pulling on a negligee, she disappeared and he heard conversation in French, parts of which he understood. "A greeting…what a lovely day…thank you, she would take the tray…would…the children later."

Then she was back, only to disappear again for several minutes. When she reappeared once more, she settled on the bed saying "Martin, would you be very cross if I asked you to have your shower in the bathroom down the passage, whilst I use this one?" She indicated the en suite facilities which were part of the master bedroom.

"Of course not," he answered.

"And would you mind very much putting your clothes in the guest room at the end of the corridor?"

He understood perfectly. The maid that he had met on his previous visit had been an older woman. He guessed that Marie's concern was for the reaction that might occur if an obvious liaison was apparent. French provincial life could be quite difficult and gossip damaging to a recently widowed woman.

"I'll pop into the guest bed for a few moments and then shower," he suggested.

Marie smiled. "I've already pulled the covers down for you."

9.30 a.m.

Later at breakfast, he was conscious of an unspoken disapproval in the maid's eyes as she cleared the table. He guessed that, no matter what Marie had said or how innocently his sudden appearance had been described, the woman, probably from a small local village, could not accept as proper the unaccompanied overnight stay of a man in her mistress's house. The presence of young children, whose voices he could now hear, probably made the situation worse.

He raised his eyebrows at Marie as the maid disappeared towards the kitchen.

"Do not worry, chéri," she said softly. "There is always gossip. I have asked her to take the children shopping after breakfast. I seem to remember that you said last night that you were free for some days?"

"Yes. I'm not hurrying anywhere."

"It seems silly staying in a hotel when I have an empty guest room." She smiled wickedly. "If your bags were in that room before Françine returns, she might believe that was where you slept."

Martin grinned. "That's an offer I cannot refuse. If you can keep her out of the room for an hour or so, I'll do what I can to convince her of the long, lonely night."

"Do not try too hard, chéri. She's from the village and they are not easily taken in."

Wednesday 2nd September 1992
9.40 a.m. Vitrolles, France

The telephone call came in the morning, as they were lying on the loungers discussing plans for a day's sailing in a boat owned by a friend. She ran to the house to answer it and when she returned several minutes later, Martin knew from the look on her face that she was troubled.

"What is it?"

"Chéri, that was a business acquaintance of Henri's. I haven't seen him since Henri died. He was…is quite important to the business and he is in the vicinity today and wished to call and see me. I had to say 'Yes' but he doesn't know about you. He might be a little…" She left the sentence to hang in the air.

"A little difficult?" he finished for her. "And you would like me away for the day?"

She nodded, clearly uncertain.

"That's no problem at all, sweet Marie. I'll take my motor and visit some of the coast that I've not yet seen. I've been far too busy until now!"

At his unconcerned tone and teasing comment, her face cleared and she laughed. "I'm probably being silly but they were discussing some business arrangement just before it all happened. He has not seen me with anyone else. I would not wish to shock him too much." She leant over Martin, kissing his scarred cheek and then his lips, her right hand caressing him intimately. "You know I cannot keep my hands off you and, if I should forget myself…"

Again she left the sentence in the air.

He reached and eased up a cup of her bikini top to caress her in turn. "How long have we got?"

"Long enough!" She pulled at his hand and, as he came to his feet, slid her hand into the front of his swimming briefs to take hold and tow him across the lawn towards the pool room and the cream leather couch.

11.30 a.m.

Martin gunned the Porsche away from the ornate gates, in the general direction of Marseilles, then thought of the seasonal crush of traffic on the roads leading to the coast and swung around at the next junction, intent upon a quieter route.

As he sat in the car studying the Michelin atlas, a black Mercedes S class saloon with darkened windows swept past.

New destination and route confirmed, Martin pulled out, retracing his steps. As he approached La Maison Vue Vitrolle, the Mercedes was stationary in the entrance. He could see the driver, a large man, speaking into the communication module. In the brief glance that he had, Martin was conscious of a passenger with a dark complexion, a shock of greying black hair and a prominent hooked nose. He saw an Italian plate on the rear of the car.

The route that he had now chosen took him towards the mountains of the Luberon and, as he found quieter roads and remote countryside, a feeling of freedom developed. In the days and nights that he had spent with Marie, there had been cocooned luxury and almost insatiable sex. It was a situation completely new to him. The routine each day had encompassed a leisurely breakfast, champagne on the sun loungers during the morning with a light lunch at midday. The maid disappeared in the early afternoon to reappear in time to prepare dinner, which Marie completed alone. The sybaritic days were punctuated by love-making, often before breakfast, always after their lunch when the maid left, and frequently again on retiring for the night. Whilst not exactly jaded, it would be nice to have a rest and he was pleased that he had insisted on taking a bag to stay away overnight. Should Marie Thé wish to invite her guest to stay for dinner, there would not be a problem.

12.10 p.m.

In fact, there was no way that Marie Thé would have wished to entertain her guest for longer than she was compelled, as the maid serving them coffee in the lounge recognised.

As she entered the room with a laden tray, the conversation, which had been in Italian, a language that she knew only a few words of, ceased. It was plain that her mistress was upset. She sat very upright in the chair, as though braced for battle. The face seemed pale beneath the tan, the fingers of one hand unconsciously twisting rings on the other.

The man opposite her, sitting in a corner of the settee, was relaxed. There was a small, almost a pleased, smile on his face, whilst the voice which she had heard as she opened the door was quiet, but powerful. As she turned to leave, he looked up at her and she shivered. It was the eyes, dark, aggressive and menacing.

Closing the door behind her, she stood for a moment, listening. The conversation had resumed immediately with Marie Thé speaking, but now in French. The words were muffled by the heavy door but the maid, as she had often before, bent towards the large old keyhole below the handle and could hear well enough.

"So what am I to tell Mr Wild? What reason can I give for changing my mind, wanting him to leave the house, but to stay in the district?"

The reply was again in Italian, as was Marie Thé's afterwards. The maid straightened up and walked silently away, wondering at this turn of events. She had been surprised and disapproving of Martin's stay at the house as a visitor and, despite the separate rooms, was scandalised by the little signs that told her of more than a friendship. However, the Englishman had proved to be pleasant to her and an unexpected bonus was that a happier mistress required less of her and seemed to welcome, rather than tolerate, requests for time off to visit an elderly mother in the next village.

She sniffed as she topped up the coffee maker, thinking, "These new men in the life of my mistress! Especially this unpleasant Italian, upsetting Madame! At least the Englishman was nice to people." Thirty minutes later, she just happened to be at an open first floor window above the front door when the Italian left. He paused, saying his farewell in French and then, "You must look to the future, Madame. I assure you that our arrangements with Henri were well advanced. Our offer to you is generous. It will enable you to live as you prefer." She thought that there was a mocking note in the voice. "This Englishman, Wild, may jeopardise your future!"

She heard her mistress's voice, cool and level now: "I will consider what you have said, Monsieur. That is all that I can promise."

Again the maid wondered. She had thought that this was a business meeting but there were disquieting undertones in the conversation overheard, from a man that the maid had never seen before. Her mistress had dealt with the death of her husband and, during all of that time, she had remained reasonably composed. Now she was obviously disturbed by a visit that seemed to impinge both on the business and on her private life. Conscious of economies that had been made in the recent past, the maid wondered apprehensively about the future.

8.10 p.m.

The evening found Martin at a little village deep in the countryside, which was not exactly what he had promised himself. The drive had been pleasant but it seemed that most of the larger villages were feeling the influence of tourism. The nicer hotels were full and prices were higher than he had anticipated. The place that he had eventually decided on had a menu which was not equalled by the chef's ability and a room which, though providing all the usual amenities lacked that most desirable of overnight facilities, a really comfortable bed.

Conscious that he had not spoken to anyone in England for a few days, he phoned John Mann for an update. There was just a note of concern in John's voice as he answered Martin's questions.

Then, "Have you been in touch with your friend Potter?" Upon receiving a negative: "Well it might be a good thing if you did. Poor chap's feeling deserted and, you never know, you may want something from him one day."

"The last time that I spoke with the Hampshire lads, I got the impression that they wanted to talk to me about some deaths in London, couple in a car on Clapham Common. I know nothing about that and really don't want to travel all the way back to ease his mind."

"You're in the clear on that, Martin. Bill Creighton rang me the other day, trying to get in touch with you. He tells me that the two at Clapham were done with a .25 and that the bullets recovered have been matched to a .25 automatic found on that guy who fell down the hillside at Dinan. One of these little ladies' handbag guns, but does the job at close range."

"That's very interesting! But why does Potter want to talk to me then?"

"I think he's getting grief from the French police. They want to talk to you further about the deaths over there. Seems Mabbett's body has now turned up. Bill tells me that they expected you back at St Malo some days ago. Impression that I got from Bill was that he wanted to speak with you before you see them."

"I'll ring him tomorrow, but I want to spend more time here before I step into Potter's arms."

"Bill tells me that Ellie May has been asking him whether he has spoken to you."

"Ah, that's a different matter. I'll ring her tonight."

"Nice to hear that you've still got proper priorities, Martin." They both laughed quietly.

Thursday 3rd September 1992
10.40 a.m. Provence, France

The mattress ensured that Martin was up early and on the road after a quick coffee. He pulled in to La Maison Vue Vitrolle mid-morning, to find a group of three people standing talking by the front door. Marie Thé was in conversation with what appeared to be a priest, whilst a second man stood by listening but taking little part.

Not wishing to interrupt, Martin remained in the Porsche with the door open. Presently the group broke up and Marie Thé came to him. He thought that she looked pale. "Are you all right, Marie?"

"Yes, chéri. Please go into the house. I will see these people away." She walked back to the visitors' car, said a few more words through the window and then followed Martin as he walked across the drive.

He waited for her at the door and, as the car disappeared towards the gates, leant forward to kiss her. She returned the kiss but was stiff. There was a slight tremor and he drew back.

"What is it?"

She babbled on inconsequentially about "unexpected visitors", not answering his question, and then excused herself, telling him to ask the maid for coffee whilst she went upstairs. He waited a moment and then quietly followed her to the bedroom. She was not visible but, through the open door he could hear noises from the en suite bathroom.

From the first day that they had spent together and Marie had asked him to use the guest room for changing and showering, Martin had avoided the bathroom attached to the main bedroom during the day, aware that Marie might prefer some privacy in at least one room.

Now he deliberately walked to the bathroom door and looked in. Marie Thé was standing by a small marble-topped side table. Her body was stiff and her eyes closed. On the table was a scattering of white powder, with two irregular lines through it. As Martin watched, with a sense of disbelief and then dismay, he saw Marie visibly relax, reach out a hand to steady herself and then open her eyes.

In the mirror above the table, he could see that they were unfocused at first and then, as she became conscious of his presence, they opened wide and her head jerked around towards him. "What are you...? "The voice was high, not normal. "I...I told you..." And then, seeing the look in his eyes, her shoulders sagged and she collapsed on a chair burying her face in her hands.

He crossed the room towards her and knelt on one knee, putting his arm around the quivering shoulders. "Marie, how long have you been using this stuff?"

"Oh, Mon Dieu, Mon Dieu," and some words in French gabbled too quickly for Martin's imperfect interpretation to catch. Then in English, "You don't understand, you don't understand!"

For some minutes the shoulders continued to quiver, but gradually she regained a degree of composure.

"Chéri, it is a long story. Where do I start?"

"Start at the beginning. I want to know everything."

She was silent for a few moments, then, "Years ago, just after my firstborn, a friend suggested that I see a particular doctor. I was a little bit down and, as the pills that I had been prescribed were having a bad effect for me, he advised that I tried marijuana. Just an occasional cigarette when I needed it. It worked for me and then, perhaps five years ago, yes it was a Bon Noel party, the first time that Henri had spent the holiday away, the same friend brought a pretty little package to the party for me, all tied up in ribbons. Inside was some white powder. It was coke. She said that it was a belated Christmas present and encouraged me to try it. Others who were at the party had used it anyway, so I did. It started from there, but I'm giving it up, truly! This is the first time that I've used it in weeks. I only have a small supply and it's only because of what has happened this morning!"

"Marijuana is one thing, sweet Marie, but cocaine can be dangerous, addictive."

"I know, I know, but it seemed such a little thing and smoking the weed had helped me and my friend told me that coke would too. I was having a bad time then, Henri was having an affair with a girl in his office. He said that he was away on business, but I thought differently. It seemed a way of getting back at him, you know. He was just starting on his 'crusade'. Making a name for himself by castigating the drugs people operating from Marseilles. It seemed such a little thing to do – so appropriate – to get back at him!"

"What was it that upset you so much this morning, made you use the stuff?"

"People in the village have been talking and the priest came with that other man, who was a close friend of Henri's in the business. They are concerned about you being here, about me having a guest with only the children here at night. I don't know what to do. I don't want you to leave but..."

Martin had expected that news of his stay would spread through the local community but had relied upon Marie's sensibilities; too much he now thought. He guessed that there were some from the wealthier set who would shrug their shoulders and smile knowingly but, from what she now told him of the recent conversation with her visitors, there were many older people in the village who were scandalised that the newly widowed Madame

Tabarde, whose husband and family were held in such high regard, should permit such an arrangement.

"If that is all, sweet Marie, then we can deal with the situation…"

"No, that is not all. There was the visit that I had yesterday, the reason that you went away. I told you that it was a business acquaintance of Henri's. Well, that is true, but he is not a nice man. It seems that he has bought into the company in some way. He is looking to buy more of the business, to take control, and I know that I must stop him."

"Can you do that?"

"I have some share options that I have not taken up. He knows this and wishes me to sell to him. I will have to buy them myself, if I can."

"Can you afford them?"

"I must afford them. All that I have comes from the company. I cannot let a man who I do not know and do not trust, take control of my life and the future of my children!"

Marie's confession seemed frank, and Martin accepted it at face value, but there was a nagging feeling that there was more to the situation than he was being told. She avoided some of his questions and, when pressed, refused to answer at all, on the grounds that their recent friendship, though so close, did not entitle him to her family's life history. He saw that he was losing the intimacy of the tears. From defensiveness, she moved to a confident refusal to answer any more questions. The snort of cocaine was having its effect.

Martin left her repairing damage to her makeup and collected the few belongings that were not already in the bag in his car. It was very evident that, whatever her thoughts on the matter, he could no longer live at La Maison Vue Vitrolle. She had two children, a position in local society and a life to rebuild. His presence could easily impair her future and there had been too much damage done to her and her family already. The brief spell of a certain sensual, sybaritic paradise was over.

With his bags in the Porsche, he sought out the maid and, when she brought him coffee on the terrace, pressed her to accept a generous gratuity for his stay. She was not surprised by the impending departure but was, pleasantly, at the size of the tip. You could never tell with these English, she seemed to be thinking as she left him.

When Marie Thé appeared, now for the first time that Martin had seen, smoking a cigarette, he told her what he had done. She reacted oddly, at first apparently relieved at his decision to go but then imploring him not to go completely away, to stay somewhere close. She had to see him again!

"But Marie, I haven't the money for an indefinite hotel stay, especially at the prices charged in the south of France! In any case, I have to sort myself out, find some work, perhaps eventually restart my business back in England."

'Chéri, I will help you find accommodation. Perhaps I can help with some work! I have many friends with businesses."

"Marie, that is lovely of you, but it will not do. I have to support myself. When I came this way I was thinking of casual work in one of the boat yards. The layup season is coming and there will be lots of boats to be lifted out and stored."

"Then I will speak with a friend who is in the marine business. He runs Nautico Commercial. They do all sorts of work on boats, although not yachts. They work on shipping, supply tugs, repair harbour installations, that sort of thing. If he has not the sort of work that you want, he may know someone who has."

At that point the conversation was interrupted by the maid. There was a telephone call for Marie. When she returned, suddenly and again oddly to Martin, she suggested that he start his search for lodgings that day, even that morning. And so Martin agreed to spend the day finding suitable lodgings and to return for lunch with Marie the following day to see what luck she had had with her Nautico friend.

He left the beautiful white house with a sense of regret, but also some relief. If he had stayed longer, he was sure that the web of luxury, beauty and sex would have entrapped him, perhaps altering life in a way that he would have later regretted. After only a few days he was missing the morning champagne! What else would he miss later in the day? With a crooked grin, he gunned the Porsche away towards the coast. He thought that if he was lucky with a job in one of the dozens of yards around Marseilles, he would need to be sleeping closer than the Vitrolle area anyway.

Martin had driven only a short distance, not even as far as his turning point of the previous day, when the smile was wiped from his face. Travelling in the opposite direction he saw a large black Mercedes. It had darkened windows but, as it swept past, he recognised the hooked nose of the passenger; with the confirmation, through his mirror, of an Italian national plate on the rear of the car. Of equal interest was the driver. He had looked large when seen the previous day, but now Martin could tell that he was a giant of a man. In the brief glance that Martin had, he seemed to be at least six inches taller than he of the hooked nose, and with shoulders that filled the large saloon's front seat.

In a rerun of the previous day, Martin pulled into the same turning space and then out again behind an old Renault van that was passing. He followed the van to see the Mercedes again pulling into the entrance of La Maison Vue Vitrolle.

With mixed emotions of curiosity, concern and a wish not to be seen to be prying, he continued after the van until a bend in the road hid the entrance and the Mercedes. Swinging onto the right hand verge, risking the Porsche exhausts, he got the car half off the road, leapt out and ran back to a gateway and then through a belt of trees to land bordering the house.

Dodging through the trees, he was in time to see the Mercedes pull up at the main entrance with Marie waiting in the open doorway. The driver got out to open the passenger's door and now the size of the man was clear – and impressive. He towered over his passenger and Martin reviewed his estimate – upwards! The man was nearly a foot taller and with the body of a weightlifter.

The two walked towards Marie, who stepped out to meet them. "Hook nose" leant forward for the customary cheek kissing. The giant did not. There was an exchange of conversation during which Marie shook her head. Then "hook nose" spoke to the giant, who turned and walked back to the car where he leant against the passenger door whilst Marie led the other into the house, closing the door after her.

Thoughtfully Martin turned and walked back to the Porsche. There was no threat apparent in the meeting. The large man was clearly an employee, probably a bodyguard, not required in the house. Had Marie known that there were visitors coming? If so, why had she said nothing? Had it been the telephone call? Was this the reason that she had suddenly decided that she wanted Martin out of the way? Concern for him or for herself?

Reaching his car, Martin extracted the binoculars that he always carried, walked back to the belt of trees and made a note of the registration number on the rear of the Mercedes. Selecting a suitably shaped tree root he settled into it to wait and watch.

It was a full forty minutes before the visitor reappeared to join his large companion and drive off. Marie Thé waited at the door until they were out of sight, then wandered slowly to the swimming pool, collected a towel from the back of a chair and walked slowly back to the house with it. It seemed to Martin that she was in deep thought. Her movements lacked the usual energetic, decisive edge and she stood for several seconds with the towel in her hand as though lost in thought.

Then the maid appeared at the kitchen door and Martin guessed that she had interrupted concentrated thought, as Marie suddenly straightened and walked towards the kitchen, where the two of them stood in conversation for some moments.

Martin did not know why, but he waited until they disappeared into the house before getting to his feet and making across the side lawns towards the front door. He had the key that Marie Thé had given him after their first days together and, using this, he let himself in. There were noises from the kitchen and, walking silently on the thick carpets, he went first to the lounge, which was empty, then the pool room, also empty, then towards the door to the kitchen. As he did so, he reached a door to a room that Marie termed as "Henri's Study". Normally it was closed and, on the only occasion that he had tried the door, it had been locked. Now the door was ajar and, peeking in, he saw Marie Thé standing in front of a large pair of double doors which were open and behind which was an array of television monitors, VCR units and control equipment.

Staggered at the size and complexity of the installation, he watched as she competently rewound and started to replay a tape. Then there was the sound of a telephone ringing, the kitchen door opening and the maid's voice calling for "Madame".

Quickly, he moved from the study door and raced silently up the stairs to the first floor landing as Marie Thé answered the maid and took the telephone call in the study. Within only a few moments, he heard her again call to the maid. She had to go out immediately and would Françine lock up if she had not returned before the maid left for the afternoon?

Martin slid quietly into the guest bedroom that he had occasionally used and waited, hearing Marie Thé go to the master bedroom and then out of the front door. There was the sound of a car starting up and Martin wondered which way she would turn on the road. It was a fifty-fifty chance that she might spot his Porsche!

Carefully, he left the guest room, went down the stairs and was reassured to hear the clink of crockery from the kitchen. The door to the study was unlocked! He entered and closed it quietly behind him. The double doors hiding the television equipment were closed. They looked like the doors to any normal office or study annexe rather than the sort of control consul that he had so often advised on or designed when a security consultant. Would they be locked? Four swift strides across the room and he found that they were not. Inside was a pair of Panasonic video recorders of a type that he knew well and control equipment identifying a number of cameras. Apart from the external camera at the Villa's gate, he had seen no others during the time that he had spent at the house, yet there were switches labelled "Lounge", "Pool", and "Study" as well as "Gates".

Martin's mind was in turmoil, questions and possible explanations raced. Switching the machine on, he found that he was looking at Marie Thé and the recent visitor, in conversation, in the lounge. The camera was apparently positioned in a corner of the room. Martin's recollection was that only a large old-fashioned movement detector, apparently connected to the intruder alarm system, had been in the lounge in that position. The CCTV camera must be a covert miniature unit inside the detector housing!

Looking up, he saw a similar detector in a corner of the study that he was in. Switching the "lounge" camera and VCR off and the "study" camera on, he was immediately rewarded with a view of the large desk, easy chairs and coffee table that occupied the centre of the room. Moving away from the consul he saw himself step into the picture.

With an odd anticipation in his belly, he switched the VCR on again and rewound it to the start of the tape. Whilst the machine was rewinding, he went to the study door, opened it and listened. There were still noises from the kitchen. Returning to the consul and the re-wound tape, he selected Pool and pressed the Play button. He watched with mixed emotions as, with the cream leather couch centre stage, first there appeared a bikini clad Marie Thé, swiftly reduced to half a bikini, followed a few moments later by his own arrival in swimming briefs that were patently too small for that sort of condition.

He switched the machine to rewind again, selected a new tape from a shelf bearing a dozen or so, still in their plastic wrappings, inserted it into the second VCR, selected Lounge and Copy and sat back to wait as the machines whirred together. Minutes later, with the copy in his pocket, he quietly made his way from the house and across the lawns.

Returning to the Porsche, he drove off slowly, looking now for a hotel where there would be a telephone, and thinking, seriously, for the first time in several days.

3.25 p.m.

Detective Jean Jibault was not having a good day. He of the big belly had seemingly "got out of bed on the wrong side" as he remembered an English expression, appearing late at work and full of questions about cases that Jean was dealing with. Inevitably there were answers that could not be given, amongst which were those concerning progress of the two "English" deaths and the whereabouts of Martin Wild. Martin's disappearance had remained a source of regret to Jean. There had been a quick bonding between the two men. They both liked the same wine which, he supposed, meant any half decent bottle and, anyway, he was anxious to continue improving his conversational English!

The telephone rang as he was on his fourth cup of coffee and starting to feel the twitches of excessive caffeine. He did not immediately recognise the voice, although he had been thinking of Martin only minutes previously.

"Martin Wild, Jean. Comment allez vous?"

A tiny ray of sunshine appeared in the top corner of his fairly grimy office window, an omen he thought. "Martin, good to hear from you, at last.

Where are you? Or is that a question that you do not understand in your, as you say, fractured French?"

Martin laughed, pleased and relieved to hear a lightness in Jean's voice.

"I'm in Provence, been following up a lead in the case," he lied smoothly. "I hope that my lack of communication has not 'blotted my copybook' – you remember the English sayings that we were exploring last?"

"You will need a lot of blotting paper for 'he of the big belly', Martin, and I do not think that the magistrate who released you to return – when was it, seven days ago? – will be too pleased either."

"Seven days ago! I must have made a mistake with my French again. I thought I had to be back today, Thursday in this week. Should I have been back on Thursday of last week?"

Jean grinned. "It won't do, Martin, you have a piece of paper to confirm the date. But I'll see what I can do, especially if this lead has led to something! I might have expected your further investigations to end up in sunny Provence rather than Normandy!"

Martin gave Jean brief details of "hook nose" and the Mercedes' registration number, without saying too much about his stay with Marie Tabarde. He then posed the question of remaining in Marseilles to continue the enquiry, but got the reply that he expected.

"Martin, this is a police matter. I have the greatest of respect for the work that you did previously, even if much of it was unorthodox and some positively dangerous for friends holding official positions. You know what the situation is. If I can present some more progress that you are responsible for, it will help against the anger of my boss, who was not a fan of the English to start with. But I have to present your body as well, to satisfy the magistrate that the police are still, nominally at least, in control. After that, we can perhaps talk of the Mercedes matter."

Martin understood perfectly and asked Jean how he could best handle his return. He then telephoned Marie Tabarde, explaining that he had to see the police again and hoped to see her soon, but not for lunch the next day, as they had arranged. He did not mention the second visit by "Hook Nose" but asked casually what sort of day she had had and listened carefully to the tone of her reply. He thought she sounded stressed as she listed a number of minor domestic traumas, but she also said nothing of her visitors.

The financial necessities of life dictated that Martin sought out the nearest gendarmerie to await Jean's travel arrangements for him, rather than spend another night in an expensive Provençal hotel. As he turned restlessly on the uncomfortably thin mattress in a small cold room, he told himself that it was good for his soul and thanked whatever Gods there were looking after him, for the luck that had accompanied his actions over recent weeks, which could so easily have resulted in yet even more uncomfortable surroundings.

The restlessness was not down to the bed alone. His mind was active with new questions raised by Marie's habit, the appearance of her visitors and by her reluctance to discuss freely those things that most lovers find easy.

On reflection, there had been no 'pillow talk' of note during their time together and he wondered whether that was as much his fault as hers. The weeks that had passed since the fatal events on the Isle of Bute, in Poole Bay and at the Rance Barrage had confirmed a change in personality. The slightly reserved character that Eileen's love had unlocked had, since the annihilations, become withdrawn and experienced dark moods, far worse than those that had concerned Eileen during their short time together. Now, there was weariness at the thought of further complications. He felt that he had enough on his plate. He had had enough for a long time. It wasn't that he regretted the vendetta, rather that the actions and the end result were totally alien to him and he had not yet adjusted to the person that he had become. Would he ever adjust? He now had dreams that relived some of the violence. He recognised the changes within himself. Sexual desire continued, but there was no wish for true intimacy. Yes, the lack of pillow talk was his fault as much as hers!

Before sleep came, he had decided that, if it was at all possible, he again needed time to himself. Somewhere away from people, all people. Those that were loved as well as those that were not. A solo boat trip would have been ideal, but boat owning was not in his financial league now. With memories of *Truly Fair*, he finally fell into a dream-laden sleep.

Wednesday 9th September 1992
11.10 a.m. Antwerp, Belgium

The cab pulled out of Antwerp Deurne airport. The wipers slapping a steady drizzle from the screen made Marie Tabarde conscious of her clothing. She had not dressed for a wet northern Europe when leaving sunny Provence that morning, had not checked the weather forecast. She shivered slightly, not only from the drop in temperature, clutching the large leather shoulder bag closer to her.

The short ride to the Queen's Hotel was not inspiring. The driver cut through side streets which seemed grey and drear. The rain did not help. At the hotel, she asked the taxi to wait and walked into the reception, the bag held tightly to her side, looking to left and right.

She saw him immediately and was surprised. She had been told that he would wear the clothes of his religion. The circular fur hat she had expected, that had been described to help identify, but hair in ringlets to his shoulders, the long skirt or culottes – she couldn't make up her mind which – with opaque black tights covering heavy legs. It made him look as though ready for a fancy dress party. He was short and fat with a red face and that did not help.

Seeing the distinctive bag with its identifying ornamentation, he rose and came to her.

"Madame Tabarde?"

She held out her hand, wondering if that was the correct thing to do. She was out of her depth on this errand in this country and she knew it. She wished that she could have had someone with her, someone that she could have trusted. She thought briefly of Martin, who she thought to be still at St Malo, but dismissed the impossible from her mind.

"I have a taxi waiting."

"Good." The greeting was perfunctory and he waddled behind her to the taxi, where he gave the driver an address and followed her into the rear of the car.

On the short journey he spoke French with what she thought was a Flemish accent. Marie had difficulty understanding him at times although French was her first tongue. That did not matter, he was only the guide. She hoped that the next man was articulate in a language that she knew.

They were approaching the main train station, she saw the rail yards off to the right. Then they were passing under a low rail arch and, as the taxi turned right, the road following the rails which were now at a higher level, she saw the row of shop fronts that had been described. Each shop occupied an arch under the railway. The arches went on and on. There must have been dozens, no scores of them. Each different but all selling, and buying, the same commodity, diamonds. So this grey street with a city's rubbish in the gutters was the so called diamond centre of Europe!

The driver stopped the cab about halfway along. The rail station entrance was in the distance. She wondered how many of these "archway shops" there were and guessed that they had passed perhaps fifty already. Surely there was not the trade in diamonds to support such a concentration?

Then they were out of the cab and her guide was speaking to a dark visaged man who stepped from a shop doorway as they arrived. She listened with dismay as her guide spoke rapidly in a language that she did not understand at all. She guessed it to be Hebrew.

The man who had been waiting, looking for them, turned to her. The eyes that gazed into hers were dark and unreadable, but he took her hand, bowed slightly and said in good French, "Madame Tabarde. It is good to meet you. Have you had a pleasant journey?"

She thanked him and said, as her previous guide returned to the taxi, "Your French is good. I was worried that I might have difficulty, as with your friend." She hesitated over the last word.

The dark eyes held a mocking light as he said, "Thank you, but we could use Italian if you prefer?"

She wondered about that. What did he know of her, of her background? How much had he been told?

She followed him into the shop. He walked straight through to a room at the back, ignoring a man and woman behind the glass topped counter to her left. The man followed them, leaving the woman sitting on a chair. In the back room was a small table with two chairs. On the table was a powerful light on an adjustable stand and a large magnifying glass on a swivelling stand. The table top was entirely covered in what looked like a fine textured baize.

The two men looked at her and, with a feeling of finality, loss and vulnerability, she opened the large bag and started to place a number of boxes of varying sizes on the table and, finally, reluctantly, a roll of suede. Within seconds, the man from the shop was examining the contents of the packages with care. He used an eyeglass as well as the large magnifying glass which, she now saw, also illuminated. As he did so, he made notes on a pad. He worked slowly and thoroughly, there was a lot to examine. Her second guide left the room to reappear with a chair for himself and she realised that it was going to take some time.

Watching the lengthening list of figures on the notepad, she wondered whether she would have enough. The sale of her home was the only alternative. She had resisted so far, preferring to sacrifice that which appealed to vanity rather than security. But there was a dreadful feeling that either one or the other would still not be enough. Damn Henri for allowing the Italian into the business – into their lives. Her income from the business was not enough, not enough by a long way. Setting up trusts for the children was all very well, but it should not have left her like this! Damn her habit as well. It was expensive, but she couldn't do without it. The last few weeks had shown that. She felt the need now and wondered where the toilet was. She debated asking the silent figure in the corner, but steeled herself to wait a little longer.

12.00 noon
St Malo, France

"But there must be something that can be done!" Martin was angry, frustrated.

"We are doing what we can," said Jean, "but you must realise that this is a big organization. The man is a big fish, not only in the criminal world, but financially and politically." And then at Martin's raised eyebrows, "Oh, he does not belong to a particular party or appear openly in government, but his businesses, his money, are the power behind certain politicians and government officers. Our budget for this sort of investigation is derisory. The result is that, whilst we occasionally pick off the little fish, the big ones continue to swim merrily, making their millions over and over again."

"And being responsible for the deaths of dozens, perhaps hundreds of people through this filthy trade. Allowing him to continue in this is like condoning mass murder!"

"But Martin, the Columbian cartels have produced the stuff for years. The Afghanistan farmers' economy has been based on it for years. The Italian mafia have controlled the distribution of it for decades. There are dozens of other organisations and countries involved in it. We are one police division in one country. The man is an Italian national who visits occasionally. All right, he has an interest in certain French companies and pays wages to crooked French politicians, but even if we had the resources and were lucky enough to close down his French operation, his organisation would continue elsewhere."

Martin was silent for a moment and then tiredly, "I know that you are right, Jean. I just cannot turn my back and ignore what I see as a friend's cry for help."

"You should have been a Frenchman, Martin, using romantic terms like that. Remember that the friend you refer to has had all of the advantages in life, is an intelligent woman, was married to a man, a Frenchman, who vigorously fought the drugs barons, and died for it. Our information is that she has been a user, perhaps a supplier of drugs, for years. But then lots are in her society. It is part of the social round."

"I saw no evidence of supply by Marie Tabarde, Jean. Surely this Italian 'Mister Big' wouldn't be at the sharp end, selling to users, no matter how wealthy they are?"

"No, you are quite right. We think that his interest in her is control of the company that her husband owned. She has a substantial share holding. A large haulage company, especially one based in Marseilles and with a good name, would be a useful addition to his business empire. He knew the husband and recognises the widow's vulnerability. The fact that she is a user may be an advantage. If our people in Marseilles are correct, then he is already spinning his web with others in her 'set' and, through them, to her. You will perhaps not know this but she left unexpectedly on a flight from Marseilles to Antwerp earlier today. She is thought to be returning tonight and we would like to know the reason for the sudden trip."

"Then perhaps I should be back in Vitrolles for when she returns. I can be more use there than I am here. The magistrate will have finished with me tomorrow for now, Jean?"

"Yes, he has. But I am not sure that you should return there just yet. I have my own position to think of. You would have been held under arrest during this investigation, if I had not agreed to act as your 'custodian'. My boss with the big belly will have me for breakfast if you disappear again before the next hearing." Jean grinned, but looked hard at Martin. "In any case, from what you have told me, I am sure that it is not all." The grin turned sceptical. "The widow Tabarde is spinning her own web and I wouldn't want you stuck to it."

Martin was silent again. Jean was right. He had run out of major funds until the insurance company paid up for the recovered painting. Apparently Marie Thé had disappeared to Belgium and he was not quite out of the woods where the investigation into the deaths of Rampton and Mabbett were concerned.

"Will you tell me when she returns, Jean?"

"'Yes. By then the magistrate may have released you from your undertaking. But you should still take care, mon ami. I am not convinced that your Madame Tabarde is not a very beautiful but very dangerous spider."

1.15 p.m.
Antwerp, Belgium

The sight of the Queen's Hotel, despite its grey and gloomy appearance, was a relief to Marie Thé. As the cab stopped and she sought money to pay the driver, the heavier weight of her shoulder bag reminded her of the parting admonition from him of the business suit.

"You're in plenty of time for your return flight. Our man will be waiting for you by your car at the Marseilles Terminal. Just hand him the packages and you will be given a package in return. It will contain the payment for the jewellery, which will be over fifty per cent more than the market value that has been quoted by our friend whom we saw this morning."

Walking into the hotel, alone again at last, she found the cloakrooms, entered a cubicle and, sitting on the seat, balanced her bag on her knees whilst she did the necessary, which included a snort from her own ration.

In the bar, she ordered a martini and sat reflectively drinking, thinking of the "friend" who had provided these contacts, of the journey home and the man waiting for the exchange. She had been given a mobile number, just in case.

Then thoughts of the last meeting with the Italian. She shivered slightly, remembering the eyes above the hooked nose, the voice soft but, although there was no direct threat, menacing and the impression of darker unplumbed depths. She wondered why she thought of him as malevolent. Nothing that he had said could be described as evil, but there was a coldness within her heart when she remembered his interest in Martin, his request, more an instruction, that she keep in touch with the English guest, whom he thought "…could be a liability…" She felt increasingly sure that the term "jeopardy" to him had many meanings, some of which she preferred not to think about.

Nerves now steady, she made a decision and enquired of Reception for a hire car company. While she waited, she wondered whether the tentacles of the organisation included hotel staff and, upon the arrival of the hire car, went to the cloakroom for a top-up from her bag. With license shown, forms completed, and her credit card debited, she was on the road, glancing nervously into the rearview mirror after every corner. The promotional map in the car's glove box was not going to be enough and, finding at last the Kennedy Tunnel which led beneath the Schelde waterway to the A14 autoroute south, she stopped at the first services area to purchase a Michelin Europe map.

From there she also made a telephone call to the mobile number that she had been given. When it connected, she answered the male voice saying in French, "Are you meeting Madame Tabarde at Marseilles this evening?"

There was a pause, then a doubtful, "Non!"

Confused, assuming the voice was a go between and that someone else would he meeting her, she said quickly, "There is a change of plan. I will not be leaving Antwerp as arranged. I will call you with a new rendezvous tomorrow at this time." She pressed the disconnect button before he could reply.

Sitting in the car with the map open on her lap, she worked out the route south, intending to drive through the night, putting as much distance between herself and Antwerp as she could. They had been in control. That must now alter. She intended making the delivery, but on her terms, now with her own guarantees. Taking another celebratory snort, she turned the key and with little care for the traffic passing the slip road in a cloud of spray, accelerated across to the fast lane, ignoring the blaze of headlights from behind.

2.00 p.m.
St Malo, France

The office was small, smaller than Martin had expected, but bright and cheerful. The woman who rose to greet him was also small, wore thick glasses and had her hair tied in an untidy, old-fashioned bun. He judged her to be about forty-five years of age and wondered whether she was the right person to do this job. The videotape recovered from the hidden television equipment at La Maison Vue Vitrolle had shocked him. The camera in the pool room had been trained accurately on the cream leather couch and the definition was good enough to show every muscle of Marie Thé's very active body. If this middle-aged lady strayed into that part of the tape, what would be the reaction? He must ensure that the translation concentrated only on the recording from the lounge camera, which covered the meeting between Marie Thé and the "Hook Nosed" Italian.

Briefly, he wondered again about the installation. He could understand more easily if it were Henri's work, but Marie must have operated the units since his death, and she had used it competently whilst he had watched.

Handing the reel to the translator, he asked that she prepare a verbatim record of the conversation on the tape, as well as give a verbal translation, but only of the forty minutes following the position that he had stopped the tape in.

Slotting the tape into the VTR, the woman swivelled a monitor screen in Martin's direction, adjusted earphones around her bun and pressed the play switch. With the sound diverted to "she of the headphones", Martin listened to the unemotional voice as the conversation in Italian and occasional French between Marie Thé and her visitor, was translated into passable English and, at the same time, typed rapidly into a word processor.

6.20 p.m.

Paris, France

Marie Thé saw the first signs for the Aeroport Charles de Gaulle as she was approaching the northern entry to the Paris périphérique. She was tired, very tired and thought of the Aeroport Orly, just off the southern section that next awaited her, where flights for Bordeaux and Marseilles were located. She stiffened her resolve. There was a greater chance of a customs search within an aeroport than on the roads. She would stick with her original plan.

The périphérique came up and, with it, the inevitable increase in traffic. It was raining again and the hypnotic arc of the wipers, now with headlights and brake lights from cars in front magnified by the mist of spray, caused her to frown and squint.

She chose the eastabout route, judging that it would be shorter and easier than the west side with its series of tunnels. She thought again of Orly and the comfort of flying and, with her right hand investigated the large shoulder bag for her private supply. The hurried snort had a quick effect and she drove aggressively, wishing to put Paris and the périphérique behind her. Once south of Paris, she felt that she would be almost on home ground and could look for a hotel for what remained of the night.

She passed the major junction with the A3 at Port de Bagnolet, then the slip roads to minor junctions. The rain was harder, the spray thicker. Traffic was moving more quickly now, the congestion over, it seemed. She was in the fast lane again, passing a huge, ten-wheeled juggernaut when, on the right-hand bend where the road dipped into the tunnels beneath the Bois de Vincennes, headlights blazed in her mirror.

Clearing the lorry, she swung into the centre lane in front of it, receiving a protesting blast from its horn and another blaze of headlights. Then, suddenly, the steering was light, non-existent for fractions of a second. The car was no longer in her control, but sliding, aquaplaning, on the standing water. She swung the wheel frantically, sawing at it as the rear of the car swung out. Everything was happening so fast! There was no response at all from the steering, just an awful, bone jarring, brain numbing impact and the sound of metal and glass shattering as the rear hit the central reservation. She was conscious of a shower of glass fragments filling the space around her head and shoulders, of centrifugal force pinning her into the seat and then throwing her against the seat belt as the car continued to gyrate.

The collision with the barrier, at some sixty mph, had spun the car in the opposite direction, out from the barrier, into the path of the juggernaut. The blaring of horns, the locked wheels on the soaking road, the desperate curses and efforts of the lorry driver were to no avail. The huge lorry with its load of metal castings hit Marie Thé's small hire car on its left hand side, at the driver's door, slamming it into the wall of the tunnel where, one after another, following vehicles smashed into the smoking wreckage and each other.

There was no pain now. She seemed to be floating. Time, which had been rushing, was slowing, now moving slowly, so slowly. Looking down, she saw the smoking wreckage below her. Remembering that she had been in a tunnel, she wondered how she could possibly look down. The scene was receding. As the edges of a dark surrounding cloud closed in, she thought, despairingly, of her two young daughters. Then the grey of the cloud enveloped her, turning to total blackness, seeming to suck all thought away.

Epilogue

One Year Later
Thursday 26th August 1993
12.40 p.m. Southampton, England

Inspector Colin Dempsey pressed the buttons on the access control at the door of the Police Club in Hulse Road and swore when it failed to release. He tried again, but was unsuccessful. They'd probably changed the code since he was last here, he decided. That was the trouble with being an infrequent visitor. The club was more a venue for the Southampton based officers, especially the older retired members, who had belonged to that city's small force, before the days of amalgamation with Hampshire County, where he had served all of his time.

He waited as another car pulled into the parking area at the front of the building, trusting to go in on the coat tails of the later arrival. He recognised the driver, Bill Creighton from Southampton CID and wondered who the second man with Bill was. He recognised the face but couldn't put a name to it. As they gathered at the door, Bill introduced his passenger as a French detective, Jean Jibault. Everything clicked into place, with reminders of their joint involvement, a year before, in the Eileen Padgett murder and the subsequent drugs enquiry.

"Jean is over with a group of IPA from St Malo," said Bill. "We're meeting here tonight for a few beers with the Hampshire Section. Why don't you join us?"

"I'm waiting for Bob Thorne. We're looking at the Function Room for his retirement do."

The three stood at the bar while drinks were ordered, then found a corner table to wait for other arrivals to their respective meetings. As they waited, for Jean's benefit, Bill referred to Colin Dempsey's role as the Liaison Inspector in the Mabbett case of a year before. Dempsey said, "What news of Martin Wild then? He dropped out of sight about then."

Bill Creighton and Jean Jibault exchanged glances. There was silence for a second or so and then Bill said, "Jean and I have just been talking about that. Martin was with Jean during the French hearings into the deaths of Mabbett and his sidekick. The bit that we didn't know on this side was that Martin had become friendly with a woman who was the widow of the French politician murdered previously. It's thought that there were links from the widow to the gang that killed her husband but, at the end of the day, nothing conclusive. Anyway, just as the Mabbett job was being wrapped up, the widow was killed in an RTA outside Paris. Apparently, when Martin heard the news, he upped and left. Jean reckons that he thought the gang had got to her too, but that wasn't so."

Jean broke in to say, "We wondered at first, but at the autopsy it was found that she was high on cocaine. In any case, witnesses insisted that it was purely bad driving in bad road conditions. No doubt the drugs added to the problems, were probably the cause of the accident – but there was no suggestion of anything other than it being an accident." He paused for a moment and then added, "The only item that no one could explain was a package of white powder, mainly talc, which was in her shoulder bag. We thought we'd got cocaine at first, but the lab soon put us right."

From Bill: "Jean tells me that Martin was useful to them in their side of the enquiry."

"When we could find him!" Jean broke in with a grin. "Had a habit of disappearing at critical times, which didn't impress some in our Judiciaire. It was after one of his disappearing acts that he surfaced with the widow Tabarde in the south of France."

Privately, he wondered again about the relationship. The video cassette given to him by Martin at their last meeting – despite one section of the tape having been wiped clean – had emphasised the involvement of a very wealthy businessman with known political and criminal connections. In Jean's mind, there was always the "birds of a feather" syndrome. Martin had introduced him to the English phrase but had disagreed with Jean's assertion that it could apply to Marie Tabarde.

He thought again of their last telephone conversation, when Martin had enquired into the investigation following Marie Thé's death. In answer to the obvious question, Jean had said, "The big fish is still swimming."

After a pause Martin said quietly, almost to himself, "Maybe one day he'll mistake a bait as prey, but not just yet. The fisherman's resting."

The comment, in English, had puzzled him and, in the hope of a better understanding, he had discussed it with Bill. Neither of them liked the conclusion that they came to.

Jean returned from his thoughts to hear Dempsey say, "And he's not been in touch since?"

From Bill: "Both Jean and I have heard from him on a couple of occasions by phone, but he's not been back to England."

"Guess there might be reasons for that," said Dempsey. "There were some questions waiting for answers in the Mabbett job on this side. Wonder what he's doing for money though. Can't live on fresh air."

"He would have been all right for a while," from Bill. "There was the insurance reward for the picture that was recovered. That would have been quite a few thousand."

"That was a bit of luck," said Dempsey. "Always was a lucky sod when he was in the job."

"Whatever luck he got professionally and financially, it couldn't have made up for the bad luck he had in other ways," said Bill Creighton. At a questioning look from Dempsey, he continued, "He lost his parents when he was young, lost his sister in a drug death and Eileen Padgett in that bomb incident. No amount of money can make up for that sort of grief."

"I didn't know about that." Jean Jibault was shocked. "He told me about his girlfriend but I didn't know of his parents and sister."

"Martin was very sensitive about his sister's death. He didn't find it easy to talk about. There was an open verdict at the inquest. No evidence to show that she had taken the drugs knowingly, but also none to say that she'd been slipped a Mickey Finn. Martin always thought the latter, but it hurt him that not everyone agreed. The result was that he left the job and we lost a good copper."

He wondered to himself about the last conversation he'd had with Martin. When asked when he was likely to come back to see a certain young lady who was continually asking after him, Martin had said that he thought he was "bad luck" and it was better if he stayed away. Bill had, after some consideration, given Ellie May a telephone number. The next time that he saw her, she asked him to help her sell her old Ford. She was taking all her available leave and adding some days that she was owed by her work for Potter, to "holiday abroad". She had a gleam in her eye and, when Bill reported Martin's comment about "bad luck", she turned in the doorway and said with an enigmatic smile, "Don't worry, Bill, we West Indians have inherited Jujus that can deal with bad luck!"

30th September 1993
4.30 p.m. Cancale, France

The small white hulled sailing boat had been anchored just half a mile southeast of the Pointe du Grouin for most of the afternoon. She was lying in seven metres of water, sheltered from the gentle westerly breeze by the high ground behind Port Mer. It had been a hot day and the only person visible on deck was a girl clad in a white bikini, lying prone beneath a faded sun awning draped over the boom.

Closer inshore was the Barbe Brûlée buoy, marking the extremity of a rocky ledge, whose seaweed encrusted sides were hidden beneath the high tide. If the coastguard had been watching from his lookout on the cliff above the Pointe, he might have seen a dark suited figure sliding away from the ledge, the air tanks of the sub aqua gear providing a steady stream of bubbles as it made for the anchored yacht.

Beneath the boat, in the shadow cast by the late afternoon sun, the figure paused and then slowly ascended to the surface inches away from the hull. The disturbance of the water roused the dozing figure and the girl rolled over and peered down. A black neoprene covered arm holding a vicious-looking spear gun came out of the water. The other hand raised the mask covering the eyes and the mouthpiece was spat out. A pair of green eyes took in the brown face looking down and a smile, slightly twisted by a scar on one cheek, parted his lips showing even white teeth. "Here's dinner. I've done my bit. It's over to you."

Ellie May regarded the grey mullet impaled on the spear with a touch of distaste. "I'll make a deal with you," she said, "I'll do salad and make your favourite dressing. You do the fish – and I'll promise to be your slave girl for afters."

"That's a deal."

Martin paddled to the stern, pulled himself onto the boarding ladder, stripped off the bottles, suit and his trunks on the bathing platform and towelled down before stepping into the cockpit. Ellie May met him with a tall glass of spritzer. He drank deeply and pulled a face.

"God, you know how to spoil a decent Muscadet," he teased.

"Well, as long as you know how to spoil an indecent maid," she giggled, glancing downwards before disappearing into the cabin.

Martin grinned, threw the towel to one side and sat with his drink, watching the dipping flight of gulls over the rocky coastline. Reminded of Scotland's west coast, his thoughts went back to Eileen and their plans to sail there from the Isles of Scilly. Eyes darkening, face now grim, his memory forwarding to Marie Thé and her love of the sea. He remembered his last conversation with Jean and the discussion about "big fish still swimming". He wondered again about the involvement between the Italian and Marie Thé. Susie had been the first victim of the drug culture and Marie Thé the last…but, before he could enter that introspective spiral, a slim brown arm appeared from the cabin, holding a bottle of Muscadet.

Draped over it were the two halves of a diminutive white bikini. A husky voice said, "Another aperitif, Lord and Master?"

Later, curled together on the narrow bunk like two spoons, Ellie awake as Martin slept, she reflected on the days spent with him. Her first visit had been an introduction to life aboard a small sailing boat, a working holiday almost. Martin had purchased the boat locally, with limited funds and was working part-time in the same boat yard to pay for the restoration of a craft that had seen better days. She did not mind the painting, enjoyed assisting where two pairs of hands were necessary, but she did mind the feeling of isolation that crept in towards the end of that holiday. It was as though Martin spent only a small part of his time in the real world, being lost in not very pleasant thoughts for much of his waking hours and beset by bad dreams at night.

With a feeling of dismayed helplessness, she thought that on her return to normality after this second visit, Bill Creighton's inevitable question would have to be answered by an admission that her 'Juju' had not been strong enough to combat the traumas that Martin had experienced.

He was a changed man whose eyes would, if reminded of the losses experienced, change from a smiling green to the cold glacial hue of arctic waters. He would then be lost in a distant introspective world that she could not enter. These periods could last for hours and were accompanied by a lack of communication and a restlessness as though of tasks, commitments, unfinished. Instinctively she knew that the dreams she had harboured as a teenager, reinforced by the happy times that they had shared before the court case had collapsed, were gone, gone forever. It seemed so unfair that the toxic world of the drug culture could reach out to curdle the life of a man who she knew to have been principled and kind.

As sleep claimed her, a tear trickled from closed eyes. Was there no end to the contamination, corruption, caused by the search by some for a chemical nirvana and the inevitable reaction of others to profit from it?

15th October 1993
5.10 p.m. The Adriatic Sea

The blue Sikorski helicopter, with Italian national markings, spiralled down towards a small island some two miles off the coast, south of Split. The passenger looked down curiously, seeing a large palatial villa positioned on the highest point of the island, the smaller bungalows off to one side and the luxurious motor yacht moored to a pier which would not have disgraced a shipping line.

The flight attendant leant over to remove his empty coffee cup. "That is the patron's new boat," he said.

"Yes. I was at the launch."

He knew that his host-to-be owned the island and wondered just how wealthy the man was. His invitation to the launch of the motor yacht, which must have cost a small fortune, had provided the introduction. Momentarily he considered the wisdom of accepting an invitation to "stay a few days" made so casually during the post launch party. Then thought of junior ministers queuing to speak and the mountain of work which awaited his return from the intergovernmental conference that he had attended and decided that he had earned a break.

The chopper touched down on a prepared pad, which reduced the inevitable dust cloud and he transferred to a waiting long wheelbase four-wheel drive which, thankfully, was air conditioned. The inside of the vehicle was a surprise, deep leather upholstery and an inlaid walnut drinks cabinet. A glass partition between the uniformed driver and the rear passengers spoke of custom building without thought of expense.

The car swept through an archway into the villa's large open courtyard, stopping before the main doors. He was conscious of fountains playing, ornate statues and the trappings of wealth before the next surprise. The person waiting to greet him at the doorway was not his host or the companion who had issued the invitation, but a very beautiful young woman, dressed in that way which speaks both of glamour and business. The light linen suit looked expensive, the skirt ending above the knees, the top through-buttoned at the front with a discreetly revealing neckline. Another surprise were her words in greeting him by name "…and I'm here to make sure that you have everything that you want."

He wondered, but looking at the smiling brown eyes, decided that he was reading too much into the greeting. She led the way to a room furnished as a comfortable lounge and surprised him again. Opening a connecting door she showed him into a luxurious bedroom with a huge bed and large en suite bathroom. This was much more than the anticipated "room". He heard the sound of a champagne cork and turned to find she of the linen suit pouring golden liquid into a tall glass. As she leant forward he found the view entrancing.

The "lovely young thing" left him to shower and change before meeting his host for dinner. As he sorted clothes, he compared his own life with that surrounding him now. Perhaps it was time to think a little more of himself and his rapidly approaching retirement and a little less of the loyalties that he owed to a perennially changing government, whose pension would not keep him in the style to which he wished to become accustomed.

Despite the air conditioning, the room was warm and, having changed, he opened the door from the lounge to the hallway by a few inches, settling in an armchair with another glass of wine. Minutes later there was a knocking on a door and, thinking it was his, he rose to answer it. On reaching the door he realised that the knock was on the door to an adjacent room, which was now also open and he could hear a conversation in low tones. The words meant nothing to him, although the low tones and his political nature excited his curiosity sufficiently to make him stand and listen.

"…The Tabarde funeral at Marseilles. They report that the Englishman, Wild, was also present. The patron is emphatic that the contract is still open."

He could not hear the reply and the conversation meant nothing to him so, as the other door closed, he returned to his chair and the glass of champagne.

At a few minutes to seven there was a knock on his door and, on opening it, he found the same girl, now dressed in a long crimson gown with a much more daring decolletage. She smiled and offered her arm, saying that his host preferred an even number at the dinner table. He again wondered about the girl, thinking now that she was more of a hostess than a secretary.

As they approached the big double doors to the dining room, he caught sight of a giant of a man off to one side of the corridor. He thought it an odd place for someone to sit but then they were through the doors to join a small grouping of expensively tanned men and beautifully groomed women. His host came forward. He was powerfully built with thick greying hair, dark eyes and the hooked nose of a predatory bird. He was grasped by the shoulders, embraced, slapped on the back and generally welcomed into the "family".

The courses came, were despatched and replaced. The conversation was good and easy. There were no politics. The wine flowed, instilling confidence, almost a feeling of regained youth. When he felt the pressure of a shapely thigh beneath the table, he was not surprised, just pleased and with the sort of anticipation that he thought he had lost, he knew now that this was the "interview" and that he could pass if he wished. He just wondered what the joining fees would be!

CPSIA information can be obtained
at www.ICGtesting.com
Printed in the USA
BVHW041425150519
548351BV00017B/1024/P